PRAISE FOR THE CRIMSON SHADOW

"A fine adventure, filled with memorable characters and compelling action."
—Terry Brooks, *New York Times*–bestselling author of *The Fall of Shannara*, on *The Sword of Bedwyr*

"Salvatore describes and choreographs battle scenes better than any other contemporary fantasist."
—*Publishers Weekly*

"A worthy, entertaining addition to fantasy literature."
—*Starlog* on *The Sword of Bedwyr*

"An epic blockbuster."
—*Cryptych*

"Swordwaving, magic, and banter."
—*Kirkus Reviews* on *The Dragon King*

"Salvatore tells a story with exciting action scenes that contain great bantering dialogue reminiscent of Indiana Jones."
—*Voice of Youth Advocates (VOYA)*

"I admire Bob Salvatore tremendously . . . He gives us a world of depth and humanity, filled with color and sound and feeling and with heroes we can't help but admire."
—Tracy Hickman, *New York Times*–bestselling coauthor of the Deathgate Cycle

"Packed from cover to cover with high-spirited derring-do and the ring of crossed steel."
—James Lowder, author of *Prince of Lies*

LUTHIEN'S GAMBLE

ALSO BY R. A. SALVATORE

Forgotten Realms

The Dark Elf Trilogy
Homeland
Exile
Sojourn

The Icewind Dale Trilogy
The Crystal Shard
Streams of Silver
The Halfling's Gem

Legacy of the Drow
The Legacy
Starless Night
Siege of Darkness
Passage to Dawn

Paths of Darkness
The Silent Blade
The Spine of the World
Sea of Swords

The Sellswords
Servant of the Shard
Promise of the Witch King
Road of the Patriarch

The Hunter's Blades Trilogy
The Thousand Orcs
The Lone Drow
The Two Swords

Transitions
The Orc King
The Pirate King
The Ghost King

Neverwinter
Gauntlgrym
Neverwinter

Charon's Claw
The Last Threshold

The Sundering
The Companions

Companions Codex
Night of the Hunter
Rise of the King
Vengeance of the Iron Dwarf

Homecoming
Archmage
Maestro
Hero

No name trilogy
Timeless

The Cleric Quintet
Canticle
In Sylvan Shadows
Night Masks
The Fallen Fortress
The Chaos Curse

War of the Spider Queen
Dissolution
Insurrection
Condemnation
Extinction
Annihilation

Stone of Tymora
Stowaway
The Shadowmask
The Sentinels

The Legend of Drizzt Anthology
The Collected Stories
Corona

DemonWars
The Demon Awakens
The Demon Spirit
The Demon Apostle
Mortalis
Ascendance
Transcendence
Immortalis

Saga of the First King

First Heros
The Highwayman
The Ancient

The First King
The Dame
The Bear

The Coven
Child of a Mad God
Reckoning of the Fallen God (2019)

Other series

The Spearwielder's Tale
The Woods Out Back
The Dragon's Dagger
The Haggis Hunters

Chronicles of Ynis Aielle
Echoes of the Fourth Magic
The Witch's Daughter
Bastion of Darkness

Crimson Shadow
The Sword of Bedwyr
Luthien's Gamble
The Dragon King

Star Wars
Star Wars Episode II: Attack of the Clones

Star Wars: The New Jedi Order
Vector Prime

Novelization
Tarzan: The Epic Adventures

LUTHIEN'S GAMBLE

THE CRIMSON SHADOW

R. A. SALVATORE

Cover illustration by Amanda Shaffer

ISBN: 978-1-5040-5585-7

This edition published in 2019 by Open Road Integrated Media, Inc.
180 Maiden Lane
New York, NY 10038
www.openroadmedia.com

To Diane, and to Bryan, Geno, and Caitlin

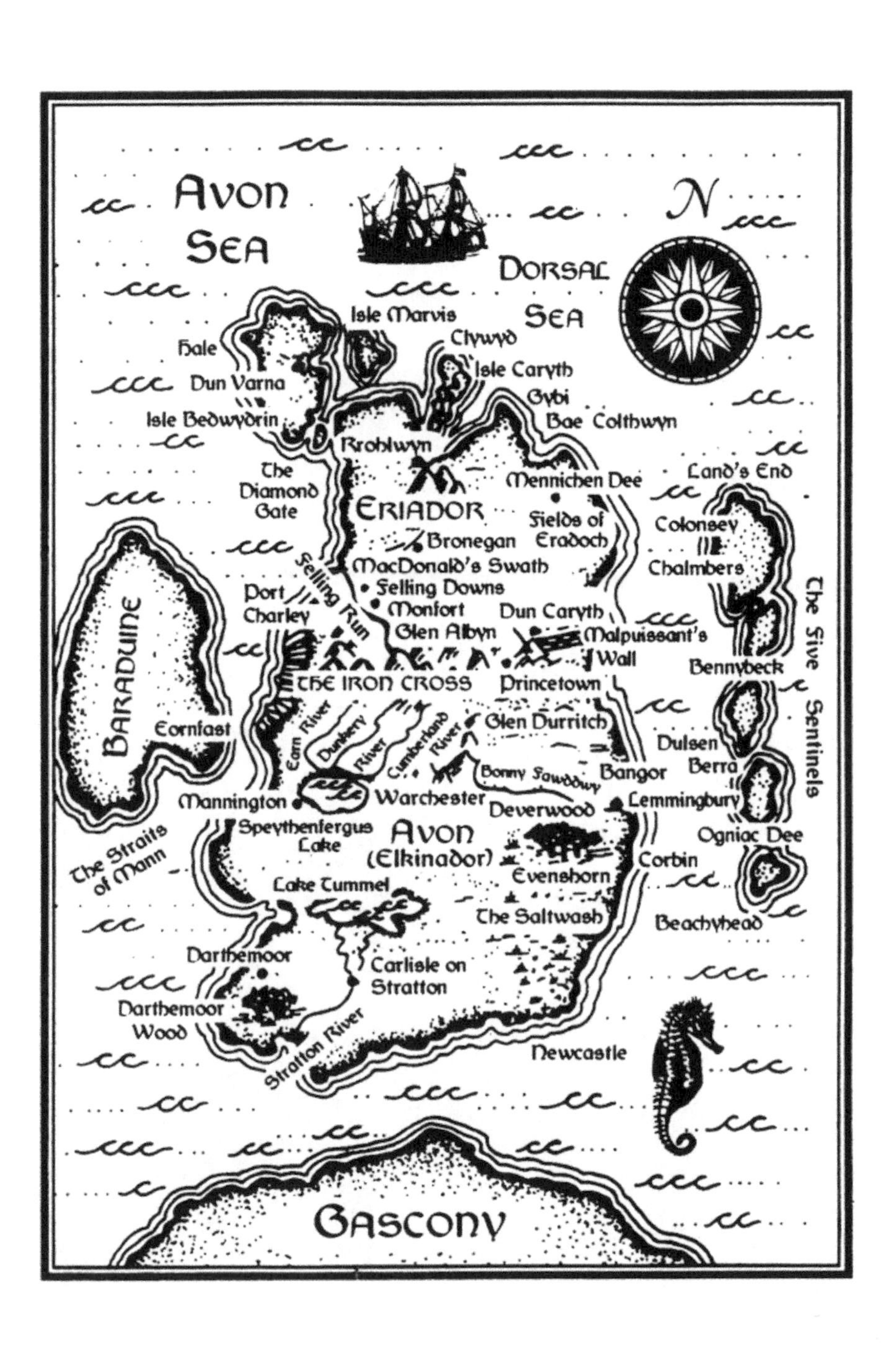

Avon
Sea
Dorsal
Sea
N
Isle Marvis
Clywyd
Isle Caryth
Gybi
Bae Colthwyn
Hale
Dun Varna
Isle Bedwydrin
Krohlwyn
The
Diamond
Gate
Eriador
Mennichen Dee
Fields of
Eradoch
Land's End
Colonsey
Chalmbers
Bronegan
MacDonald's Swath
Selling Run
Selling Downs
Port
Charley
Monfort
Glen Albyn
Dun Caryth
Malpuissant's
Wall
Baraduine
The Iron Cross
Princetown
Bennybeck
The Five Sentinels
Glen Durritch
Eornfast
Eorn River
Dunkery River
Cumberland River
Bonny Sawddwy
Bangor
Dulsen
Berra
Mannington
Warchester
Deverwood
Lemmingbury
Speythenfergus
Lake
Avon
(Elkinador)
Ognaic Dee
Corbin
The Straits
of Mann
Lake Tummel
Evenshorn
The Saltwash
Beachyhead
Darthemoor
Carlisle on
Stratton
Darthemoor
Wood
Stratton River
Newcastle
Gascony

LUTHIEN'S
GAMBLE

PROLOGUE

IT WAS A time in Eriador of darkness, a time when King Greensparrow and his wizard-dukes blanketed all the Avonsea Islands in a veil of oppression and when the hated cyclopians served as Praetorian Guard, allied with the government against the common folk. It was a time when the eight great cathedrals of Avonsea, built as blessed monuments of spirituality, the epitome of homage to higher powers, were used to call the tax rolls.

But it was a time, too, of hope, for in the northwestern corner of the mountain range called the Iron Cross, in Montfort, the largest city in all of Eriador, there arose cries for freedom, for open revolt. Evil Duke Morkney, Greensparrow's pawn, was dead, his skinny body hanging naked from the tallest tower of the Ministry, Montfort's great cathedral. The wealthy merchants and their cyclopian guards, allies of the throne, were sorely pressed, bottled up in the city's upper section, while in the lower section, among the lesser houses, the proud Eriadorans remembered kings of old and called out the name of Bruce MacDonald, who had led the victory in the bitter cyclopian war centuries before.

It was a small thing really, a speck of light in a field of blackness, a single star in a dark night sky. A wizard-duke was dead, but the wizard-king could easily replace him. Montfort was in the throes of fierce battle, rebels pitted against the established ruling class and their cyclopian guards. The vast armies of Avon had not yet marched, however, with winter thick about the land. When they did come on, when the might that was Greensparrow flowed to the north, all who stood against the wizard-king would know true darkness.

But the rebels would not think that way, would fight their battles one at a time, united and always with hope. Such is the way a revolution begins.

Word of the fighting in Montfort was not so small a thing to the proud folk of Eriador, who resented any subjugation to the southern kingdom of Avon. To the proud folk of Eriador, uttering the name of Bruce MacDonald was never a small thing—nor were the cries for Eriador's newest hero: the slayer of Morkney, the unwitting leader of a budding revolution.

Cries for the Crimson Shadow.

CHAPTER 1

THE MINISTRY

THE REVOLT HAD begun here, in the huge nave of the Ministry, and the dried blood of those killed in the first battle could still be seen, staining the wooden pews and the stone floor, splattered across the walls and the sculpted statues.

The cathedral was built along the wall separating the city's merchant class from the common folk, and thus held a strategic position indeed. It had changed hands several times in the weeks since the fighting began, but so determined were the revolutionaries that the cyclopians still had not held the place long enough to climb the tower and cut down Duke Morkney's body.

This time, though, the one-eyed brutes had come on in full force, and the Ministry's western doors had been breached, as well as the smaller entrance into the cathedral's northern transept. Cyclopians poured in by the score, only to be met by determined resistors, and fresh blood covered the dried blood staining the wooden pews and the stone floor.

In mere seconds, there were no obvious battle lines, just a swarming mob of bitter enemies, hacking at each other with wild abandon, killing and dying.

The fighting was heard in the lower section of the city, the streets belonging to the rebels. Siobhan, half-elven and half-human, and her two-score elvish companions—more than a third of all the elves in Montfort—were quick to answer the call. A secret entrance had been fashioned in the wall of the great cathedral, which it shared with lower Montfort, cut by cunning dwarfs in those rare times when there was a lull in the fighting. Now Siobhan and her companions rushed from the lower section of town, scrambling up preset ropes into the passageway.

They could hear the fighting in the nave as they crawled along the crude tunnel. The passage split, continuing along the city's dividing wall, then curving as it traced the shape of the cathedral's apse. The dwarfs had not had a hard time fashioning the passage, for the massive wall was no less then ten feet thick in any place, and many tunnels were already in place, used by those performing maintenance on the cathedral.

Soon the elves were traveling generally west. They came to an abrupt end in the tunnel at a ladder that led them up to the next level. Then they went south, west again, and finally north, completing the circuit of the southern transept. Finally Siobhan pushed a stone aside and crawled out onto the southern triforium, an open ledge fifty feet up from the floor that ran the length of the nave, from the western door all the way to the open area of the crossing transepts. The beautiful half-elf gave a resigned sigh as she brushed the long wheat-colored tresses from her face and considered the awful scene below.

"Pick your shots with care," Siobhan instructed her elven companions as they crowded out behind her and filtered along the length of the ledge. The command hardly seemed necessary as they viewed the jumble of struggling bodies below. Not many targets presented themselves, but few archers in all of Avonsea could match the skill of the elves. The great longbows sang out, arrows slicing through the air unerringly to take down cyclopians.

A quarter of the elvish force, with Siobhan in the lead, ran along the triforium all the way to its western end. Here a small tunnel, still high above the floor, ran across the western narthex and crossed the nave, opening onto the northern triforium. The elves rushed among the shadows, around the many statues decorating that ledge, to its opposite end, the base of the northern transept. More cyclopians poured in through the door there, and there were few defenders to stem their flow in this area. The ten elves bent their bows and fired off arrow after arrow, devastating the invading cyclopians, filling the northern transept with bodies.

Below in the nave, the tide seemed to turn, with the cyclopians, their reinforcements dwindling, unable to keep up the momentum of their initial attack.

But then there came an explosion as a battering ram shattered the doors at the end of the southern transept, destroying the barricades that had been erected there. A new wave of cyclopians charged in, and neither the archers on the triforium nor the men fighting in the nave could slow them.

"It is as if all the one-eyes of Montfort have come upon us!" the elf standing behind Siobhan cried out.

Siobhan nodded, not disagreeing with the assessment. Apparently Viscount Aubrey, the man rumors named as the new leader of the king's forces in Montfort, had decided that the Ministry had been in enemy hands long enough. Aubrey was a buffoon, so it was said, one of the far too many fumbling viscounts and barons in Eriador who claimed royal blood, lackeys all to the unlawful Avon king. A buffoon by all accounts, but nevertheless Aubrey had taken control of the Montfort guards, and now the viscount was throwing all of his considerable weight at the rebel force in the cathedral.

"Luthien predicted this," Siobhan lamented, speaking of her lover, whom the fates had chosen as the Crimson Shadow. Indeed, only a week before, Luthien had told Siobhan that they would not be able to hold the Ministry until spring.

"We cannot stop them," said the elf behind Siobhan.

Siobhan's first instinct was to yell out at the elf, to berate him for his pessimism. But again Siobhan could not disagree. Viscount Aubrey wanted the Ministry back, and so he would have it. No longer was their job the defense of the great building. Now all they could hope to do was get as many allies out alive as possible.

And, in the process, inflict as much pain as possible on the cyclopians.

Siobhan bent her bow and let fly an arrow that thudded into the chest of a one-eyed brute an instant before it thrust its huge sword into a man it had knocked to the floor. The cyclopian stood perfectly still, its one large eye staring down at the quivering shaft, as though the brute did not understand what had happened to it. Its opponent scrambled back to his feet and brought his club in a roundhouse swing that erased the dying brute's face and hastened its descent to the floor.

The man spun and looked to the triforium and Siobhan, his fist raised in victory and in thanks. Two running strides put him in the middle of yet another fight.

The cyclopians advanced in a line along the southern end of the swarming mob, linking up with allies and beating back resisters.

"Back to the southern triforium," Siobhan ordered her companions. The elves stared at her; if they rejoined their kin across the way, they would be surrendering a valuable vantage point.

"Back!" Siobhan ordered, for she understood the larger picture. The nave would soon be lost, and then the cyclopians would turn their eyes upward to the ledges. The only escape for Siobhan's group was the same route that had brought them in: the secret passage that linked the far eastern wall with the southern triforium. The half-elf knew that she and her companions had a long way to go, and if that small tunnel above the western doors was cut off by the cyclopians, the northern ledge, and Siobhan's group, would be completely isolated.

"Run on!" Siobhan called, and her companions, though some still did not understand the command, did not pause to question her.

Siobhan waited at the base of the northern triforium looking back across the nave as her companions rushed by. She remained confident that her elven band, the Cutters by name, would escape, but feared that not a single man who was now defending the nave would get out of the Ministry alive.

All the elves passed her by and were moving along the tunnel. Siobhan turned to follow, but then looked back, and a wave of hope washed over her.

As she watched, a small, perfectly squared portion of the back end of the cathedral, directly below the secret tunnel that her group had used to enter the Ministry, fell in. Siobhan expected a resounding crash, and was surprised to see that the wall did not slam to the floor but was supported by chains, like some drawbridge. A man rushed in, scrambling over the angled platform, his crimson cape flowing behind him. He leaped to the floor, and two short strides brought him to the altar, in the center of the apse. Up he leaped, holding high his magnificent sword. Siobhan smiled, realizing that those cunning dwarfs had been at work on more than the secret entrance. They had fashioned the drawbridge, as well, probably at Luthien's bidding, for the wise young man had indeed foreseen this dangerous day.

The defenders of the Ministry fought on—but the cyclopians looked back and were afraid.

The Crimson Shadow had come.

"Dear Luthien," Siobhan whispered, and she smiled even wider as Luthien's companion, the foppish halfling Oliver deBurrows, rushed to catch up to the man. Oliver held his huge hat in one hand and his rapier in the other, his purple velvet cape flowed out behind him. He got to the altar and leaped as high as he could, fingers just catching the lip. Kicking and scrambling, the three-foot-tall Oliver tried desperately to clamber up beside Luthien, but he would not have made it except that Luthien's next companion rushed up behind, grabbed the halfling by the seat of his pants, and heaved him up.

Siobhan's smile faded as she regarded the newcomer, though surely the half-elf was glad to see Luthien in such strong company. This one was a woman, a warrior from Luthien's home island of Bedwydrin, tall and strong and undeniably beautiful, with unkempt red hair and eyes that shone green as intensely as Siobhan's own.

"Well met, Katerin O'Hale," the half-elf whispered, putting aside the moment of jealousy and reminding herself that the appearance of these three, and of the three-score warriors that poured over the drawbridge behind them, might well be the salvation of those trapped defenders in the nave.

Crossing the tunnel within the west wall was no easy task for the elves, for Siobhan's fears that the cyclopians would cut them off were on the mark, and the one-eyed brutes were waiting for them in the crawl spaces above the western narthex. The defense had not yet been organized, though, and the elves, with help from their kin from the southern tunnel, fought their way through to the southern triforium with only a few minor injuries

Coming out onto that ledge, Siobhan saw that the fighting below had shifted somewhat, with the defenders gradually rolling toward the east, toward the escape route that Luthien and his force had opened.

"Fight to the last arrow," Siobhan told her companions. "And prepare ropes that we might go down to the southern wing and join with our allies."

The other elves nodded, their faces grim, but truly they could not have expected such an order. The Cutters were quick-hitters: in, usually with their bows only, and out before the enemy could retaliate. This was the Ministry, though, and it was about to be lost, along with many lives. Their usual tactics of hit and retreat be damned, Siobhan explained hurriedly, for this battle was simply too important.

Luthien was in the fighting now, his great sword *Blind-Striker* cutting down cyclopians as he spearheaded a wedge of resistance. Oliver and Katerin flanked him, the halfling—tremendous hat back upon his long and curly brown locks—fighting with rapier and main gauche, and the woman deftly wielding a light spear. Oliver and Katerin were formidable fighters, as were the men holding the lines behind them, a wedge of fury working out from the semicircular apse, felling enemies and enveloping allies in their protective shield.

For the cyclopians, though, the focus of the march was Luthien, the Crimson Shadow, slayer of Morkney. The one-eyes knew that cape and they had come, too, to know the remarkable sword, its great golden and jewel-encrusted hilt sculpted to resemble a dragon rampant, outspread wings serving as the secure crosspiece. Luthien was the dangerous one: he was the one the Eriadorans rallied behind. If the cyclopians could kill the Crimson Shadow, the revolt in Montfort might quickly be put down. Many cyclopians fled the determined stalk of the mighty young Bedwyr, but those brave enough put themselves in Luthien's way, eager to win the favor of Viscount Aubrey, who would likely be appointed the next duke of the city.

"You should fight with main gauche," Oliver remarked, seeing Luthien engaged suddenly with two brutes. To accentuate his point, the halfling angled his large-bladed dagger in the path of a thrusting spear, catching the head of the weapon with the dagger's upturned hilt just above the protective basket. A flick of Oliver's deceptively delicate wrist snapped the head off the cyclopian's spear, and the halfling quick-stepped alongside the broken shaft and poked the tip of his rapier into the brute's chest.

"Because your left hand should be used for more than balance," the halfling finished, stepping back into a heroic pose, rapier tip to the floor, dagger hand on hip. He held the stance for just a moment as yet another cyclopian came charging in from the side.

Luthien smiled despite the press, and the fact that he was fighting two against one. He felt a need to counter Oliver's reasoning, to one-up his diminutive friend.

"But if I fought with two weapons," he began, and thrust with *Blind-Striker*, then brought it back and launched a wide-arcing sweep to force his opponents away, "then how would I ever do this?" He grabbed up his sword in both hands, spinning the heavy blade high over his head as he rushed forward. *Blind-Striker* came angling down and across, the sheer weight of the two-handed blow knocking aside both cyclopian spears, severing the tip from one.

Around went the blade, up over Luthien's head and back around and down as the young man advanced yet again, and again the cyclopian spears were turned aside and knocked out wide.

Blind-Striker continued its furious flow, following the same course, but this time the young man reversed the cut, coming back around from the left. The tip drew a line of bright blood from the closest cyclopian's shoulder down across its chest. The second brute turned to face the coming blade, spear held firmly in front of its torso.

Blind-Striker went right through that spear, right through the brute's armor, to sink deeply into its chest. The cyclopian staggered backward and would have fallen, except that Luthien held the sword firmly, and the blade held the brute in place.

The other cyclopian, wiping away its own blood, fell back and scrambled away, suddenly having no desire to stand against this young warrior.

Luthien yanked his sword free and the cyclopian fell to the floor. He had a moment before the next cyclopian adversary came at him, and he couldn't resist glancing back to see if he had taken the smile from Oliver's face.

He hadn't. Oliver's rapier was spinning circles around the tip of a cyclopian sword, the movement apparently confusing the dim-witted brute.

"Finesse!" the halfling snorted, his strong Gascony accent turning it into a three-syllable word. "If you fought with two weapons, you would have killed them both. Now I might have to chase the one you lost and kill the most ugly thing myself!"

Luthien sighed helplessly and turned back just in time to lift *Blind-Striker* in a quick parry, intercepting a wicked cut. Before Luthien could counter, he saw a movement angle in under his free hand at his left. The cyclopian jerked suddenly and groaned, Katerin O'Hale's spear deep in its belly.

"If you fought more and talked less, we'd all be out of here," the woman scolded. She tugged her spear free and swung about to meet the newest challenge coming in at her side.

Luthien recognized her bluster for what it was. He had lived and trained beside Katerin for many years, and she could fight with the best and play with them, too. She had taken an immediate liking to Oliver and his swaggering bravado, an affection that was certainly mutual. And now, despite the awful battle, despite the fact that the Ministry was about to fall back into Aubrey's dirty hands, Katerin, like Oliver, enjoyed the play.

At that moment, Luthien Bedwyr understood that he could not be surrounded by better friends.

A cyclopian roared and charged in at him, and he went into a crouch to meet the rush. The brute jerked weirdly, though, and then crashed onto its face, and Luthien saw an arrow buried deep in its skull. He followed the line of that shot, up and to the left, fifty feet above the floor, to the triforium and to Siobhan, who was eyeing him sternly—and he got the distinct feeling that she was not pleased to see him at play beside Katerin O'Hale.

But that was an argument for another day, Luthien realized as yet another brute came on, and several more beside it. The wedge had passed out of the apse and crossed the open transept areas by this point, and the narrow formation could effectively go no farther, for now Luthien and his companions were fighting on three sides. Many of the trapped defenders of the Ministry had joined their ranks, but one group of a half-dozen was still out of reach, only thirty feet ahead of where Luthien stood.

Only thirty feet, but with at least a dozen cyclopians between them and the rescuers.

"Organize the retreat," Luthien called to Katerin, and as soon as she looked back to him she knew what he meant to do. It seemed overly daring, even suicidal, and Katerin's instincts and her love of Luthien made her want to try the desperate charge beside the man. She was a soldier, though, duty-bound and understanding of her role. Only Luthien or Oliver or she could lead the main group back across the apse and through the breached eastern wall, back into the streets of the lower section, where they would scatter to safety.

"Oliver!" Luthien yelled, and then was forced to fight off the attack of a burly and ugly cyclopian. When he heard a weapon snap behind him, he knew that Oliver had heard his call. With a great heave, Luthien sent the cyclopian's arms and weapon up high. At the same time, the young warrior hopped up on his toes and spread his legs wide.

Oliver rolled through, coming back over to his feet with his rapier tip angled up. This was a tall cyclopian, and short Oliver couldn't make the hit as he had planned, driving his rapier up through the brute's diaphragm and into its lungs . . . but he settled for a belly wound instead, his fine blade sliding all the way in until it was stopped by the creature's thick backbone.

Luthien pushed the dying brute aside.

"You are sure about this?" Oliver asked, seeing the barrier between them and the trapped men. The question was rhetorical, and merely for effect, for the halfling waited not for an answer but leaped ahead into the throng of cyclopians, weaving a dance with his blade that forced the attention of the nearest two down to his level.

"You have met my fine friend?" the halfling asked as *Blind-Striker* swept in just above his head and above the defenses of the two brutes, slashing them away. Oliver shook his head incredulously at the continued stupidity of cyclopians. He and Luthien had used that trick twenty times in the last two weeks alone, and it hadn't failed yet.

Back at the main group, Katerin, too, shook her head, amazed once again at the fighting harmony Luthien and Oliver had achieved. They complemented each other perfectly, move for move, and now, despite all odds, they were making fine progress through the cyclopians, down the middle aisle between the high-backed pews.

Up on the triforium ledge, Siobhan and her cohorts realized what Luthien and Oliver were trying to do and understood that the only way the young warrior and his halfling friend, along with the six trapped men, could possibly escape was if they got support from the archers. Katerin had the main group in organized retreat by then, fighting back across the open transept area and fast approaching the apse, so Siobhan and her friends concentrated their fire directly before, and behind, Luthien and Oliver.

By the time the two companions got to the pews where the fighting continued, only four of the men were left standing. One was dead; another crawled along the wooden bench, whimpering pitifully, his guts torn.

A cyclopian leaned over the back of the high pew behind him, spear poised to finish the job. Luthien got there first, and *Blind-Striker* lived up to its name, slashing across the brute's face.

"Run on! To the breach!" Oliver instructed, and three of the four men gladly followed that command, skittering behind the halfling. The fourth turned and tried to follow, but got a spear in his back and went down heavily.

"You must leave him!" Oliver cried out to Luthien as cyclopians closed all around them. "But of course you cannot," the halfling muttered, knowing his friend. Oliver sighed, one of his many sighs for the duties of friendship, as Luthien beat back another brute, then dropped to his knees, hauling the wounded man up onto his free shoulder.

The two got back out of the pew easily enough, but found the aisle fully blocked with so many cyclopians in front of them they couldn't even see the three retreating men who had come out just before them.

"At least he will serve as a shield," Oliver remarked, referring to the man slung over Luthien's shoulder.

Luthien didn't appreciate the humor, and he growled and rushed ahead, amazed when he took down the closest cyclopian with a single feint-thrust maneuver.

But it was blind luck, he realized, as the next cyclopian came in, pressing him hard. Unbalanced, he had to fight purely defensively, his sword barely diverting each savage thrust. Luthien understood the danger of delay, knew that time was against him. Cyclopians were coming out of the pews to either side and charging down the aisle behind him. Grabbing the wounded man had cost him his life, he suddenly realized, but still, Luthien Bedwyr didn't regret the decision. Even knowing the result, if the situation was before him again, he would still try to save the wounded man.

His vision impeded by the rump of the unconscious man, Luthien could hardly see his opponent when the brute dodged to the left. Had the cyclopian been smart enough to rush in from that angle, it surely would have cut Luthien down. But it came back out to the right, and Luthien saw, though the cyclopian did not, a slender blade following its path. The cyclopian stopped and cut back to the left again, right into Oliver's rapier.

That deadly rapier blade angled down for some reason that Luthien did not understand. He turned to regard Oliver, and found the halfling balancing on top of the pew back.

"Follow me!" Oliver cried, hopping ahead to the next high back, thrusting as he landed to force the nearest cyclopian to give ground.

"Behind you!" Luthien cried, but Oliver was moving before he ever spoke the words, turning a perfect spin on the narrow plank. The halfling leaped above a sidelong cut and struck as he landed, again with perfect balance, his rapier tip poking a cyclopian in the eye.

The brute threw its weapon away and fell on its back to the bench, grasping at its torn eye with both hands.

"So sorry, but I have no time to kill you!" Oliver yelled at it, and the halfling waved to Luthien and rushed to the side, down the pew instead of down the aisle.

Luthien wanted to follow, but could not, for a horde of cyclopians beat him to the spot, and he could feel the hot breath of many more at his heels. He roared and slashed wildly, expecting to feel a spear tip at any moment.

The tumult that suddenly erupted about him sounded like a swarm of angry bees, buzzing and whipping the air every which way. Luthien yelled out at the top of his lungs and continued to strike blindly throughout the terrifying moment, not really understanding.

And then it was over, as abruptly as it had begun, and all the cyclopians near the young man lay dead or dying, stung by elvish arrows. Luthien spared no time to glance back to the triforium; he skittered along between the pews in fast pursuit of Oliver.

When they exited the other end, along the northern wall of the cathedral, they were glad to see that the three men they had rescued were beyond the altar, clambering over the tip of the angled drawbridge, where Katerin and others waited.

Oliver and Luthien made the edge of the northern transept, and saw Katerin holding her ground as cyclopians scrambled to close the escape route.

Few cyclopians blocked the way to the apse, and those fled when one was taken down by Siobhan's last arrow. On ran the two companions, Luthien still carrying the wounded man.

The altar area teemed with one-eyed brutes, and the allies holding the breach were overwhelmed and forced to fall back.

"No way out," Oliver remarked.

Luthien growled and sprinted past the halfling, to the base of the apse, then up the few stairs to the semicircular area. He didn't go straight for the altar, though, but veered to the left, toward the arched northern wall. "Close it!" he yelled to his friends at the drawbridge.

After a moment of stark horror and shock, Oliver calmed enough to figure out Luthien's reasoning. The halfling quickly gained the angle that would put him ahead of his encumbered friend. He made the wall, ripping aside an awkwardly hanging torn tapestry to reveal a wooden door.

Another barrage of arrows from the triforium kept the path clear momentarily as Oliver stood aside and let Luthien lead the way into the narrow passage, a steeply angled and curving stair that wound its way up the Ministry's tallest tower, the same stair the two companions had chased Morkney up before their fateful encounter. Oliver slammed the door behind him, but cyclopians soon tore it from its meager hinges and took up the chase.

The first thing Luthien noticed when he went into the dark stair was how very cold it was. Twenty steps up, the young man came to understand why the cyclopians, on those few occasions since the uprising when they had occupied the Ministry, had not cut down the body of their fallen leader. The normally treacherous steps and the curving walls were thick and slick with ice, snow, and water no doubt pouring into the tower from the open landing at its top.

In the darkness, Luthien had to feel his way. He put one foot up after the other, as quickly as he could go, more often than not leaning heavily against the man he carried, who was, in turn, wedged against the frozen wall.

Then Luthien slipped and stumbled, banging his knee hard against the unyielding stone. He felt movement to his side and saw the halfling's silhouette as Oliver passed, low to the floor, using his main gauche as an impromptu ice pick, stabbing it, setting it, and pulling himself along.

"Yet another reason to fight with both hands," the halfling remarked in superior tones.

Luthien grabbed Oliver's cape and used it to regain his balance. He heard the cyclopians right behind, struggling, but coming on determinedly.

"Care!" Oliver warned as one block of ice cracked free of a step, sliding down past his friend and nearly taking Luthien with it.

Luthien heard a commotion behind him, just around the bend, and knew that the closest cyclopian had gone down.

"Leave a rope end," the young warrior instructed when he came up to the cleared step.

Oliver immediately tugged his silken rope from his belt and dropped one end close to Luthien, then pressed up the stairs with all speed.

Luthien didn't dare lay the unconscious man on the floor, fearing he would slide away to his doom. He turned on the cleared step and braced himself, readying his sword.

He couldn't see the cyclopian's look of horror, but could well imagine it, when the first creature stumbled around the bend right below him, only to find that the quarry was no longer in flight!

Blind-Striker hit hard and the brute went down. Luthien stumbled as he struck, falling against the wall, and he winced when he heard the agonized groan of the unconscious man.

Down the dying brute slid, taking out the next in line, and the next behind that, until all the cyclopians were in a bouncing descent down the curving stair.

Luthien shifted the man to a more secure position on his shoulder, took up the rope, waited for Oliver to tighten the other end about a jag in the uneven wall, and began his determined climb. It took the companions more than half an hour to get up the three hundred steps to the small landing just a few steps below the tower's top. There they found the way blocked by a wall of snow. Behind them came the pounding footsteps of cyclopians closing in once more.

Oliver dug into the snow with his main gauche, the dagger's thick blade chipping and cutting away the solid barrier. Half frozen, their hands numb from the effort, they finally saw light. Dawn was just beginning to break over Montfort.

"Now what are we to do?" Oliver yelled through chattering teeth and the howling, biting wind as they pushed through to the tower's top.

Luthien laid the unconscious man down in the snow and tried to tend his wound, a wicked, jagged cut across his abdomen.

"First we are to be rid of those troublesome one-eyes," Oliver answered his own question, while he searched about the tower top until he found the biggest and most solid block of ice.

He pushed it to the top of the stairwell and shouldered it through the opening with enough force so that it slid down the five steps and across the landing, then down the curving stairwell below that. A moment later, Oliver's efforts were rewarded by the screams—rapidly diminishing screams—of surprised cyclopians.

"They will be back," Luthien said grimly.

"My so young and foolish friend," Oliver replied, "we will be frozen stiff before they ever arrive!"

It seemed a distinct possibility. Winter was cold in Montfort, nestled in the mountains, and colder still three hundred feet up atop a snow-covered tower, with no practical shielding from the brutal northern winds.

Luthien went to the tower's side, to the frozen rope Oliver had tied off weeks ago around one of the block battlements. He shielded his eyes from the stinging wind and peered over, down the length of the tower, to the naked body of dead Duke Morkney, visible, though still in shadow, apparently frozen solid against the stone.

"You have your grapnel?" Luthien asked suddenly, referring to the enchanted device the wizard Brind'Amour had given to the halfling: a black puckered ball which once had been affixed to the now frozen rope.

"I would not leave it up here," Oliver retorted. "Though I did leave my fine rope, holding the dead duke. A rope you can replace, you see, but my so fine grapnel . . ."

"Get it out," Luthien shouted, having no patience for one of Oliver's legendary orations.

Oliver paused and stared hard at the young man, then cocked an eyebrow incredulously. "I have not enough rope to get us down the tower," the halfling explained. "Not enough rope to get us halfway down!"

They heard the grunts of approaching cyclopians from the entrance to the stairwell.

"Get it ready," Luthien instructed. As he spoke, he tugged hard on the frozen rope along the tower's rim, freeing some of it from the encapsulating ice.

"You cannot be serious," Oliver muttered.

Luthien ran back and gingerly lifted the wounded man. Another cyclopian growl emanated from the curving tunnel, not so far below.

Oliver shrugged. "I could be wrong."

The halfling got to the frozen rope first. He rubbed his hands together vigorously, blowing on them several times, and into his green gauntlets, as well, before he replaced them. Then he took up his main gauche in one hand and the rope in the other, and went over the side without hesitation. He worked his way down as quickly as he could, using the long-bladed dagger to free up the rope as he went, knowing that Luthien, with his heavy load, would need a secure hold.

Oliver grimaced as he came down to the rope's end, gingerly setting his foot atop the frozen head of the dead Duke Morkney. Settling in, he glanced all about in the growing light trying to find a place where he could use his magical grapnel, a place that could get him to another secure footing.

Nothing was apparent, except one tiny window far below. To make matters worse, Oliver and Luthien were coming down the northern side of the Ministry. The courtyard below was on the wrong side of the dividing wall and was fast-filling with cyclopians, looking and pointing up.

"I have been in worse places," Oliver said flippantly as the struggling Luthien joined him, the poor wounded man slipping in and out of consciousness and groaning with every bounce.

Luthien braced himself, putting one foot on Morkney's frozen shoulder. He turned so that he could clench the rope with the same hand that held the unconscious man, and tugged his other hand free.

"There was the time that you and I hung over the lake," Oliver went on. "A so huge turtle below us, a dragon to our left, and an angry wizard to our right . . ."

Oliver's story trailed off in a sympathetic "Ooh," when Luthien held up his hand to show that the rope had cut right through his gauntlet and into his skin as well. He would have been bleeding, except that what little blood had come out had already darkened and solidified on his palm.

Cyclopians gained the tower top just then and hung over the edge, leering down at Luthien and Oliver.

"We have nowhere to go!" the frustrated Oliver cried suddenly.

Luthien considered the apparent truth of the words. "Throw your grapnel around to the east," he instructed.

Oliver understood the wisdom—around the eastern corner would put them back on the right side of Montfort's dividing wall—but still, the command seemed foolish. Even if they swung around that way, they would be hanging more than two hundred feet above the street, with no practical way to get down.

Oliver shook his head, and both friends looked up to see a spear hanging down from the tower's lip, then rapidly dropping their way.

Luthien drew out *Blind-Striker* (and nearly tumbled away for the effort) and lifted the solid blade just in time to deflect the missile.

Cyclopians howled, both above and below the companions, and Luthien knew that the parry was purely lucky and that sooner or later one of those dropped spears would skewer him.

He looked back to Oliver, meaning to scold him and reiterate his command, and found that the halfling had already taken out the curious grapnel and was stringing out the length of rope. Oliver braced himself and flung the thing with all his strength, out to the northwest. As the rope slipped through his fingers, Oliver deftly applied enough pressure and brought himself around toward the east, turning the angle of the flying ball.

A final twist slapped Oliver's hand against the icy wall to the east, and the smooth-flying ball disappeared around the bend.

Neither companion dared to breathe, imagining the ball striking sidelong against the eastern wall.

The rope didn't fall.

Oliver tugged gingerly, testing the set. They had no way of knowing how firmly the grapnel had caught, or if turning its angle as they swung around would free it up and drop them to their deaths.

Another spear fell past them, nearly taking the tip from Luthien's nose.

"Are you coming?" the halfling asked, holding the rope up so that Luthien could grab on.

Luthien took it and hugged it closely, securing himself and the unconscious man, and looping the rope below one foot. He took a deep breath—Oliver did, too.

"You have never been in a worse place," Luthien insisted.

Oliver opened his mouth to reply, but only a scream came out as Luthien slipped off the frozen duke, his weight taking the surprised halfling along for the ride.

An instant later, a better-aimed cyclopian spear buried itself deeply into the top of Duke Morkney's frozen head.

The trio slid along and down the icy-smooth tower wall, flying wide as they swung around the abrupt corner, and crashed back hard, sliding to a jerking stop forty feet below the enchanted grapnel.

They found no footing, and looked down, way down, to yet another gathering below, this one of their allies. Even as they watched, the last of the Cutters came out of the secret eastern door, using a rope to descend the twenty feet to the ground, past the drawbridge, which had been closed and secured. There was no way for those allies to help them, no way for Katerin, or even the agile elves, to scale the icy tower and get to them.

"This is a better spot," Oliver decided sarcastically. "At least our friends will get to see us die."

"Not now, Oliver," Luthien said grimly.

"At least we have no spears falling at our heads," the halfling continued. "It will probably take the dim-witted one-eyes an hour or more to figure out which side of the tower we are now on."

"Not now, Oliver," Luthien said again, trying to concentrate on their predicament, trying to find a way out.

He couldn't see even a remote possibility. After a few frustrating moments, he considered just letting go of the rope and getting the inevitable over with.

A spear plummeted past, and the pair looked up to see a group of brutes grinning down at them.

"You could be wrong," Luthien offered before Oliver could say it.

"Three tugs will free the grapnel," Oliver reasoned, for that indeed was the only way to release the enchanted device once it had been set. "If I was quick enough—and always I am—I might reset it many feet below."

Luthien stared at him with blank amazement. Even the boastful Oliver had to admit that his plan wasn't a plan at all, that if he pulled free the grapnel, he and Luthien, and the wounded man as well, would be darker spots on a dark street, two hundred feet below.

Oliver said no more, and neither did Luthien, for there was nothing more to say. It seemed as though the legend that was the Crimson Shadow would not have a happy ending.

Brind'Amour's grapnel was a marvelous thing. The puckered ball could stick to any wall, no matter how sheer. It was stuck now sidelong, the eye-loop straight out to the side and the weighted rope hanging down.

Luthien and Oliver felt a sudden jerk as their weight finally made the ball half-turn on the wall and straighten out, shifting so that it was in line above the hanging rope. Then, suddenly and unexpectedly, the pair found themselves descending, the ball sliding along the icy surface.

Luthien cried out. So did Oliver, but the halfling kept the presence of mind to jab at the stone with his main gauche. The dagger's tip bit into the ice, threw tiny flecks all about, drawing a fine line as the descent continued.

Up above they heard cyclopian curses, and another spear would have taken Oliver had he not thrust his main gauche above his head, knocking it away. Down below, they heard cries of "Catch them!"

Luthien kicked at the wall, tried to scratch at the ice with his boot heels, anything to maintain some control along the sliding descent. He couldn't tell how high he was, how far he had to go. Every so often, the puckered ball came to a spot that was not so thick with ice and the momentum of the slide was lessened. But not completely stopped. Down went the friends, sometimes fast and sometimes slow, screaming all the way. Luthien noted the secret door forty feet to the side and an instant later he felt hands reaching up to grab his legs, heard groans all about him as comrades cushioned the fall and the ground rushed up to swallow him.

Then he was down, in a tumble, and Oliver was above him, the halfling's fall padded by Luthien's broad chest.

Oliver leaped up and snapped his fingers. "I told you I have been in worse places," he said, and three tugs freed his enchanted grapnel.

A moment later, thunderous pounding began at the closed drawbridge, the cyclopians outraged that they had lost their prize. Blocks split apart and fell outward, the brutes using one of the many statues within the cathedral as a battering ram.

Luthien was helped to his feet; the wounded man was scooped up and carried away.

"Time to go," said Katerin O'Hale, standing at the stunned young Bedwyr's side, propping him by the elbow.

Luthien looked at her, and at Siobhan standing beside her, and let them pull him away.

In the blink of a cyclopian eye, the Eriadorans disappeared into the streets of Montfort's lower section, and the cyclopians, standing helplessly as they finally breached the wall, didn't dare to follow.

Some distance away, Oliver pulled up short and bade his companions to wait. They all looked back, following the halfling's gaze up the side of the Ministry's tower. The ice-covered eastern wall shone brilliantly in the morning light, and the image the halfling had spotted was unmistakable, and so fitting.

Two hundred feet up the wall loomed a red silhouette, a crimson shadow. Luthien's wondrous cape had worked another aspect of its magic, leaving its tell-tale image emblazoned on the stones, a fitting message from the Crimson Shadow to the common folk of Montfort.

CHAPTER 2

TO THE BITTER END

"YOU SHOULD NOT be up here," Oliver remarked, his frosty breath filling the air before him. He grabbed the edge of the flat roof and pulled himself over, then hopped up to his feet and clapped his hands hard to get the blood flowing in them.

Across the way, Luthien didn't reply, other than to nod in the direction of the Ministry. Oliver walked up beside his friend and noted the intensity in Luthien's striking cinnamon-colored eyes. The halfling followed that gaze to the southwest, toward the massive structure that dominated the Montfort skyline. He could see the body of Duke Morkney still frozen against the cathedral wall, the spear still stuck in the dead man's head. The rope around his neck, however, now angled out from the building, its end pushed away from the buttress where it had been tied.

"They cut the rope," the halfling howled, thinking the garish scene perfectly outrageous. "But still the dead duke stays!" Indeed the cyclopians had cut the rope free from the tower top, hoping to dislodge Morkney. Farther down the tower side, though, the rope remained frozen and so the cyclopians had done nothing more than create what looked like a ghastly antenna, sticking up from Morkney's head as if he were some giant bug.

Luthien jutted his chin upward, toward the top of the tower, and shifting his gaze, Oliver saw cyclopians bumbling about up there, cursing and pushing each other. Just below the lip, the tower glistened with wetness and some of the ice had broken away. The halfling realized what was happening a moment later when the cyclopians hoisted a huge, steaming cauldron and tipped it over the edge. Boiling water ran down the side of the tower.

One of the cyclopians slipped, then roared in pain and whirled away, and the hot cauldron toppled down behind the water. It spun along its descent, but stayed close to the wall, and slammed into the butt of the spear that was embedded in Morkney's head. On bounced the cauldron, bending the spear out with it, and the soldiers on the roof winced as Morkney's head jerked forward violently, nearly torn from his torso. The spear did come free, and it and the cauldron fell to the courtyard below, to the terrified screams of scrambling cyclopians and the derisive hoots from the many common Eriadorans watching the spectacle from the city's lower section.

The pushing atop the tower became an open fight and the offending cyclopian, still clutching the hand he had burned on the cauldron, was heaved over the battlement. His was the only scream from that side of the dividing wall, but the hoots from the lower section came louder than ever.

"Oh, I do like how they bury their dead!" Oliver remarked.

Luthien didn't share the halfling's mirth. The Ministry had been lost to Aubrey, and it was Luthien's decision to let the viscount keep it, at least for the time being. The cost of taking the building back, if they could indeed roust the cyclopians from the place, would not be worth the many lives that would be lost.

Still, Luthien had to wonder about the wisdom of that decision. Not because he needed the cathedral for strategic purposes—the huge building could be defended, but the open courtyards surrounding it made it useless as a base of offensive operations—but because of its symbolic ramifications. The Ministry, that gigantic, imposing temple of God, the largest and greatest structure in all of Eriador, belonged to the common folk who had built it, not to the ugly one-eyes and the unlawful Avon king. The soul of Montfort, of all of Eriador, was epitomized by that cathedral; every village, no matter how small or how remote, boasted at least one family member who had helped to build the Ministry.

The next cauldron of boiling water was dumped over the side then, and this time, the cauldron itself was not dropped. The hot liquid made it all the way down to the duke, and the rope, freed of its icy grasp, rolled over and hung down. A few seconds later, the upper half of Morkney's frozen torso came free of the wall and the corpse bent out at the waist.

The two friends couldn't see much on the top of the tower, of course, but after a long period when no cyclopians appeared near the edge, Luthien and Oliver surmised that the brutes had run out of hot water.

"Is a long way to climb with a full cauldron," the halfling snickered, remembering the winding stair, a difficult walk even without the cold and the ice.

"Aubrey believes that it is worth the effort," Luthien said, and his grim tone tipped Oliver off to his friend's distress.

Oliver stroked the frozen hairs of his neatly trimmed goatee and looked back to the tower.

"We could take the Ministry back," he offered, guessing the source of Luthien's mood.

Luthien shook his head. "Not worth the losses."

"We are winning this fight," Oliver said. "The merchant-types are caught in their homes and not so many cyclopians remain." He looked at the wall and imagined the scene in the northern courtyard. "And one less than a moment ago," he said with a snort.

Luthien didn't disagree. The Eriadorans were close to taking back their city—Caer MacDonald, it had been called—from Greensparrow's lackeys. But how long would they hold it? Already there were reports of an army coming from Avon to put down the resistance, and while those were unconfirmed and possibly no more than the manifestation of fears, Luthien couldn't deny the possibility. King Greensparrow would not tolerate an uprising, would not easily let go of Eriador, though he had never truly conquered the land.

Luthien thought of the plague that had ravaged Eriador some twenty years before, in the very year that he had been born. His mother had died in that plague, and so many others as well, nearly a third of the Eriadoran populace. The proud folk could no longer continue their war with Greensparrow's armies—forces comprised mostly of cyclopians—and so they had surrendered.

And then another plague had come over Eriador: a blackening of the spirit. Luthien had seen it in his own father, a man with little fight left in him. He knew it in men like Aubrey, Eriadorans who had accepted Greensparrow with all their heart, who profited from the misery of the commonfolk.

So what exactly had he and Oliver started that day in the Ministry when he had killed Morkney? He thought of that battle now, of how Morkney had given over his body to a demon, further confirmation of the wickedness that was Greensparrow and his cronies. The mere thought of the evil beast, Praehotec by name, sent shudders coursing through Luthien, for he would not have won that fight, would not have plunged Oliver's rapier through the duke's skinny chest, had not Morkney erred and released the demon to its hellish home, the human thinking to kill the battered Luthien on his own.

Looking back over the events of these last few weeks, the blind luck and the subtle twists of fate, Luthien had to wonder, and to worry—for how many innocent people, caught up in the frenzy of the fast-spreading legend of the Crimson Shadow, would be punished by the evil king? Would another plague, like the one that had broken the hearts and will of Eriador when Greensparrow first became king of Avon, sweep over the land? Or would Greensparrow's cyclopian army simply march into Montfort and kill everyone who was not loyal to the throne?

And it would go beyond Montfort, Luthien knew. Katerin had come from Isle Bedwydrin, his home, bearing his father's sword and news that the uprising was general on the island, as well. Gahris, Luthien's father, had apparently found his heart, the pride that was Eriador of old, in the news of his son's exploits. The eorl of Bedwydrin had declared that no cyclopian on Isle Bedwydrin would remain alive. Avonese, once Aubrey's consort and passed on by Aubrey to become the wife of Gahris, was in chains.

The thought of that pompous and painted whore brought bile into Luthien's throat. In truth, Avonese had begun all of this, back in Bedwydrin. Luthien had unwittingly accepted her kerchief, a symbol that he would champion her in the fighting arena. When he had defeated his friend, Garth Rogar, the wicked Avonese had called for the vanquished man's death.

And so Garth Rogar had died, murdered by a cyclopian that Luthien later slew. While the ancient rules gave Avonese the right to make such a demand, simple morality most definitely did not.

Avonese, in pointing her thumb down, in demanding the death of Garth Rogar, had set Luthien on his path. How ironic now that Aubrey, the man who had brought the whore to Bedwydrin, was Luthien's mortal enemy in the struggle for Montfort.

Luthien wanted Aubrey's head and meant to get it, but he feared that his own, and those of many friends, would roll once King Greensparrow retaliated.

"So why are you sad, my friend?" Oliver asked, his patience worn thin by the stinging breeze. No more cyclopians had appeared atop the tower, and Oliver figured that it would take them an hour at least to descend, fill another cauldron, and haul the thing up. The comfort-loving halfling had no intention of waiting an hour in the freezing winter wind.

Luthien stood up and rubbed his hands and his arms briskly. "Come," he said, to Oliver's relief. "I am to meet Siobhan at the Dwelf. Her scouts have returned with word from the east and the west."

Oliver hopped into line behind Luthien, but his step quickly slowed. The scouts had returned?

The worldly Oliver thought he knew then what was bothering Luthien.

The Dwelf, so named because it catered to nonhumans, particularly to dwarfs and elves, was bustling that day. It was simply too cold outside to wage any major battles, and many of the rebels were using the time to resupply their own larders and relax. Located in one of Montfort's poorest sections, the Dwelf had never been very popular with any except the nonhuman residents of Montfort, but now, as the favored tavern of the Crimson Shadow, the hero of the revolution, it was almost always full.

The barkeep, a slender but rugged man (and looking more fearsome than usual, for he hadn't found the time to shave his thick black stubble in nearly a week), wiped his hands on a beer-stained cloth and moved up to stand before Oliver and Luthien as soon as they took their customary seats at the bar.

"We're looking for Siobhan," Luthien said immediately.

Before Tasman could answer, the young Bedwyr felt a gentle touch on his earlobe. He closed his eyes as the hand slid lower, stroking his neck in the sensuous way only Siobhan could.

"We have business," Oliver said to Tasman, then looked sidelong at the couple. "Though I am not so sure which business my excited friend favors at this time."

Luthien's cinnamon eyes popped open and he spun about, taking Siobhan's hand as he turned and pulling it from his neck. He cleared his throat, embarrassed, to find that the half-elf was not only not alone, but that one of her companions was a scowling Katerin O'Hale.

The young man realized then that the gentle stroke of his neck had been given for Katerin's benefit.

Oliver knew it, too. "I think that the war comes closer to my home," he whispered to Tasman. The barkeep snickered and slid a couple of ale-filled mugs before the companions, then moved away. Tasman's ears were good enough to catch everything important that was said along his bar, but he always tried to make sure that those conversing didn't know he was in on the discussion.

Luthien locked stares with Katerin for a long moment, then cleared his throat again. "What news from Avon?" he asked Siobhan.

Siobhan looked over her left shoulder to her other companion, an elf dressed in many layers of thick cloth and furs. He had rosy cheeks and long eyelashes that glistened with crystals of melting ice.

"It is not promising, good sir," the elf said to Luthien, with obvious reverence.

Luthien winced a bit, still uncomfortable with such formal treatment. He was the leader of the rebels, put forth as the hero of Eriador, and those who were not close to him always called him "good sir" or "my lord," out of respect.

"Reports continue that an army is on the way from Avon," the elf went on. "There are rumors of a great gathering of cyclopian warriors—Praetorian Guard, I would assume—in Princetown."

It made sense to Luthien. Princetown lay diagonally across the Iron Cross to the southeast. It was not physically the closest to Montfort of Avon's major cities, but it was the closest to Malpuissant's Wall, the only pass through the great mountains that an army could hope to navigate, even in midsummer, let alone in the harsh winter.

Still, any march from Princetown to Montfort, crossing through the fortress of Dun Caryth, which anchored Malpuissant's Wall to the Iron Cross, would take many weeks, and the rate of attrition in the harsh weather would be taxing. Luthien took some comfort in the news, for it didn't seem probable that Greensparrow would strike out from Princetown until the spring melt was in full spate.

"There is another possibility," the elf said grimly, seeing the flicker of hope in the young Bedwyr's eyes.

"Port Charley," guessed Katerin, referring to the seaport west of Montfort.

The elf nodded.

"Is the rumor based in knowledge or in fear?" Oliver asked.

"I do not know that there is a rumor at all," the elf replied.

"Fear," Oliver decided, *and well-founded,* he silently added. As the realities of the fighting in Montfort had settled in and the rebels turned their eyes outside the embattled city, talk of an Avon fleet sailing into Port Charley abounded. It seemed a logical choice for Greensparrow. The straits between Baranduine and Avon were treacherous in the winter, and icebergs were not uncommon, but it was not so far a sail, and the great ships of Avon could carry many, many cyclopians.

"What allies—" Luthien began to ask, but the elf cut him short, fully expecting the question.

"The folk of Port Charley are no friend of cyclopians," he said. "No doubt they are glad that one-eyes are dying in Montfort, and that Duke Morkney was slain."

"But . . ." Oliver prompted, correctly interpreting the elf's tone.

"But they have declared no allegiance to our cause," the elf finished.

"Nor will they," Katerin put in. All eyes turned to her, some questioning, wondering what she knew. Luthien understood, for he had often been to Hale, Katerin's home, an independent, free-spirited town not so different from Port Charley. Still, he wasn't so sure that Katerin's reasoning was sound. The names of ancient heroes, of Bruce MacDonald, sparked pride and loyalty in all Eriadorans, the folk of Port Charley included.

"If a fleet does sail, it must be stopped at the coast," Luthien said determinedly.

Katerin shook her head. "If you try to bring an army into Port Charley, you will be fighting," she said. "But not with allies of Greensparrow."

"Would they let the cyclopians through?" Oliver asked.

"If they will not join with us, then they will not likely oppose Greensparrow," Siobhan put in.

Luthien's mind raced with possibilities. Could he bring Port Charley into the revolution? And if not, could he and his rebels hope to hold out against an army of Avon?

"Perhaps we should consider again our course," Oliver offered a moment later.

"Consider our course?" Katerin and Siobhan said together.

"Go back underground," the halfling replied. "The winter is too cold for much fighting anyway. So we stop fighting. And you and I," he said to Luthien, nudging his friend, "will fly away like wise little birds."

The open proclamation that perhaps this riot had gotten a bit out of hand sobered the mood of all those near to the halfling, even the many eavesdroppers who were not directly in on the conversation. Oliver had reminded them all of the price of failure.

Siobhan looked at her elvish companion, who only shrugged helplessly.

"Our lives were not so bad before the fight," Tasman remarked, walking by Luthien and Oliver on the other side of the bar.

"There is a possibility of diplomacy," Siobhan said. "Even now. Aubrey knows that he cannot put down the revolt without help from Avon, and he dearly craves the position of duke. He might believe that if he could strike a deal and rescue Montfort, Greensparrow would reward him with the title."

Luthien looked past the speaker, into the eyes of Katerin O'Hale, green orbs that gleamed with angry fires. The notion of diplomacy, of surrender, apparently did not sit well with the proud warrior woman.

Behind Katerin, several patrons were jostled and then pushed aside. Then Katerin, too, was nudged forward as a squat figure, four feet tall but sturdy, sporting a bushy blue-black beard, shoved his way to stand before Luthien.

"What's this foolish talk?" the dwarf Shuglin demanded, his gnarly fists clenched as though he meant to leap up and throttle Luthien at any moment.

"We are discussing our course," Oliver put in. The halfling saw the fires in Shuglin's eyes. Angry fires—for the dwarf, now that he had found some hope and had tasted freedom, often proclaimed that he would prefer death over a return to subjugation.

Shuglin snorted. "You decided your course that day in the Ministry," he roared. "You think you can go back now?"

"Not I, nor Luthien," the halfling admitted. "But for the rest . . ."

Shuglin wasn't listening. He shoved between Luthien and Oliver, grabbed the edge of the bar, and heaved himself up to stand above the crowd.

"Hey!" he roared and the Dwelf went silent. Even Tasman, though certainly not appreciating the heavy boots on his polished bar, held back.

"Who in here is for surrendering?" Shuglin called.

The Dwelf's crowd remained silent.

"Shuglin," Luthien began, trying to calm his volatile friend.

The dwarf ignored him. "Who in here is for killing Aubrey and raising the flag of Caer MacDonald?"

The Dwelf exploded in cheers. Swords slid free of their sheaths and were slapped together above the heads of the crowd. Calls for Aubrey's head rang out from every corner.

Shuglin hopped down between Oliver and Luthien. "You got your answer," he growled, and he moved to stand between Katerin and Siobhan, his gaze steeled upon Luthien and muscular arms crossed over his barrel chest.

Luthien didn't miss the smile that Katerin flashed at the dwarf, nor the pat she gave to him.

Of everything the dwarf had said, the most important was the ancient name of Montfort, Caer MacDonald, a tribute to Eriador's hero of old.

"Well said, my friend," Oliver began. "But—"

That was as far as the halfling got.

"Bruce MacDonald is more than a name," Luthien declared.

"So is the Crimson Shadow," Siobhan unexpectedly added.

Luthien paused for just an instant, to turn a curious and appreciative look at the half-elf. "Bruce MacDonald is an ideal," Luthien went on. "A symbol for the folk of Eriador. And do you know what Bruce MacDonald stands for?"

"Killing cyclopians?" asked Oliver, who was from Gascony and not Eriador.

"Freedom," Katerin corrected. "Freedom for every man and woman." She looked to Siobhan and to Shuglin. "For every elf and every dwarf. And every halfling, Oliver," she said, her intent gaze locking with his. "Freedom for Eriador, and for every person who would live here."

"We talk of halting what we cannot halt," Luthien put in. "How many merchants and their cyclopian guards have been killed? How many Praetorian Guards? And what of Duke Morkney? Do you believe that Greensparrow will so easily forgive?"

Luthien slipped off his stool, standing tall. "We have begun something here, something too important to be stopped by mere fear. We have begun the freeing of Eriador."

"Let us not get carried away," Oliver interjected. "Or we might get carried away . . . in boxes."

Luthien looked at his diminutive friend and realized how far Oliver—and many others, as well, given the whispers that had reached Luthien's ears—were sliding backward on this issue. "You are the one who told me to reveal myself in the Ministry that day," he reminded the halfling. "You are the one who wanted me to start the riot."

"I?" Oliver balked. "I just wanted to get us out of there alive after you so foolishly jumped up and shot an arrow at the Duke!"

"I was there to save Siobhan!" Luthien declared.

"And I was there to save you!" Oliver roared right back at him. The halfling sighed and calmed, patted his hand on Luthien's shoulder. "But let us not get carried away," Oliver said. "In boxes or any other way."

Luthien didn't calm a bit. His thoughts were on destiny, on Bruce MacDonald and the ideals the man represented. Katerin was with him, so was Shuglin, and so was his father, back on Isle Bedwydrin. He looked toward Siobhan, but could not read the feelings behind the sparkle of her green eyes. He would have liked something from her, some indication, for over the past few weeks she had quietly become one of his closest advisors.

"It cannot be stopped," Luthien declared loudly enough so that every person in the Dwelf heard him. "We have started a war that we must win."

"The boats will sail from Avon," Oliver warned.

"And so they will be stopped," Luthien countered, cinnamon eyes flashing. "In Port Charley." He looked back out at the crowd, back to Siobhan, and it seemed to him as if the sparkle in her eyes had intensified, as if he had just passed some secret test. "Because the folk of that town will join with us," Luthien went on, gathering strength, "and so will all of Eriador." Luthien paused, but his wicked smile spoke volumes.

"They will join us once the flag of Caer MacDonald flies over Montfort," he continued. "Once they know that we are in this to the end."

Oliver thought of remarking on just how bitter that end might become, but he held the thought. He had never been afraid of death, had lived his life as an ultimate adventure, and now Luthien, this young and naive boy he had found on the road, had opened his eyes once more.

Shuglin thrust his fist into the air. "Get me to the mines!" he growled. "I'll give you an army!"

Luthien considered his bearded friend. Shuglin had long been lobbying for an attack on the Montfort mines, outside of town, where most of his kin were imprisoned. Siobhan had whispered that course into Luthien's ear many times, as well. Now, with the decision that this was more than a riot, with the open declaration of war against Greensparrow, Luthien recognized that action must be taken swiftly.

He eyed the dwarf directly. "To the mines," he agreed, and Shuglin whooped and hopped away, punching his fist into the air.

Many left the Dwelf then, to spread the word. It occurred to Oliver that some might be spies for Aubrey and were even now running to tell the viscount of the plan.

It didn't matter, the halfling decided. Since the beginning of the revolt in the city's lower section, Aubrey and his forces had been bottled up within the walls of the inner section and could not get word to those cyclopians guarding the Montfort mines.

"You are crazy," Siobhan said to Luthien, but in a teasing, not derisive, manner. She moved near to the man and put her lips against his ear. "And so exciting," she whispered, but loud enough so that those closest could hear. She bit his earlobe and gave a soft growl.

Looking over her shoulder, glimpsing Katerin's scowl, Luthien recognized again that Siobhan's nuzzle, like her earlier display of affection, was for the other woman's sake. Luthien felt no power, no pride, with that understanding. The last thing the young Bedwyr wanted to do was bring pain to Katerin O'Hale, who had been his lover—and more than that, his best friend—those years on Isle Bedwydrin.

Siobhan and her elvish companion left then, but not before the half-elf threw a wink back at Luthien that changed to a superior look as she passed Katerin.

Katerin didn't blink, showed no expression whatsoever.

That alone made Luthien nervous.

Not so long afterward, Luthien, Oliver, and Katerin stood alone just inside the door of the Dwelf. It was snowing again, heavily, so many of the patrons had departed to stoke the fires in their own homes.

The talk between the three was light, but obviously strained, with Oliver pointedly keeping the subject on planning the coming assault on the Montfort mines.

The tension between Luthien and Katerin did not diminish, though, and finally Luthien decided that he had to say something.

"It is not what it seems," he stammered, interrupting the rambling Oliver in midsentence.

Katerin looked at him curiously.

"With Siobhan, I mean," the young man explained. "We have been friends for some time. I mean . . ."

Luthien found no words to continue. He realized how stupid he must sound; of course Katerin—and everyone else!—knew that he and Siobhan were lovers.

"You were not here," he stuttered. "I mean . . ."

Oliver groaned, and Luthien realized that he was failing miserably and was probably making the situation much worse. Still, he could not bring himself to stop, could not accept things as they were between him and Katerin.

"It's not what you think," he said again, and Oliver, recognizing the scowl crossing Katerin's face, groaned again.

"Siobhan and I . . . we have this friendship," Luthien said. He knew that he was being ultimately condescending, especially considering the importance of the previous discussion. But Luthien's emotion overruled his wisdom and he couldn't stop himself. "No, it is more than that. We have this . . ."

"Do you believe that you are more important to me than the freedom of Eriador?" Katerin asked him bluntly.

"I know you are hurt," Luthien replied before he realized the stupidity of his words.

Katerin took a quick step forward, grabbed Luthien by the shoulders and lifted her knee into his groin, bending him low. She moved as if to say something, but only trembled and turned away.

Oliver noted the glisten of tears rimming her green eyes and knew how profoundly the young man's words had stung her.

"Never make that mistake about me again," Katerin said evenly, through gritted teeth, and she left without turning back.

Luthien gradually straightened, face white with pain, his gaze locked on the departing woman. When she disappeared into the night, he looked helplessly at Oliver.

The halfling shook his head, trying not to laugh.

"I think I'm falling in love with her," Luthien said breathlessly, grimacing with the effort of talking.

"With her?" Oliver asked, pointing to the doorway.

"With her," Luthien confirmed.

Oliver stroked his goatee. "Let me understand," he began slowly, thoughtfully. "One woman puts her knee into your cabarachees and the other puts her tongue into your ear, and you prefer the one with the knee?"

Luthien shrugged, honestly not knowing the answer.

Oliver shook his head. "I'm very worried about you."

Luthien was worried, too. He didn't know what he was feeling, for either Katerin or for Siobhan. He cared for them both—no man could ask for a dearer friend or lover than either woman—and that made it all the more confusing. He was a young man trying to explore emotions he did not understand. And at the same time, he was the Crimson Shadow, leader of a revolution . . . and a thousand lives, ten thousand lives, might hinge on his every decision.

Oliver started for the door and motioned for Luthien to follow. The young man took a deep and steadying breath and readily complied.

It was good to let someone else lead.

CHAPTER 3

BREAKOUT

HALF A DOZEN cyclopians, the leaders of the operation at the Montfort mines, turned dumbfounded stares to the door of their side cave—a door that they thought had been locked—when the man and the halfling casually strode in, smiles wide, as though they had been invited. The two even closed the door behind them, and the halfling stuck a pick into the lock opening and gave a quick twist, nodding as the tumblers clicked again.

The closest brute scrambled for its spear, which was lying across hooks set into the squared cave's right-hand wall, but faster than its one eye could follow, the man hopped to the side, whipped a magnificent sword from its sheath on his hip, and brought it swinging down across the spear shaft, pinning the weapon. The cyclopian shifted, meaning to run the man down. But it paused, confused, at the sight of the man standing calmly, unthreateningly, his hand held up as though he wanted no fight.

Before another cyclopian could react, the halfling rushed between the closest two chairs and leaped atop the table, rapier in hand. He didn't threaten any of the brutes, though. Rather, he struck a heroic pose.

A chair skidded from behind the table and one cyclopian, the largest of the group, stood tall and ominous. Like Luthien over to the side, Oliver waved his hand in the air as though to calm the brute.

"Greetings," the halfling said. "I am Oliver deBurrows, highway-halfling, and my friend here is Luthien Bedwyr, son of Eorl Gahris of Bedwydrin."

The cyclopians obviously didn't know how to react, didn't understand what was going on. The Montfort mines were some distance south of the city itself, nestled deep in the towering mountains. The place was perfectly secluded; the brutes didn't even know that the battle for Montfort was raging, for they had heard nothing from the city since before the first snows. Except for the prisoner caravans, which wouldn't resume until the spring melt, no one visited the Montfort mines.

"Of course, you would know him better as the Crimson Shadow," Oliver went on.

The large cyclopian at the end of the table narrowed its one eye dangerously. There had been a breakout at the mines just a few months before, when two invaders, rumored to be a human and a halfling, had slipped in, killed more than a few cyclopians, and freed three dwarven prisoners. The entire group of guards in this small side room had been on a shift far underground on that occasion, but these two certainly fit the descriptions of the perpetrators. The cyclopian and its allies couldn't be sure of anything, though, for this sudden intrusion was too unexpected, too strange.

"Now I wanted for me and my friend here, and for our two hundred other friends outside"—that turned more than one cyclopian's head toward the closed door—"to just come in here and kill you very dead," Oliver explained. "But my gentle friend, he wanted to give you a chance to surrender."

It took a moment for the words to register, and the large cyclopian caught on first. The brute roared, overturning the table.

Oliver whirled away from the brute on his heel, expecting the move. He scrambled and leaped, flicking his rapier to the left, then to the right, slicing the two closest cyclopians across their faces.

"I will consider that a no," the halfling said dryly, falling into a roll as he landed and turning a complete somersault to find his center of balance.

The cyclopian nearest to Luthien growled and lowered its shoulder to charge, but Luthien pointed toward the trapped spear. "Look!" the young Bedwyr cried.

The stupid brute complied, turning to see Luthien's sword rapidly ascending, as Luthien snapped a wicked backhand. *Blind-Striker*'s heavy, fine-edged blade cracked through the brute's forehead.

Luthien leaped over the corpse as it crumbled.

"I told you they would not surrender!" yelled Oliver, who was engaged with two cyclopians, including one of the two he had stabbed in the face. The halfling's aim on the other had been better, his rapier taking the creature directly in the eye. Like its companion, the brute had stumbled out of its chair, but had then tripped over the chair, and it squirmed about on the floor, flailing its arms wildly.

Luthien charged the side of the tipped table, lowering his shoulder as though he meant to ram it and knock it into the cyclopian across the way. The one-eye, outweighing the man considerably, likewise dropped its massive shoulder, more than willing to oblige. At the last moment, Luthien cut to the side, behind the upturned table, and the brute hit the furniture alone. Overbalanced, the cyclopian came skidding by, and Luthien hardly gave it a thought as he snapped *Blind-Striker* once to the side, into the cyclopian's ribs.

The young Bedwyr cleared the jumble and squared his footing, facing evenly against the largest brute, who had retrieved a huge battle-ax.

"One against one," he muttered, but in truth Luthien figured that this particular cyclopian, seven feet tall, at least, and weighing near to four hundred pounds, counted for one and a half.

The two facing Oliver, neither holding any weapon, gingerly hopped and skittered from side to side, looking for an opening so that they could grab the miserable rat and his stinging blade.

Oliver casually shifted and turned, poking his rapier's tip into grasping hands and seeming as though he was truly enjoying every moment of this fight.

"And I haven't even drawn my second blade," the halfling taunted. One of the cyclopians lurched for him, and he responded by sinking his rapier through its palm, the tip sliding several inches deep into the brute's forearm.

The cyclopian howled and grasped its wrist, falling to its knees with the pain, and the movement temporarily trapped the rapier. Quick-thinking, Oliver drew out his main gauche, but he found that the other cyclopian was not coming for him. The brute had rushed to the side to retrieve a nasty-looking ax.

In it charged, and Oliver sprang atop the shoulders of the kneeling cyclopian and squared to meet the attack, eyes-to-eye.

The halfling sprang away, though, as the kneeling cyclopian reached up to grab at his feet and the charging brute launched a wicked overhead chop.

The descending ax missed—missed Oliver, at least—and the attacking cyclopian groaned as the head of its kneeling fellow split apart.

"Oh, I bet that hurt," the fleeing halfling remarked.

Luthien pivoted to retreat from a sidelong swipe. He went right down to one knee and lurched forward in a thrust, scoring a hit on the advancing brute's thigh.

It was a grazing blow, though, and did not halt the giant cyclopian's charge; Luthien had to dive forward in a headlong roll to avoid the next swipe.

He came up to his feet, spiraling back the other way, and scored another hit on his opponent, this time slashing the one-eye's rump. The monster growled and spun, and the heavy ax knocked *Blind-Striker* aside.

"Remember not to parry," Luthien told himself, his hand stinging from the sheer weight of the hit. He raised his sword in both hands then, and hopped back into a defensive crouch.

"We told you that you should surrender," Luthien teased, and in looking around at the carnage, the large brute could hardly argue. Three of its comrades were dead or dying, a fourth was blinded, struggling to regain its feet and swiping wildly at the empty air. Even as the largest brute started to yell out a warning, Oliver stuck the blind cyclopian in the butt as he rushed past.

The blind brute wheeled, turning the wrong way around, and was promptly knocked flat by the cyclopian chasing Oliver. The charging brute stumbled over its falling companion, but lurched forward in an impromptu attack, swinging with all its might.

Oliver skipped aside and the ax drove deep into the upturned table.

On its knees, off balance and fully extended, with its blind comrade grabbing at its waist, the outraged cyclopian had no leverage to extract the stuck blade.

"Do let me help you," Oliver offered, rushing up and slipping his main gauche into his belt. He reached for the ax, but shifted direction and thrust his rapier through the cyclopian's throat instead.

"I changed my mind," Oliver announced as the gurgling cyclopian slipped to the floor.

Luthien's sword went up high as his monstrous opponent brought its ax overhead. The young man rushed forward, knowing that he had to move quickly before the huge one-eye gained any momentum. He slammed hard into his adversary. *Blind-Striker* struck against the ax handle and took a finger from the brute's right hand, and the attack was stopped before it ever truly began.

Still clutching the sword hilt in both hands, Luthien spun to his right and took a glancing blow on the hip from a thrusting knee. Luthien kept his back in close to the brute as he rotated; he knew that this routine would bring victory or defeat, and nothing in between. He dropped his blade over his right shoulder and bent low, then came up straight hard, slicing his blade right to left.

Blind-Striker caught the one-eye under its upraised left arm, tearing muscle and bone and nearly severing the limb.

The cyclopian's ax banged off its shoulder and fell to the floor. The brute stood a moment longer, staring blankly at its wound and at Luthien. Then it staggered a step to the side and fell heavily against the wall, its lifeblood pouring freely.

Luthien turned away to see Oliver tormenting the blind cyclopian, the halfling darting this way and that, poking the helpless creature repeatedly.

"Oliver!" Luthien scolded.

"Oh, very well," the halfling grumbled. He skipped in front of the brute, waited for its flailing arms to present an opening, then rushed in with a two-handed thrust, his rapier sliding between cyclopian ribs to find the creature's heart, his main gauche scoring solidly on its neck.

"You really should grow another eye," Oliver remarked, skipping back as the brute fell headlong, dead before it hit the floor.

Oliver looked at Luthien almost apologetically. "They really should."

■ ■ ■

A hundred feet east along the mountain wall from the side cave Luthien and Oliver had entered, Katerin O'Hale came running out of a tunnel in full flight, more than a dozen drooling cyclopians close behind.

The woman, her sword dripping blood from her first kill inside, started as though she meant to run down the road toward Montfort, but turned instead and rushed at a snow berm.

A spear narrowly missed her, diving deep into the snow, and Katerin was glad that cyclopians, with one eye and little depth perception, were not good at range weapons. Elves were much better.

Over the berm she went, diving headlong, the brutes howling only a couple of dozen feet behind her.

How they skidded and scrambled when Siobhan and the rest of the Cutters popped up over the lip of that banking, their great longbows bent back! Like stinging bees, the elvish arrows swarmed upon the cyclopians; one fell with eight arrows protruding from its bulky chest. A handful managed to turn and run back toward the mine entrance, but more arrows followed to strike them.

Only one cyclopian limped on, several arrows sticking from its back and legs. Another bolt got it in the back of the shoulder as it neared the cave, but it stubbornly plowed on and got inside.

Shuglin the dwarf and a host of rebels, mostly human, but with several other dwarfs among them, were fast in pursuit. Soon after the blue-bearded Shuglin dashed into the cave, the wounded cyclopian shrieked a death cry.

Behind the berm, Katerin squinted against the glare off the white snow and looked to the west. The door of the side cave was open again, just a bit, and an arm waved up and down, holding Oliver's huge hat.

"No need to fear for those two when they are together," Siobhan remarked, standing at Katerin's side.

Katerin looked at the half-elf, her rival for Luthien's attention. She was undeniably beautiful, with long and lustrous wheat-colored hair that made Katerin self-conscious of her own red topping.

"They have more than their share of skill, and more than their share of luck," Siobhan finished, flashing a disarming grin. There was something detached about her, Katerin recognized, something removed and superior. Still, Katerin felt no condescension directed toward her personally. All the elves and half-elves shared that cool demeanor, and Siobhan was among the most outgoing of the lot. Even their obvious rivalry over Luthien seemed less bitter than it could have been, or would have been, Katerin knew, had her rival been another proud woman from her homeland.

Siobhan and her band filtered over the snow berm, following the others into the mine entrance. Siobhan paused and waited, looking back at Katerin.

"Well done," the half-elf said as she stood among the cyclopian corpses, her sudden words catching Katerin off guard. "You baited the brutes perfectly."

Katerin nodded and rolled over the banking, sliding to her feet on the other side. She hated to admit it, but she had to, at least to herself: she liked Siobhan.

They went into the cave side by side.

Much farther down the tunnel, Shuglin and his charging band had met with stiff resistance. A barricade was up, slitted so that crossbows could be fired from behind it. Cyclopians were terrible shots, but the tunnel was neither high nor wide, and the law of averages made any approach down the long and straight run to the barricade treacherous.

Shuglin and his companions crouched around the closest corner, angered at being bottled up.

"We must wait for the elven archers," one man urged.

Shuglin didn't see the point, didn't see what good Siobhan's band might do. The cyclopians were too protected by their barricade; one or two shots might be found, but even skilled elves would not do much damage with bows.

"We got to charge," the dwarf grumbled, and the chorus around him was predictably grim.

Shuglin peeked around the bend, and nearly lost his nose to a skipping bolt. By the number of quarrels coming out and the briefness of the delay between volleys, he figured that there must be at least a dozen cyclopians on the other side of the barrier. Three times that number of fighters stood beside the dwarf, and twenty times that number would soon filter in, but the thought of losing even a few allies here, barely into the mines, didn't sit well.

The dwarf pushed his way back from the corner, coming up to a man who carried a great shield. "Give it to me," Shuglin instructed, and the man eyed him curiously for only a moment before he complied.

The shield practically covered the dwarf from head to toe. He moved back to the corner, thinking to spearhead the charge.

A cyclopian groaned from behind the barrier. Then another.

Shuglin and his allies looked to each other, not understanding.

Then they heard the slight twang of a bow, far down the tunnel ahead of them, and behind the barrier another one-eye screamed out.

Shuglin's powerful legs began pumping; he verily threw himself around the corner. His allies took up the battle cry and the charge.

"Silly one-eye," came a voice with a familiar Gascon accent from beyond the barrier. "One poke of my so fine rapier blade and you cannot see!"

A quarrel skipped off Shuglin's shield. A man flanking him took a hit in the leg and went down.

Hearing swords ringing, the dwarf didn't pause long enough to look for an opening. He lowered his strong shoulder and plowed into the barricade. Wood and stone shook loose. Shuglin didn't get through, but his allies used him as a stepping-stone and the barrier was quickly breached. By the time the dwarf regained his wits and clambered over the rubble, the fight was over, without a single rebel killed or even seriously wounded.

Luthien pointed to a fork in the passage, just at the end of the lamplight. "To the left will take you to the lower levels and your enslaved kin."

Shuglin grunted; Luthien knew where the fighting dwarf wanted to be. Shuglin had been in the mines before, but for only a short while. The dwarf had been taken prisoner in Montfort for aiding Luthien and Oliver in one of their many daring escapes. He had been sentenced to hard labor in the mines as all convicted dwarfs were, along with two of his fellows. But Oliver, Luthien, and the Cutters had rescued the three dwarfs before the cyclopians had had the chance to take them down to the lower levels.

"And where are you off to?" Shuglin wanted to know, seeing that Luthien and Oliver weren't moving to follow him.

Luthien shrugged and smiled, and turned to leave. Oliver tipped his hat. "There are many smaller side tunnels," the halfling explained. "Look for us when you need us most!"

With that heroic promise, Oliver scampered off after Luthien, the two of them going right at the fork, back to the narrow passage that had led them here from the guard room. They had indeed found many tunnels leading off that passage, several of which sloped steeply down. The main entrance to the lower mines, where the dwarfs were kept as slaves, was to the left at the fork, as Luthien had told Shuglin, but Luthien and Oliver figured that if they could get down lower in secret, they could rouse the enslaved dwarfs and strike at the cyclopian guards from behind.

They did make their way down and in the lower tunnels found a score of dirty, beleaguered dwarfs for every cyclopian guard. Though battered and half-starved, the tough bearded folk were more than ready to join in the cause, more than ready to fight for their freedom. Pickaxes and shovels that had been used as mining tools now served as deadly weapons as the growing force made its way along the tunnels.

Shuglin's group, rejoined with the rest of their allies, including Katerin and the Cutters, found their reception exactly the opposite. The main entrance to the lower mines also housed the largest concentration of cyclopians. They fought a bitter battle in the last room of the upper level, and predictably, the large platform that served as an elevator to the lower level was destroyed by the cyclopians.

Using block and tackle and dozens of ropes, Shuglin and his dwarfs quickly constructed a new transport. Getting down was a different matter, and many were lost in the first assault, despite the fine work of the elvish archers. Once the lower chamber was secured, the group faced a difficult, room-to-room march, and there were at least as many well-armed cyclopians as there were rebels.

But there were as many dwarf slaves as both forces combined, and when Luthien and Oliver and their makeshift army showed up behind the cyclopian lines, the defense of the mines fell apart.

That same night, the dwarfs crawled out of the Montfort mines, many of them looking upon stars for the first time in more than a decade. Almost without exception, they fell to their knees and gave thanks, cursing King Greensparrow and singing praises to the Crimson Shadow.

Shuglin put a strong hand on Luthien's shoulder. "Now you've got your army," the blue-bearded dwarf promised grimly.

With five hundred powerful dwarfs camped about him, Luthien didn't doubt those words for a moment.

Standing off to the side, Oliver's expression remained doubtful. He had previously offered to Luthien that perhaps the dwarfs should run off into the mountains, and that he and Luthien and whoever else would come could ride north, into the wilder regions of Eriador, where they might blend into the landscape, so many more rogues in a land of rogues. Despite the victorious and heartwarming scene around him now, Oliver seemed to be holding to those thoughts. The pragmatic halfling understood the greater nations of the wider world, including Avon, and he could not shake the image of Greensparrow's army flowing north and crushing the rebels. Many times in the last few weeks, Oliver had pondered whether Avon used the gallows or the guillotine.

Oliver the highwayhalfling longed for his life out on the road, an outlaw, perhaps, but not so much an outlaw that an entire army would search for him!

"We cannot flee," Luthien said to him, recognizing the forlorn expression and understanding its source. "It is time for Montfort to fall."

"And for Caer MacDonald to rise," Katerin O'Hale quickly added.

CHAPTER 4

A WISE MAN'S EYES

THE MANY WINTERS had played hard on the old wizard Brind'Amour's broad shoulders, and the crow's-feet that creased his face were testament to his many hours of study and of worry. No less were his worries now—indeed, he suspected that Eriador, his beloved land, was in its most critical time—but his shoulders were not stooped, and anyone looking at the wizened face would likely not notice the crow's-feet, too entranced by the sheer intensity of the old man's deep blue eyes.

Those eyes sparkled now, as the wizard sat in the high-backed chair before his desk in a roughly circular cave, its perfectly smooth floor the only clue that this was no natural chamber. A single light, sharp like a spark of lightning, illuminated the room, emanating from a perfectly round crystal ball sitting atop the desk between a human skull and a tall, treelike candelabra.

Brind'Amour leaned back in his chair as the light began to fade and considered the images that the enchanted ball had just shown to him.

The dwarfs were free of the Montfort mines and had come into the city beside Luthien and Oliver.

The dwarfs were free!

Brind'Amour stroked his snow-white beard and brushed his hand over his white hair, which he had tied back in a thick ponytail. He could trust these images, he reminded himself, because he was looking at things as they were, not as they might be.

He had done that earlier, looked into the future. A risky business, and an exhausting one. Of all the magical enchantments a wizard might cast, prophesying was perhaps the most troublesome and dangerous, for looking into the future involved more than harnessing simple energies, such as a strike of lightning, and more than sending one's consciousness to another real-time place, as in simple scrying. Looking into the future meant bringing together all the known elements of the present in one place, a crystal ball or a mirror, then forcing logical conclusions to each, as well as resultant new conflicts. Truly such prophesying was a test of a wizard's intelligence and intuition.

Brind'Amour rarely dared such prophesying because, despite his curiosity, he realized that the future was not dependable. He could cast the spell over his crystal ball, huddle close, and study the fleeting images—and they were always fleeting, flickers, and partial pictures—but he could never know which were true and which were only possibilities. And of course, the mere fact that some prying wizard had glimpsed into the potential future made it more likely that the natural outcome would be altered.

Brind'Amour hadn't been able to resist a quick glance this one day, and he had come away with one image that seemed plausible, even likely: a man atop a tall tower in Montfort. Brind'Amour had a general idea of the current events in the city—he had visited Montfort mentally on a couple of occasions, looking through the eyes of a half-elf—and though he didn't recognize the man on the tower, he knew from the rich clothes and ample jewelry that this was obviously one of Greensparrow's supporters.

The wizard leaned back in his chair. A man atop a tower, he thought. Taunting the populace. A leader, a symbol of what remained in Montfort of King Greensparrow. Something would have to be done about that, Brind'Amour mused, and he knew that he could work this change himself, without great expense and no risk at all. Perhaps his journey into the realm of what might be had been worth the cost this time.

The cost . . . he remembered the many warnings his masters of centuries ago had given him concerning prophesying. The risk . . .

Brind'Amour shook all that from his mind. This time was different. This time he had not looked primarily at what might be, but at what *was*. And "what was" was a full-scale revolt in Montfort, one that might turn into a revolution for all of Eriador. In a roundabout way, Brind'Amour had begun it. He was the one who had given the crimson cape to Luthien Bedwyr; he was the one who had set the Crimson Shadow and his halfling cohort on the road to Montfort. At that time, Brind'Amour had only hoped Luthien could cause some mischief, perhaps renewing the whispered legend of the Crimson Shadow, hero of old. Brind'Amour had dared to hope that in the years to come he might build upon the whispers surrounding Luthien to gradually diminish Eriador's acceptance of wicked King Greensparrow.

Fate had intervened to rush events much more quickly than the old wizard had anticipated, but Brind'Amour was not saddened by that fact. He was excited and hopeful. Above all else, Brind'Amour believed in Eriador and her sturdy folk, Luthien Bedwyr among them.

His divining had shown him that several villages, including Luthien's own of Dun Varna on the Isle Bedwydrin, had taken up the cause. Just that morning a fleet, mostly converted fishing boats, had put out from Dun Varna, braving the icy waters of the Dorsal on the short trip to neighboring Isle Marvis. Aboard were reinforcements for the eorl of Marvis as he, like Gahris, eorl of Bedwydrin, tried to rid his land of the hated cyclopians.

Brind'Amour whispered a few words and snapped his fingers three times, and the many tips of the candelabra flickered to flaming life. He rose from his chair, smoothing his thick and flowing blue robes as he made his way near a table that lay deeply buried under a pile of parchments. Brind'Amour shuffled them about, finally extracting a map of the Avonsea Islands. Thousands of colored dots, green and red and yellow, covered the map, representing concentrations of people and the sides they represented in the conflict. South of the mountains, in Avon proper, those dots were nearly all green, for those loyal to the throne, or yellow, indicating a neutral bent. North of the mountains showed many green concentrations, as well—the merchant section of Montfort remained one green blob—and most of the others were yellow still. But the red dots, symbolizing the rebels, were growing in number.

The wizard held the map up before him and closed his eyes, reciting the words of another spell. He recalled everything the crystal ball had just shown him, the new events in Montfort and the fleet in the north, and when he opened his eyes, the map now indicated the changes, with a wave of red flowing toward Isle Marvis and a red wall thickening about Montfort's entrapped merchant quarter.

"What have I begun?" the old wizard mused, and he chuckled. He hadn't anticipated this, not for another hundred years, but he believed that he was ready for it, and so was Eriador. Luthien had retrieved Brind'Amour's staff from the lair of the dragon Balthazar, and now Luthien, with handy Oliver beside him, and a growing number of other leaders surrounding them both, was showing remarkable progress.

Brind'Amour replaced the map on the table and pinned down its corners with paperweights that resembled little gargoyles. He sighed deeply and looked back to the immense desk and the dancing flames of the candelabra, throwing more light than normal candles ever could. The crystal ball tugged at his curiosity, as it had for many weeks, not to look at Eriador, but to explore beyond the land's southern borders to see what was brewing in Avon.

Brind'Amour sighed again and realized he was not prepared for that dangerous venture. Not yet. He needed to rest and gather his strength, and let the budding rebellion grow to full bloom. Briefly, he regretted having looked upon the future earlier, for the present continued to call out to him and he was too tired to answer. Scrying the future was taxing, but for a wizard in Brind'Amour's secret position, sending his magical energies over the miles to view the present events of the wide world was simply dangerous. Such energies could be detected by Greensparrow and his dukes, and since few wizards remained in the world, any of Brind'Amour's scrying attempts could be traced to this most secret of caves in the Iron Cross.

The wizard spoke a word of magic and gently puffed, and the flames atop the candelabra flickered wildly, then blew out. Brind'Amour turned and went through the door, down a narrow passage which led to his bedchamber. He had one more thing to accomplish before he could lie down for a well-deserved sleep. He trusted in his vision of what might soon come in Montfort, of Greensparrow's man standing atop that tall tower, and he knew what to do about it.

He stopped at a side room along the corridor, a small armory, and searched among the hodgepodge of items until he located a specific, enchanted arrow. Then he delivered it—a simple magical spell, really—to a certain beautiful half-elf in Montfort, one who always seemed to be in the middle of the trouble.

The wizard went to his rest.

Luthien woke with a start. He spent a long minute letting his eyes adjust to the dim lighting and looking about his small room, making sure that all was aright. The fireplace glowed still—it could not be too late—but the flames were gone, the pile of logs consumed to small red embers, watchful eyes guarding the room.

Luthien rolled out of bed and padded across the floor. He sat on the stone hearth. Its warmth felt good against his bare flesh. He moved the screen aside, took up the poker and stirred the embers, hardly considering the movements, for he was too filled with a multitude of emotions that he did not understand. He put a couple of logs on the pile and continued blowing softly until the flames came up again.

He watched them for some time, allowing their tantalizing dance to bring him back to Bedwydrin, back to Dun Varna and a time before he had taken this most unexpected road. He remembered the first time he and Katerin had made love on the high hill overlooking the city and the bay.

Luthien's smile was short-lived. He reminded himself that he needed his sleep, that the next day, like all the others, would be filled with turmoil, with fighting and decisions that would affect the lives of so many people.

Luthien replaced the poker in its iron stand near the hearth and stood up, brushing himself off. As he approached the bed, the light greater now that the fire was up once more, he paused.

The covers had rolled over when he got up, the thick down blanket bunched up high, and beneath it he could see Siobhan, lying naked on her belly, fast asleep. The young man gently sat down on the edge of the bed. He put his hand under the edge of the cover, on the back of Siobhan's knee, and ran it up slowly, feeling every inch of her curving form until he got to her neck.

Then he spread his fingers in her lustrous hair. Siobhan stirred, but did not wake.

She was so smooth, so beautiful, and so warm. Luthien couldn't deny the half-elf's overwhelming allure; she had captured his heart with a single glance.

Why, then, had he just been thinking of Katerin?

And why, the young man wondered as he crawled back under the covers, snuggling close to Siobhan, was he feeling so guilty?

In the days she had been in Montfort, Katerin had given no sign that she wanted to be back together with Luthien. She had not uttered a single word of disapproval about the relationship Luthien had fostered with Siobhan.

But she did disapprove, Luthien knew in his heart. He could see it in her green eyes, those beautiful orbs that had greeted him at dawn after the night he had become a man, on a hill in Dun Varna, in a world that seemed so many millions of miles and millions of years away.

It was all lace and frills, niceties and painted ladies who served the court well. The sight revealed in the crystal ball turned Brind'Amour's stomach, but at the same time, it gave him hope. Carlisle on Stratton, in Avon far to the south of Eriador, had been built for war, and by war, centuries before, a mighty port city bristling with defenses. Greensparrow had come to the throne ruthlessly, in a bloody and bitterly fought battle, and the first years of his reign had been brutal beyond anything the Avonsea Islands had seen since the Huegoth invasions of centuries before.

But now Carlisle was lace and frills, an overabundance of sweetened candies and carnal offerings.

Brind'Amour's magical eye wove its way through the palace. The wizard had never before been so daring, so reckless, as to send his mind's eye so near to his archenemy. If Greensparrow detected the magical emanations . . .

The thick stone walls of Brind'Amour's mountain hideaway would be of little defense against Greensparrow's allies, mighty demons from the pits of hell.

The sheer bustle of the palace amazed the distant wizard. Hundreds of people filtered through every room on the lower level, all drinking, all stuffing their faces with cakes, many stealing away to whatever darkened corner they could find. Burly cyclopians lined the walls of every room. How ironic, the wizard mused; many of the one-eyes stood before tapestries that depicted ancient battles in which their ancestors were defeated by the men of Avon!

The eye moved along, the images in the crystal ball flitting past. Then Brind'Amour felt a sensation of power, a magical strength, and for a moment, he thought that Greensparrow had sensed the intruding energy and he nearly broke the connection altogether. But then the old wizard realized that this was something different, a passive energy: the strength of Greensparrow himself, perhaps.

Brind'Amour leaned back and considered that point. He recalled Luthien's battle with the wizard Duke Morkney atop the tower of the Ministry. Morkney had called in a demon, Praehotec, and had given the beast his own body to use. In watching that battle, Brind'Amour had felt this very same sensation, only it was stronger here.

The old wizard understood, and he was filled with revulsion. With a low growl, he leaned forward, throwing all his concentration into the divining device and moving the eye along, following the beacon of Greensparrow's energy. It sailed up the back stairs of the palace, to the second floor where there weren't so many people, though even more one-eyed Praetorian Guards. It went down a maze of thickly carpeted hallways and came to a closed door.

Brind'Amour felt a jolt as the eye came up to that door. He tried to force it through, but found that a barrier was in place: the room had been magically sealed.

Greensparrow was behind that door. Brind'Amour knew it, but knew, too, that if he sent enough of his own energy to break through the blocking ward, the wizard-king would surely sense it.

Suddenly, the image in the crystal ball went dark as a huge cyclopian passed through the insubstantial eye. The door opened, and Brind'Amour was quick to urge his eye to follow the brute through.

The room beyond was relatively empty, considering the lavish furnishings throughout the rest of the palace. A single throne was centered in the square chamber, atop a circular dais, two steps up from the floor, and while the chair was ornate, decorated with glittering gemstones of green and red and violet, the floor was bare, except for narrow strips of red carpeting running from each of the room's four doors to the dais.

Greensparrow—Brind'Amour knew it was the wretch, though he hadn't seen the man in centuries, and had never known him well—lounged in the throne, fiddling with a huge ring upon the middle finger of his left hand. His hair was long and black and curly, and his face was painted and caked, though the makeup did little to hide the obvious toll his years of study and dealings with demons had taken. He appeared foppish, but Brind'Amour was not fooled. When Greensparrow looked out to regard the approaching cyclopian, his amber-colored eyes flickered with intelligence and intensity.

Brind'Amour wisely kept his magical eye near the cyclopian, hoping the strength of the imposing brute would somewhat mask the magical energy.

"What news, Belsen'Krieg?" the king asked, seeming bored.

Brind'Amour dared to move his magical eye out enough to get a good look at the brute. Belsen'Krieg was among the sturdiest and ugliest cyclopians the old wizard had ever seen. Rotting tusks stuck up over Belsen'Krieg's upper lip, which had been split in half diagonally just below its wide, flattened nose. The brute's eye was huge and bloodshot and a thick brow hung out over it like an awning on a storefront. Scars crossed both of Belsen'Krieg's cheeks, and his neck, as thick as a child's chest, seemed to be a yellow-green blob of scar tissue. His black-and-silver Praetorian Guard uniform, though, was perfectly neat, with gold brocade stitched on both shoulders and an assortment of medals and ribbons making his massive chest seem huger still.

"We have heard nothing from Montfort, my King," the cyclopian snorted, his diction impressive for one of his race, but his articulation difficult to understand due to his almost constant snuffling.

"Morkney's other cannot get back into the city," Greensparrow said, more to himself than to Belsen'Krieg.

"Morkney's other?" Brind'Amour whispered, thinking the choice of words odd. Was the wizard-king implying that all of his dukes had personal relationships with specific demons?

"So we must assume that the fool duke is dead," Greensparrow went on.

"A minor inconvenience," Belsen'Krieg offered.

"Is my ship ready to sail?" Greensparrow asked, and Brind'Amour held his breath, thinking that the king meant to go to Eriador personally to put down the revolt. If that happened, the old wizard knew, Luthien and his friends didn't have a chance.

"The waters are clear of ice all the way to Chaumadore Port," Belsen'Krieg replied immediately.

Gascony? Brind'Amour's heart leaped with sudden hope. Greensparrow was going to Gascony!

"And the waters to the north?" the king asked, and again, Brind'Amour held his breath.

"Less so, by all reports," the cyclopian answered.

"But you can get through," Greensparrow replied, and the words were not a question but a command.

"Yes, my King."

"Such silly business." Greensparrow shook his head as though the whole affair was thoroughly distasteful. "We must show them their folly," he went on, and rose from his chair, straightening his fine purple baldric and the thick and ruffled cloak. "Kill every man, woman, and child associated with the rebels. Make an example of them that Eriador will not forget for centuries to come."

He had said it so casually, so ruthlessly.

"Yes, my King!" came the predictably eager reply. No cyclopian ever questioned an order to slaughter humans.

"And I warn you," Greensparrow added, just before exiting the chamber through the back door, "if my vacation is interrupted, I will hold you personally responsible."

"Yes, my King," Belsen'Krieg responded, and the cyclopian didn't seem to be worried. Indeed, to the fearful old wizard watching from more than five hundred miles away, the cyclopian seemed to be rejoicing.

Brind'Amour cut the connection and leaned back in his chair. The crystal ball went dark, and so did the room, but the wizard didn't command his enchanted candelabra to light.

He sat in the dark, considering the connection his enemies held with demons, a relationship that was apparently still very strong. Brind'Amour thought of the fateful decision of the brotherhood those many, many years ago. The cathedrals had been built, the islands knew peace, and few cared much for the wizards, old men and women all. Their time had passed, the brotherhood had decided—even the great dragons had been put down, destroyed or imprisoned in deep caves, as Brind'Amour and his fellows had sealed up Balthazar. Brind'Amour had lost his staff in that encounter, and so convinced was he that his time was ended, that he did not even try to regain it.

All of the brotherhood had gone to sleep, some to eternal rest. Others, such as Brind'Amour, sent themselves into a magical stasis in private castles or caves. All of them . . . except for Greensparrow. He had been only a minor wizard in the old days, but one who had apparently found a way to extend the time of wizards.

Brind'Amour had chosen stasis over death because he believed that one day he might be useful to the world once more. Thus, when he had gone to his magical slumber, he had enacted spells of alarm that would call to him when the day was dark. And so he had awoken, just a few years before, to find Greensparrow seated as king of Avon and deep in unholy alliances with demons.

Brind'Amour sat in the dark considering his enemies, both human and fiend. He sat in the dark, wondering if he had been wise to set Luthien, and Eriador, on such a collision course against such an enemy as this.

CHAPTER 5

INCH BY INCH

"IT IS NOT so deep," Shuglin grumbled, the end of his blue beard slick with slime.

"I am not so tall," Oliver retorted without hesitation.

The frustrated dwarf looked over to Luthien, who promptly hoisted the complaining halfling under one arm and struggled on through the ice and the muck.

"Oliver deBurrows, walking a sewer!" Oliver grumbled. "If I had known how low I would sink beside the likes of you . . ."

His complaint became a muffled groan as Luthien pitched suddenly to the side, slamming them both against the wall.

They came up apart, Oliver hopping to his feet and slapping at the muck on his blue pantaloons, crying "Ick! Ick! Ick!"

"We're under the merchants," Shuglin put in, his gravelly voice thick with sarcasm. "You probably should be quiet."

Oliver cast a hopeless glance at Luthien, but he knew that his friend was more amused than sympathetic. And he knew, too, that his complaints were minor; in light of the importance of this day, even Oliver could not take them seriously. Only a week after the opening of the mines, the rescued dwarfs had shown their value, repairing old weapons and armor, fashioning new equipment, and opening up the sewers under the embattled merchant quarter. Now Luthien and Oliver, Shuglin and three hundred of his bearded kin, were creeping along several parallel routes and would come up right in the midst of their enemies.

Still, the halfling figured that he didn't have to enjoy the journey. The lanterns lit the tunnels well enough, but they did nothing to ward off the dead cold. Ice lined the sewer tunnels and was thick about the floor's rounded center, but there was fresh waste above the ice and it would take more than a freeze to defeat the awful stench of the place.

"They had barricaded the openings," Shuglin explained, "but we got through in more than a dozen and killed four cyclopians who were nearby in the process."

"None escaped to warn of our approach?" Luthien asked for the tenth time since the expedition had set out from the city's lower section.

"Not a one," Shuglin assured him, also for the tenth time.

"I would so enjoy marching through this muck only to find the enemy waiting for us," Oliver added sarcastically.

Shuglin ignored him and took up the march again, moving swiftly down the straight tunnel. A few moments later, the dwarf stopped and signaled for those following to do likewise.

"We are found," the dismal halfling said.

Shuglin took the lantern from another dwarf and held it high in front of the mouth of the passage. He nodded as a like signal came from across the intersection, and he poked his stubby thumb upward. "All in time," the dwarf remarked, motioning for the others to move along once more.

They came into a small cubby at the side of the passage. A ladder—of new dwarfish construction—was secured against one wall, leading up a dozen feet to a wooden trapdoor.

Luthien motioned to Oliver. It had been agreed that the stealthy halfling would lead them out of the sewer, and Oliver was happy to oblige, happy to be out of the muck even if the entire cyclopian force was waiting for him above. He sprang nimbly and silently to the ladder and started up.

Before he neared the top, the trapdoor creaked open. Oliver froze in place and those down below went perfectly silent.

"Oh, no," the halfling moaned as a naked pair of cyclopian buttocks shifted over the hole. Oliver buried his face in his arms, hoping his wide-brimmed hat would protect him. "Oh, please shoot him fast," he whispered, not thrilled with the possibilities.

He breathed easier when Luthien's bow twanged and he felt the rush of air as an arrow whipped past. He looked up to see the bolt bury itself deep in the unwitting cyclopian's fleshy bottom. The brute howled and spun, and took a dwarfish crossbow quarrel right in the face as it foolishly leaned over the opening. The screaming went away and the friends heard the cyclopian fall dead on the floor of the small room above.

Oliver adjusted his hat and looked to the upturned faces below. "Hey," he called out softly, "the one-eyes, they look the same from both ends!"

"Just go on!" Luthien scolded.

Oliver shrugged and scampered up the ladder, coming into a small, square room, where the smell was nearly as bad as down below. Some brute was knocking on the door.

"Bergus?" it called.

Oliver turned back, putting his face over the opening, lifting his finger over pursed lips and motioning for the others to clear out of the way. Then he padded silently to the door. It rattled as the brute outside jostled it, for only a small hook held it closed.

"Bergus?" the brute growled again, and Oliver could tell that it was fast growing impatient.

The door shook as the cyclopian hit it harder, perhaps with his shoulder. Oliver looked to the dead cyclopian and considered the angle.

"You all right?" came a call, and the door shook again. Oliver slipped to the side of it and drew out his rapier.

Three loud knocks.

"Bergus?"

"Help me," Oliver grunted softly, trying to imitate the low tones of a cyclopian and to sound as though he was in trouble. As soon as he spoke the words, he brought his rapier flicking up, unhooking the latch. An instant later the cyclopian hit the door shoulder first, barreling through, and Oliver stung the inside of its knee with his rapier point, then kicked the brute's back foot in behind its leading one.

The overbalanced cyclopian pitched right over its fallen companion. Oliver was quick in the chase, guiding its flight so that it nearly tumbled right into the hole. A strong arm lashed out to the side, though, and the brute was able to hold itself up, with only its head and shoulders and one arm going over the lip.

Oliver jumped back and moved to strike, but he heard a twang from below and the cyclopian jerked violently, then went still. The halfling rushed back to the door and closed it once more, checking to ensure that no one else was around. Then he went to the cyclopian and heaved the creature into the hole.

"Good shot," he said to Luthien when he saw the man step over the body to get to the ladder. "But do you know which end of the thing you hit?"

Luthien didn't even look up. He didn't want to encourage Oliver, didn't want the halfling to see his amused smile.

All across the quiet upper section of the city, the invaders filtered out of several such outhouses and other privies located inside merchant dwellings. The air was still cold and dark before the dawn, and they could hear fighting over at the wall, near the Ministry.

"Right on time," Oliver said, for the diversion—an attack by forces from the lower section—was not unexpected.

Luthien nodded grimly. Right on time. Everything was going according to plan. He looked about, his eyes adjusting to the dim light, and he nodded, seeing lines of grim-faced dwarfs, who had lived for years as slaves under the tyranny of Greensparrow, filtering into nearly every shadow.

The young Bedwyr started off, Oliver in tow, heading in the general direction of the fighting. They quick-stepped along the shadows of one lane, coming to an abrupt stop at a corner when they heard footsteps fast approaching from the other way.

A cyclopian skidded around the bend, its one eye going wide with surprise.

"This is too easy," the halfling complained, and stuck his rapier into the monster's chest. A second later, *Blind-Striker* split the brute's skull down the middle.

Luthien started to answer, but both he and Oliver jumped and spun as a fight exploded behind them. A group of cyclopians had rushed out of a side avenue, also heading for the fight, but they found battle sooner than expected as two bands of dwarfs, Shuglin among them, caught them in a squeeze, overwhelming them in the street.

Skirmishes erupted all across the merchant section, and the fighting increased when the sun broke the horizon, sending slanting rays into the turmoil of war. Luthien and Oliver encountered only minimal resistance—two cyclopians, which they quickly defeated—on their way to the wall near the Ministry, where they would link with their allies, but found that a number of dwarfs had beaten them to the spot. Already the cyclopians holding the position were hard-pressed.

"Keep alert!" Luthien ordered the halfling. The young man took out his folded bow, opened and pinned it in a single movement and had an arrow ready to fly. While Oliver guarded his back and flanks, he picked his shots, one by one.

Grappling hooks came sailing over the wall, and with the dwarfs engaging the defenders on this side, others roaming the streets to cut off any reinforcements, the cyclopians could not resist. Elves and men streamed up and over the wall, joining the fighting throng.

Luthien tried to put an arrow up quickly, seeing one man slip down and a cyclopian moving in, sword high for the kill.

"Damn!" the young Bedwyr shouted, knowing he could not make the shot in time.

The cyclopian halted suddenly. Luthien didn't understand why, but didn't question the luck as he finally got his arrow sighted.

The brute fell headlong before he could let fly, two arrows protruding from its back. Following their line, back along the wall, Luthien spotted a familiar figure, beautiful and lithe, with the angular features of a half-elf.

"Siobhan," Oliver said behind him, the halfling obviously pleased and inspired by the fine figure she cut, standing tall atop the wall in the shining morning light.

Before Luthien remembered that he had a bow of his own, the half-elf held hers up again and fired, and another cyclopian fell away.

"Are you going to watch or play?" Oliver cried, running by the young man. Luthien looked back to the main fight, which was on in full now, at the wall and in the courtyard beside the towering Ministry. He slung his bow over his shoulder and drew out *Blind-Striker*, running to catch up with his friend.

Both spotted Katerin, leaping down off the wall into the middle of the fray, right in between two cyclopians.

Oliver groaned, but Luthien knew the sturdy woman of Hale better than to be afraid for her.

Back and forth she worked her spear, parrying and slapping at the surprised brutes. She thrust forward viciously, driving the spear tip into one's belly, then tore it free and shifted her angle as she reversed direction, the spear's butt end slamming the other cyclopian in the face. Katerin twirled the weapon in her hands and jabbed the tip the other way, slicing the brute's throat, then rotated it again and came back furiously, finishing the one that was holding its spilling guts.

Luthien, obviously pleased, looked at Oliver. "Two to two," he remarked.

"Say that five times fast," the halfling replied.

Before Luthien could begin to respond, Oliver poked his finger back toward the wall, and Luthien turned just as Siobhan felled another brute from the wall with her deadly bow.

"One up," Oliver said smugly, and it seemed to the two as if they had unintentionally taken sides.

"Not so!" Luthien was quick to call, and Oliver turned to see Katerin running full out. She skidded down into a crouch and hurled her spear, catching a fleeing cyclopian right in the back of the neck, dropping it to skid across the cobblestones on its ugly face.

"It would seem as if they were evenly matched," Oliver said, and his sly tone made Luthien realize that he was talking about more than fighting.

Luthien didn't appreciate the comment; Oliver saw that as soon as he had uttered the words. He rushed off, rapier held high. "Are you to watch or to play?" he cried again.

Luthien let go of his anger, put aside his confusion and all thoughts of the two wonderful women. Now wasn't the time for deep thinking. He caught up to Oliver and together they rushed headlong into the battle.

Merchant houses were raided by the dozen that fateful morning in Montfort and scores of slaves were freed, most of whom gladly joined in the fight. Hundreds of cyclopians were beaten down.

The human merchants, though, were not summarily killed, except for those who fought back against the rebels and would not surrender. Giving them the option to surrender was Luthien's doing, the first order he had given to his rebels before the assault had begun. Luthien did not comfortably assume the role of leadership, but in this matter he was as forceful as anyone had ever seen him, for the young man believed in justice. He knew that not all of Montfort's merchants were evil men, that not all of those who had prospered during Greensparrow's time necessarily adhered to or agreed with the wicked king's edicts.

The final fight for the city was a bitter one, but in the end the cyclopian guards, city and Praetorian, were simply overwhelmed and the taking of Montfort was completed.

Except for the Ministry. The rebels had avoided attacking the place until all else was accomplished because it was too defensible. The five doors which led into the cathedral, including the secret one that had been cut in the eastern wall and the broken section of that same wall, had been secured and braced and could withstand tremendous punishment.

But now the Ministry was all that remained as a bastion for those loyal to the king of Avon. And with the mines taken, those brutes bottled up inside could not look anywhere close for support.

Luthien and Oliver headed back for the place after a tour of the conquered merchant quarter. Luthien had hoped to find Viscount Aubrey alive, but had seen no sign of him. He wasn't surprised; vermin like Aubrey had a knack for survival and Luthien suspected that he knew exactly where to find the man.

The two companions joined the bulk of their army, which had gathered in the courtyards about the great structure of the Ministry, hurling taunts, and occasionally an arrow, at any cyclopian that revealed itself in any window or atop the smaller towers.

"We can get in there!" Shuglin the dwarf declared, running up and grabbing Luthien by the arm.

"They have nowhere to run," Luthien assured him, his voice soothing in its tone of complete confidence. "The battle is over."

"There could be near to five hundred of them in there," Katerin O'Hale interjected doubtfully, joining the three.

"Better reason to stay outside and wait," Luthien was quick to reply. "We cannot afford the losses."

The friends moved about the courtyard, helping out with the tending of the wounded and trying to organize the forces. Now that the cyclopian threat was ended, a myriad of other problems presented themselves. There was looting by many of the frustrated commonfolk who had lived so long with so little, and more than one merchant house had been set ablaze. Skirmishes took place between dwarfs and men, two races who had not lived beside each other in any numbers since Morkney had shipped most of the dwarfs off to the mines, and decisions still had to be made concerning the fate of the captured merchants.

Early that afternoon, Luthien finally caught sight of Siobhan again, the half-elf walking determinedly his way.

"Come with me," she ordered, and Luthien recognized the urgency in her voice.

From across the courtyard, Katerin and Oliver watched him go.

"It is business, that is all," Oliver said to the woman.

Katerin scowled at him. "What makes you believe that I care?" she asked, and walked away.

Oliver shook his head, and admired Luthien more at that moment than ever before.

"This is the most dangerous time," Siobhan said to Luthien after she had escorted him far away from the crowd. She went on to tell of the looting and of dissatisfied murmurs among the rebels.

Luthien didn't understand the seemingly illogical reactions, but he saw what was happening around him and could not deny Siobhan's fears. This should have been their moment of glory, and indeed it was, but mingled with that glory was a tumult of confusing emotions. The rebel mob did not move with a unified purpose, now that the actual battle had ended.

"The fighting will ebb for many weeks perhaps," Siobhan said.

"Our only strength is in unity," Luthien replied, beginning to catch on to her reasoning. Their goals had been met; even the Ministry could hold out only as long as the food inside lasted. The cyclopians bottled within the massive cathedral could not threaten them in any substantial way, for the rebels held strong defensive positions across the open plazas that surrounded the Ministry. If the cyclopians came charging out, their numbers would be decimated by archers before they ever engaged in close combat.

So Montfort had been taken, but what did that mean? In the weeks before the final attack, Luthien and the other leaders had clearly defined the goal, but they had not devised a plan for what would follow.

Luthien looked away from the open plaza, westward over the merchant section, and the plume of black smoke from the torched houses showed him beyond doubt that this was indeed a dangerous time. He understood the responsibilities before him and realized that he had to act quickly. They had taken Montfort, but that would mean nothing if the city now fell into disarray and anarchy.

The young Bedwyr inspected himself carefully, noted the muck from the sewer and the blood of enemy and friend alike. The magnificent crimson cape, though, showed no stains, as if its magic would tolerate no blemishes.

"I have to clean up," Luthien said to Siobhan.

She nodded. "A washbasin and a clean change of clothes have already been prepared."

Luthien looked at her curiously. Somehow he was not surprised.

Less than an hour later, with less time to prepare than he would have liked, but with the breakdown of order growing among the celebrating populace, Luthien Bedwyr walked out into the middle of the plaza in front of the Ministry. The young man's head swirled as he considered the mass of onlookers: every one of his rebel warriors, every one of Shuglin's kin, the Cutters, and thousands of others, had all come to hear the Crimson Shadow, all come to learn their fate, as though Luthien served as the mouth of God.

He tried not to look at their faces, at the want and need in their eyes. He was not comfortable in this role and hadn't the slightest idea of how or why this responsibility had befallen him. He should get Oliver to address them, he thought suddenly. Oliver could talk, could read the needs of an audience.

Or Siobhan. Luthien looked at her closely as she guided him along to the steps of a gallows that was under construction for those captured cyclopians or merchants who were deemed worthy of such an end. Perhaps he could get Siobhan to speak.

Luthien dismissed the thought. Siobhan was half-elven and more akin to elves than to men. Yet if ten thousand people were now gathered about the plaza, watching from the streets, the wall, and no doubt even below the wall in the lower section, where they could not see but could hear the relayed whispers, not seven hundred of them had any blood other than human.

He walked up the steps beside Siobhan and took some comfort in the familiar faces of Oliver, Katerin, and Shuglin standing in the front row. They looked expectant and confident; they believed in him.

"Do not forget the city's true name," Siobhan whispered in his ear, and then she stepped to the side of the platform. Luthien, the Crimson Shadow, stood alone.

He had prepared a short speech, but the first words of it would not come to him now. He saw cyclopians in the windows of the Ministry, staring down at him as eagerly as the gathered crowd, and he realized that their fate, and the fate of all Eriador and all of Avon, was held in this moment.

That notion did little to calm the young man.

He looked to his friends below him. Oliver tipped his monstrous hat, Katerin threw Luthien a wink and a determined nod. But it was Shuglin, standing patiently, almost impassive, burly arms across his chest and no telling expression on his bearded face, who gave Luthien the heart he needed. Shuglin, whose people had suffered so horribly in slavery under the tyranny of Duke Morkney. Indomitable Shuglin, who had led the way to the mines and would hear no talk of ending the fight for Montfort until the job was done.

Until the job was done.

His cinnamon eyes steeled, Luthien looked out to the crowd. No longer did he try to recall the words of his speech, rather he tried to decipher the feelings in his heart.

"My allies!" he shouted. "My friends! I see before me not a city conquered."

A long pause, and not a whisper rippled about the gathering.

"But a city freed!" Luthien proclaimed, and a huge roar went up. While he waited for the crowd to quiet, Luthien glanced over at Siobhan, who seemed perfectly at ease, perfectly confident.

"We have taken back a small part of what is rightfully ours," the young Bedwyr went on, gaining momentum, gaining heart. He held up his hand, thumb and finger barely an inch apart. "A small part," he reiterated loudly, angrily.

"Montfort!" someone yelled.

"No!" Luthien quickly interjected, before any chant could begin.

"No," the young Bedwyr went on. "Montfort is just a place on a map, a map in the halls of King Greensparrow." That name brought more than a few hisses. "It is a place to conquer, and to burn." Luthien swept his hand around to the plume of smoke behind him, diminished now, but still rising.

"What gain in taking Montfort and burning Montfort?" he called out above the confused murmurs. "What gain in possessing buildings and items, in holding things, simple things, that Greensparrow can come back and take from us?

"No gain, I say," Luthien continued. "If it was Montfort that we conquered, then we have accomplished nothing!"

A thousand shrugs, a thousand whispers, and a thousand curious questions filtered back to Luthien as he paused and held his conclusion, baiting the crowd, building their anxiety.

"But it was not Montfort!" he cried at last, and the whispers diminished, though the curious, confused expressions did not. "It was nothing that King Greensparrow—no, simply Greensparrow, for he is no king of mine—can take from us. It was not Montfort, I say. Not something to conquer and to burn. It was Caer MacDonald that we took back!"

The plaza exploded in roars, in cheers—for Luthien, for Caer MacDonald. The young Bedwyr looked at the beaming Siobhan. Remember the city's true name, she had coached him, and now that he had spoken the words, Siobhan looked different to Luthien. She seemed as if the cloud had passed from her face, she seemed vindicated and confident. No, more than confident, he realized. She seemed secure.

Siobhan, who had been a merchant's slave, who had fought secretly against the ruling class for years and who had stood beside Luthien since his rise in the underground hierarchy, seemed free at last.

"Caer MacDonald!" Luthien yelled when the gathering had quieted somewhat. "And what does that mean? Bruce MacDonald, who fought the cyclopians, what did he fight for?"

"Freedom!" came a cry directly below the platform, and Luthien did not have to look down to know that it was the voice of Katerin O'Hale.

The call was echoed from every corner of the plaza, around the city's dividing wall, and through the streets of the city's lower section. It came to the ears of those who were even then looting the wealthiest houses of the city, and to those who had burned the merchants' houses, and they were ashamed.

"We have taken back not a place, but an ideal," Luthien explained. "We have taken back what we were, and what we must be. In Caer MacDonald, we have found the heart of our hero of old, but it is no more than a small piece, a tiny gain, a candle's flicker in a field of darkness. And in taking that, in raising the flag of Caer MacDonald over the Ministry once more . . ." He paused, giving the crowd the moment to glance at the great structure's tall tower, where some figures were stirring.

"And we shall!" Luthien promised them when they looked back, and he had to pause again until the cheering died down.

"In taking back this piece of our heritage, we have accepted a responsibility," he went on. "We have lit a flame, and now we must fan that flame and share its light. To Port Charley, in the west. To the isles, Bedwydrin, Marvis, and Caryth, in the north. To Bronegan, south of the northern range, and to Rrohlwyn and their northern tip. To Chalmbers and the Fields of Eradoch in the east and to Dun Caryth, until all the dark veil of Greensparrow is lifted, until the Iron Cross and Malpuissant's Wall divide more than land. Until Eriador is free!"

It was the perfect ending, Luthien thought, played to the perfect syllable and perfect emphasis. He felt exhausted but euphoric, as tired as if he had just waged a single-handed battle against a hundred cyclopians, and as satisfied as if he had won that fight.

The thrill, the camaraderie, was back within the swelled ranks of the rebels. Luthien knew, and Siobhan knew, that the danger had passed at least for the moment.

The armies of Greensparrow would come, but if Luthien and his friends could maintain the sense of higher purpose, could hold fast to the truths that lay in their hearts, they could not lose.

Whatever ground Greensparrow reclaimed, whatever lives his army claimed, they could not lose.

The rally did not lose momentum as the minutes slipped past; it would have gone on all the day, it seemed, and long into the night. But a voice sounded from the top of the Ministry, an answer to the claims of Luthien Bedwyr.

"Fools, all!" cried a figure standing tall atop the tower's battlements, and even from this distance, some four hundred feet, Luthien knew it to be Viscount Aubrey. "What have you taken but a piece of land? What have you won but a moment's reprieve and the promise of swift and terrible vengeance?"

That stole more than a little of the mirth and hope.

Luthien considered the man, his adversary. Even with all that had transpired, Aubrey appeared unshaken, still meticulously groomed and powdered, still the picture of royalty and strength.

Feigned strength, the battle-toughened Luthien pointedly told himself, for though Aubrey wore the weapons and ribbons of a warrior, he was better at ducking a fight than waging one.

Luthien hated him, hated everything he stood for, but could not deny the man's influence over the crowd, which did not recognize the ruse for what it was.

"Do you think that you can win?" Aubrey spat with a derisive snicker. "Do you think that King Greensparrow, who has conquered countries, who even now wages war in lands south of Gascony, and who has ruled for twenty years, is even concerned? Fools, all! Your winter snows will not protect you! Bask in the glories of victory, but know that this victory is a fleeting thing, and know that you, every one, will pay with your very souls for your audacity!"

Oliver called up to Luthien, getting the man's attention. "Tell him that he was stupid for not better blocking the sewers," the halfling said.

Luthien understood Oliver's motives, but doubted the value of his methods. Aubrey had a powerful weapon here, a very real fear among the rebels that they had started something they could not hope to finish. Montfort—Caer MacDonald—was free, but the rest of their world was not, and the force they had beaten in this city was a tiny fraction of the might Greensparrow could hurl at them.

They all knew it, and so did confident Aubrey, standing tall atop the impervious tower, apparently beyond their reach.

When Luthien did not move to answer, Oliver did. "You talk so brave, but fight so stupid!" the halfling yelled out. A few half-hearted cheers arose, but did not seem to faze the viscount.

"He didn't even block the sewers," Oliver explained loudly. "If his king fights with equal wisdom, then we will dine in the palace of Avon by summer's end!"

That brought a cheer, but Aubrey promptly quenched it. "The same king who conquered all of Eriador," he reminded the gathering.

It could not go on, Luthien realized. They could gain nothing by their banter with Aubrey and would only continually be reminded of the enormity of the task before them. Oliver, sharp-witted as he was, had no ammunition to use against the viscount, no verbal barbs which could stick the man and no verbal salves to soothe the fears that Aubrey was inciting.

Luthien realized then that Siobhan had moved to stand beside him.

"Finish your speech," the half-elf said to him, lifting a curious arrow out of her quiver. It looked different from her other bolts, its shaft a bright red hue, its fletching made not of feathers but of some material even the half-elf did not know. She had discovered the arrow that morning, and as soon as she had touched it, it had imparted distinct telepathic instructions, had told her its purpose, and for some reason that she did not understand, the telepathic voice seemed familiar to her.

With her elven blood, Siobhan understood the means and ways of wizards, and so she had not questioned the arrow's presence or its conveyed message, though she remained suspicious of its origins. The only known wizards in all of the Avonsea Islands, after all, were certainly not allies of the rebels!

Siobhan kept, the arrow with her, though, and now, seeing this situation, the exact scene which had been carried on telepathic waves, her trust in the arrow and in the wizard who had delivered it to her was complete. A name magically came into her head when Luthien took the arrow from her, a name that the half-elf didn't recognize.

Luthien eyed the bolt. Its shaft was bright red, its fletchings the whitish yellow of a lightning bolt. It possessed a tingle within its seemingly fragile shaft, a subtle vibration that Luthien did not understand. He looked at Siobhan, saw her angry glower turned to the tall tower, and understood what she meant for him to do.

It struck Luthien then how influential this quiet half-elf had been, both to him and to the greater cause. Siobhan had been fighting against the merchants and the cyclopians, against the reign of Greensparrow, much longer than Luthien. Along with the Cutters, she had been stealing and building the network that became Luthien's army. Siobhan had embraced Luthien, the Crimson Shadow, and had prodded him along. It was she, Luthien recalled, who had informed him that Shuglin had been captured after the dwarf had helped Oliver and Luthien escape a failed burglary. It was Siobhan who had pointed Luthien toward the Ministry, and then to the mines, and the Cutters had arrived at those mines when Luthien and Oliver went to rescue Shuglin.

It was Siobhan's own trial that had brought Luthien to the Ministry again, on that fateful day when he killed Duke Morkney, and she had followed him all the way up the tower in pursuit of the evil man.

And now Siobhan had given Luthien this arrow, which he somehow knew would reach its mark. Siobhan had led him to his speech and now she had told him to end that speech. Yet she carried a longbow on her shoulder, a greater bow than Luthien's, and she was a better archer than he. If this arrow was what Luthien suspected, somehow crafted or enchanted beyond the norm, Siobhan could have made the shot easier than he.

That wasn't the point. There was more at stake here than the life of a foolish viscount. Siobhan was propagating a legend; by allowing Luthien to take the shot, she was holding him forward as the unmistakable hero of the battle for Caer MacDonald.

Luthien realized then just how great a player Siobhan had been in all of this, and he realized, too, something about his own relationship with the half-elf. Something that scared him.

But he had no time for that now, and she wouldn't answer the questions even if he posed them. He looked back at the crowd and Aubrey and focused on the continuing banter between the viscount and Oliver.

Oliver drew occasional laughter from those around him with his taunts, but in truth, he had no practical responses to the fears that Aubrey's threats inspired. Only a show of strength now could keep the rebels' hearts.

Luthien pinned open his folding bow, a gift from the wizard Brind'Amour, and fitted the arrow to its string. He brought it in line with Aubrey and bent the bow back as far as it would go.

Four hundred feet was too far to shoot. How much lift should he allow over such a distance and in shooting at such a steep angle? And what of the winds?

And what if he missed?

"For the heart." Siobhan answered his doubts in an even, unshakable tone. "Straight for the heart."

Luthien looked down the shaft at his foe. "Aubrey!" he cried, commanding the attention of all. "There is no place in Caer MacDonald for the lies and the threats of Greensparrow!"

"Threats you should heed well, foolish son of Gahris Bedwyr!" Aubrey retorted, and Luthien winced to think that his true identity was so well-known.

He had a moment of mixed feelings then, a moment of doubt about killing the man and the role he had unintentionally assumed.

"I speak the truth!" Aubrey shouted to the general gathering. "You cannot win but can, perhaps, bargain for your lives."

Just a moment of doubt. It was Aubrey who had come to Isle Bedwydrin along with that wretched Avonese. It was Aubrey who had brought the woman who had called for Garth Rogar's death in the arena, who had changed Luthien's life so dramatically. And now it was Aubrey, the symbol of Greensparrow, the pawn of an unlawful king, who stood as the next tyrant in line to terrorize the good folk of Montfort.

"Finish the speech," Siobhan insisted, and Luthien let fly.

The arrow streaked upward and Aubrey waved at it, discarding it as a futile attempt.

Halfway to the tower the arrow seemed to falter and slow, losing momentum. Aubrey saw it and laughed aloud, turning to share his mirth with the cyclopians standing behind him.

Brind'Amour's enchantment grabbed the arrow in mid-flight.

Aubrey looked back to see it gaining speed, streaking unerringly for the target Luthien had selected.

The viscount's eyes widened as he realized the sudden danger. He threw his hands up before him frantically, helplessly.

The arrow hit him with the force of a lightning stroke, hurling him back from the battlement. He felt his breastbone shatter under the weight of that blow, felt his heart explode. Somehow he staggered back to the tower's edge and looked down at Luthien, standing atop the gallows.

The executioner.

Aubrey tried to deny the man, to deny the possibility of such a shot. It was too late; he was already dead.

He slumped in the crenellations, visible to the gathering below.

All eyes turned to Luthien; not a man spoke out, too stunned by the impossible shot. Even Oliver and Katerin had no words for their friend.

"There is no place in Caer MacDonald for the lies and threats of Greensparrow," Luthien said to them.

The hushed moment broke. Ten thousand voices cried out in the exhilaration of freedom, and ten thousand fists punched the air defiantly.

Luthien had finished his speech.

CHAPTER 6

OUT OF HIS ELEMENT

"WE COULD TAKE it down on top of them," Shuglin offered. The dwarf continued to study the parchment spread wide on the table before him, all the while stroking his blue-black beard.

"Take it down?" Oliver asked, and he seemed as horrified as Luthien.

"Drop the building," the dwarf explained matter-of-factly. "With all the stones tumbling down, every one of those damned one-eyes would be squashed flat."

"This is a church!" Oliver hollered. "A cathedral!"

Shuglin seemed not to understand.

"Only God can drop a church," the halfling insisted.

"That's a bet I would take," Shuglin grumbled sarcastically under his breath. The place was strongly built, but the dwarf had no doubt that by knocking out a few key stones . . .

"And if God had any intention of destroying the Ministry, he would have done so during Morkney's evil reign," Luthien added, his sudden interjection into the conversation taking Shuglin away from his enjoyable musings.

"By the whales, aren't we feeling superior?" came a voice from the door, and the three turned to see Katerin enter the room in Luthien and Oliver's apartment on Tiny Alcove, which still served as headquarters for the resistance even though great mansions and Duke Morkney's own palace lay open for the taking. Staying on Tiny Alcove in one of the poorest sections of Montfort was Luthien's idea, for he believed that this was a cause of the common folk, and that he, as their appointed leader, should remain among them, as one of them.

Luthien eyed Katerin carefully as she sauntered across the room. The apartment was below ground, down a narrow stair from the street, Tiny Alcove, which was, in truth, no more than an alleyway. Luthien could see the worn stairs rising behind Katerin and the guards Siobhan had posted relaxing against the wall, taking in the warm day.

Mostly, though, the young Bedwyr saw Katerin. Only Katerin. She was one to talk about feeling superior! Ever since the incident in the Dwelf, Katerin had taken on cool airs whenever she was around Luthien. She rarely met his eyes these days, seemed rather to look past him, as though he wasn't even there.

"Of course we are," Oliver answered with a huff. "We won."

"Not superior," Luthien corrected, his tone sharp—sharper than he had intended. "But I do not doubt the evil that was Morkney, and that is Greensparrow. We are not superior, but we are in the right. I have no—"

Katerin's expression grew sour and she held up her hand to stop the lecture before it had even begun.

Luthien winced. The woman's attitude was getting to him.

"Whatever you intend to do with the Ministry, you should do it soon," Katerin said, suddenly grim. "We have news of a fleet sailing off the western coast, south of the Iron Cross."

"Sailing north," Oliver reasoned.

"So say the whispers," Katerin replied.

Luthien was not surprised; he had known all along that Greensparrow would respond with an army. But though he understood that the war was not ended, that Greensparrow would come, the confirmation still hit him hard. Caer MacDonald wasn't even secured yet, and there were so many other tasks before the young man, more decisions each day than he had made in his entire life. Fifteen thousand people were depending on him, looking to him to solve every problem.

"The weather-watchers believe that the warm will stay," Katerin said, and though that sounded like good news to the winter-weary group, her tone was not light.

"The roads from Port Charley will be deep with mud for many weeks," Luthien reasoned, thinking he understood the woman's dismay. The snow was not so deep, but traveling in the early spring wasn't much better than a winter caravan.

Katerin shook her head; she wasn't thinking at all of the potential problems coming from the west. "We have dead to bury," she said. "Thousands of dead, both man and cyclopian."

"To the buzzards with the cyclopians!" Shuglin growled.

"They stink," Katerin replied. "And their bloated corpses breed vermin." She eyed Luthien squarely for the first time in several days. "You must see to the details. . . ."

She rambled on, but Luthien fell back into a chair beside the small table and drifted out of the conversation. He must see to it. He must see to it. How many times an hour did he hear those words? Oliver, Siobhan, Katerin, Shuglin, and a handful of others were a great help to him, but ultimately the last say in every decision fell upon Luthien's increasingly weary shoulders.

"Well?" Katerin huffed, drawing him back to the present conversation. Luthien stared at her blankly.

"If we do not do it now, we may find no time later," Oliver said in Katerin's defense. Luthien had no idea what they were talking about.

"We believe that they are sympathetic to our cause," Katerin added, and the way she spoke the words made Luthien believe that she had just said them a minute ago.

"What do you suggest?" the young Bedwyr bluffed.

Katerin paused and studied the young man, as though she realized that he hadn't a clue of where the discussion had led. "Have Tasman assemble a group and go out to them," Katerin said. "He's knowing the farmers better than any. If there's one among us who can make certain that food flows into Caer MacDonald, it is Tasman."

Luthien brightened, glad to be back in on the conversation and that this was one decision he didn't have to make alone. "See to it," he said to Katerin.

She started to turn, but her green eyes lingered on Luthien for a long while. She seemed to be sizing him up, and . . .

And what? Luthien wondered. There was something else in those orbs he thought he knew so well. Pain? Anger? He suspected that his continuing relationship with Siobhan did hurt Katerin, though she said differently to any who would listen.

The red-haired woman turned and walked out of the room, back up the stairs past the elven guards.

Of course, the proud Katerin O'Hale would never admit her pain, Luthien reasoned. Not about anything as trivial as love.

"We'll find no volunteers to bury one-eyes," Oliver remarked after a moment.

Shuglin snorted. "My kin will do it, and me with them," the dwarf said, and with a quick bow to Luthien, he, too, turned to leave. "There is pleasure to be found in putting dirt on top of cyclopians."

"More pleasure if they are alive when you do," Oliver snickered.

"Think on dropping that building," the dwarf called over his shoulder, and he seemed quite eager for that task "By the gods, if we do it, then the cyclopians inside will already be buried! Save us the trouble!"

Shuglin stopped at the door and spun about, his face beaming with an idea. "If we can get the one-eyed brutes to take their dead inside, and then we drop the building . . ."

Luthien waved at him impatiently and he shrugged and left.

"What *are* we to do about the Ministry?" Oliver asked after moving to the door and closing it.

"We have people distributing weapons," Luthien replied. "And we have others training the former slaves and the commoners to use them. Shuglin's folk have devised some defenses for the city, and I must meet with them to approve the plans. Now we have dead men to bury and food to gather. Alliances to secure with neighboring farm villages. Then there is the matter of Port Charley and the fleet that is supposedly sailing north along the coast. And, of course, the dead cyclopians must be removed."

"I get the point," Oliver said dryly, his Gascon accent making the last word into two syllables, "po-went."

"And the Ministry," exasperated Luthien went on. "I understand how important it is that we clear that building before Greensparrow's army arrives. We may have to use it ourselves, as a last defense."

"Let us hope the Avon soldiers do not get that far inside the city," Oliver put in.

"Their chances of getting in will be much greater if we have to keep a quarter of our forces standing guard around the cathedral," Luthien replied. "I know it, and know that I must come up with some plan to take the place."

"But. . ." Oliver prompted.

"Too many tasks," Luthien answered. He looked up at Oliver, needing support. "Am I to be the general, or the mayor?"

"Which would you prefer?" Oliver asked, but he already knew the answer: Luthien wanted to fight against Greensparrow with his weapons, not his edicts.

"Which would be the better for the cause of Eriador?" the man replied.

Oliver snorted. There was no doubt in the halfling's mind. He had seen Luthien lead the warriors, had watched the young man systematically free Montfort until it became Caer MacDonald. And Oliver had observed the faces of those who fought beside Luthien, those who watched in awe his movements as he led them into battle.

There came a knock on the door, and Siobhan entered. She took one look at the pair, recognizing the weight of their discussion, then excused herself from those who had come with her, waving them back out into the street and closing the apartment door. She moved quietly to the table and remained silent, deferring to the apparently more important discussion. This was not an unusual thing, Siobhan had a way of getting in on most of Oliver and Luthien's conversations.

"I do not think the Crimson Shadow would be such a legend if he was the mayor of a town," the halfling answered Luthien.

"Who then?" Luthien wanted to know.

The answer didn't come from Oliver, but, unexpectedly, from the half-elf, who had already surmised the problem. "Brind'Amour," she said evenly.

As soon as the weight of that name registered, both the friends nearly fell over with surprise—Luthien would have had he not been sitting already.

"How do you know that name?" Oliver, finding his voice first, wanted to know.

Siobhan put on a wry smile.

Oliver looked at Luthien, but the young Bedwyr shrugged, for he had not mentioned the old wizard to anybody in the city.

"You know of Brind'Amour?" Luthien asked her. "You know who he is and where he is?"

"I know of a wizard who lives still, somewhere in the north," Siobhan answered. "I know that it was he who gave to you the crimson cape, and the bow."

"How do you know?" Oliver asked.

"It was he who gave to me the arrow that you used to slay Viscount Aubrey," Siobhan went on, and that was explanation enough.

"Then you have spoken to him?" Luthien prompted.

The half-elf shook her head. "He has . . ." She paused, trying to find the right way to put it. "He has looked at me," she explained. "And through my eyes." She noted the surprise—hopeful surprise—on both her companions' faces. "Yes, Brind'Amour understands what has happened in Montfort."

"Caer MacDonald," Luthien corrected.

"In Caer MacDonald," Siobhan agreed.

"But will he come?" Oliver wanted to know, for the suggestion seemed perfect to the halfling. Who better than an old wizard to see to the day-to-day needs of a city?

Siobhan honestly did not know. She had felt the presence of the wizard beside her and had feared that presence, thinking that Greensparrow was watching the movements of the rebels. Then Brind'Amour had come to her in a dream and had explained who he was. But that was the only contact she had made with the old wizard, and even it was foggy, perhaps no more than a dream.

Although, considering the arrow she had found in her quiver, and Luthien and Oliver's confirmation of the existence of such a man, she now knew, of course, that it had been much more than a dream.

"Do you know where he is?" Luthien asked her.

"No."

"Do you know how to speak with him?"

"No."

At a loss, Luthien looked to Oliver.

"He is a fine choice," the halfling said, the exact words Luthien wanted to hear.

Luthien knew that the wizard's cave was somewhere within the northern-most spurs of the Iron Cross, to the north and east of Caer MacDonald, on the southern side of a wide gap called Bruce MacDonald's Swath. The young Bedwyr had been there only once, along with Oliver, but unfortunately on that occasion neither of them had found the chance to spy out the locale. A magical tunnel had brought them into the cave, whisking them off the road right in the midst of cyclopian pursuit. The pair had left via a magical tunnel, as well, Brind'Amour setting them down on the road to Montfort. Judging from where they were taken by the wizard, and where he had dropped them off, Luthien could approximate the location, and he knew that Brind'Amour's sight was not limited by stone walls.

Within the hour, the eager young man selected messengers, a dozen men he sent out from the city with instructions to ride to the northern tips of the Iron Cross, separate, and find high, conspicuous perches, and then read loudly from parchments Luthien gave to each of them, a note that the young man had written for the old wizard.

"He will hear," Luthien assured Oliver when the two saw the dozen riders off.

Oliver wasn't sure, or that the reclusive Brind'Amour would answer the call if he did hear. But Oliver did understand that Luthien, weary of the business of governing, had to believe that relief was on the way, and so the halfling nodded his agreement.

"So bids Luthien Bedwyr, present Lord of Caer MacDonald, which was Montfort," the young man called out, standing very still, very formal and tall, on a flat-topped hillock.

Some distance away, another man slipped off his horse and unrolled a parchment similarly inscribed. "To the wizard Brind'Amour, friend of those who do not call themselves friends of King Greensparrow . . ."

And so it went that morning in the northernmost reaches of the Iron Cross, with the twelve messengers, two days out from Caer MacDonald, each going his own way to find a spot which seemed appropriate for such a call into the wind.

Brind'Amour woke late that morning, after a refreshing and much-needed rest: twelve solid hours of slumber. He felt strong, despite his recent journeys into the realm of magic, always a taxing thing. He did not know yet that Viscount Aubrey was dead, slain by the arrow he had delivered into Siobhan's quiver, for he had not peered into his crystal ball in many days.

He still wasn't certain of Luthien and the budding revolt, of how long Montfort could hold out against the army that would soon sail up the coast, or about his own role in all of this. Perhaps this was all just a prelude, he had told himself the night before as he crawled into his bed. Perhaps this rumbling in Eriador would soon be quieted, but would not be forgotten, and in a few decades . . .

Yes, the old wizard had decided. In a few decades. It seemed the safer course, the wiser choice. Let the tiny rebellion play itself out. Luthien would be killed or forced to flee, but the young Bedwyr had done his part. Oh, yes, the young warrior from Isle Bedwydrin would be remembered fondly in the years to come, and the next time Eriador decided to test the strength of Avon's hold, Luthien's name would be held up beside that of Bruce MacDonald. And Oliver's, too, and perhaps that would inspire some help from Gascony.

Yes, to wait was the wiser choice.

When first he woke, feeling lighthearted, almost jovial, Brind'Amour told himself that he was happy because he was secure now with his decision to stay out of the fight and let it play out to the bitter end. He had chosen the safe road and could justify his inaction by looking at the greater potential for Eriador's future. He had done well in giving Luthien the cape; Luthien had done well in putting it to use. They had all done well, and though Greensparrow would not likely grow old—the man had lived for several centuries already—he might become bored with it all. After twenty years, Greensparrow's grip had already loosened somewhat on Eriador, else there never could have been such a rebellion in Montfort, and who could guess what the next few decades would bring? But the people of Eriador would never forget this one moment and would crystallize it, capture it as a shining flicker of hope, frozen in time, the legend growing with each retelling.

The old wizard went to cook his breakfast full of euphoria, full of energy and hope. He might do a bit more, perhaps when the battle was renewed in Montfort. Maybe he could find a way to aid Luthien, just to add to the legend. Greensparrow's army would no doubt regain the city, but perhaps Luthien could take on that ugly brute Belsen'Krieg and bring him to a smashing end.

"Yes," the wizard said, congratulating himself. He flicked his wrist, snapping the skillet and sending a pancake spinning into the air.

He heard his name and froze in place, and the pancake flopped over the side of the skillet and fell to the floor.

He heard it again.

Brind'Amour hustled down the passageways of his cavern home, into the room he used for his magic. He heard his name again, and then again, and each time he heard it, he tried to move faster, but only bumbled about.

He thought it was Greensparrow come calling, or one of the king's lesser wizards, or perhaps even a demon. Had he erred in sending his sight out to the palace in Carlisle? Had Greensparrow postponed his announced vacation in Gascony to deal first with troublesome Brind'Amour?

Finally, the old wizard got the thick cloth off of his crystal ball, put the item on the desk in front of him, and calmed himself enough to look into its depths.

Brind'Amour sighed loudly, so very relieved when he learned that the call was not from a wizard but from a mere man, apparently a messenger.

Relief turned to anger as Brind'Amour continued to seek and he came to know that there were several men calling for him.

"Fool!" Brind'Amour grumbled at Luthien as soon as he realized exactly what was going on. "Daring fool," he whispered. This was not Montfort; these lands were still in the hands of cyclopians and others loyal to Greensparrow. No open revolt had come, at least not as far as Brind'Amour knew.

And to speak Brind'Amour's name so clearly, so loudly, where Greensparrow's ears might hear! If the king of Avon realized that Brind'Amour was somehow connected to the revolt in Montfort, if he knew that Brind'Amour was even awake from his centuries-long sleep, then his eyes would surely focus more closely on Eriador; he would not go to vacation in Gascony and would turn all of his attention north instead. The cause would be crushed.

The cause.

For a long, long time, Brind'Amour, ever cautious, had tried to convince himself that the cause was not so important, that the fight in Montfort was just a prelude to what might happen many decades down the road. But now, fearing that all of the rebellion was in jeopardy, considering the deep feelings rushing through him, he had to wonder if he had been fooling himself. He might justify letting this rebellion die in Montfort, but only for a short while. When it was done, when the blood had washed from the fields and the city's walls, Brind'Amour would lament the return of Greensparrow, the opportunity for freedom—for freedom *now*—lost.

Whatever course he now considered, Brind'Amour knew that he had to silence those silly boys with their silly scrolls. He felt strong indeed this morning and discovered that he dearly wanted to test his magic.

The wizard moved to the side of his desk, opened a drawer, and took out a huge, black leather-bound book, gently opening it. Then he began to chant, falling into the archaic runes depicted on the pages, falling deeper into the realm of magic than he had gone for nearly four hundred years.

The twelve men on their twelve hills had been reading and rereading their scrolls for more than two hours. But their instructions had been to read on from sunrise to sunset, day after day, until their call was answered.

Now their call *was* answered, but not in any way they, or Luthien, had anticipated.

A sudden black cloud rolled over the peaks of the Iron Cross, south of the readers. The blackest of clouds, a ball of midnight against the blue sky. A stiff wind kicked up, ruffling the parchments.

All twelve of the men held stubborn, loyal to Luthien and convinced of the importance of their mission.

On came the cloud, dark and ominous, blocking out the sun, except for twelve tiny holes in the blackness, twelve specific points that caught the rays of day and focused them through a myriad of ice crystals.

One by one, those holes released the focused ray of light under the cloud, and each of those beams, guided by a wizard looking into a crystal ball in a cave not so far away, found its mark, shooting down from the heavens to strike unerringly at the unfurled parchments.

The brittle paper ignited and burned, and one by one, the readers dropped the useless remnants and ran to their nearby mounts. One by one, they emerged from the foothills at a full gallop. Some linked up, but those who had charged out first did not stop and look back for their companions.

In the cave, Brind'Amour settled back and let the crystal ball go dark. Only a few minutes earlier he had felt refreshed and full of vigor, but now he was tired and old once more.

"Foolish boy," he muttered under his breath, but he found that he did not believe the words. Luthien's judgment in sending out callers might have been amiss, but the young man's heart was true. Could Brind'Amour say the same for himself? He thought again of the uprising, of its scale and of its importance, of his own insistence that this was just a prelude.

Was he taking the safe route or the easy one?

CHAPTER 7

THE CRIMSON SHADOW

"COULD WE NOT have gone in the lower door?" Oliver asked, thoroughly cold and miserable and with still more than a hundred feet of climbing looming before him.

"The door is blocked," Luthien whispered, his mouth close to Oliver's ear, the cowl of his crimson cape covering not only his head but the halfling's as well. "You did not have to come."

"I did not want to lose my rope," the stubborn halfling replied.

They were scaling the eastern wall of the Ministry, more than halfway up the tallest tower. The night air was not so cold, but the wind was stiff this high up, biting at them and threatening to shake them free. Luthien huddled tight and checked the fastenings of his magical cape. He couldn't have it blowing open up here, leaving him and Oliver exposed halfway up the wall!

He had been wearing his cape daily since the rebellion began, for it was the symbol that the common folk of the city had rallied behind. The Crimson Shadow, the legend of old come to life to lead them to freedom. But the cape was much more than a showpiece. Cloistered within its protective magics, the cape tight about him and the cowl pulled low, Luthien was less than a shadow, or merely a shadow blended into other shadows—for all practical measures, completely invisible. He had only used the cape in this camouflaging manner a couple of times during the weeks of fighting to go over the wall and scout out enemy positions. He had thought of trying to find Aubrey, to kill the man in his house, but Siobhan had talked him out of that course, convincing him that the bumbling viscount was, in reality, a blessing to the rebels.

This time, though, Luthien would not be talked out of his plan; in fact, he had told no one except Oliver of his intentions.

So here they were, in the dark of night, almost up the Ministry's tallest wall. There were cyclopians posted up there, they both knew, but the brutes were likely huddled close around a fire. What would they be on watch against, after all? They could not see the movements of men on the streets below, and they certainly did not expect anyone to come up and join them!

Oliver's last throw had been good, heaving the magical grapnel up to the end of the rope, but after climbing the fifty feet to the puckered ball, the companions found few places to set themselves. There were no windows this high up on the tower, and the stones had been worn smooth by the incessant wind.

Luthien hooked his fingers tight into a crack, his feet barely holding to a narrow perch. "Hurry," he bade his companion.

Oliver looked up at him and sighed. The halfling, his feet against the wall, was tucked in tight against Luthien's belly—the only thing holding Oliver aloft was Luthien. Oliver fumbled with the rope, trying to loop it so that he could fling it up the remaining fifty feet, all the way to the tower's lip.

"Hurry," Luthien said more urgently, and Oliver understood that the young man's hold was not so good. Muttering a curse in his native Gascon tongue, the halfling reached out and tossed the magical grapnel as high as he could. It caught fast, no more than twenty feet above them.

Again came that whispered Gascon curse, but Luthien dismissed it, for he saw something that the halfling did not.

Oliver quieted and held on tight to Luthien, who took up the rope and climbed only a few feet, coming to a stop atop a jutting stone.

"Make the next throw the last throw," Luthien whispered, planting himself firmly.

Oliver tugged three times on the rope, the signal for the grapnel to loosen. It slipped down silently and Oliver reeled it in. Now, since Luthien had solid footing, so did Oliver, and the halfling took his time and measured his throw.

Perfect: the grapnel hit the wall with the slightest of sounds just a foot below the tower's lip.

Again Oliver grabbed on and Luthien took up the rope, ready to climb. Oliver grabbed his wrist, though, and when Luthien paused, he, too, heard the movement up above.

Luthien ducked low under the protective cape, sheltering himself and Oliver. After a long moment, the young Bedwyr dared to look up and saw the silhouette of a cyclopian peering over the wall down at him.

Luthien thought the game was up, but the brute made no move and no sound, gave no indication at all that it had seen the companions.

"Nothing," the cyclopian grumbled, and walked away from the rim, back to the warmth of the fire.

Oliver and Luthien shared a sigh, and then the young Bedwyr hauled them both up the rope to the tower's lip.

They heard the cyclopians—three, at least—about a dozen feet away.

Oliver's head came over the lip first, and he confirmed the number and the distance. Luck was with the halfling, then, for he noted, too, the movement of a fourth brute, milling about on the landing just a few stairs down from the tower's top.

Oliver signaled his intent to Luthien, and then, like a weasel slipping along a riverbank, the halfling picked his way along the top of the wall, around and over the battlements without a sound.

Luthien silently counted; Oliver had asked for a count of fifty. That completed, the young Bedwyr pulled himself up to the tower's lip, peering at the three brutes huddled about their small fire. Luthien slid up to sit on the wall, gently rolled his legs over, and put a hand to his sword's hilt. He would have to strike fast and hard and could only hope that Oliver would take care of the one by the stairs—and hopefully, there was only one at the stairs!

No time for those thoughts now, Luthien scolded himself. They were three hundred feet up the tower and fully committed. He slipped down off the wall, took a deep breath as he set his feet firmly, then charged, drawing his blade.

Blind-Striker hit the first cyclopian where it crouched, slashing diagonally across the back of the brute's shoulder, severing the backbone. The cyclopian fell without a sound, and Luthien whipped the sword across as the second leaped up, spinning to face him. His blade got the creature through the chest—two dead—but snagged on a rib and would not immediately come free at Luthien's desperate tug.

The third cyclopian did not charge, but turned and fled for the stairs. It jerked weirdly halfway there, then stopped altogether, went to its knees, and fell over on its back, dead. Luthien noted Oliver's main gauche embedded deeply in its chest, a perfect throw.

Oliver came out of the stairwell and casually stepped over and retrieved his thrown weapon. "What were they eating?" the halfling inquired, walking past the kill toward the small fire. He picked up a stick, a chunk of cooking mutton on its other end.

"Ah, so fine," the halfling said, delighted, and sat down.

A few moments went by before Oliver looked up to see Luthien staring at him incredulously. "Do hurry," the halfling bade the young man.

"You are not coming?" Luthien asked.

"I said I would get you up the tower," Oliver replied, and went back to the mutton feast.

Luthien chuckled. He pulled off his pack and dropped another silken cord, this one as long as the tower was tall, at Oliver's feet. "Do prepare the descent," he bade the halfling.

Oliver, face deep in the mutton, waved him away. "Your business will take longer than mine," he assured Luthien.

Luthien snickered again and started away. It made sense of course, that he should go down alone. Once inside the Ministry, he would have to move quickly, and he could not do that with Oliver tucked under the folds of his cape.

He found the fourth cyclopian, dead of a rapier thrust, on the landing just below the tower level. An involuntary shudder coursed Luthien's spine as he recognized how efficient his little friend could be. All for the good cause, he reminded himself, and started down the longer, curving stair. He met no resistance all the three hundred steps to the floor, and to his relief found that the door at the bottom of the stair, along the curving wall of the cathedral's eastern apse, was ajar.

Luthien peered into the vast nave. A few torches burned; he heard the snores of dozens of cyclopians stretched out on the many benches. Only a few of the brutes were up, but they were in groups, talking and keeping a halfhearted watch.

They were confident, Luthien realized. The cyclopians were convinced that the rebels wouldn't accept the losses they would no doubt suffer if they attacked the fortified Ministry. A good sign.

Luthien came out of the door and crept among the shadows, silent and invisible. He noted more cyclopians milling about on the triforium ledges, but they, too, were not paying much attention. Luthien went right, to the north, and scouted out the transept. The doors down there were heavily barricaded, as expected, and a group of cyclopians sat in a circle before them, apparently gambling.

They were bored and they were weary—and soon they would have nothing to eat.

Luthien thought of going all around the transept, back into the nave and down to the west. He changed his mind and went back to the apse instead, then around the semicircle and into the southern transept.

Halfway down, he found what he was looking for: a huge pile of foodstuffs. The young Bedwyr smiled wickedly and moved in close. He took out a small black box, which Shuglin had designed for him, and then six small pouches, filled with a black powder that the dwarfs used in their mining. He considered the pile for a few moments, placing the pouches strategically. He set two between the three kegs of water he found on one side of the pile, probably the only drinking water the brutes had.

Next came some flasks of oil, wrapped in thick furs so that they would not clang together. Carefully, the invisible intruder doused the pile of provisions. One of the cyclopians near to the southern transept's door sniffed the air curiously, but the smell of Luthien's oil was not easily detected over that of the lanterns already burning throughout the Ministry.

When the cyclopian went back to its watch at the door, Luthien huddled under his cape with the black box, perfectly square and unremarkable, except that the top had a small hole cut into it. Luthien carefully opened the box. He tried to study Shuglin's design to see what was inside, but in the dim light he could make out little. There were two small glass vials, that much he could see, and the strike plate and wick were in between them.

Luthien looked up, glanced around to make sure that no cyclopians were nearby. Then he huddled low beside the pile, making sure that his cape and the piled provisions shielded the box. He flicked the strike plate. It sparked, but the wick did not catch.

Luthien glanced about again, then repeated the motion.

This time, the wick lighted, burning softly. Now Luthien could see Shuglin's design, the amber liquid in one glass, the reddish liquid in the other, and the leather pouch below, probably filled with the same black powder.

Intriguing, but Luthien had no time to study it further; Shuglin guaranteed him a count of twenty-five, no longer. He closed the box and crept away, back into the shadows, back into the apse, through the door and onto the lowest stairs. There, he paused, watching.

With a hiss and a sputter, the black box exploded, igniting the pile. Cyclopians hooted and shouted, charging in all directions.

A second explosion sounded, and then a third and a fourth, close together, and the water kegs burst apart.

Luthien turned and sprinted up the stairs, smiling as he heard four more distinctive blasts.

"I take it that we are done," Oliver remarked between bites of mutton when the young man, huffing and puffing, stumbled out onto the tower's top.

"We have to go and tell the guards around the plaza to be alert," Luthien replied. "The cyclopians will try to break out soon."

Oliver took one last bite, wiped his greasy hands on the furred cape of one of the dead cyclopians, and moved to the wall, where the grapnel and rope were already fastened to the longer cord that reached all the way to the street, ready to take them down.

Inside the Ministry, the cyclopians found most of their provisions ruined and nearly all of their potable water lost. They jostled and fought amongst themselves, every one blaming another, until one brute found the answer in the form of a crimson shadow of a caped man, indelibly stained on the wall of the eastern apse.

Luthien's enchanted cape had left its mark.

Word raced up Avon's western coast, across the mountains into Eriador, and from village to village, to Caer MacDonald and beyond. A great fleet was sailing, bracing the freezing waters: at least fifty Avon ships, enough to carry more than ten thousand Praetorian Guards. And those ships were low in the water, said the rumors, low and brimming with soldiers.

The news was received stoically at the Dwelf. Luthien and his companions had expected the army, of course, but the final confirmation that it was all more than rumor, that Greensparrow was indeed aware of the rebellion and responding with an iron fist, sobered the mood.

"I will set out for Port Charley in the morning," Luthien told his gathered commanders. "A hard ride will get me there before the Avon fleet arrives."

"You cannot," Siobhan replied simply, with finality.

Luthien looked hard at her, as did Oliver, who was about to volunteer to ride off beside his friend (all the while hoping that he might turn Luthien north instead, back into hiding in the wilds).

"You govern Caer MacDonald," the half-elf explained.

"Do not leaders often sally forth from the place they lead?" Oliver remarked.

"Not when that place is in turmoil," the half-elf answered. "We expect a breakout from the Ministry any day."

"The one-eyes will be slaughtered in the open plaza," Oliver said with all confidence, a confidence that was widespread among all the rebels.

"And Luthien Bedwyr must be there," Siobhan went on without hesitation. "When that fight is done, the city will be ours, wholly ours. It would not be appropriate for that important moment to pass with the leader of the rebellion halfway to Port Charley."

"We cannot underestimate the importance of Port Charley," Luthien interjected, feeling a little left out of it all, as if he weren't even in the room, or at least as though he didn't have to be in the room. "Port Charley will prove critical to the rebellion and to Caer MacDonald. Even as we sit here bantering, Shuglin's people work frantically to prepare the defenses of the city. If the whispers speak truly, then an army equal in size to our own force will soon march upon our gates."

"Equal odds favor the defense," Katerin O'Hale remarked.

"But these are Praetorian Guards," Luthien emphasized. "Huge and strong, superbly trained and equipped, and no doubt the veterans of many campaigns."

"You doubt our own prowess?" Katerin wanted to know, her tone sharply edged with anger.

"I want the best possible outcome," Luthien firmly corrected. In his heart, though, he did indeed doubt the rabble army's ability to hold against ten thousand Praetorian Guards, and so did everyone else in the room, proud Katerin included.

"Thus, Port Charley is all-important," Luthien went on. "They have not declared an alliance, and as you yourself have pointed out," he said to Katerin, "they will not be easily convinced."

The red-haired woman leaned back in her chair and slid it out from the table, visibly backing off from the conversation.

"We must bottle that fleet up in the harbor," Luthien explained. "If the folk of Port Charley do not allow them to pass, they will have to sail on, and might waste many days searching for a new place to land."

"And every day they are at sea is another day they might encounter a storm," Oliver said slyly.

Luthien nodded. "And another day that they will tax their provisions and, knowing cyclopians, their patience," he agreed. "And another day that Shuglin and his kin have to complete their traps around the outer walls of Caer MacDonald. The fleet must be kept out. We cannot fail in this."

"Agreed," Siobhan replied. "But you are not the one to go." Luthien started to respond, but she kept on talking, cutting him off. "Others are qualified to serve as emissaries, and it will not look as good as you believe to have the leader of the rebellion walking into Port Charley, to say nothing of the reaction from the cyclopians already in that town.

"You think that you will impress them with your presence," Siobhan went on, brutally honest, but her tone in no way condescending. "All that you will impress them with is your foolishness and innocence. Your place is here—the leaders of Port Charley will know that—and if you show up there, you will not strike them as a man wise enough for them to follow into war."

Luthien, slack-jawed, his shoulders slumped, looked over at Oliver for support.

"She's not so bad," the halfling admitted.

Luthien had no way to disagree, no arguments against the simple logic. Again he felt as if Siobhan, and not he, was in control, as if he were a puppet, its strings pulled by that beautiful and sly half-elf. He didn't like the feeling, not at all, but he was glad that Siobhan was at his side, preventing him from making foolish mistakes. Luthien thought of Brind'Amour then, realizing more clearly than ever that he was out of his element and in desperate need of aid.

"Who will go, then?" Oliver asked Siobhan, for Luthien, by his expression alone, had obviously conceded the floor to her on this matter. "Yourself? I do not think one who is half-elven will make so fine an impression."

Oliver meant no insult, and Siobhan, concerned only for the success of the rebellion, took none.

"I will go," Katerin promptly put in. All eyes turned her way, and Luthien leaned forward again on his stool, suddenly very interested and worried.

"I know the people of Port Charley better than anyone here," Katerin stated.

"Have you ever been there?" Oliver asked.

"I am from Hale, a town not so unlike Port Charley," Katerin answered. "My people think the same way as those independent folk. We have never succumbed to the rule of Greensparrow. We have never succumbed to any rule save our own, and tolerate kings and dukes only because we do not care about them."

Luthien was shaking his head. He wasn't sure that he wanted to be away from Katerin right now. And he didn't want her riding off alone to the west. Word of the fight in Caer MacDonald had spread throughout the southland of Eriador, and none of them knew what dangers might await any emissary on the road.

"There is another reason you cannot go," Katerin said to Luthien. "If the men of Port Charley do not join in our alliance, they will have all the ransom they need for Greensparrow with the Crimson Shadow delivered into their hands."

"You doubt their honor?" Luthien asked incredulously.

"I understand their pragmatism," Katerin replied. "They care nothing for you, not yet."

Katerin's point did not make Luthien feel any better about letting her go. She, too, would prove a fine bartering point with the king of Avon!

"Katerin is right," came word from an unexpected ally for the woman of Hale. "You cannot go, and she can accomplish what we need better than anyone in Caer MacDonald," Siobhan reasoned.

Katerin looked hard at the half-elf, suspicious of her rival's motives. For an instant she wondered if Siobhan wanted her to go so that she would perhaps be killed or taken prisoner, but looking into the half-elf's green eyes—sparkling, intense orbs so like her own—Katerin saw no animosity, only genuine hope and even affection.

Luthien started to protest, but Siobhan stopped him short. "You cannot let your personal feelings block the path to the general good," the half-elf scolded, turning to glare at the young man. "Katerin is the best choice. You know that as well as anyone." Siobhan looked back to Katerin, smiled, and nodded, and the woman of Hale did likewise. Then Siobhan turned back to Luthien. "Do I speak truly?"

Luthien sighed, defeated once more by simple logic. "Take Riverdancer," he bade Katerin, referring to his own horse, a shining highland Morgan, as fine a steed as could be found in all of Eriador. "In the morning."

"Tonight," Katerin corrected grimly. "The Avon fleet does not drop sail when the sun sleeps."

Luthien did not want her to go. He wanted to run across the room and wrap her in a tight hug, wanted to protect her from all of this, from all the evils and all the dangers in the world. But he realized that Katerin and Siobhan were right. Katerin was the best choice, and she needed no protection.

Without another word, she turned and left the Dwelf.

Luthien looked to Oliver. "I will return when I return," the halfling explained with a tip of his hat, and he moved to follow Katerin.

Luthien eyed Siobhan, expecting her to stop the halfling, dissuade him as she had Luthien.

"Ride well," was all the half-elf said, and Oliver tipped his hat to her as well, and then he, too, was gone.

Those remaining in the Dwelf had many other things to discuss that night, but they sat quietly, or in small, private conversations. Suddenly a man rushed in.

"The Ministry!" he cried.

It was all he had to say. Luthien leaped down from his stool and practically stumbled headlong for the door. Siobhan caught him by the arm and supported him, and he paused, straightening, and eyed her directly.

Her smile was infectious, and Luthien knew that, despite the fact that Oliver and Katerin were likely already on the road, he would not fight alone this night.

The desperate cyclopians charged out of the Ministry through the north, west, and south doors, roaring and running, trying to get across the plaza and into the shadows of the alleyways. Swarms of arrows met them from every side, and then the rebels didn't even wait for the cyclopians to charge; they rushed out to meet them, matching desperation with sheer fury.

Luthien and the others from the Dwelf did not go over the wall. Rather, they pounded their way through the eastern wall, where it had been breached before, up from the city's lower section and back into the Ministry once again. As the slaughter continued in the plaza, more than a few cyclopians thought to turn and flee back into the cathedral. There was still some food remaining, after all, and they figured that if they could get back in and barricade the doors once more, there would be fewer of them left to share it.

But Luthien's small group met them and kept the cathedral's main door thrown wide so that rebels, too, could get inside. Once more the hallowed floor of the great cathedral ran deep with blood. Once more a place of prayer became a place of cries, shouts of anger, and shrieks of the wounded.

It was finished that night. Not a single cyclopian remained alive in the city of Caer MacDonald.

CHAPTER 8

PORT CHARLEY

PORT CHARLEY WAS a huddled village, white-painted homes built in tight, neat rows up a series of cut steps along the foothills of the Iron Cross and overlooking the tumultuous Avon Sea. It was said that on the clearest of days the shining white and green cliffs of Baranduine, far to the west, could be seen from those highest perches, beckoning the souls of men. Port Charley was a dreamy place, and yet cheery on those rare days that the sun did shine, bouncing gaily off the white-faced houses, off the white fences outlining every yard and bordering each of the city's tiers.

Such was the day, bright and sunny and cheery, when Oliver and Katerin came in sight of the village. They noted that there was no snow in or about the town, just windblown rock, white and gray streaks amidst the squared and neat cottages. Splotches of green and brown dotted the landscape, and a few trees stood bare, poking high and proud between cottage and stone.

"Too early to bloom," Oliver remarked. He kicked Threadbare, his yellow pony, to a faster trot.

Katerin spurred Riverdancer on, the powerful white stallion easily pacing the smaller pony.

"I have been here in the spring," Oliver explained. "You really should see Port Charley in the spring!" The halfling went on to describe the blossoming trees and the many flowers peeking from sheltering crevices in the stones and from the many, many window boxes, but Katerin only half-listened, for she needed no descriptions. To her, Port Charley was Hale, on a larger scale, and the young woman remembered well the land of her youth, the wind blowing off the cold waters, the spattering of bright color, purple mostly, against the gray and white. She heard the sound of the tide, that low rumble, the growl of the earth itself, and she remembered Isle Bedwydrin and taking to the sea in a craft that seemed so glorious and huge tied up at the wharf, but so insignificant and tiny once the land became no more than a darker line on the gray horizon.

And Katerin remembered the smell, remembered that most of all, heavy air thick with salt and brine. Heavy and healthy, primal somehow. Port Charley and Hale, these were places to be most alive, where the soul was closest to the realities of the tangible world.

Oliver noted the dreamy, faraway look in the woman's green eyes and went quiet.

They came in from the northeast, down the single road that forked, going right to the dunes and the sea, and left to the lowest section of the village. Oliver started left, but Katerin knew better.

"To the wharves," she explained.

"We must find the mayor," Oliver called after her, for she did not slow.

"The harbormaster," Katerin corrected, for she knew that in Port Charley, as in Hale, the person who controlled the docks controlled the town as well.

Their mounts' hooves clattered loudly on the wooden boardwalk that snaked through the soft sandy beach to the wharves, but once they approached those docks, where water lapped loudly and many boats bumped and banged against the wooden wharf, the sound of their mounts became insignificant. Gulls squawked overhead and bells sounded often, cutting the air above the continual groan of the rolling surf. One boat glided toward the docks at half-sail, a swarm of gray and white gulls flapping noisily above it, showing that the crew had landed a fine catch this day.

Squinting, Oliver could see that a man and a woman were at work on the deck of the boat, chopping off fish heads with huge knives and then tossing the unwanted portions into the air straight overhead, not even bothering to look up, as if they knew that no piece would ever find its way through the flock to fall back down.

Katerin led the way up a ramp to the long boardwalk that fronted the village. Seven long spurs jutted out into the harbor, enough room for perhaps two hundred fishing boats, five times Hale's modest fleet. An image of those small boats darting in and around massive war galleons flashed in Katerin's mind. She hadn't seen many ships of war, just those that occasionally docked in Dun Varna, and one that had passed her father's boat out on the open sea off Isle Bedwydrin's western coast; she had no idea what one of those ships could do. She could well imagine their power, though, and the image sent a shudder along her spine.

She shook the disturbing thoughts away and looked at the harbor. She hoped it had a shallow sounding, too shallow for the great ships to put in. If they could get the enemy into smaller landing craft, the fishermen of Port Charley would make a landing very difficult indeed.

Katerin realized that she was getting ahead of herself. Formulating battle plans by the folk who knew these waters best would come later. Right now, Katerin and Oliver merely had to convince the folk of Port Charley to stand against the invading force and keep Greensparrow's army out in the harbor.

Riverdancer's hooves clomped along the boardwalk, Threadbare right behind. Katerin understood the wharf's design, similar to the one in Hale, and so she made her way to the fourth and central pier.

"Should we not walk the horses?" Oliver asked nervously, his gaze locked on the slits in the boardwalk, and the spectacle of the dark water far below them. The tide was out and soon Oliver and Katerin were a full thirty feet above the level of the water.

Katerin didn't answer, just kept her course straight for the small cottage built beside the pier. Only a couple of boats were in—it was still early in the afternoon—and a few crusty old sea dogs waddled along the various piers, turning curious glances at the strange newcomers, particularly at the foppish halfling, so colorful and out of place in the wintry village.

An old woman, her face brown and cracked and her white hair thin, as though the incessant sea breeze had blown half of it away, came out to greet them before they reached the cottage.

She nodded at them as they dismounted, and smiled, showing more gum than tooth: her few remaining teeth were crooked and stained. Her eyes were the lightest of blue, almost washed of color, and her limbs and fingers, like the teeth, were crooked and bent in awkward angles, with knuckles and joints like knobby bumps on her old frame.

But she was not an unattractive sight. There was a goodness about her, a genuinely noble and honest soul, someone who had walked a straight path despite the crooked limbs.

"Yer won't find passage south fer another two-week," she said in nasal tones. "And not fer north fer another two-week after that."

"We do not seek passage at all," Katerin replied. "We seek the harbormaster."

The old woman spent a long moment regarding Katerin, studying the hard texture of her hands and the way she held herself straight despite the stiff breeze. Then she extended her arm warmly. "Yer found her," she said. "Gretel Sweeney."

"Katerin O'Hale," the young woman replied, and her mention of the port town to the north brought a smile and a nod of recognition from Gretel. The old harbormaster recognized a fellow seagoer when she saw one. She didn't know what to make of Oliver, though, until she thought back across the years. Gretel had been Port Charley's harbormaster for nearly two decades, and she made it a point of watching every foreign ship dock and unload. Of course she did not remember everyone who passed through her village, but Oliver was one who was hard to forget.

"Gascon," she said, shifting her arm toward the halfling.

Oliver took the offered hand and brought it to his lips. "Oliver de-Burrows," he introduced himself, and when he let go of Gretel's hand, he dipped into a sweeping bow, his hat brushing the wooden decking.

"Gascon," Gretel said again to Katerin with a wink and a nod.

Katerin got right to the point. "You have heard of the fighting in Montfort?" she asked.

Gretel's almost white eyes twinkled with comprehension. "Strange to make a Gascon an emissary," she said.

"Oliver is a friend," Katerin explained. "A friend to me and a friend to Luthien Bedwyr."

"Then it's true," the old woman said. "The son of Bedwydrin's eorl." She shook her head, her expression sour. "To be sure, he's a long way from home," she remarked, as Katerin and Oliver looked to each other, each trying to gauge Gretel's reaction. "As are yerselves!"

"Trying to make that home whole again," Katerin was quick to respond.

Gretel didn't seem impressed. "I've got tea a'brewing," she said, turning toward the cottage. "Ye've got much to tell me, and no doubt to offer me, so we may as well be comfortable during the talking."

Oliver and Katerin continued to look at each other as Gretel disappeared into the cottage.

"This will not be easy," Oliver remarked.

Katerin slowly shook her head. She had known that the folk of Port Charley wouldn't be impressed with any rebellion. The place was so much like Hale. Why should they rebel, after all, when they were already free? The fisherfolk of Port Charley answered to no one but the sea, and with that as their overlord, Luthien and his fight in Montfort, and indeed, even King Greensparrow himself, did not seem so important.

A young boy bounded out of the cottage, running down the boardwalk and toward the town as the two friends tied up their mounts.

"Gretel is calling in some friends," Katerin explained.

Oliver's hand immediately and instinctively went to the hilt of his rapier, but he pulled it away at once, remembering the noble look in Gretel's eye and feeling foolish for entertaining such a fear even for a moment.

"Tea?" Katerin asked resignedly. She was thinking of the task before her, of convincing Gretel and her compatriots of the importance of the rebellion, of asking these people to risk their lives in a fight they likely cared nothing at all about. Suddenly she felt very tired.

Oliver led the way into the cottage.

Gretel would hear nothing of the troubles in Montfort, which Katerin insisted on calling Caer MacDonald, and nothing of the old legends come to life until the others arrived.

"Old fisherfolk," the harbormaster explained. "Too old for the boats and so we of Port Charley use their wisdom. They know the sea."

"Our troubles do not concern only the sea," Oliver politely reminded the woman.

"But the sea be our only concern," Gretel said, a stinging retort that reminded Oliver and especially Katerin of just how difficult this mountain would prove to climb.

Gretel wanted to talk about Hale; she knew some of the northern village's older fisherfolk, had met them at sea during the salmon runs many years before, when she was young and captained her own boat. Though she was an impatient sort, a woman of action and not idle talk (especially not with cyclopian ships sailing fast for Eriador's coast!), Katerin obliged, and even found that she enjoyed Gretel's stories of the mighty Avon Sea.

Oliver rested during that time, sipping his tea and taking in the smells and sounds of the seaside cottage. The other old sea dogs began arriving presently, one or two at a time, until Gretel's small cottage was quite filled with brown, wrinkled bodies, all smelling of salt and fish. The halfling thought he recognized one of the men, but couldn't quite place him, his suspicions only heightened when the fellow looked Oliver's way and gave a wink. Perhaps this had been one of the crew on the boat that had taken Oliver into Port Charley several years before, or one of the others at the boardinghouse where Oliver had stayed until he had grown bored of the port and departed for Montfort.

After a moment of studying the old creature, tucked protectively, even mysteriously, under a heavy blanket, even though he was sitting near the burning hearth, Oliver shrugged and gave it up. He couldn't place the man.

Despite that, Oliver thought it a perfectly grand gathering, and Katerin felt at home, more so than she had since she had left Hale at the age of fourteen to go into training in the arena at Dun Varna.

"There, then," Gretel announced after one particularly bawdy tale concerning ships that didn't quite make it past each other in the night. "Seems we've all gathered."

"This is your ruling council?" Oliver asked.

"These are all the ones too old to be out in the boats," Gretel corrected. "And not old enough yet to be stuck lying in their beds. Them soon returned with the day's catch will hear what we've to say."

She looked at Katerin and nodded, indicating that the floor was hers.

Katerin rose slowly. She tried to remember her own proud village and the reactions of her people if they were faced with a similar situation. The folk of Hale didn't much care for Greensparrow, didn't talk much about him, didn't waste many words on him—neither did the folk of Port Charley—but what she needed here and now was action, and ambivalence was a long way from that.

She rose slowly and moved to the center of the room, leaning on the small round table for support. She thought of Luthien in Caer MacDonald and his stirring speech in the plaza beside the Ministry. She wished that he was here now, dashing and articulate. Suddenly she blamed herself for being so arrogant as to think to replace him.

Katerin shook those negative thoughts from her mind. Luthien could not reach these folk—Katerin's folk. His words were the sort that stirred people who had something to lose, and whether it be Greensparrow, or Luthien or anyone else claiming rulership of Eriador, and thus, of Port Charley, the folk here recognized only one king: the Avon Sea.

Katerin continued to hesitate, and the fisherfolk, men and women who had spent endless hours sitting quiet on open, unremarkable waters, respected her delay and did not press her.

The young woman conjured an image of Port Charley, considered the neat rows and meticulous landscaping, a pretty village cut from the most inhospitable of places. So much like Hale.

But not so much like most of the more southern Eriadoran towns, Katerin realized, especially those in the shadows of the Iron Cross. The young woman's face brightened as she realized the course of her speech. The folk of Port Charley cared little for the politics of the land, but they, as much as any group in Eriador or Avon, hated cyclopians. By all accounts, very few of the one-eyes lived in or near Port Charley; even the merchants here usually kept strong men as guards, not the typical cyclopian escort.

"You have heard of the rebellion in Caer MacDonald," she began. She paused for a moment, trying to gauge the reaction, but there was none.

Katerin's eyes narrowed; she stood straight and tall away from the table. "You have heard that we killed many cyclopians?"

The nods were accompanied by grim, gap-toothed smiles, and Katerin's course lay open before her. She spoke for more than an hour before the first questions came back at her, then answered every one, every concern.

"All we need is time," she finally pleaded, mostly to Gretel. "Keep the Avon fleet bottled in your harbor for a week, perhaps. You need not risk the life of a single person. Then you will see. Caer MacDonald will fend off the attack, destroy Greensparrow's army in the field, and force a truce from the southern kingdom. Then Eriador will be free once more."

"To be ruled by . . . another king," one man interrupted.

"Better he, whoever it may be," Katerin replied, and she thought she knew who the next king of Eriador would be, but saw no sense in speaking of him specifically at this time, "than the demon-allied wizard. Better he than the man who invites cyclopians into his court and appoints them as his personal Praetorian Guard."

The heads continued to nod, and when Katerin looked at Oliver, she found that he, too, was nodding and smiling. Quite pleased with her performance, the young woman turned directly to Gretel, her expression clearly asking for an answer.

At that moment, a middle-aged man, his hair salt-and-pepper, his face ruddy and showing a few days of beard, burst into the cottage, wide-eyed and out of breath.

"Ye've seen them," Gretel stated more than asked.

"Anchorin' five miles to the south," the man explained.

"Too close in to sail through the dark."

"Warships?" Katerin asked.

The man looked at her, and then at Oliver, curiously. He turned his gaze to Gretel, who motioned that he should continue.

"The whole damned Avon fleet," he replied.

"As many as fifty?" Katerin needed to know.

"I'd be puttin' it more at seventy, milady," the man said. "Big 'uns, too, and low in the water."

Katerin looked again at Gretel, amazed at how composed the old woman, indeed the whole gathering, remained in light of the grim news. Gretel's smile was perfectly comforting, perfectly disarming. She nodded, and Katerin thought she had her answer.

"The two of yer will stay with Phelpsi Dozier," Gretel said. "On the *Horizon*, a worthy old tub."

Dozier, the oldest man at the gathering, perhaps the oldest man Katerin had ever seen, stepped up and tipped his woolen cap, smiling with the one tooth remaining in his wide mouth. "She's mostly at the docks nowadays," he said, almost apologetically.

"I'll have my boy see to yer horses," Gretel continued, and her tone seemed to indicate that the meeting was at its end. Several of those gathered stood up and stretched the soreness out of their muscles and headed for the door. Night had fallen by then, dark and chill, the wind groaning off the sea.

"We have many preparations," Katerin tried to put in, but Gretel hushed her.

"The folk of Port Charley've made them preparations before yer were even born, dear girl," the old harbormaster insisted. "Yer said yer needing a week, and we're knowing how to give it to yer."

"The depth of the harbor?" Katerin asked, looking all around. She didn't doubt Gretel's words, but could hardly believe that seventy Avon warships could be taken this lightly.

"Shallow," answered the old man by the hearth, the one Oliver thought he recognized. "The ships will have only the last forty feet of the longest two piers beside which to dock. And that section can be easily dropped."

The halfling noted then that the man's accent didn't match the salty dialect of the others, but that clue only left Oliver even more befuddled. He realized that he should know this man, but for some reason, as though something had entered his brain and stolen away a memory, he could not call him to mind.

He dismissed it—what else could he do?—and left with Katerin and Phelpsi Dozier. They found the *Horizon* tied up near to shore on the next pier in line and Phelpsi let them into the hold, surprisingly well furnished and comfortable, considering the general condition of the less-than-seaworthy old boat.

"Get yer sleep," old Dozier invited them, tossing pillows out to them from a closet. He nodded and started for the door.

"Where are you going?" Oliver was confused, for he thought that this was the man's home.

Dozier wheezed out a somewhat lewd laugh. "Gretel's to let me stay with her this night," he said. He tipped his wool hat once more. "See yer at the dawn."

Then he was gone, and Oliver tipped his hat toward the door, hoping that he would possess such fires when he was that old. The halfling kicked off his high boots and fell back onto one of the two cots in the tiny hold, reaching immediately to turn the lantern down low. He noted Katerin's look of a caged animal and hesitated.

"I thought you would be at home in such a place," he remarked.

Katerin's eyes darted his way. "Too much to be done," she replied.

"But not by us," Oliver insisted. "We have ridden a hard and long road. Take the last offered sleep, silly girl, for the road back is no shorter!"

Katerin remained uneasy, but Oliver turned down the lantern anyway. Soon Katerin was lying back on her cot, and soon after that, the gentle rhythm of the lapping waves carried her away into dreams of Hale.

A stream of light woke her, and Oliver, too: the first ray of dawn. They heard the outside commotion of people running along the wooden pier and realized that the fleet was probably in sight. Together, they jumped from their cots, Katerin rushing for the door while Oliver pulled on his boots.

The door was locked, barred from the other side.

Katerin put her shoulder against it hard, thinking it stuck.

It would not budge.

"What silliness is this?" Oliver demanded, coming up to her side.

"No silliness, my halfling hero," came a voice from above. The two looked up to see a hatch swinging open. They had to squint against the intrusion of sudden light, but could see that the opening was barred. Gretel knelt on the deck above, looking down at them.

"You promised," Katerin stuttered.

Gretel shook her head. "I said that we could give yer a week if we had a mind to. I didn't say we had a mind to."

For a moment, Katerin thought of grabbing the main gauche off of Oliver's belt and whipping it the old harbormaster's way.

But Gretel smiled at her, as though she read the dangerous thoughts completely. "I, too, was young, Katerin O'Hale," the old woman said. "Young and full of the fight. I know the fire that burns in yer veins, that quickens the beat of yer heart. But no more. My love fer the sword's been tempered by the wisdom o' years. Sit quiet, girl, and hold faith in the world."

"Faith in a world filled with deceit?" Katerin yelled.

"Faith that yer don't know everything," Gretel replied. "Faith that yer own way might not be the best way."

"You will let the one-eyes through Port Charley?" Oliver asked bluntly.

"Two of the Avon ships have already put in," Gretel announced. "Move them along, so we decided. In one side and out the other, and good riddance to them all!"

"You damn Caer MacDonald!" Katerin accused.

Gretel seemed pained by that for a moment. She dropped the hatch closed.

Katerin growled and threw herself at the door once more, to no avail. It held tight and they were locked in.

Soon they heard the unified footsteps and drum cadence of the first cyclopian troops marching in from the pier. They heard one brutish voice above the others, surprisingly articulate for one of the one-eyed race, but neither of them knew of Belsen'Krieg.

Belsen'Krieg the Terrible had come with nearly fifteen thousand hardened warriors to crush the rebellion and bring the head of Luthien Bedwyr back to his king in Carlisle.

CHAPTER 9

PREPARATIONS

LUTHIEN WALKED THE length of the Caer MacDonald line, the area beyond the city's outer wall. Caer MacDonald had three separate fortifications. The tallest and thickest wall was inside the city, dividing the wealthy merchant section from the poorer areas. Next was the thick, squat fortification that surrounded the bulk of the city, and finally, fifty feet out from that, the outer defense, a bare and thin wall, half again a short man's height, and in some places no more than piled stones.

Beyond this outer wall, the land was open, with few trees or houses. Sloping ground, good ground to defend, Luthien thought. The cyclopians would have to come in a concentrated formation—en masse, as Oliver had called it—for the city could only be attacked from the north or the west. East and south lay the mountains, cold and deep with snow, and though a few of the one-eyes might swing around that way, just to pressure the defenders, the main group would have to come uphill, across open ground.

And that ground was being made more difficult by Shuglin's industrious dwarfs. Every one of them greeted Luthien as he walked past, but few bothered to look up, would not interrupt this most vital of jobs. Some dug trip trenches, picking through the still-frozen earth inch by inch. These were only about two feet deep and fairly narrow, and would afford little cover, but if a charging cyclopian stumbled across one, his momentum would be halted; he might even break his leg. Other dwarfs took the trip trenches one step further, lining the ridge closest to the city with sharp, barbed pickets.

Luthien grew hopeful while watching the quiet, methodical work, but, in truth, there were few dwarfs on the field. Most were over by the wall, and that was where the young Bedwyr found Shuglin.

The blue-bearded dwarf stood with a couple of friends by a small table, poring over a pile of parchments and every so often looking up toward the wall and grunting, "Uh huh," or some other noise. Shuglin was pleased to see Luthien, though he didn't even notice the man's approach until Luthien dropped a hand on his shoulder.

"How does it go?" the young Bedwyr asked.

Shuglin shook his head, didn't seem pleased. "They built this damned wall well," he explained, though Luthien didn't quite understand the problem. Wasn't a well-built wall a good thing for defenders?

"Only eight feet high and not so thick," Shuglin explained. "Won't stop the cyclopians for long. A ponypig could knock a hole in the damned thing."

"I thought you just said they built it well," Luthien replied.

"The understructure, I mean," said Shuglin. "They built the understructure well."

Luthien shook his head. Why would that matter?

Shuglin paused and realized it would be better to start from the beginning. "We decided not to hold this wall," he said, and pointed up Caer MacDonald's second wall.

"Who decided?"

"My kin and me," Shuglin answered. "We asked Siobhan and she agreed."

Again Luthien felt that oddly out-of-control sensation, like Siobhan was tugging hard at those puppet strings. For an instant, the young man was angry at being left out of the decision, but gradually he calmed, realizing that if his trusted companions had to come to him for approval on every issue, the whole of them would be bogged down and nothing important would ever get done.

"So we're thinking to fight from here, then retreat back to the city," Shuglin continued.

"But if the cyclopians gain this wall, they'll have a strong position from which to reorganize and rest up," Luthien reasoned.

The dwarf shrugged. "That's why we're trying to figure out how to drop this damned wall!" he grumbled, his frustration bubbling over.

"What about that powder you put in the box?" Luthien asked after a moment's thought. "The box I used to destroy the supplies in the Ministry."

"Not nearly enough of the stuff!" Shuglin huffed in reply, and Luthien felt foolish for not realizing that the cunning dwarfs would have considered the powder if it was a practical option. "And hard to make," Shuglin added. "Dangerous."

The dwarf finally looked up from the parchments, running his stubby fingers through his bushy blue-black beard. He reminded himself then that Luthien was only trying to help, and was even more desperate about the defense of Caer MacDonald than were Shuglin's folk.

"We'll use some of the powder," the dwarf elaborated, "on the toughest parts of the wall, but damn, they built it well!"

"We could knock it down now and just begin our defense from the second wall," Luthien offered, but Shuglin began shaking his head before the young man even finished the thought.

"We'll get it down," the dwarf assured Luthien. "The trick is to get it to fall *out*, on top of the stupid one-eyes."

Shuglin went back to his parchments; another dwarf asked him a question. Luthien nodded and walked away, reassured by the competence of those around him. Shuglin and his kin were trying hard to steal every advantage from their enemies, to hurt the cyclopians at every turn.

They would have to, Luthien knew. They would have to.

The two trapped friends sat glumly, listening to the passage all morning long. Marching feet, thousands of them, the clanking and bristling of heavy armor and shields, and the clomp of hooves: ponypigs, the cyclopians' favorite mount, smaller than horses and not as swift, but thicker and more muscular. The two heard the caissons roll, packed with weapons, no doubt, and food.

It went on, and on, and on, and Katerin and Oliver could do nothing to stop it. Even if they found some way out of the *Horizon*'s hold, there was nothing they could do anymore to slow the Avon army, nothing anyone could do.

"When they are gone, we will be freed," Oliver reasoned, and Katerin agreed, for it seemed to her that Gretel and the people of Port Charley held no grudge against the rebels. They merely wanted no trouble in their town. To proud Katerin, though, that position was not acceptable. The war had come, and in her mind, any Eriadoran that did not join them was, at best, a coward.

"Then we must ride so swiftly," Oliver went on. "North and east around the army, to warn our friends." He almost said "our friends in Caer MacDonald," but at that moment, with the unending, unnerving rumble of the army on the dock above him, it seemed to the halfling that the city in the mountains might soon be known as Montfort again.

"For whatever good that will do," Katerin replied, her tone bitter. She pounded a fist against the unyielding door and slumped back on her cot.

The procession outside continued, all through the morning and into the early hours of afternoon. Oliver's mood brightened when he found some food in a compartment under his cot, but Katerin wouldn't even eat, her mouth too filled with bitterness.

Finally, the clamor outside began to lessen somewhat. The solid rumble became sporadic and the voices of cyclopians were fewer, much fewer. And then, at last, a knock on the door.

It swung open before either could respond, and Gretel entered, her face somber but without apology.

"Good," she said to Oliver, "I see ye've found the food we left yer."

"I do so like my fish!" the happy halfling replied. "Oh," he said, his eyes cast down when he noticed the scowl Katerin was aiming at him.

"You promised," Katerin growled at Gretel.

The old woman held up her hand, waving away the remark as though it was insignificant. "We do what we must," she said. "We do what we must."

"Even if that means dooming fellow Eriadorans?" Katerin retorted.

"It was in all our best interests fer us to let the cyclopians pass, to treat them as friends," Gretel tried to explain.

But Katerin wasn't hearing it. "Our only hope was to bottle the fleet in the harbor, to keep them off-shore until the defense of Caer MacDonald could be completed and support could be mustered throughout the land," she insisted.

"And what would yer have us do?"

"Deny the docks!" the woman of Hale yelled. "Drop the outer piers!"

"And then what?" Gretel wanted to know. "The brutes'd sit in the harbor, whittling sticks? Yer smarter, girl. They'd've gone to the north and found a beach o' their own, and put in, and we could not have stopped them!"

"It would have bought us time," Katerin answered without hesitation.

"We are a town o' but three thousand," Gretel explained. "We could not have stopped them, and if they then marched back to Port Charley . . ."

She let the words hang unfinished in the air, dramatic and ominous, but still Katerin didn't want to hear the reasoning.

"The freedom of Eriador is all that matters," she said through gritted teeth, green eyes flashing dangerously. She flipped her fiery hair back from her face so that Gretel could see well her unrelenting scowl.

"Gretel echoes my own words," came a voice from just outside the door, and an old man walked into the small room. His hair and beard were snowy white, hair tied back in a ponytail, and his robes, rich and thick, were bright blue.

Oliver's mouth drooped open, and he realized then who the man at the meeting, the man at the hearth, had been. Clever disguise!

"I do not know you," Katerin said, as if to dismiss him, though from his clothing, and indeed his demeanor, he was obviously a man of some importance. She feared for a moment that he might be one of Greensparrow's remaining dukes.

"Ah, but I know you, Katerin O'Hale," the old man said. "The best friend Luthien Bedwyr ever had."

"Oh?" said Oliver, hopping up from his cot.

Katerin looked to the halfling, and then to the old man, and saw that there was recognition between them, smiles friends might exchange. It hit her suddenly.

"Brind'Amour?" she breathed.

The old man fell into a graceful, sweeping bow. "Well met, Katerin O'Hale, and long overdue," he said. "I am an old man," he winked at Oliver, "and getting older every day, but still I can appreciate such beauty as yours."

Katerin's first instinct was to punch him. How dare he think of such an unimportant thing at this time? But she realized that there was no condescension in his tone, realized somehow that the beauty he referred to was much more than the way she looked. He seemed to her, all at once, like a father, a wise overseer of events, watching them and measuring them, like the old fisherfolk of Hale who trained the novices in the ways of the sea. Brind'Amour was akin to those old fisherfolk, but the training he offered was in the way of life. Katerin knew that instinctively, and so when she realized what he had first said in support of Gretel's words, she found some comfort and began to hope that there was some other plan, some better plan, in motion.

"We must let the brutes through Port Charley," Brind'Amour said to the pair, mostly to Katerin, as though he realized that she would be the hardest to convince. "We must let them, and Greensparrow, think that the revolt in Montfort—"

"Caer MacDonald," Katerin corrected.

"No," said Brind'Amour. "Not yet. Let them think that the revolt in Montfort is a minor thing, an isolated thing, and not desired by any outside of that one city. We must plan long term."

"But the defenses will not be completed in time!" Katerin replied, her pleading voice almost a wail.

"Long term!" Brind'Amour said sharply. "If Eriador is indeed to be free, then this one force of cyclopians will prove the least of our troubles. Had we kept them out of the harbor, had we shown them that Eriador was in general revolt, they would have simply sent one of their ships sailing back to the south to inform Greensparrow and return with reinforcements. In the meantime, those cyclopians remaining would have overrun Port Charley and secured the defenses of this city, giving Greensparrow an open port north of the Iron Cross.

"How many warriors do you think Luthien would lose in trying to uproot fourteen thousand Praetorian Guards from Port Charley?" the old wizard asked grimly, and Katerin's sails had no more wind. She hadn't seen that possibility—neither had Luthien apparently—but now that Brind'Amour spoke, it seemed perfectly logical and perfectly awful.

"We are not ye enemies, Katerin O'Hale," Gretel put in.

Katerin looked hard at her, the young woman's expression clearly asking the question that was on her mind.

"But we are enemies of the one-eyes," Gretel confirmed. "And whoever rules Eriador should be of Eriador, not of Avon."

Katerin recognized the sincerity in the old woman's face and understood that Port Charley had indeed joined the alliance against Greensparrow. Again because of her knowledge of her own town, Katerin understood that Gretel would not have made such a bold and absolute statement if she didn't have the backing of her townsfolk.

"I still think that it would have been easier to keep them out of the docks," Katerin had to say. "Perhaps we might have even sunk one or two of their ships, taking half a thousand cyclopians to the bottom with them!"

"Ah, yes," Brind'Amour agreed. "But then they would have kept those ships we did not sink." Katerin and Oliver looked at the old man, his face widening with a wicked grin. "Not tomorrow night, but the night after that," he said, and he and Gretel exchanged a serious nod.

Brind'Amour turned back to the expectant companions. "The night after next will be a dark one," he explained. "Dark enough for us to board the Avon ships. In two nights, Eriador will have a fleet."

The wizard's smile was infectious. The halfling spoke for Katerin and himself: "I do like the way you think."

CHAPTER 10

MOSQUITOES

THE WORD RAN ahead of the marching force like windswept fire, crossed from town to town, raced along the roads and the mountain trails, and came to Caer MacDonald before the whole of the Praetorian Guard had even marched out beyond Port Charley's eastern borders.

Luthien took the news stoically, putting on a bold face for his companions, telling them that the cyclopians' passage through the port city had been expected, and though he had hoped for more time, the defenses would be ready. A rousing cheer accompanied his every remark: after the victory in Caer MacDonald and the raising of Eriador's ancient flag over the Ministry—the decorated mountain cross, its four equal arms flared at their corners, on a green field—the rebels were ready for a fight, eager to spill more cyclopian blood.

Luthien appreciated that attitude and took heart in it, joining in the "celebration" Shuglin began in the Dwelf, the theme of the party giving praise for so many one-eyes to kill. The young Bedwyr left early, though, explaining that he had much to do the next day and reminding them that many small villages, most of them not shown on any maps or even named by any but those who lived there, lay between Caer MacDonald and Port Charley. When he left the Dwelf, the young Bedwyr did not go back to his apartment in Tiny Alcove. Rather, he slipped around to the back of the tavern and climbed the rain gutter to the roof.

"What have we begun?" Luthien asked the starry night. The air was crisp, but not too cold, and the stars glistened like crystalline ornaments. He considered the news from the west; the cyclopians hadn't even been slowed in Port Charley, and that could only mean that the folk of the port town had not embraced the rebellion.

"We need them all," Luthien whispered, needing to hear his thoughts aloud. He felt as if he was preparing a speech, and considering the way things had gone, he knew that he might well be. "All of Eriador. Every man, every woman. What good may our efforts be if those we seek to free do not take up arms in their own defense? What worth is victory if it is not a shared win? For then, I do not doubt, those who are free because of our sacrifice will not embrace that which we have accomplished, will not see the flag of Eriador as their own."

Luthien moved to the western edge of the roof, kicked away a piece of hardened snow and knelt upon the bare spot. He could see the massive silhouette of the Ministry, where so many brave folk had died. The Ministry, built as a symbol of man's spirit and love of God, but used by Greensparrow's pawn as a house of tax collection, and as a courtroom. Not even a courtroom, Luthien mused, for under Morkney, the Ministry was a place of condemnation and not of justice.

Stars twinkled all about the tallest tower, as though the structure reached right up into the heavens to touch the feet of God. Truly it was a beautiful night, calm and quiet. Few lights burned in the city, and the streets were quiet, except right in front of the Dwelf, where the impromptu celebration continued and an occasional soul wandered outside. Beyond the city's wall, Luthien could see the fires of the dwarven encampment. Some were blazing, but most had burned down to low embers, an orange glow in the darkened field.

"Sleep well," the young Bedwyr whispered. "Your work is not yet done."

"Nor is our own," Luthien heard behind him, and he turned to see Siobhan's approach, her step so light and quiet that she wasn't leaving an impression in the hardened snow that covered most of the roof.

Luthien looked back to the Ministry and the stars. He did not flinch, did not tense at all, as Siobhan put her hand under his ear and ran it gently down his neck to his shoulder.

"Katerin and Oliver have failed," Luthien said, bitter words indeed. "We have failed."

Siobhan cleared her throat, and it sounded to Luthien as more of a snicker than a cough. He turned to regard her.

How beautiful she appeared in the quiet light of evening; how fitting she seemed to the time of starlight, her eyes twinkling like those stars in the heaven above, her skin pale, almost translucent, and her hair flowing thick and lustrous, in such contrast to the delicate and sharp angles of her elven features.

"You declare defeat before the battle is even begun," Siobhan answered, her voice calm and soothing.

"How many cyclopians?" Luthien asked. "And they're not ordinary tribe beasts, but Praetorian Guard, the finest of Greensparrow's army. Ten thousand? Fifteen? I do not know that we could hold back half that number."

"They will not be as many when they get to Caer MacDonald," Siobhan assured him. "And our own numbers will grow as villagers flock in from the western towns." Siobhan slid her hand down Luthien's shoulder, across his chest, and leaned close, kissing him on the temple.

"You are the leader," she said. "The symbol of free Eriador. Your will must not waver."

Once more Luthien Bedwyr felt as if he had become a pawn in a game that was much too large for him to control. Once more he felt himself in the embrace of the puppeteer. Siobhan. Beautiful Siobhan. This time, though, Luthien did not resist that touch, the pulling of his strings. This time the presence of the half-elf, a tower of strength and determination, came as a welcome relief to him.

Without Siobhan beside him, behind him, Luthien believed that he would have broken that night, would have lost his purpose as he lost his hope. Without Siobhan, his guilt for those who would soon die, and who had already died, would have overwhelmed the prospects of the future, for with such a tremendous force marching toward the liberated city, the thought of a free Eriador seemed a fleeting, twinkling fantasy, as unreachable as the stars that flanked the tower of the Ministry.

Siobhan led him from the roof and back to the apartment in Tiny Alcove.

Katerin did not sleep well that night, too worried for her homeland, but she heard Oliver's contented snores in the room next to hers, comfortable quarters at a small inn high up the levels of Port Charley. The next morning, though, the woman of Hale was not tired, too excited by the sight of the departing army as she and Oliver joined Brind'Amour near to the eastern road.

The main body of the Avon force was long out of sight, several miles from the town already, and now came the supporting troops, mostly driving wagons loaded with provisions. Gretel directed its departure, working side by side with one of the largest and ugliest cyclopians either Katerin or Oliver had ever seen.

"The very ugliest!" Oliver assured his companions. "And I have seen many cyclopians!"

"Not as many as I," Brind'Amour interjected. "And Belsen'Krieg, for that is the brute's name, is truly the most imposing."

"Ugly," Oliver corrected.

"In spirit as well as in appearance," Brind'Amour added.

"He will ride out soon to join with his force." Katerin's tone was anxious.

"Belsen'Krieg will lead them, not follow," Brind'Amour confirmed. The wizard motioned to a powerful ponypig, heavily armor plated, with sharpened spikes protruding from every conceivable angle. Just looking at the monstrous thing, both Oliver and Katerin knew that it was Belsen'Krieg's. Only the most ugly cyclopian would choose such a gruesome and horrible mount.

"As soon as Belsen'Krieg and his soldiers are away, we can stop the wagons," Katerin reasoned, her face brightening suddenly. That light dimmed, though, as she regarded the old wizard.

"The wagons will roll throughout the day," Brind'Amour explained. "And a smaller group will depart tomorrow. But all the food that leaves with that second group will be tainted, and their drinking supply will be salted with water from the sea. That should give Belsen'Krieg enough good supplies to get him more than halfway to Montfort, fully committed to his march. Above all else, we must prevent him from turning back to Port Charley. Let them reach their goal, hungry and weary, and not ready for the fight, with Luthien before them and our army on their heels."

Both Oliver and Katerin looked curiously at the wizard, reacting to that last remark.

"Yes," Brind'Amour explained. "Port Charley will send a fair force after the cyclopians, and the one-eyes will be pecked every mile of their march, for every village between here and Montfort has joined in our cause."

Katerin was no longer arguing with the wizard, though she wasn't sure if he was stating fact or hope. Her instincts, her anger, continually prompted her to act, to strike out in any way she could find against the cyclopians and the foreign King Greensparrow. Already Brind'Amour had earned her trust. She realized that he, and not she, had brought Port Charley into the rebellion, before she and Oliver had even arrived. If the wizard's claim was correct, he had also secured alliance with the other southern Eriadoran villages, and if the wizard was right about Port Charley, Eriador would soon possess a fleet of great warships that was probably nearly as large as Greensparrow's remaining fleet in Avon.

Still, Katerin could not forget the army marching east, marching to Caer MacDonald and her beloved Luthien. Could Caer MacDonald hold?

She had to admit, to herself at least, that Brind'Amour was right as well in his argument about letting the cyclopians march upon that city. In the larger picture, if Eriador was indeed to be free, this force led by Belsen'Krieg—a mere token of what Greensparrow could ultimately hurl at them—might be among the least of their troubles.

That truth brought little comfort to Katerin O'Hale and sent a shudder along her spine.

Siobhan's predictions were proven accurate the very next day, when villagers from the towns nearest Caer MacDonald began flocking into the city. Mostly, it was the young and the old who came in, in orderly fashion and all carrying provisions, ready to fight if necessary, to hold out against the wicked king of Avon to the last. And every group that came in spoke of their hardiest folk, who were moving to the west to meet with and hinder the approach of the cyclopian force.

Luthien didn't have to ask to know that this was somehow Siobhan's doing, that while he sat up on the roof, mulling over what seemed like an assured defeat, the half-elf and her stealthy cohorts were out and about, rousing the towns, telling them that the time for their independence had come.

The response from those towns was overwhelming. That day and the next, Luthien watched his garrison within the city grow from six thousand to ten thousand, and though many of the newer soldiers were elderly and could not match a powerful cyclopian in close combat, they had grown up on the Eriadoran plains hunting deer and elk, and they were skilled with their great yew bows.

So also were those younger warriors that went out in bands from the smaller villages, and Belsen'Krieg's army found itself under assault barely two days and ten miles out from Port Charley.

The damage to the massive force was not excessive. Every once in a while a cyclopian went down, usually wounded, but sometimes killed, and flaming arrows whipped into the supply wagons, causing some excitement. More important, though, was the effect of the skirmishers on the army's morale, for the cyclopians were being hindered and stung by an enemy that hit fast from concealment, then flittered away like a swarm of bees in a swift wind—an enemy they could not see and could not catch.

Belsen'Krieg kept them together and kept them marching straight for Montfort, promising them that once the city was overrun, they could slaughter a thousand humans for every dead cyclopian.

Oliver looked out at the heavy fog that came up that night, the third after the cyclopians had put into Port Charley, and he knew that this was no natural event. Since he had met up with Brind'Amour, the wizard had constantly complained about how weakened magic had become, but Oliver thought this enchantment wonderful, the perfect cover for this night's business.

Seventy ships from Avon lay anchored out in the harbor, great warships, many with catapults or ballistae set on the poop deck. In studying those magnificent vessels that day, Oliver and Katerin had agreed that it was a good thing Brind'Amour had intervened in Port Charley. Had they followed their original plan and tried to keep the cyclopians out in the water, this picturesque and enchanting town would have been reduced to piles of rubble.

Katerin, Brind'Amour, and Gretel joined Oliver at the dock a short while later. Immediately, the young woman scowled at Oliver, and the halfling pretended that he did not understand.

Katerin grabbed the plumed hat off his head and ruffled his purple cape. "Could you not have dressed better for the occasion?" she grumbled.

Oliver pulled the hat back from her and put his free hand over his heart, as though she had just mortally wounded him. "But I am!" he wailed. "Do you not understand the value of impressing your enemy?"

"If we are successful this night," Brind'Amour put in, "then our enemy will never see us."

"Ah, but they will," Oliver assured him. "I will wake at least one and let him see his doom before my rapier blade pierces his throat."

Katerin smiled. She loved the halfling's accent, the way he made rapier sound like "rah-pee-yer." She wasn't really angry with Oliver's dress; she was just teasing him a bit to get the edges off her own nerves. Katerin was a straightforward fighter, an arena champion, and this stealthy assassination technique was not much to her liking.

There was no other choice, though, and she understood that. Seventy ships, nearly a thousand cyclopian crewmen. There could be no mistakes; not a ship could escape to sail south and warn Greensparrow.

Port Charley was bustling that night. Many of the cyclopian sailors were ashore, even most of those who were supposed to be on watch out at the boats, lured in by the promise of fine food and drink, and other, more base, pleasures. The town's three taverns were bursting with excitement, and so were the more than a dozen private homes that had been opened up to accommodate the crews.

The killing would begin at midnight, when most of the one-eyes were too drunk to realize what was happening. By that time, a hundred small boats would be well on their way through the fog, out to the anchored ships.

"The signal!" Gretel motioned toward a flickering light to the north. She held up her own lantern to the south, unhooded it for just a moment, then again, and the message was relayed all down the line.

Brind'Amour, Oliver, and Katerin stepped into their small boat along with two of Port Charley's folk, a husband and wife.

"In Gascony we have such bugs as we are this night," Oliver said to them, quieting his tone as both Brind'Amour and Katerin *shhh'd* him. "They come from Espan, mostly, and so does their name," the halfling continued in a whisper. "Mosquitoes. Clever bugs. You hear them in your ear and swat at them, but they are not there. They are somewhere else on your body, taking drops of your blood.

"We are mosquitoes," the halfling decided. "Mosquitoes on Greensparrow."

"Then let us hope that enough mosquitoes can suck a body dry," Brind'Amour remarked, and they all went silent, drifting out from the docks, the oars barely touching the water, for stealth and not speed was the order of business this night.

Oliver was first up the anchor rope of the first ship they came upon, the halfling swiftly climbing hand over hand to the rail. He paused there, and then, to everyone's disbelief, he began talking.

"Greetings, my one-eyed, bow-legged, wave-riding, so ugly friend," he said, and reached under his cloak and produced a flask. "You are missing all the fun, but fear not, I, Oliver deBurrows, have brought the fun to you!"

Most alarmed were the villagers in the rowboat, but Katerin, who was beginning to figure this strange halfling out (and was beginning to understand why Luthien liked Oliver so much), stood up and steadied herself in the boat, taking the longbow from her shoulder.

They couldn't see what was transpiring beyond the rail, just Oliver's back, his purple cape fluttering in the breeze. "I have brought you a woman, as well," the halfling said. "But that will cost you a few of your so fine Avon gold pieces."

Predictably, the eager cyclopian leaned over the rail to get a look at the goods, and Katerin wasted no time in putting her arrow into the brute's head.

Even as the bolt struck the mark, Oliver grabbed the cyclopian by the collar and heaved. The one-eye hit the water between the ship and the rowboat, bobbing facedown after the initial waves had settled.

Brind'Amour wanted to call up and scold Oliver, for the noise was too great. Suppose other cyclopians were about on the deck? But Oliver was out of sight.

There was indeed another cyclopian awake and roaming the deck, but by the time Katerin, the next up the rope, had made the rail, it was already dead, Oliver standing atop its massive chest, wiping his bloodstained rapier blade on its cloak.

"Mosquitoes," the halfling whispered to her. "Buzz buzz."

And so it went up and down the line, with every ship boarded and taken.

Back on shore, the killing commenced as well, and in only two of the twelve houses and one of the taverns did the cyclopians have enough wits about them to even put up a struggle.

When the wizard's fog cleared later that night, nearly twenty of Port Charley's folk were dead, another seven wounded, but not a cyclopian remained alive in the town, or in the harbor, and the rebels now possessed a fleet of seventy fine warships.

"It was too easy," Brind'Amour said to Oliver and Katerin before the three retired that night.

"They did not expect any trouble," Katerin replied.

Brind'Amour nodded.

"They underestimate us," Oliver added.

Still the wizard nodded. "And if that truth holds, Montfort will not be taken," he said. The wizard dearly hoped he was right, but he remembered the image of mighty Belsen'Krieg, sophisticated, yet vicious, and doubted that the days ahead would be as easy as this night.

Late the next morning, so that the mosquitoes had the time for a good night's rest, the town of Port Charley organized its own force, nearly a thousand strong. With Katerin upon Riverdancer, Oliver on Threadbare, and Brind'Amour on a fine roan stallion, joining old Phelpsi Dozier—who had been a commander in the first war against Greensparrow twenty years before—at the head of the column, the soldiers started out toward the east.

Heading for Montfort, which Brind'Amour would not yet let them call Caer MacDonald.

CHAPTER 11

TAINTED

BELSEN'KRIEG, HIS UGLY face a mask of outrage, pulled the cord from one of the sacks piled in the back of the wagon and reached inside with his huge hand. Those terrified cyclopians around him didn't have to wait for their general to extract the hand to know what would be found.

"Tainted!" the ugly general bellowed. He yanked his hand from the sack and hurled the worthless supplies—part foodstuffs, but mostly fine beach sand—high into the air.

Montfort was only thirty miles from Port Charley, as the bird flies, but given the rough terrain and the season, with some trails blocked by piled snow and tumbled boulders and others deep with mud, the cyclopian general had planned on a five-day march. The army had done well; as far as Belsen'Krieg could determine, they had crossed the halfway point early that morning, the third day out. And now their route could be directly east, sliding away from the mountains to easier ground for more than half the remaining distance.

But they were nearly out of food. The soldiers had left Port Charley with few supplies, the plan being that the wagons would continually filter in behind them on the road. So it had gone for the first two days, but when the wagons had left the afternoon of that second day to go back to Port Charley and resupply, they had been attacked and burned.

Belsen'Krieg had promptly dispatched a brigade of a thousand of his finest troops to meet the next east-moving train. Despite a few minor skirmishes with the increasing numbers of rebels, that caravan had gotten through, to the cheers of the waiting army. Those cheers turned to silent frowns when the soldiers discovered they had been deceived, that the supplies which had gone out of the port city on the second day were not supplies at all.

The cyclopian leader stood and stared back to the west for a long, long time, fantasizing about the torture and mayhem he would wreak on the fools of Port Charley. Likely it was a small group of sympathizers for the rebels—the fact that the wagons got out of the town at all made Belsen'Krieg believe that the criminals in Port Charley were few. That wouldn't hinder Belsen'Krieg's revenge, though. He would flatten the town and sink all of their precious fishing boats. He would kill . . .

The cyclopian dismissed the fantasy. Those were thoughts for another day. Right now, Belsen'Krieg had too many pressing problems, too many decisions. He considered turning the force back to Port Charley, crushing the town and feasting well, maybe on the meat of dead humans. Then he looked back to the east, to the easier ground, the rolling fields of white and brown that lay before them. They were more than halfway to Montfort, and of the twelve or so miles remaining, at least ten of them would be away from the treacherous mountains. With a good hard march, the army could reach Montfort's walls by twilight the next day. They might even happen upon a village or two, and there they could resupply.

There they could feast.

The cyclopian began to nod his huge head, and those around him stared hopefully, thinking that their magnificent leader had found a solution.

"We have two more hours of good light," Belsen'Krieg announced. "Double-step!"

A couple of groans emanated from the gathering about the general, but Belsen'Krieg's scowl silenced them effectively.

"Double-step," he said again, calmly, evenly. Had this been an ordinary cyclopian tribe, one of the wild groups that lived in the mountains, Belsen'Krieg's life would likely have been forfeit at that moment. But these were Praetorian Guards; most had spent their entire lives in training for service to Greensparrow. The grumbling stopped, except for the unintentional rumblings of empty stomachs, and the army resumed its march and gained another two miles before the sun dipped below the horizon and the chill night breeze came up.

Belsen'Krieg's advance scouts came back to the army soon after it had pitched camp, reporting that they had discovered a village ahead, not far off the trail, only a few miles to the north of Montfort. The place was not deserted, the scouts assured Belsen'Krieg, for as dusk fell, lamps were lit in every house.

The brutish cyclopian leader smiled as he considered the news. He still did not know what to make of this rebellion, did not know how widespread it might be. Going into a small village might be risky, might incite more Eriadorans to join in the fight against Greensparrow. Belsen'Krieg considered his own soldiers, their morale dwindling with their supplies. They would go into the town, he decided, and take what they needed, and if a few humans were killed and a few buildings burned, then so be it.

That rumor spread through the cyclopian encampment quickly, eagerly, and the soldiers bedded down with hope.

As the darkness settled in deep about the camp though, the night, like the one before, became neither quiet nor restful, and hope shifted to uneasiness. Bands of rebels circled the camp, peppering the brutes with arrows, some fire-tipped, others whistling invisibly through the dark to thud into the ground or a tree, a tent pole or even a cyclopian, surprising and unnerving all those around. At one point, a volley of nearly a hundred burning bolts streaked through the night sky, and though not a single cyclopian was slain in that barrage, the effect on the whole of the army was truly unsettling.

Belsen'Krieg realized that the small rebel bands would do little real damage, and he knew that his soldiers needed to rest, but for the sake of morale, he had to respond. So bold an attack could not go unanswered. Companies were formed up and sent out into the darkness, but they saw nothing among the snowy and muddy fields and heard nothing except the taunts of the elusive Eriadorans, who knew this ground, their home ground.

One company, returning to the encampment, was attacked openly, if only briefly, as they neared the crest of a small hill. A group of men sprang up from concealment atop that hillock and charged down through the cyclopian ranks, swatting at the brutes with clubs and old swords, poking at them with pitchforks and slicing with scythes. They ran right through the cyclopians with no intention of stopping for a pitched fight, and rushed out, disappearing into the darkness. A few seconds of frenzy, another small thorn poked into the side of the huge army.

In truth, only a dozen Praetorian Guards were killed that long night, and only a score or so were wounded. But few of the brutes slept, and those who did, did not sleep well.

"The bait is set?" Luthien asked Siobhan soon before dawn of the next day, an overcast, rainy, and windswept day. He looked out from Caer MacDonald's northern wall, across the lightening fields and hedgerows. He noted the lighter shade of gray, the last remnants of snow, clinging to the dark patches, losing the battle with spring.

"Felling Downs," the half-elf replied. "We had fifty soldiers in there all the yesterday, and burned the lights long into the night." Siobhan chuckled. "We expected to be attacked by the cyclopians' advance scouts, but they stayed out."

Luthien glanced at her sidelong. He had wondered where she had been the previous night, and now he thought himself foolish for not realizing that Siobhan would personally lead the group out to the small village north of Caer

MacDonald as bait. Wherever the fighting might be, Siobhan would find her way to the front. Even Shuglin and the other dwarfs, so tortured under Greensparrow's rule, were not as fanatical. Everything in Siobhan's life revolved around the rebellion and killing cyclopians.

Everything.

"How many have gone?" Luthien asked.

"Three hundred," came the quick reply.

Again Luthien looked at the half-elf. Three hundred? Only three hundred? The cyclopian force numbered fifty times that, but they were supposed to go out and deal the brutes a stinging blow with only three hundred warriors? His expression, eyebrows arching high over his eyes, clearly asked all of those questions.

"We cannot safely cover more in the ground to the north," Siobhan explained, and from her tone it was obvious that she wished they could send out the whole of their force. She, perhaps even more than Luthien, wanted to hit hard at the cyclopian army. "We cannot risk many lives on the open field."

Luthien nodded. He knew the truth of what Siobhan was saying; in fact, he had initially argued against going out from Caer MacDonald at all. But the ambush plan was a good one. For the cyclopians to take the easiest and most logical route into Caer MacDonald, they would have to cross a small river west of Felling Downs, then turn south, through the town and straight to the foothills and the walled city. There was only one real bridge across that river anywhere in the vicinity, northwest of Felling Downs, but Luthien and his cohorts could cross the water in the rougher ground just to the west of Caer MacDonald. They would then strike out to the north and take up a secretive position in the hedgerows and other cover just south of the bridge—a bridge which Shuglin's folk had already rigged for collapse. When the bulk of the enemy army got across, heading out for Felling Downs, that bridge would be taken down and those cyclopians caught on the western side would face the wrath of Luthien's marauders.

"Know this as an important day," the young Bedwyr remarked. "The first true test of Avon's army."

"And of our own," Siobhan added.

Luthien started to argue, was going to remark that the taking of Montfort had been their first test, but he stopped, admitting the truth of Siobhan's words. This would be the first time the rebels battled with a large contingent of Praetorian Guards, a trained and prepared army.

"The group is away?" Luthien asked.

Siobhan nodded, and unconsciously looked to the west.

"And you will soon set out to join with them?" Luthien asked. The question was rhetorical, for of course Siobhan would rush to catch up with those who would soon see battle. "Then we must hurry," the young Bedwyr quickly added.

The fact that he had suddenly included himself in the ambush was not lost on Siobhan. She stared long and hard at Luthien, and he could not determine if her look was approving or not.

"You are too valua—" came the beginning of her response.

"We are all too valuable," the young Bedwyr said, determined that he would not be turned away this time. Lately, every time Luthien included himself in plans that would likely lead to fierce combat, someone, usually Siobhan, would pipe in that he was too valuable to risk himself so.

Siobhan knew better than to argue. She could convince Luthien of many things, could guide him through many decisions, but she had learned during the taking of Montfort that no amount of coercion would keep the brave young man out of harm's way.

"This is the test of Avon's army," Luthien explained. "And I must see how they respond."

Siobhan thought of several arguments against that course, primarily that the defense of Caer MacDonald, and the morale of the rebels, would be weakened indeed if Luthien Bedwyr, the Crimson Shadow, was killed before the cyclopians even reached the city walls. She kept her doubts private, though, and decided to trust in Luthien. He had been in on every major skirmish within the city, and whether it was skill or just dumb luck, he had come through it all practically unscathed.

They set out together almost immediately, running west and then north, along with a few elven archers. Less than an hour after the dawn, the three hundred warriors, hand-picked for this important battle, lay in wait within a mile south of the bridge over the small river known as Felling Run. Across the water to the east, the marauders could see the plumes of smoke rising from the chimneys of Felling Downs, more bait for the cyclopians.

And soon after, to the north, they caught their first glimpse of Avon's army, a huge black and silver mass, tearing up the turf, shaking the ground as they stomped determinedly on. Luthien held his breath for many moments after he realized the extent of that force. He thought of Oliver and the halfling's plan to abandon the rebellion and flee to the northland, and he wondered, for the first time, if Oliver might not have been right.

CHAPTER 12

FELLING DOWNS

THE PLUMES OF smoke rising from the chimneys of Felling Downs were in sight as the cyclopian force plodded along, traveling generally southeast now. They came to Felling Run, a small river, a swollen stream really, being no more than twenty feet across and averaging about waist deep. Running water was visible from the high banks, but most of the river remained frozen over, patches of gray ice lined by white snow.

Belsen'Krieg walked his sturdy ponypig right up to the bank, just south of the one bridge in sight, and considered the water and the town beyond. They could cross here and turn directly south for Montfort, crushing the village on their way, or they could turn south now and head into the foothills west of the city. The huge and ugly cyclopian leader still wanted to sack this town, still thought that the blood and the supplies would do his force good, but he was leery for some reason that he did not understand. Perhaps it was that the town was too tempting, too easy a kill. The people here knew that the cyclopians were on the way. Belsen'Krieg was certain of that, especially considering the peppering his force had taken all the way from Port Charley. Everyone in the south of Eriador knew about the march, and many obviously did not approve. So why would the folk of the village across the river remain in their homes, knowing that the cyclopians would be coming through? And why, Belsen'Krieg pondered, had the rebels in Montfort left this bridge, obviously the easiest route to the captured city, standing?

"A delay, my lord?" came a question from behind, startling the unusually introspective cyclopian. Belsen'Krieg looked over his shoulder to see four of his undercommanders astride their ponypigs, eyeing him curiously.

"The soldiers grow impatient," remarked the undercommander who had spoken before, a slender cyclopian with long and curly silver hair and great muttonchops sideburns, both attributes highly unusual for the race. The brute was called Longsleeves for his penchant for wearing fine shirts, buttoned high on the neck, with sleeves that ran all the way to the top of his thin hands.

Belsen'Krieg looked back across the Felling Run, to the plumes of smoke. The inviting plumes of smoke; the cyclopian knew that Longsleeves spoke truthfully, that his soldiers were verily drooling at the sight.

"We have to move them," another of the undercommanders put in.

"Across, or to the south?" Belsen'Krieg asked, more to himself than the others.

"To the south?" Longsleeves balked.

"We can go to the south, into the foothills, and approach Montfort from the western fields," answered a lesser cyclopian, just an aide to one of the mounted undercommanders. Longsleeves moved to strike the impertinent brute, but his master held the slender cyclopian back, explaining that this brute among the group was the most familiar with this region, having spent many years in the Montfort city garrison.

"Continue," Belsen'Krieg ordered the aide.

"Felling Run ain't much up that way," the brute went on, pointing to the south. "Just a few streams all runnin' together. We could go right up and walk across them, and still have two miles a'goin' before we got to Montfort."

The aide's excitement wasn't shared by the undercommanders, who understood the importance of sacking this town, giving their tired soldiers some play and some food. Belsen'Krieg recognized that fact and sympathized with his undercommanders and their fears of desertion. The town was just across the river, half a mile away perhaps, across rolling, easy fields. Quick and easy plunder.

But still that nagging sensation remained with the general. Belsen'Krieg had seen many, many battles, and like all of the finest warriors, he possessed a sixth sense concerning danger. Something here simply didn't smell right to him.

Before he could act upon those feelings, though, to explain them or simply to order the army to the south, his undercommanders hit him with every argument for crossing and sacking that they could find. They sensed the way their general was leaning and feared that they would lose this one easy battle before the pitched fight at Montfort's walls.

Belsen'Krieg listened to them carefully. He feared that he might be getting paranoid, upset about ghosts. Much of Eriador apparently sided with the rebels in Montfort—the bandits attacking his camps and the wagons of tainted supplies proved that—but by all appearances, most of the country remained quiet, not loyal to Greensparrow, perhaps, but certainly cowed.

The undercommanders continued to argue; they wanted a taste of blood and maybe some food. Belsen'Krieg doubted that they would find much of either in the inconsequential town across the river, but he relented anyway. He marched with a force of nearly fifteen thousand Praetorian Guards, after all, and the easier ground to Montfort was indeed on the other side of the river.

"We cross here," the general stated, and the faces of the four undercommanders brightened. "The town will be flattened," he further offered to their wicked smiles. "But," he said sternly, stealing the growing mirth, "we must be in sight of Montfort's walls before the day ends!"

The undercommanders each looked to Belsen'Krieg's aide, who bobbed his head eagerly. Montfort was no more than five miles of easy ground beyond the village of Felling Downs.

Not so far to the south, crouched behind hedgerows, crawling amidst tumbles of boulders, even in trenches dug along the back of a ridge, Luthien and his three hundred waited nervously. They had expected the cyclopians to swarm right across the bridge on the way to Felling Downs, but for some reason they did not understand, the army had paused.

"Damn," Luthien muttered as the moments passed uneventfully. They had gambled on the cyclopians crossing; if the brutes turned south before the river, then Luthien and his raiders would have to flee back to Caer MacDonald with all speed. Even if they got away without much fighting, as Luthien believed they could, nothing would be gained, only lost, for the few hundred here could have been better served by remaining in the city, in helping with the continuing defensive preparations.

"Damn," the young Bedwyr said again, and Siobhan, crouched beside him, had no words to comfort him this time. She, too, knew the gamble, and she sat quietly, chewing on her bottom lip.

Together they watched as several cyclopians ran ahead of the halted mass, running for the bridge. The brutes pulled up to a trot, then a walk as they neared the structure and began pointing out specific places to each other, making it quickly apparent that they had gone out to inspect the structure.

"Damn," came the predictable lament among the raiders, and this time it was Siobhan, not Luthien, who spoke the words.

The bridge across Felling Run was not a large structure. It was made completely of wood and stood no more than fifteen feet above the ice-covered stream. It was wide and solid, and had stood with only minor repairs for longer than anyone could remember. Ten horses, or seven wide ponypigs, could cross it abreast, and its gently arching roadway was grooved by the countless merchant wagons that had crossed it, making their way from Port Charley to Montfort.

The five cyclopians sent to inspect the structure were not tentative in the least as they came upon the solid wood. The fall to the river was only fifteen feet, after all, and the river was obviously shallow and not very swift running. The brutes fanned out, two to a side and one in the middle, directing the inspection. They went down to their knees, gripping the edges and bending over to take a look at what was underneath.

The great oak beams appeared to be solid, unbreakable. Even the cyclopians, never known for feats of engineering or construction of any kind, could appreciate the strength of the bridge. The call of "yok-ho," the cyclopian signal that all was well, came from one, then another, both on the right side of the bridge.

The brute peeking over the bridge's left-hand side, nearest to the eastern bank, noticed something strange. The wood under here was weathered and gray, except for two pegs the cyclopian spotted: new pegs, with sawdust still clinging to their visible edge.

"Yok-ho!" called the first brute on the left, who then joined the curious cyclopian near the eastern bank, the only one who had not given the signal.

"Yok-ho?" he asked, bending low to see what had so sparked his companion's interest.

The curious brute pointed out the new pegs.

"So?" his companion prompted. "It's been a tough winter blow. The bridge needed fixing."

The other cyclopian was not so certain. He had a nagging suspicion, and he wanted to crawl over the edge and snake in for a closer look. His companion wasn't thrilled with that idea, though.

"Call out yok-ho," the one-eye insisted.

"But the peg—"

"If you don't call it out, we'll be turning south," the other growled.

"If it falls—" the curious cyclopian tried to explain, but again he was cut short.

"Then those on it will tumble down," the other replied. "But those who get across, and we'll be in the front of that group, will get to the town and get to the food. My stomach's been growling all the day, and all of yesterday! So call it out, or I'll put my fist into your eye!"

"What do you see?" demanded the cyclopian standing in the middle of the bridge.

The curious one took a last look at the pegs, then at the scowl of his companion. "Yok-ho!" he cried out, and the brute in the middle, as eager as any to get to the town, didn't question the delay any further.

Word was relayed back to the waiting army, and they began to move immediately, tightening ranks so that they could get across the bridge as quickly as possible.

Under that bridge, tucked into cubbies between the great beams near to the center of the understructure, three dwarfs, who had heard the conversation at the lip of the bridge and now the thunder of marching footsteps and ponypig hooves on the planks above, breathed deep sighs of relief. Each dwarf carried a large mallet, ready to knock out designated pegs and drop the bridge when the signal came from the south.

Down to the south, Siobhan, Luthien, and all the others breathed relieved sighs, as well, as they watched the Avon army crossing over to the east. Luthien took out his folding bow and pinned it open; the others fitted long arrows to their bowstrings. Then they waited.

Half the force got across, including all of the cavalry, and still the raiders held their shots.

The lines of cyclopians stretched out across the way, nearing Felling Downs. The brutes would find the town deserted and all supplies gone, though the villagers had left more than a few traps, snares, and oil-soaked buildings, flint and steel attached to door jambs waiting for a cyclopian to walk in.

For the waiting marauders, the timing had to be perfect. They didn't want to trap too many cyclopians on this side of the bridge, but it would take them a couple of minutes to get down there to engage the brutes and they didn't want to wait so long as to allow all the cyclopians to run across. One elf was dug in less than two hundred feet from the bridge, in a deep hole beneath a lone tree. Her job was to count the remaining one-eyes and signal back, and so Luthien and the others waited for the flash of a mirror.

Most of the army was across, the trailing brutes growing more confident and less structured in their formations now. Siobhan nodded up and down the line and great bows bent back, anticipating the call.

The mirror flashed; the air hummed with the vibrations of bowstrings. The first volley went out to the bank just east of the bridge, a three-hundred arrow barrage to prevent any of the brutes who had already gone over from running back across before the bridge fell.

Confusion erupted from the cyclopians as the stinging, deadly darts whipped in. Howls and cries filtered up and down the ranks; to the south, a horn blew.

So much confusion hit those upon the bridge, scrambling brutes trying to decide which way to run, that the one-eyes never even heard the pounding as the dwarfs took up their mallets, slamming out the pegs.

The second barrage came flying from the south, this time plucking into the ranks of some three hundred brutes remaining on the western bank.

Commands rang out all along the cyclopian line, the army trying to turn about to meet the unexpected foe. Those cyclopians near the bridge scrambled to get into formation on both banks, lining up their great shields to deflect the next volley.

One group of cavalry, a dozen ponypig riders, including undercommander Longsleeves, came galloping onto the bridge from the west, trying to get back and take command of the force left behind.

Beams groaned and creaked; below came a tremendous cracking sound from the ice and splashes. The cavalry unit was more than halfway across, scattering cyclopian infantry, even knocking a few over the side.

The bridge collapsed beneath them.

Now all of the bowshots from the south were concentrated on those unfortunate cyclopians trapped on the west. Each barrage took less of a toll as more and more got into their tight defensive posture, great shields lined edge to edge.

With cries of "Free Eriador!" and "Caer MacDonald!" the raiders leaped up from their concealment, bows twanging as they charged. Within twenty feet of their opponents, the cyclopians came out of their metal shell and charged ahead, eager for close combat. But this tactic was known and had been anticipated, and almost as one, the rebels skidded down to one knee, pulling back for one more shot, point-blank, into their enemies.

That last volley decimated the cyclopian ranks, killed nearly a hundred of the brutes, and sent those remaining into a scramble of pure confusion.

Out came *Blind-Striker*, and Luthien Bedwyr, his crimson cape billowing in the morning breeze, led the charge.

Across the river, the cyclopian army hooted and cursed. Some threw their long spears, others fired crossbows, but cyclopians, having only one eye and no depth perception, were not adept at missile fire, and their barrage, however heavy, was ineffective.

Still, the enemy was in sight, and the cyclopians were hungry for blood. Many picked a careful course along the angled logs of the bridge which had not fallen, while others, on orders from their tyrant commander, swarmed down the banks, trying to cross on the ice.

Some got almost halfway before the ice broke apart, dropping them into the freezing waters.

On the western bank, the massacre was on in full. Outnumbered by more than two to one, the remaining cyclopians, Praetorian Guard all, put up a good fight initially. But as more died, and as it became apparent that little if any help would cross over from the eastern bank, groups of the brutes began to run off, back to the west, the way they had come, wishing they could run all the way to Carlisle in Avon!

They didn't get nearly that far. Barely a hundred yards from the bridge, they found more enemies, those independent rebel bands that had peppered the force since it had left Port Charley.

The rebels from Caer MacDonald saw the unexpected help as well, and their hearts soared and the cyclopians' heart for the battle fell apart. Above it all was Luthien, running from fight to fight, slashing with *Blind-Striker* and calling out for Eriador, inspiring his warriors.

Those cyclopians across the river, particularly one huge and ugly brute atop a huge and ugly ponypig, also noticed the Crimson Shadow. Belsen'Krieg called for a crossbow.

Siobhan and the hundred elves who took part in the raid broke free of the melee as soon as it became apparent that the cyclopians would be easily slaughtered. Taking up their bows, the elves lined the western bank, more than willing to trade missile volleys with the one-eyes. Mostly, they concentrated their fire on those brutes splashing in the river, or crawling along the remains of the bridge. Half of the elves provided cover fire as the three courageous dwarfs crawled out of the bridge's wreckage and picked their way up the western bank.

In short order, the bridge was clear of one-eyes, and those still alive in the suddenly red-running river had turned about and were scrambling for their own ranks.

Luthien came up to the bank beside Siobhan, *Blind-Striker* in hand and dripping cyclopian blood. He looked to the half-elf—and then both fell away suddenly as a crossbow bolt cut the air between them. Turning to look across the bank, they recognized Belsen'Krieg and knew that this huge brute had been the one to shoot at them—to shoot at Luthien. It had been no random attempt.

The elves kept up their barrage, but the cyclopian army, willing to abandon comrades for the sake of their own hides, was fast pulling back, understanding that they could not trade volleys with the likes of elves.

Belsen'Krieg remained, statuesque atop his ponypig. The one-eyed general and Luthien stared at each other long and hard. The armies would meet in full very soon, of course, but suddenly it seemed to Luthien as if those forces, all of the men and dwarfs and elves, and all of the cyclopians, were no more than extensions of their two generals. Suddenly, the impending fight for Montfort, for Caer MacDonald, became a personal duel.

Before Luthien could stop her, Siobhan put up her bow and let fly, her arrow streaking across the river to strike Belsen'Krieg in the broad shoulder.

The cyclopian general hardly flinched. Without taking his unblinking stare from Luthien, the brute reached up and snapped off the arrow shaft. He nodded grimly, Luthien answered with a similar nod, and then Belsen'Krieg wheeled his ponypig and galloped away, riding through a hail of arrows, though if any hit him or his mount, it wasn't apparent.

Luthien stood silent on the bank, watching the monstrous brute depart. The enemy was real to him now, very real, and as awestricken and afraid as he had been when first he glimpsed the black and silver swarm that was the army of Avon, he was even more so having looked upon the powerful leader of that force.

On the western bank, it was over in a matter of minutes, with less than four-score casualties to the raiders, mostly wounds that would heal, and more than three hundred cyclopian dead littering the snowy and muddy field.

A complete victory for the rebels, but as the Avon army flowed away from the bridge, toward Felling Downs and Caer MacDonald beyond that, Luthien wondered how much this minor skirmish would ultimately affect the final outcome.

Later that morning, Oliver and Katerin and the force from Port Charley, still many miles to the west, saw the plumes of black smoke rising in the east, as Felling Downs was consumed by the fires, the rage, of the cyclopian army.

The sight was bittersweet, for the marching force had heard from the independent bands of the ambush set at Felling Downs that the fight went well. Still, those plumes of smoke reminded them all that the war would not be without cost, and on a more practical and immediate level, that they still had a long march ahead of them and a long fight after that.

As twilight settled in deep over Eriador, the folk from Port Charley set their last camp before the fight. Oliver rode out alone from their ranks, prodding Threadbare across the ghostly gray fields. He came up a hillock—a high ridge for this far north of the Iron Cross—and he saw the fires.

Hundreds of fires, thousands of fires, a vast sea of cyclopians. More enemies than boastful Oliver had ever seen gathered in one place, and the halfling was sorely afraid, more for Luthien and those in Montfort than for himself, for he understood that no matter how hard they marched and how early they left, the force from Port Charley would not come on the field until the end of the next day.

"Luthien will hold," came a voice that startled Oliver, nearly dropping him from his mount. Brind'Amour walked up beside him.

Oliver looked all about, but saw no mount nearby, and he understood that the old man had used a bit of wizardry to get out here.

"Luthien will hold for the first fight," Brind'Amour assured Oliver, as if he had read the halfling's every thought, every worry.

The words were of small comfort to Oliver as he continued to scan that vast encampment to the south and east.

▪ ▪ ▪

Those cyclopian campfires were visible from the high towers of Caer MacDonald as well, and Luthien and Siobhan, atop the Ministry's highest platform, marked them well and watched them for a long time in silence.

They knew, too, that if those fires were visible to them, then Caer MacDonald's dark walls were visible to the hungry and angry cyclopians.

The city was quiet this night, deathly still.

CHAPTER 13

AGAINST THE WALL

THE NEXT WAS not a bright dawn, the sky hazy gray with the first high clouds of yet another gathering storm. When shafts of sunlight did break through, the fields sparkled with wetness, as did the helms and shields and glistening speartips of the Avon army, forming into three huge squares, four to five thousand soldiers in each.

Luthien watched the spectacle from atop the low gatehouse of the city's inner wall. He and his group had crawled in just ahead of the Avon force, leaving the cyclopians to set their camp on the field, for the one-eyes had met up with more minor resistance in the foothills between Felling Downs and Montfort. No groups had actually engaged the vast army; they had just stung the one-eyes enough to keep them diverted, allowing Luthien's band to slip far to the south and cross the river, then dash back into the protection of the city as the night had deepened around them.

Before Luthien lay a hundred feet of empty ground, all structures and wagons having been removed by the dwarfs. The empty field ended at the lower outer wall, the base of which had been chopped and wedged, ready to drop outward, away from the city. Thick ropes pulled taut ran back into the courtyard, a third of the distance to the inner wall. These were pegged solidly into the ground, and beside each stood an ax-wielding dwarf.

Those dwarfs would have a long wait, Luthien hoped. The first defense would come from that outer wall; its low parapets were lined shoulder-to-shoulder by archers and pikemen. Luthien spotted Siobhan among that line, her long wheat-colored tresses hanging low out of a silvery winged helmet, her great longbow in hand.

The young Bedwyr next looked for Shuglin, but could not find the dwarf. In fact, Luthien saw none of the bearded folk, except for those twenty dwarfs ready to chop the lines and one or two in place along the outer wall. Luthien looked up and down his own line along the inner wall, but still, for some reason he did not understand, he found no dwarfs. He looked back to Siobhan instead, admiring her fierce beauty, her sheer strength of character. All those around looked to her for guidance as surely as they looked to the Crimson Shadow.

The whooshing sound of a catapult behind him, from the Ministry, brought the young man from his contemplations of the fair half-elf. He lifted his gaze beyond the outer wall and saw the three black and silver masses approaching, a row of solid metal, with shields butted together perhaps sixty-five fronting each of the squares. Oliver had warned Luthien that they would do this, calling the formations "testudos," but no words could have prepared Luthien for the splendor of this sight. One testudo was directly north of the city, a second northwest, and the third almost directly west, a three-pronged attack that would pressure the two main outer walls. At least they weren't surrounded, Luthien thought, but of course, Caer MacDonald could not easily be surrounded, since its southern and eastern sections flowed into the towering mountains, virtually impassable at this time of year.

Any relief that Luthien might have realized with that thought was lost as the Avon march progressed. The cyclopians came like a storm cloud, slowly, deliberately. Above the din of the march and the excitement along the wall, Luthien heard the cyclopian drummers striking a rhythmic, monotonous beat.

A heartbeat, continuous, inevitable.

A ball of flaming pitch hit the field in front of the brutes—some of those in the front rank were splattered. But their shields deflected the missiles and they never slowed.

A lump of panic welled in Luthien's throat, a sudden urge to run away, out of Caer MacDonald's back gate and into the mountains. He hadn't foreseen that it would be like this, so controlled and determined. He had expected the cyclopian leader to make some announcement, expected some horns to blow, followed by a roaring charge.

This was too calculated, too confident. The Praetorian Guard held tight ranks; their line hardly fluttered as the next catapult shot hit in their midst. A few were killed or wounded—some had to have been—but the mass didn't reveal any losses in the least, just rolled on to the cadence, continuous, inevitable. To Luthien, so, too, seemed the impending fall of Caer MacDonald.

Luthien glanced all around. All was suddenly quiet on his side of the wall, and he realized that the men and women around him were entertaining similar fears. A voice in Luthien's head told him that it was time for him to be the leader, the true leader. The rebels had hit a critical moment before the battle had even been joined.

Luthien climbed to the top of the battlement and drew *Blind-Striker* from its scabbard. "Caer MacDonald!" he cried. "Eriador free!"

Those waiting behind the outer wall glanced back, some confused, but some, like Siobhan, knew and appreciated what the young Bedwyr was up to.

Luthien ran along the wall to the gatehouse on the other side of Caer MacDonald's huge front gate. He continued his cry, and it became a chant, taken up by every soldier manning the city wall.

Those on the outer wall, with the enemy fast closing into range, did not cry out, but surely they were heartened by the cheering behind them. Up came the lines of bows, arrows fitted and ready.

The cyclopian army continued its slow and steady march. Fifty feet away. Forty.

Still Siobhan and her companions held their bows bent, seeing little to shoot at along the barricade of metal shields. Another catapult lob landed in the midst of the army, far back among the ranks, and then a ballista bolt, driving down from one of the Ministry's towers, slammed into the front line, and no shield could hold it back. It buckled the blocking metal in half and blasted through, skewering one cyclopian, and the force of the hit knocked those brutes flanking him from their feet, causing a temporary break in the line.

The archers were quick to let fly and the stinging arrows penetrated the mass, taking their toll.

Barely twenty feet away, the cyclopian square at the northwest bend in the outer wall broke ranks and charged, screaming wildly. The bow strings hummed; pikemen jabbed down from their higher perches, trying to keep the brutes from the eight-foot barrier.

Siobhan, farther to the north with her elves, called for a volley before the square facing them even broke ranks. It was a calculated gamble, and one that paid off, for at close range the powerful elfish longbows drove arrows right through the blocking shields, and the elves were quick enough to fit their next arrows so that they fired again almost immediately.

A third and fourth volley followed before the cyclopians could finish closing the twenty feet, but as devastating as the bow fire was, it hardly dented the great mass, five thousand Praetorian Guards to this square alone. The brutes did not panic, did not weep for their fallen. They swarmed the wall and clambered up it, often climbing over the backs of their own dead.

Siobhan's elves fought brilliantly—so did the folk, mostly humans, holding the northwestern corner and the western expanse—but their line was thin, far too thin, and in a matter of moments, the wall was breached in several places.

From the inner wall came three short blasts of a horn, and all on the outer wall who were able broke ranks and fled back for the city gate.

To their credit, those dwarfs ready with the axes waited until the very last moment, gave everyone fighting along the outer wall every possible second to get away. But then they could wait no more; cyclopians were inside the line and bearing down on them and if they did not put their axes to quick work on the ropes, they would find themselves engaged in close combat instead.

One by one, the ropes snapped, each with a huge popping sound, and the stones of the outer wall groaned.

Luthien held his breath; the wall seemed to hang in place for a long, long while, perhaps held up by the sheer bulk of the force on the other side. Finally, it tumbled, breaking from the west around to the north like a great wave upon a beach.

In truth, not too many cyclopians were killed by the falling wall. It didn't collapse, but rather fell like a tree, and many of the brutes were able to scramble back out of harm's way. But their formation was broken by the ensuing confusion, and when Luthien's line along the inner wall loosed their first barrage of arrows, more hit cyclopian flesh than blocking shields.

Luthien didn't witness that devastating barrage. He and fifty others were down in the courtyard behind the main gates, mounted on the finest steeds that could be found within the city. Caer MacDonald's inner doors were swung wide, and ropes and ladders were dropped over the wall to aid in the flight of those allies coming in from the outer wall. Archers picked their shots carefully, taking down the leading cyclopians so that as few as possible of the defenders would be caught in combat outside the city.

Out from the gates came the cavalry, led by Luthien, crimson cape and reddish hair flying wild behind him, *Blind-Striker* held high to the gray morning sky.

Beyond the rubble of the outer wall, Belsen'Krieg and his undercommanders regrouped quickly and sent on a new and furious charge. Luthien and his mounted allies prepared to meet it and slow it, so that those running from the outer wall could get to safety. The young Bedwyr regrouped the cavalry around him, set the line for the charge. The bulk of the cyclopians were sixty feet away, twenty feet inside the rubble of the outer wall.

Luthien's eyes widened in amazement as the ground erupted right at the feet of the enemy force, as Shuglin and his five hundred dwarfs crawled up from their concealment, hacking and chopping their hated, one-eyed enemies with abandon.

Another volley of arrows whipped down from the wall behind Luthien; the ballista atop the Ministry blasted a huge hole in one rank of the cyclopian line.

"Eriador free!" Luthien bellowed, and out he charged, fifty horsemen alongside him, running headlong into the writhing black-and-silver mass.

The most horrible and confusing minutes of Luthien Bedwyr's young life ensued, amidst a tangle of bodies, the whir of arrows, the screams of the dying. Every way he turned, Luthien found another cyclopian to slash; his horse was torn out from under him and he was caught by a dwarf whom he never got the chance to thank, for they were soon separated by a throng of slashing enemies.

Luthien got hit, several times, but he hardly noticed. He drove *Blind-Striker* halfway through one cyclopian, then yanked it free and slashed across, gouging the bulbous eye of another. The first one he had hit, though, was not quite dead, too enraged and confused and horrified all at once to lie down and die.

Luthien felt the warmth of his own blood rolling down the side of his leg. He spun back and moved to finish the grievously wounded brute, but never got the chance as another wave rolled in between them, pushing them far apart. Always before, even in the scrambles in and around the Ministry, Luthien's battles had been personal, had been face-to-face with an opponent, or side by side with a friend, until one could move along to the next fight. Not this time, though. Half the cyclopians Luthien engaged were already carrying wounds from previous encounters; most of the friends he spotted were carried away by the sheer press of that murderous frenzy before he could even acknowledge them.

With the archers who had fled the outer wall bolstering the line, the fire from the inner wall was devastating. And with Luthien's cavalry and the dwarfs scrambling amid the cyclopian ranks, the brutes could not form up into any defensive shell.

The momentum of the ambushing groups had played out, however, and though the cyclopian line had bent, it had not broken. The confusing battle turned into a frenzied retreat for Luthien's group and the dwarfs, what few could manage to get away from the roiling mass of Praetorian Guards.

They came out in bunches mostly, every one trailing blood, from weapon and from body, and not a single dwarf or rider would have made it back to the city had not the archers on the wall covered their retreat.

Luthien thought his life was surely at its end. He killed one cyclopian, but his sword got hooked on the creature's collarbone. Before he could extract the weapon and turn to defend himself, he got swatted on the ribs by a heavy club. Breathless and dizzy, the young Bedwyr spun and tumbled.

The next thing he knew, he was half-running, half-carried from the throng, heading for the wall. He heard the growls of cyclopians on his heels, heard the buzz of arrows above his head, but he was distant from it somehow.

Then he was dragged up a ladder, caught from above by several hands, and hauled over the wall. He looked back as he tumbled, and the last thing he saw before his consciousness left him was the face and blue-black beard of Shuglin as the dwarf, his dear friend, came over the wall behind him.

"You are needed up on the wall," came a call in Luthien's head, a distant plea, but a voice that he recognized. He opened bleary eyes to see Siobhan bending over him.

"Can you rise?" she asked.

Luthien didn't seem to understand, but he didn't resist as Siobhan lifted his head from the blanket and took up his arm.

"The wall?" Luthien asked, sitting up and shaking the daze from his mind. All the memories of earlier that morning, the horror of the pitched battle, the blood and the screams, flooded back to him then, like the images of a nightmare not yet forgotten in the light of dawn.

"We held," Siobhan informed him, prodding him on, forcing him to his feet. She took hold of him as he stood, steadying him. "We scattered them and stung them. Their dead litter the field."

Luthien liked the words, but there was something in Siobhan's words, an edge of anxiety, that told him she was trying to convince herself more than him. He wasn't surprised when she continued.

"But they have re-formed their lines and are advancing," the half-elf explained. "Your wounds are not so bad, and your presence is needed at the wall." Even as she spoke, she was dragging him along, and Luthien felt like an ornament, a figurehead, symbol of the revolution. At that moment, he didn't doubt that if he had died, Siobhan wouldn't tell anybody; she'd just prop him up against the wall, tie *Blind-Striker* to his upraised hand, and shove a dwarf under his cape to call out glorious cheers.

When Luthien got up to the wall, though, he began to appreciate the cold edge of Siobhan's actions. The field before Caer MacDonald, all the way to the rubble of the outer wall, was covered in bodies and red-soaked with blood, huge puddles of blood that couldn't find its way into the frozen ground. Every so often, someone from the wall would hurl something down to the field and the air would throb with beating wings as countless carrion birds lifted off into the gray sky—a sky that had grown darker as the day progressed.

It was such a surreal, unbelievable scene of carnage that Luthien could hardly sort it out. Most of the dead were cyclopians, all silver and black and red with blood, but among them were the corpses of many men and women, a few elves, and many, many of Shuglin's bearded folk.

That's what Luthien saw most of all: the dead dwarfs. The brave dwarfs who had sprung up in the midst of the marching army, causing chaos and destruction, though they knew they would pay dearly for their actions. It seemed to the young Bedwyr as if all of them were out there broken and torn, sacrificed not to save Caer MacDonald but only to ward off the first cyclopian charge.

His face ashen, breathing hard, Luthien looked at Siobhan. "How many?" he asked.

"More than three hundred," she replied grimly. "Two hundred of them dwarfs." Siobhan stood straighter suddenly, squared her shoulders and her delicate jaw. "But five times that number of cyclopians lay dead," she estimated, and it seemed to Luthien that there were at least that many bodies covering the field.

Luthien looked away, back to the field, then beyond the field and the rubble, to the swarming black-and-silver mass, the Avon army coming on once more. He took note of a lighter patch of gray in the sky and figured that it was not yet noon, yet here they came again, to repeat the scene of carnage, to cover the dead with a second layer.

"All in one morning," the young man whispered.

Luthien examined his line. There would be no falling outer wall this time, no ambush by Shuglin's people. This time, the cyclopians would march right to the inner wall, and if they overcame its defenders, if they got into the city, Caer MacDonald would be lost.

Would be lost, and the rebellion would be at its end, and Eriador would not be free. Luthien did not consider the personal implications of it all, did not even think that he might die in the next hours, or wonder about the consequences to himself if he did not die and the city was lost. Now, up on this wall, the situation was larger than that; there was too much more at stake.

Strength flowed through Luthien's battered limbs; he hoisted his sword high into the air, commanding the attention of all those nearby.

"Eriador free!" came the cheer. "Caer MacDonald!"

Next to Luthien, Siobhan nodded approvingly. She half-expected the young Bedwyr to pass out from his wounds and knew that he would find this next battle difficult indeed. But he had accomplished what she needed of him, and if he was among the dead after this attack, she would cultivate the legend; she would have every remaining soldier defending Caer MacDonald add the name of Luthien Bedwyr to the cheer.

Those thoughts were for another time, the half-elf told herself. The catapults fired, the ballistae twanged, and the squared cyclopian groups—two now, not three as in the first attack—plodded on. Upon the wall, a thousand bows bent back and fired, and then again, and again, and again, a thick hail of arrows whistling and thumping against shields, occasionally slipping through a crack in the cyclopian defensive formation.

Still they came on, the black-and-silver, undeniable flood. They crossed the rubble of the outer wall, stepped over or on top of the dead. An incessant popping noise, the rapid bursts of arrows slamming against metal, became one long drone, mixing with the hum of bowstrings, the very air vibrating.

The Praetorian Guard broke ranks less than fifty feet from the wall. Ladders appeared; dozens twirled ropes with heavy grapnels as they charged the wall. One large group supported a felled tree between their lines and charged the main gates.

Arrow volleys from the gatehouses decimated the group holding the battering ram, but many other cyclopians were nearby to take up the tree.

Now the ring of swords, steel on steel, was heard up and down the wall. Cries of rage mingled with cries of agony, snarls and wails, hoots of victory that became horrifying, agonizing shrieks a moment later as the next opponent struck hard.

At first, cyclopians died by the score, ten to one over the defenders. But as more grapnels came sailing over the wall, as more and more Praetorian Guards gained footing, stretching the line of the defenders, the ratio began to shift.

Soon it became five to one, then two to one.

Luthien seemed to be everywhere, running along the battlements, striking hard and fast before racing on to the next fight, chopping a taut cyclopian climbing rope on his way. He lost track of his kills and wasn't really certain how many brutes he actually finished anyway. He felt that the defenders would hold, though the price would be heavy indeed.

An explosion, a shudder along the wall near to the gatehouses, nearly knocked the young Bedwyr from his feet and did indeed tumble a couple of men and cyclopians nearby.

A second followed, then a third, accompanied by the sound of hammers working furiously.

"The door!" someone shouted, and Luthien understood. He glanced over the wall and saw the mass congregating, saw the end of the dropped tree, its mission completed.

Down from the wall leaped Luthien, into the courtyard, into the tangle. He believed that he was rushing to his death, but couldn't stop himself. The cyclopians were in the courtyard, pouring through the broken gates. This was where Caer MacDonald would fall or hold, and this was where Luthien Bedwyr had to be.

Soon, as it had been out in the courtyard for the first fight, there were no defined lines, just a mass of soldiers, killing and dying. Luthien tripped over one dying man, and the stumble saved his life, for as he lurched low, a cyclopian sword, still dripping with blood of the victim Luthien had tripped across, whipped high, just above the young Bedwyr's bent back. Luthien realized that if he stopped, he would be killed before he could turn and face this adversary, so he threw his weight ahead, plowing into another group.

Right into the midst of three cyclopians.

▪ ▪ ▪

Up on the wall, Siobhan and her elves continued sending a stream of arrows into the mass outside of Caer MacDonald's wall, while the larger and stronger humans battled with those brutes stubbornly scrambling up the ropes and ladders.

"Find their leaders!" the half-elf commanded, and many of her archers were already doing just that. They scanned the mob, seeking out any one-eye giving orders, and whenever an elf spotted one, he called all those archers near to him to bear a concentrated barrage.

One by one, Belsen'Krieg's undercommanders went tumbling to the dirt.

Luthien went down to his knees in a spin, completing a semicircle and whipping his sword across, straight out, driving two of the cyclopians back. The young man brought his lead foot under him, coming about and up, batting the third brute's blade high and lunging forward, gutting the one-eye.

Luthien rushed forward, tearing free *Blind-Striker* as he passed, then cutting right around, using the falling brute as a shield from the other two, who were close on his heels. He came out behind the tumbling cyclopian, slashing and charging.

One of the cyclopians wielded a trident, the other a sword, and both weapons were knocked aside in that furious charge. The cyclopian with the trident jumped back, put one hand over the butt end of the weapon, and launched it straight for Luthien's head.

Luthien, quick as a cat, dropped down and parried, sword coming high and deflecting the angle of the deadly missile. He didn't let the trident fly past him, though, but caught it halfway along its shaft in his free hand as the sword defeated its momentum, then reversed its angle, bringing its butt to the ground just in front of him and angling it out to the side, setting it against the charge of the sword-wielder.

The cyclopian skidded to a stop, but got poked in the shoulder.

Luthien wasn't paying attention. He left the trident the moment it was set, rushing out the other way, toward the brute that had hurled the weapon. The cyclopian scrambled, trying to pull a short sword from its belt. It got the weapon out, but too late, while Luthien's sword slammed hard against its hilt, knocking it from the one-eye's grasp.

Straight up went *Blind-Striker*, cutting like a knife, slicing the brute's face from chin to forehead. The sword spun around and down in a diagonal swipe, tearing at the brute's collarbone, across its lower throat and down and under its right breast. Luthien managed yet another stab as the brute fell away, again in the belly.

The young Bedwyr whirled about, instinctively slashing his sword before him, just in time to pick off the sword of the remaining brute. Back came *Blind-Striker*, parrying the weapon again, and then a third time, and with each pass, Luthien gained ground, forced his opponent to backpedal. Pure rage drove the young man; this was his homeland; his Eriador. He stabbed and slashed, dropped and cut at the brute down low, then leaped up and poked at the cyclopian's eye.

"How many can you block?" he screamed into the brute's face, pushing it back, ever back, up on its heels until it stumbled.

A club knocked free from a nearby melee hit Luthien on the leg and he, too, stumbled, and the cyclopian tried to reverse the momentum, tried to go on the offensive. It jabbed with its short sword, but wasn't able to throw its weight into the thrust. Luthien fell back, then came forward in a rush, beyond the extended weapon, *Blind-Striker* driving straight into the brute's heart.

It had all happened in the span of a few moments; three kills before the blood had even dripped from the blade. Luthien tore his sword free and jumped about, expecting to be overwhelmed in the crush. He was surprised, for suddenly there seemed to be many fewer cyclopians in the courtyard. He looked at the doors and saw that Shuglin's tough three hundred had fought in a line to seal the courtyard, and now many dwarfs had their shoulders to the battered doors, holding them fast. Still, by Luthien's estimation, there should have been more cyclopians, more frenzied fighting, in the courtyard.

Luthien sprinted to a stack of crates piled nearby and leaped atop it, and from the better vantage point, he understood the cyclopian tactics. Instead of fighting a pitched battle just inside the gates, many of the one-eyes had broken away and were running and scattering along Caer MacDonald's streets.

A cry from the wall above Luthien declared that the cyclopians outside were in retreat. It was repeated all along the defensive line, accompanied by rousing cheers. With the slaughter becoming more and more one-sided inside the gates, the second assault, like the first, had been repelled.

Luthien didn't feel much like cheering. "Clever," he whispered, a private applause for his adversary, no doubt the huge and ugly cyclopian he had seen at Felling Run.

Siobhan was beside him a moment later, her shoulder wet with fresh blood. "They have broken away," the half-elf reported.

"And many have slipped into the city," Luthien replied grimly.

"We will hunt them down," Siobhan promised, a vow Luthien did not doubt. But Luthien knew, and Siobhan did, too, that hunting the brutes would be an expensive proposition. The fact that they would have to take the effort to search out these cyclopians was exactly the point of the maneuver, for it would take as many as ten defenders to search out each creature that had slipped into the many alleyways of Caer MacDonald.

Somewhere far away from the wall came the cry of "Fire!" and a plume of black smoke began a slow and steady ascent over the interior of the city. The cyclopians were already at work.

Luthien looked to the wall and thought again of his clever adversary, a tactician far better than he would expect from the crude one-eyed race. There were, perhaps, twenty thousand enemies facing each other, another few thousand already lying dead, but suddenly it all seemed to be a personal struggle to Luthien, as it had out by Felling Run. The ugly cyclopian against him.

And if he lost, then all of Caer MacDonald would pay the dear price.

CHAPTER 14

TWILIGHT

"IT WILL SNOW tonight," Siobhan remarked to Luthien and the others manning the wall around them. In the city behind them, several fires raged. Many cyclopians had been hunted down during the course of that afternoon, but others were still out there, prowling the shadows.

"He'll not wait," Luthien assured her.

The half-elf looked at the young man. The way he had spoken the words, and his referral to the enemy leader, and not to the Avon army, gave her insight into what the young Bedwyr might be thinking.

Siobhan looked over her shoulder, back toward the city, and saw another group of warriors, their faces covered in soot, emerging from one lane, heading for the wall. Below her, Shuglin's dwarfs worked hard at reinforcing the gate, but it had never been designed as a ward against so large a force. Up to now, battles for the city had usually been relatively small-scale, mostly against rogue cyclopian tribes. The main doors, though large, were not even bolstered by a portcullis, and though the plans had been drawn up to put one in place, the other defensive preparations, such as rigging the outer wall for collapse, had taken precedence.

"Replace them on the wall," Luthien instructed another man near to him, referring to the group coming out of the city. "And send a like number back into the city to hunt and join with the children and the elderly in battling the fires." The man, his face grim, nodded and left.

"March on," Luthien whispered into the biting wind as he looked back out over the fields, and Siobhan knew that he was calling to his enemy. This was a brutal battle, and only growing worse. All the able-bodied men and women had been fighting at the walls, but now even the children and the elderly, even those fighters who had been sorely wounded, had been forced to join in to fight cyclopians, or to fight flames. "Let us be with it."

"You are so certain that the one-eyes will come," Siobhan stated.

"The storm will be a big one," Luthien replied. "He knows. Their march to the city will be more difficult in the morning, if they can even come through the storm. Uphill and through blowing snow." Luthien shook his head. "No," he assured those around him. "Our enemy will not wait. The time to strike is now, with the sun still in the sky and the fires burning behind us, with our position weakened at the wall and the doors still hanging loose from the last assault."

"The dwarfs work well," one other man remarked, needing to report on some positive news.

Luthien didn't argue the point.

"They will come on," Siobhan agreed. "But can we hold?"

Luthien looked at her for just a moment, then glanced all around, at the faces of those nearby who had suddenly become quite interested in the conversation. "We will hold," Luthien said determinedly, teeth clenched. "We will drive them from our gates once more, kill them in the field, and then let the storm stop them and freeze what few are left alive. Eriador free!"

An impromptu cheer erupted from that section of the wall. Siobhan didn't join in. She stared long and hard at Luthien, though he, looking over the fields, didn't seem to notice her. She knew the truth of his little speech, knew that any apparent conviction in his words was for the sake of the others nearby. Luthien was no fool. Three, four, maybe even five thousand cyclopians were dead or wounded too badly to continue to fight, but between the defenders' dead and those who were within the city's interior, hunting cyclopians and battling flames, the force along the wall was at least as badly depleted, and every defender lost, every lost archer, who might fire a dozen arrows before the brutes even got near to the wall, was worth several cyclopians.

They had almost lost the wall in the last attack, and the odds then had been much more in their favor, the defenses more solid.

Luthien directed a sharp glance at the half-elf, as though he had somehow heard her silent reasoning. "Send the word throughout the city," he instructed. "Get everyone who is not at the wall or otherwise engaged, within the walls of the merchant section. Let most go into the Ministry."

Siobhan bit her lip. She was cold from loss of blood and the freezing wind, and from the confirmation that Luthien shared her doubts. These were plans of retreat, a contingency based on his belief that the outer wall, and thus, the outer city, would be lost before the nightfall.

"And give them all weapons," Luthien added as the half-elf started away. "Even the children. Even the very old."

Siobhan did not look back because she did not want Luthien to see her wince. The gravity of the potential defeat weighed heavily on her, as it did on

Luthien. After the fighting, the victorious cyclopians would not show much mercy.

They were all seasoned to this type of battle now, after only a single day, and so there was no panic along the wall when the black-and-silver mass appeared again, in two huge squares, marching slowly toward them.

The heartbeat of the drums; the thunder of the footsteps. An occasional bow twanged, but at this distance, even arrows from the great elvish longbows had no chance of penetrating the blocking shield wall. Luthien wanted to pass the word along the line to hold all shots. The cyclopians would get closer, after all, much closer.

Luthien kept quiet, though, realizing that his desire to scold his own was wrought of his ultimate frustration and fear, and understanding that those same emotions guided the defenders who did fire their bows. The archers might not be doing any real damage to the cyclopian line, but they were bolstering their own courage.

It occurred to Luthien that courage and stupidity might not be so far apart.

The young Bedwyr shook that nonsense from his mind and from his heart. This was Caer MacDonald, his city, his Eriador, and there was nothing stupid about dying here for this concept called freedom, which Luthien had never truly known in the short two decades of his life.

The cyclopians reached the rubble of the outer wall and came over it, like an indomitable wave of black-and-silver death. Now the bows sang out, one after another, many at a time, and the catapults and ballistae fired off as fast as the crews manning them could reload baskets of stones or heavy spears. But how many could they kill? Luthien had to wonder as he, too, let fly with his bow. A hundred? Five hundred? Even if that were the case, the cyclopians could spare the losses. The air about Luthien hummed with the song of quivering bowstrings, but the cyclopian ranks did not falter. As the defenders on the wall had become quickly seasoned to the type of battle on this field, so had the Praetorian Guard, and the defenders of Caer MacDonald had nothing new or unexpected to throw at them.

The squares dissolved into a rushing mob. Out came the grapnels and hundreds of ropes, out came the ladders, dozens and dozens of stripped trees with branches pegged or tied on as cross-steps, for the cyclopians had not been idle during the hours of midday. Caer MacDonald's wall was not high enough to delay the charge; the defenders did not have the time to slaughter enough of the brutes, or cut enough of the ropes, or knock away enough of the ladders.

Luthien wondered if he should call the retreat immediately, run back to the inner wall by the Ministry with his soldiers, surrender the outer section of the city. In the few moments that he took to make up his mind, the decision was made for him. The battle was joined in full.

Shuglin's battered dwarfs, as solid a force as could be found, held the courtyard, ready for another breach along the main gates. Looking out from the gatehouse, Luthien realized that the dwarfs would not be enough. A swarm of Praetorian Guards battered at the barricaded doors. A line of cavalry waited behind them, the heavy ponypigs and the largest and strongest of the cyclopians. Luthien spotted the ugly general among those ranks. He wanted to call for a concentrated volley to that spot, but in looking around, he understood that it was too late; few on the wall still held their bows, and most of those who did were swinging the weapons like clubs, battering at the cyclopians as the brutes climbed up in stubborn, unending lines.

Luthien sprinted along the wall. He cut one rope, then a second, then heard a shout below and decided that the best place for him would be among the dwarfs. The breaches along the wall were dangerous, of course, but if the courtyard was lost, then so, too, would be the bulk of the city.

As he came down among Shuglin's throng, Luthien saw that the fighting had already begun at the gate. One of the doors was gone, buried under the weight of the press, and in the bottleneck at the gates, the dwarven and cyclopian dead began to pile up.

Luthien came across Shuglin and grabbed his friend by the shoulder, a farewell salute.

"We'll not hold them this time," the dwarf admitted, and Luthien could only nod as he had no words to reply to the grim, and apparently accurate, argument.

The cyclopians began to gain ground at the gate, the press of one-eyes forcing the dwarfs back. And each step back widened the area of battle, allowed room for more cyclopians to pour into the fight.

"Eriador free," Luthien said to Shuglin, and the two exchanged smiles, and together they rushed in to die.

Tears rimmed Siobhan's green eyes as she darted from position to position atop the wall, bolstering the defenses wherever a cyclopian had gained a foothold. Her sword carried dozens of nicks, from chopping through ropes and banging against the stone of the walltop, but the imperfections were hardly noticeable beneath the thick layer of blood and gore that stained the blade.

She ran on toward yet another break in the line, but skidded to a stop, nearly tumbling in a bloody slick, as she noticed a silver helmet coming up over the wall. Her sword crashed down, cleaving the helm, cleaving the cyclopian's skull.

Siobhan allowed herself a moment to catch her breath and survey the wall. Cyclopians were coming over in large numbers; soon they would be a virtual waterfall of bodies, leaping down into the city, Caer MacDonald, wiping out whatever gains the rebellion had made. Montfort's flag would fly again, it seemed, along with the pennant of Greensparrow, and under them, Siobhan's people, the Fairborn elves, would know slavery once more.

The half-elf shook her head and screamed at the top of her lungs. She would not play whore again for some merchant in Greensparrow's favor. No, she would die here, this day, and would kill as many Praetorian Guards as she could, in the hope—and it was fast becoming a fleeting hope—that her efforts would not be in vain, that those who came after her would be better off for her sacrifice.

Another silver helm appeared above the battlement; another cyclopian fell dead to the field below.

Luthien was fighting now, beside Shuglin, yet they were nowhere near the broken gate. The dwarven ranks could not hold tight enough to stem the cyclopian flow. It was like grabbing fine sand, too much fine sand to fit into your hand. And still the brutes were coming in an endless, incessant wave.

Luthien wondered when the enemy cavalry would burst through. He hoped that he would get a chance, just one chance, at the ugly cyclopian leader. He hoped that he might at least win a personal victory, though the war was surely lost.

Blind-Striker cut a circular parry, narrowly deflecting a cyclopian spear. Luthien realized the price of his distraction, feared for an instant that his fantasizing about the enemy leader had put him in a perilous position indeed, up on his heels with no room to retreat!

His one-eyed opponent noted the opening, too, and came on fiercely. But suddenly the cyclopian lurched and fell away, and standing in its place was Shuglin, who offered a wink to his human friend.

"To the door?" the dwarf asked through the tangle of his blue-black beard.

"Is there any other place for us to be?" Luthien answered wistfully, and together they turned, looking for an opening that would lead them to the front lines of the fight.

They stopped suddenly as a sharp hissing sound erupted from the stone above the broken doors. Green sparks and green fire sputtered about the structure, and the fighting stopped as dwarfs, cyclopians, and men turned to watch.

There came a sparkling burst of bright fire, a puff of greenish-gray smoke, and then, as abruptly as it had appeared, it was extinguished, and where it had been, instead of smooth, unremarkable stone, loomed a portcullis—a huge portcullis!

"Where in the name of Bruce MacDonald . . ." Shuglin started to cry out, among the astonished cries of everyone else who witnessed the remarkable spectacle, particularly those unfortunate cyclopians directly below the massive, spiked creation.

Down came the portcullis, crushing the one-eyes below it, blocking the advance of those beyond the gate and preventing the retreat of the brutes inside.

The dwarfs didn't wait for an explanation, but fell into a battle frenzy, hoping to clear the courtyard quickly that they might bolster the defense of the wall.

Luthien spent a few moments marveling at the portcullis. He knew it was a creation of magic—he was one of the few in the battle who had ever personally witnessed such a feat before—but he wondered if someone in the fight had caused it, or if it was some unknown magic of Caer MacDonald, some magical ward built into the stones of the city to come forth when the rightful defenders were in dire need.

A horn from far across the field and cheers from those defenders on the wall who had a moment to consider the scene answered Luthien's questions. He broke free of the tangle in the courtyard, scrambled up to the parapet, and witnessed the charge of allies.

Luthien's gaze focused immediately on two mounts, a shining white stallion and an ugly yellow pony, and though they and their riders were but specks on the distant field, Luthien knew then that Oliver and Katerin had come.

Indeed they had, along with a force that had swelled to almost two thousand, the militia of Port Charley's ranks more than doubled by bands of rebels joining them along their march.

Arrows rained on the confused one-eyes outside of the wall. Here and there, bursts of flame erupted above the cyclopian heads, releasing shards of sharpened steel to drop among the brutes, stinging and blinding them.

Luthien knew magic when he saw it, and in considering the allies approaching, he knew who else had come to the call of Caer MacDonald. "Brind'Amour," he whispered, his voice filled with gratitude and sudden hope.

Siobhan was beside him then, wrapping him in a tight hug and kissing him on the cheek. Luthien wrapped one strong arm about her and did a complete pivot, a quick turn of pure joy.

"Katerin has come!" Siobhan cried. "And Oliver! And they've brought some friends!"

The moment of elation for the pair, and for all the other defenders, was quickly washed away by the reality of the continuing fight. Luthien surveyed the scene, trying to find some new plans. Even though the defenders were still outnumbered, he entertained the thought of destroying the entire cyclopian army on the field, there and then. If the confusion among the one-eyes could hold, if there was any desertion among their ranks . . .

But these were Praetorian Guards, and Luthien had not overestimated the cunning of their leader. Belsen'Krieg, too, paused and considered the battle, and then he turned his forces, all of them who were not trapped inside the city.

"No!" Luthien breathed, watching the thousands of black-and-silver clad Praetorian Guard forming into a new line as they ran straight toward the approaching reinforcements. Even from this distance, he could estimate the numbers of his allies, and he put them at no more than two thousand, less than one-fourth the number of enemies that would soon overwhelm them.

The young Bedwyr called for archers to fire into the ranks of the departing brutes; he wanted to organize a force that could rush out of the city to the aid of Katerin and Oliver. But the battle along the wall and in the courtyard was not yet won, and Luthien could only watch.

"Run," he whispered repeatedly, and his heart lifted a bit when the approaching force turned about in an organized retreat.

The Avon army gave chase, but Oliver and his companions had not been caught off guard by the cyclopians' turn. They had expected to be chased from the field, and were more than happy to oblige, running all the way back to Felling Run and across the river on makeshift bridges they had left behind, into defensible positions on the other bank.

Then the bridges were pulled down, and the cyclopians came upon a natural barrier they could not easily cross, especially with hundreds of archers peppering their ranks once more.

Frustration boiled in Belsen'Krieg, but he was no fool. He had lost the day, and probably near to two thousand soldiers, but now he was confident that the rebels had played out their last trick. Even with these unexpected reinforcements, the cyclopian leader did not fear ultimate defeat.

Tomorrow would be another day of war.

And so the cyclopian force moved north. The sun settled on the western horizon, somehow finding an opening among the thickening clouds to peek through and shine upon the walls of the city that was still known as Caer MacDonald.

At least for one more day.

CHAPTER 15

CHESS GAME

THE FIGHTING WITHIN the city did not end at twilight. The wall and courtyard were cleared soon enough, but many cyclopians had slipped into the shadows of Caer MacDonald; several fights broke out in alleyways, and several buildings went up in flames.

Soon after sunset, too, the storm that Siobhan had predicted broke in full. It began as heavy sleet, drumming on the roofs of the houses within the city, drenching the fires of the encampments from Avon and Port Charley. As the night deepened and the temperature dipped, the sleet became a thick, wet snow.

Luthien watched it from the gatehouse, and later from the roof of the Dwelf. It seemed to him as if God, too, was sickened by the sight of the carnage, and so He was whitewashing the grisly scene. It would take more than snow, however deep it lay, to erase that image from Luthien Bedwyr's mind.

"Luthien?" came a call from the street below—Shuglin's throaty voice. Luthien cautiously picked his way across the slippery roof and peered down at the dwarf.

"Emissary from Oliver's camp," Shuglin explained, pointing to the tavern door.

Luthien nodded and headed for the rain gutter that would allow him to climb down to the street. He had expected that their allies would send an emissary; he had wondered if perhaps the whole force might come into the city.

Apparently that was not the case, for the night grew long and the fires of the encampment still burned far in the west, beyond Felling Run. The emissary would explain the intentions of the force to him so that he could coordinate the movements of Caer MacDonald's defenses. Luthien found that his heart was racing as he slipped down the rain gutter, lighting gently on the street, which was already two inches deep with snow.

Perhaps it was Katerin who had come in, Luthien hoped. He hadn't realized until this very moment how badly he wanted to see the fiery, red-haired woman of Hale.

When he rushed into the Dwelf, he found that the emissary wasn't Katerin, or Oliver, or even Brind'Amour. It was a young woman, practically a girl, by the name of Jeanna D'elfinbrock, one of Port Charley's fisherfolk. Her light eyes sparkled when she looked upon Luthien, this legend known as the Crimson Shadow, and Luthien found himself embarrassed.

The meeting was quick and to the point—it had to be, for Jeanna had to get back to the encampment long before dawn, dodging cyclopian patrols all the way. Oliver deBurrows had wanted to bring Port Charley's force in, the young woman reported, but they could not safely cross Felling Run. The cyclopians were not so far to the north, and they were alert and would not allow such a move.

Luthien wasn't surprised. Many of Caer MacDonald's defenders were dead or wounded too badly to man the walls. If the two thousand or so reinforcements were allowed inside the city, the holes in the city's defenses would be plugged, and the cyclopians would have to resume their assault practically from the same place they had begun it the previous day.

"Our deepest thanks to you and all your force," Luthien said to Jeanna, and now it was her turn to blush. "Tell your leaders that their actions here will not be in vain, that Caer MacDonald will not fall. Tell Oliver, from me personally, that I know he will show up where most we need him. And tell Katerin O'Hale to take care of my horse!" Luthien couldn't help a sidelong glance at Siobhan as he spoke of Katerin, but the half-elf did not seem bothered in the least.

With that, Jeanna D'elfinbrock left the Dwelf and the city, picking her careful way across the snowy fields back through the raging storm the few miles to the Port Charley encampment.

Later that night, Luthien and Siobhan lay in bed, discussing the day past and the day yet to come. The wind had kicked up, shaking the small apartment in Tiny Alcove, humming down the chimney against the rising heat so that the air in the small room had a smoky taste.

Siobhan snuggled close to Luthien, propped herself up on one elbow, and considered the concentration on the young man's fair face. He lay flat on his back, staring up at the dark. But he was looking somewhere else, the perceptive half-elf knew.

"They are fine," Siobhan whispered. "They have campfires blazing and know how to shelter themselves from the weather. Besides, they have a wizard among them, and from what you've told me of Brind'Amour, he'll have a trick or two to defeat the storm."

Luthien didn't doubt that, and it was a comforting thought. "We could have swung them to the south and brought them into the city along the foothills," the young man reasoned.

"We did not even know the extent and location of their camp until well after sunset," Siobhan replied.

"It would only have taken a couple of hours," Luthien was quick to answer. "Even in the storm. Most of the lower trails are sheltered, and there was little snow on them to begin with." He breathed a deep, resigned sigh. "We could have gotten them in."

Siobhan didn't doubt what he was saying, but the last thing she wanted now for Luthien was added guilt. "Oliver knows the area as well as you," she reminded Luthien. "If the folk of Port Charley wanted to get into Caer MacDonald, they would have."

Luthien wasn't so certain of that, but the argument was moot now, for it was well past midnight and he couldn't do anything about the camp's location.

"Shuglin informs me that he and his kin have some new traps ready for the cyclopians," the half-elf said, trying to shift the subject to a more positive note. "When our enemies come on again, they'll find the wall harder to breach, and if they're caught out in the open for any length of time, Oliver and his force will squeeze them from behind."

"Oliver hasn't enough soldiers to do that."

Siobhan shook her head and chuckled. "Our allies will strike from a distance!" she insisted. "Hit with their bows at the back of the cyclopians, and run off across the fields."

Luthien wasn't so certain, but again he did not wish to press the argument. He continued to stare up at the ceiling, at the flickering shadows cast by the wind-dancing flames of the hearth. Soon he felt the rhythmic breathing of the sleeping Siobhan beside him, and then he, too, drifted off to sleep.

He dreamed of his adversary, the huge and ugly cyclopian. All the tactics of the day filtered through his thoughts, all the moves the brute had executed: the first powerful probe at the city; the second assault, the feint, where many cyclopian arsonists slipped in; and the tactic when the new army appeared on the field, the sudden and organized turn of the skilled Praetorian Guard. They would have been destroyed on the field then and there, would have been squeezed and in disarray, caught defenseless. But their leader had reacted quickly and decisively, had swung about and chased the folk from Port Charley all the way back across Felling Run.

Luthien's eyes popped open wide, though he had been asleep for only a little more than an hour. Beside him, Siobhan opened a sleepy eye, then buried her cheek against his muscular chest.

"He is not coming back," Luthien said, his voice sounding loud above the background murmur of the wind.

Siobhan lifted her head, her long hair cascading across Luthien's shoulder.

"The cyclopians," Luthien explained, and he slipped out from Siobhan's grasp and propped himself up on his elbows, staring at the red glow of the hearth. "They are not coming back!"

"What are you saying?" Siobhan asked, shaking her head and brushing her hair back from her face. She sat up, the blankets falling away.

"Their leader is too smart," Luthien went on, speaking as much to himself as to his companion. "He knows that the arrival of the new force will cost him dearly if he goes against our walls again."

"He has come to take back the city," Siobhan reminded.

Luthien pointed a finger up in the air, signaling a revelation. "But with everything that has happened, and with the storm, he knows that he may lose."

Siobhan's expression revealed her doubts more clearly than any question ever could. Cyclopians were a stubborn, single-minded race for the most part, and both she and Luthien had heard many tales of one-eye tribes charging in against overwhelming odds and fighting to the last living cyclopian.

Luthien shook his head against her obvious reasoning. "These are Praetorian Guards," he said. "And their leader is a cunning one. He will not come against the city tomorrow."

"Today," Siobhan corrected, for it was after midnight. "And how do you know?"

Luthien had an answer waiting for her. "Because I would not attack the city tomor—today," he replied.

Siobhan looked at him long and hard, but did not openly question his rationale. "What do you expect of him?" she asked.

Until that very moment, Luthien had no idea of what his adversary might be up to. It came to him suddenly, crystal clear. "He's going across the river," the young Bedwyr asserted, and by the end of this sentence, he was finding breath hard to come by.

Siobhan shook her head, doubting.

"He will go over the river and catch the folk of Port Charley out in the open," Luthien pressed, growing more anxious.

"His goal is the city," Siobhan insisted.

"No!" Luthien replied sharply, more forcefully than he had intended. "He will catch them in the open field, and when they are destroyed, he can come back at us."

"If he has enough of a force left to come back at us," Siobhan argued. "And by that time, we will have many more defenses in place." She shook her head again, doubting the reasoning, but could see by Luthien's stern visage that he was not convinced.

"Time works against our enemy," Siobhan reasoned. "By all accounts, they are practically without food, and they are far from home, weary and wounded."

Luthien wanted to remind her again that these were not ordinary cyclopians, were Praetorian Guard, but she kept going with her reasoning.

"And if you are right," she said, "then what are we to do? Oliver and the others are not fools. They will see the brutes coming, and then the way will be clear for them to get into Caer MacDonald."

"Our enemy will not leave an open path," Luthien said grimly.

"You have to trust in our allies," Siobhan said. "Our responsibilities are in defending Caer MacDonald." She paused and took note of Luthien's hard breathing. Clearly, the man was upset, confused, and worried.

"There is nothing for us to do," Siobhan said, and she bent low and kissed Luthien, then sat back up, making no move to cover her nakedness. "Trust in them," she said. Her hand moved along Luthien's cheek and down his neck, and his muscles relaxed under her gentle touch.

"But there is something," he said suddenly, sitting up and looking directly into Siobhan's eyes. "We can go out before dawn, along those trails in the north. If we circle . . ."

Luthien stopped, seeing the look of sheer incredulity on the half-elf's face.

"Go out from the city?" she asked, dumbfounded.

"Our enemy will catch them in the open," Luthien pleaded. "And then, if he decides that he hasn't enough of a force remaining to capture the city, he'll turn about and march for Port Charley, now wide open to him. The cyclopians will slaughter that town and dig in, and with the season moving toward spring, Greensparrow will have an open port in Eriador and will send a second, larger force across the mountains."

"How many are you thinking to send out?" the half-elf asked, concerned by Luthien's reasoning.

"Most," Luthien replied without hesitation.

Siobhan's expression turned grim. "If you send most out, and our enemy comes back against Caer MacDonald, he will be entrenched within the city before we can strike back at him. We will be defeated and without shelter, scattering across Eriador's fields."

Luthien expected that criticism, of course, and there was indeed much truth in what Siobhan was arguing. But he didn't think that his adversary would come back at the city right away. Luthien's gut told him that the cyclopians would cross the river.

"Is this because of her?" Siobhan asked suddenly, unexpectedly.

Luthien's jaw dropped open. The reference to Katerin in such a way pained him, even more because for just a moment, he wondered if it might be true.

Siobhan saw his wounded reaction. "I am sorry," she said sincerely. "That was a terrible thing to say." She leaned close and kissed Luthien again.

"I know that your heart is for Caer MacDonald," Siobhan whispered. "I know that your decisions are based on what is best for all. I never doubt that." She kissed him again, and again, deeply, and he put his arms about her and hugged her close, feeling her warmth, needing her warmth.

But then, in this night of revelations, Luthien pushed Siobhan out to arm's length, and his puzzled expression caught her off guard.

"This is not about me, is it?" he asked, accusingly.

Siobhan didn't seem to understand.

"All of this," Luthien said candidly. "The love we make. It is not me, Luthien Bedwyr, that you love. It is the Crimson Shadow, the leader of the rebellion."

"They are one and the same," Siobhan replied.

"No," Luthien said, shaking his head slowly. "No. Because the rebellion will end, one way or the other, and so might I. But then again, I might not die, and what will Siobhan think of Luthien Bedwyr then, when the Crimson Shadow is needed no more?"

Even in the quiet light, Luthien could see that Siobhan's shoulders, indeed her whole body, slumped. He knew that he had wounded her, but he realized, too, that he had made her think.

"Never doubt that I love you, Luthien Bedwyr," the half-elf whispered.

"But . . ." Luthien prompted.

Siobhan turned away, looked at the glowing embers in the hearth. "I never knew my father," she said, and the abrupt subject change caught Luthien by surprise. "He was an elf, my mother human."

"He died?"

Siobhan shook her head. "He left, before I was born."

Luthien heard the pain in her voice, and his heart was near to breaking. "There were problems," he reasoned. "The Fairborn—"

"Were free then," Siobhan interjected. "For that was before Greensparrow, nearly three decades before Greensparrow."

Luthien quieted, but then realized that Siobhan's tale made her nearly sixty years old! Much came into perspective for the young man then, things he hadn't even considered during the wild rush of the last few weeks.

"I am half-elven," Siobhan stated. "I will live through three centuries, perhaps four, unless the blade of an enemy cuts me down." She turned to face Luthien directly, and he could see her fair and angular features and intense green eyes clearly, despite the dim light. "My father left because he could not bear to watch his love and his child grow old and die," she explained. "That is why there are so few of my mixed heritage. The Fairborn can love humans, but they know that to do so will leave them forlorn through the centuries."

"I am a temporary companion," Luthien remarked, and there was no bitterness in his voice.

"Who knows what will happen with war thick about us?" Siobhan put in. "I love you, Luthien Bedwyr."

"But the rebellion is paramount," Luthien stated.

It was a truth that Siobhan could not deny. She did indeed love Luthien, love the Crimson Shadow, but not with the intensity that a human might love another human. Elves and half-elves, longer living by far, could not afford to do that. And Luthien deserved more, Siobhan understood then.

She slipped out of the bed and began pulling on her clothes.

A part of Luthien wanted to cry out for her to stay. He had desired her since the moment he had first seen her as a simple slave girl.

But Luthien stayed quiet, understanding what she was saying and silently agreeing. He loved Siobhan, and she loved him, but their union was never truly meant to be.

And there was another woman that Luthien loved, as well. He knew it, and so did Siobhan.

"The cyclopians will not come into the city tomorrow," Luthien repeated as Siobhan pulled her heavy cloak over her shoulders.

"Your reasoning calls for a tremendous gamble," the half-elf replied.

Luthien nodded. "Trust in me," was all that he said as she walked out the door.

CHAPTER 16

LUTHIEN'S GAMBLE

LUTHIEN BARELY SLEPT the rest of that night, just lay in his bed, staring at the shadows on the ceiling, thinking of Siobhan and Katerin, and the enemy. Mostly the enemy: *his* enemy, the hulking, ugly cyclopian, more cunning than any one-eye Luthien had ever known.

Siobhan returned to the apartment an hour before dawn to find Luthien fully awake, dressed, and sitting in a chair before the hearth, staring into the rekindled flames.

"He's not going to come," Luthien said to her, his voice even, certain. "He's going to take his army across the river and catch Oliver's force unawares."

After a few moments of silence, with Siobhan making no move to reply, Luthien glanced over his shoulder to regard the half-elf. She stood by the door, holding his cloak.

Luthien pulled on his boots and went to her, taking the garment and following her out of the apartment.

The city was already awake, full of activity, and most of the bustle was nearby. Siobhan had gathered practically all of the army, ready to follow Luthien out of Caer MacDonald. The snow had turned into sleet and then to rain, but the wind had not abated. A thoroughly miserable morning, and yet, here they were, the thousands of Caer MacDonald's makeshift militia, ready to march hard and fast to the west, ready to brave the elements and the cyclopians. Luthien knew who had prompted them.

He looked at the half-elf then, standing calmly by his side, and his eyes were moist with tears of gratitude. He understood the depth of his gamble—if he was wrong and his adversary struck again against Caer MacDonald, the city would be overrun. Siobhan knew that, too, and so did every man and woman, every elf and dwarf, who had come out here this morning. They would take the gamble; they would trust in Luthien.

The young Bedwyr felt a huge weight of responsibility upon his shoulders, but he allowed himself only a moment of doubt. He had played this out in his mind over and over throughout the night and was confident that he understood his adversary, that he was correctly anticipating the enemy's move.

Siobhan and Shuglin pulled him to the side.

"I am not going with you," the dwarf informed him.

Luthien looked at Shuglin curiously, not knowing what to make of the unexpected declaration.

"The dwarfs will comprise most of the defenders left in Caer MacDonald," Siobhan explained. "They are best with the ballistae and catapults, and they have rigged traps that only they know how to spring."

"And we are not much good in the deep snow," Shuglin added with a chuckle. "Beards get all icy, you know."

Luthien realized then that Shuglin's hesitance to go out had nothing to do with any doubts the dwarf might harbor. Caer MacDonald had to remain at least moderately defended, for even if Luthien's assessment proved correct, the cyclopians might send a token force at the city to keep the defenders within the walls distracted.

"You have all the horses," Shuglin began, turning to the business at hand and unrolling a map of the region. "There are a few among you who know well the trails you'll need—we have even dispatched scouts to report back as you go along, in case the weather forces you to take an alternate route." As he spoke, the dwarf moved his stubby finger along the map, through the foothills beyond Caer MacDonald's southern gate, out to the west, around the Port Charley encampment, and then circling back to the north, back to the fields where they would meet the cyclopians.

They set out without delay, a long stream of six thousand desperate, determined warriors. All of the elves were among the ranks, and all of the cavalry group, though fewer than two hundred fit horses could be found in the entire city. Like ghosts in the predawn dark, they went without lights, without any bustle. Quietly.

Many carried longbows, each archer weighed down by several quivers of arrows. One group carried packs of bandages and salves, and the two dozen dwarfs that did go along were broken into groups of four, each group supporting a huge log across their shoulders. The going was slow on the slick trails—Luthien and the other horsemen had to walk their mounts all the way through the foothills—but the rain had cut hard into the snow. Every now and then they encountered a deep drift, and they bored right through it, using swords and axes as ice picks and shovels.

As the sky lightened with the approach of dawn, the Port Charley encampment came into sight in the fields to the north, just across Felling Run. Luthien found a high perch and stared long and hard in that direction, looking for some sign of the cyclopians.

Beyond the Port Charley encampment, the field was empty.

Doubts fluttered about the young Bedwyr. What if he was wrong? What if the cyclopians went to Caer MacDonald instead?

Luthien fought them away, concentrated on the chosen course. The ground leveled out just a few hundred yards to the north; a rider could get into the Port Charley encampment within twenty minutes. Luthien dispatched three, with information for Oliver. He told them to pick their way through the remaining rough terrain, then split up as they crossed the field in case cyclopian assassins were about.

Luthien saw those same three riders milling about the still-moving column a short while later. He went to them, confused as to why they were still there, and found that Siobhan had overruled him.

"My scouts near the base of the foothills have spotted cyclopian spies in the field," the half-elf explained.

Luthien looked again to the north, to the encampment. "Our friends should be informed of our position," he reasoned.

"We have little enough cover where we are," Siobhan replied. "If we are found out. . ." She let that notion hang heavily in the air, and Luthien didn't have to press the point. If his adversary found out about the move before the army of Avon marched, then their target would surely become Caer MacDonald.

Again doubts filled Luthien's mind. If cyclopian scouts were in the field between his column and the Port Charley encampment, might they already have learned of the march?

Siobhan saw a cloud cross the young man's face, and she put a comforting hand on Luthien's forearm.

The entire force took up a position northeast of the Port Charley camp, filtering down to the edge of the fields, out of sight, but ready to charge across and meet the foes. It was good ground, Luthien decided, for their rush, when it came, would be generally downhill into cyclopians marching across slippery, uneven ground.

When it came, Luthien wondered, or *if it* came? He continued to peer across the whitened fields, empty save the blowing rain.

A long hour passed. The day brightened and the rain turned into a cold drizzle. The folk of the Port Charley encampment were stirring, breaking down their tents, readying their gear.

Another hour, and still no sign.

Siobhan waited with Luthien. "Our allies do not cross the river," she kept saying, the implication being that Caer MacDonald was not under attack, that the cyclopians hadn't moved.

This did little to calm Luthien. He had thought that his adversary would attack at first light, hard and fast. He wondered if the cyclopians might be going the other way, around to the east, to come in against the city. If the cyclopians could manage the rough terrain, that would be a fine plan, for then the Avon army would not be caught in between the defenders and the Port Charley group—indeed, the reinforcements from Port Charley would have to swing all the way around the city, or cross through the city itself, just to get into the battle.

Near panic, Luthien looked around at his camp, at the cavalry rubbing down the dripping horses, at the dwarfs, oil-soaking their great logs, at the archers testing the pull of their bows. The young Bedwyr suddenly felt himself a fool, suddenly believed that he had set them all up for disaster. He wanted to break down the camp then, march back swiftly to Caer MacDonald, and he almost called out commands to do just that.

But he could not. They were too fully committed to change their minds. All they could do was sit and wait, and watch.

Another hour, and the rain picked up again, mixing with heavy sleet. Still no word from Caer MacDonald, though a plume of black smoke had risen into the gray sky above the city.

Another single arsonist, Luthien told himself. Not a full-scale battle—certainly not!

He was not comforted.

He looked at Siobhan, and she, too, seemed worried. Time worked against them and their hoped-for ambush, for if the cyclopians were not attacking, they were likely gathering information.

"We should try to get word to the Port Charley group," Luthien said to her.

"It is risky," she warned.

"They have to know," Luthien argued. "And if the cyclopians move against the city, we must be informed immediately to get in at their backs before they overrun the wall."

Siobhan considered the reasoning. She, like Luthien, knew that if the cyclopians did indeed throw their weight on the city, no amount of forewarning would matter, but she understood the young man's need to do something. She felt that same need as well.

She was just beginning to nod her agreement when the word came down the line, anxious whisper by anxious whisper.

"To the north!"

Luthien stood tall, as did all of those nearby, peering intently through the driving rain. There was the black-and-silver mass, finally making its way to the south, a course designed to encircle the Port Charley encampment and cut off any retreat to the west.

Luthien's heart skipped a beat.

■ ■ ■

Belsen'Krieg thought himself a clever brute. Unlike most of his one-eyed race, the burly cyclopian was able and bold enough to improvise. His goal was Montfort, and if he didn't get the city, he certainly would have some explaining to do to merciless Greensparrow.

But Belsen'Krieg knew that he could not take Montfort, not now, with this second force on the field, and likely with more rebels flocking in to join the cause. And so the cunning general had improvised. He split his remaining eleven thousand Praetorian Guards, sending three thousand straight south on the eastern side of Felling Run, to use the river as a defensive position as the Port Charley folk had used it against him. This group was not likely to see much fighting this day, but they would hold the encamped army to the western bank, where Belsen'Krieg and his remaining eight thousand would make short work of them.

The cyclopian main group had marched all morning, up to the north, then across Felling Run, and then back to the south, giving the enemy a wide berth so that they would not be discovered until it was too late. There was good ground west of the encampment, the cyclopian leader knew. He would squash this rebel rabble, and then, depending on his losses and the weather, he could make his decision: to go again against Montfort, or to turn back to the west and crush Port Charley.

Now the enemy was in sight; soon they would understand that they could not cross the river, and by the time they recognized the trap and were able to react to it, they would have no time to go in force into the mountains, either. Some might scatter and escape, but Belsen'Krieg had them.

Yes, the cyclopian leader thought himself quite clever that morning, and indeed he was, but unlike Luthien, Belsen'Krieg had not taken into account the cleverness of his adversary. As the cyclopian's force pivoted to the good ground in the west, another force had even better ground, up above them, in the foothills to the south.

"This is not so good," Oliver remarked to Katerin when word of the cyclopian move reached them. They stood together under a solitary tree, Threadbare and Riverdancer standing near to them, heads down against the driving sleet.

"Likely they've got the river blocked," Katerin reasoned, and she motioned that way—there was some movement on the fields to the east, across Felling Run. "We have to go into the mountains, and quickly."

"So smart," Oliver whispered, honestly surprised. The halfling didn't like the prospects. If the cyclopians chased them into the broken ground to the south, they could not hold their force together in any reasonable manner. Many would be slain, and many more would wander helplessly in the mountains to starve or freeze to death, or to be hunted down by cyclopian patrols.

But where else could they go? Certainly they couldn't fight the Avon army on even, open ground.

A pop and flash, and a smell of sulfur, came out of the tree above them, and they looked up just as Brind'Amour, materializing on a branch above and to the side, found his intended perch too slippery and tumbled to the ground.

The old wizard hopped up, slapping his hands together and straightening his robes as though he had intended the dive all along. "Well," he said cheerily, "are you ready for the day's fight?"

Katerin and Oliver stared at the happy wizard incredulously.

"Fear not!" Brind'Amour informed them. "Our enemies are not so many, and not so good. They are hungry and weary and a long, long way from home. Come along, then, to the horses and to the front ranks."

Oliver and Katerin couldn't understand the man's lightheartedness, for they did not know that the wizard had been watching through the night and the morning with far-seeing, magical eyes. Brind'Amour had known of the cyclopian pivot for some time, and he knew, too, about the secret friends perched in the south.

No need to tell Oliver and Katerin, Brind'Amour figured. Not yet.

Katerin brushed a lock of drenched hair back from her face and looked at Oliver. They exchanged helpless shrugs—Brind'Amour seemed to know what he was doing—retrieved their mounts, and followed the wizard. All the Port Charley camp came astir then, digging into defensible positions, preparing to meet the cyclopian charge.

"I do hope he has some big booms ready for them," Oliver said to Katerin after the wizard left them in the front ranks. The halfling stared across the open ground at the masses of black and silver.

"They are not so many," Katerin replied sarcastically, for the cyclopian force dwarfed them four to one, at least.

"Very big booms," Oliver remarked.

It seemed fitting to them both that the storm intensified with a burst of snow just as the cyclopians began their roaring charge.

To their credit, the hardy fisherfolk of Port Charley did not break ranks and flee. Word filtered down the line that a cyclopian group had indeed entrenched on the eastern riverbank, and it seemed as if the roaring mass of enemies would simply plow over them. But they did not flee. Their bowstrings took up a humming song, and the folk began to sing, too, thinking this to be their last stand.

Brind'Amour stood back from the front ranks, his skinny white arms uplifted to the sky, head tilted far back and eyes closed as he reached out with his magic toward the storm, to the energy of the thick clouds. Many of those simple fisherfolk about him were afraid, for they did not know of magic and had grown up all of their lives hearing that it was a devil-sent power. Still, none dared to try to interrupt the wizard's spell, and old Dozier, who remembered a time before Greensparrow, stayed close to the wizard, trying to comfort and reassure his frightened comrades.

Brind'Amour felt as if his entire body was elongating, stretching up to the sky. Of course it was not, but his spirit was indeed soaring high, reaching into those clouds and grasping and gathering the energy, focusing it, shaping it, and then hurling it down in the form of a lightning bolt into the front ranks of the charging cyclopians.

Black- and silver-clad bodies rebounded with the shock. One unfortunate brute took the blow full force, his metal armor crackling with blue sparks.

"Oh, that was very good!" Oliver congratulated. He looked up to his right, to Katerin on Riverdancer, sitting much higher than he. She wasn't watching the scene ahead, wasn't even looking back over her shoulder at the wizard. Rather, she was looking left, over Oliver, to the south.

"Not as good as that!" she replied.

Oliver spun about just as the horns sounded, just as Luthien's cavalry led the charge. The halfling spotted four plumes of black smoke as the dwarfs lit the logs, so soaked with oil that they defied the storm. Ropes had been strung around flat-headed pegs on each end of those logs, two dwarfs holding on to each end, running blindly, full out down the slope, rushing down with their rolling, burning rams.

"Luthien," Katerin whispered.

"I really do love the man," Oliver declared.

"So do I," Katerin said, under her breath, but Oliver caught every word, and he smiled, warmed by the thought (and more than a little jealous of his sandy-haired friend!).

The cyclopian formation became a mass of madness. The brutes fell all over each other trying to get out of the way; many hurled spears or even threw their swords in sheer desperation.

But the sturdy dwarfs held true to their course, came right up to the brutes before letting go of the logs, bowling down dozens of the one-eyes.

Right behind the dwarfs, firing bows as they came, charged Siobhan and her kin and the many men and women of Caer MacDonald. There was no way to stop on the slippery turf, but the force had no intention of stopping, or even slowing. They barreled on, their sheer momentum trampling down many enemies and sending many more running from the battle.

Tucked in the center of the line near the back of the cyclopian formation, Belsen'Krieg watched in pure frustration. The ugly general had never dreamed that the humans would be daring enough to come out of Montfort.

Another lightning bolt exploded among his troops. It killed only a few, but struck terror into the hearts of all those nearby. The battle had just begun, the folk of Port Charley hadn't even joined in yet, but Belsen'Krieg recognized the danger. His soldiers were exhausted and weak from hunger. He had lost some to desertion during the night, something practically unheard of in the Praetorian Guard. They needed a victory now, and Belsen'Krieg had thought he would gain one, an easy one, against the small encampment.

So he had thought.

Another bolt from the skies jolted the ground near the cyclopian leader, close enough so that he was splattered with the blood of a blasted brute.

The huge one-eye took up his sword. He focused on the battle that was drawing near; with typical cyclopian savagery, Belsen'Krieg decided to lead by example.

He encountered his first enemy a minute later. A quick pass with his ponypig, a quick swipe with his sword, and the brute moved on, his weapon dripping blood.

Luthien's group of a hundred and seventy cavalry were the first to hit the cyclopian line. Like those running behind them, the riders couldn't hope to slow down on the slick slope, and so they didn't try, using the sheer bulk of their strong mounts to run down the first ranks of one-eyes.

There were no targets to pick, only a mass to slash at, and Luthien did just that, connecting on every swing, cleaving helms and skulls, turning his horse this way and that, stabbing at anything that moved below him. He heard the shrieks of terror to the east, the rumble of the burning, rolling logs, and the screams as the bearded folk loosed their fury. He heard the hum of bowstrings and the clang of steel against steel and knew that all his forces had come crashing in.

A lightning bolt jolted the ground, another soon after, and Luthien, who had witnessed the fury of wizards, was glad that Brind'Amour was on his side.

Then, from up front came more screams, more ringing steel, and Luthien understood that the Port Charley folk had joined. He thought of Oliver and Katerin, on Threadbare and Riverdancer, and he hoped that his friends would survive.

But these were all fleeting, distant thoughts to the young Bedwyr, for the sea of black and silver churned below him. He took a hit on his thigh, a glancing blow that stung his horse more than it stung him. Luthien brought *Blind-Striker* whipping about, looking to pay the brute back. But the one-eye was already gone, had already moved along in the tangle. No problem for Luthien, though, for many other enemies were within striking distance. His great sword rushed down, smashing the side of a helmet with enough force to snap the neck of the creature wearing it.

And so it went for many minutes. A third of the horsemen had been pulled down, but many more cyclopians than that were dead around them, and many more scrambled to get away.

Luthien pressed on, followed the mass, hacking with abandon. Every so often he yelled out, "Eriador free!" and he sighed every time he was answered, every time he found confirmation that he had not been totally separated from his comrades.

It was not a long battle—not like the assault on Caer MacDonald's walls, or even like the swirling mass within the courtyard after the gates had been breached. The cyclopians, their morale low, seeing an easy victory become something terrible, broke apart wherever they were hit hard, scattering, trying to re-form into some defensive posture. But each time, they were hit again by the fierce Eriadorans; each time, their pocket formations were blasted apart.

By the time the cyclopians had come to fully understand the weight of the unexpected force from the south, several hundred were dead, and the presence of a wizard among the ranks of the fisherfolk, indeed a very powerful wizard, struck terror into their hearts. They had grown up under Greensparrow, the personal force of the wizard-king, and they knew.

They knew.

There was more organization and more determination wherever Belsen'Krieg and his mounted undercommanders made their appearance, but even the huge one-eyed general understood this disaster. He kept hoping that the three thousand across the river would join in, but that was not what he had instructed them to do. Belsen'Krieg recognized the limitations of his own race. The Praetotian Guard were fabulous soldiers, disciplined and brave (for cyclopians), but they did not improvise. They were led by a single figurehead, in this case Belsen'Krieg, and they moved as extensions of his will to direct and straightforward commands. Those brutes across the river had been told to dig in and hold the ground, and so they would, sitting there stupidly while the main force was massacred on the field.

The cyclopian general spotted Luthien and the Caer MacDonald cavalry, chopping his ranks apart directly south of his position. As soon as he recognized the young Bedwyr, the crimson-caped man from the river, Belsen'Krieg understood who had precipitated this ambush. As Luthien had recognized him as the cyclopian general, so he recognized Luthien's authority.

The cyclopian was too filled with rage to tip his shining helm at his cunning adversary. He wanted to pound his ponypig over to Luthien and chop the man down! But Belsen'Krieg was smarter than that. His formation, the classic military square at the start of the charge, was no more, and he could not reorganize any significant portion of his frightened and weary force. Not now. Not with the press from two sides and a wizard hurling lightning from the skies.

He thought of gathering as many as he could and charging straight to the east, toward the river, in an attempt to link up with his other force, but the scouts he sent out among the ranks came back shaking their ugly heads, for the main host from Caer MacDonald had come in at the southeastern corner and had already joined with the folk of Port Charley.

Belsen'Krieg looked again to the south, spotted Luthien for just a moment, crimson cape flying, sword swinging high. *That one again*, the cyclopian thought. *That miserable human has done this, all of this.*

The word came from Belsen'Krieg then, a command the Praetorian Guard were not used to following. "Run away!"

Luthien gradually came out of the mass of fighters, or rather, the mass gradually diminished about him. He had to work harder to search out targets then, and whenever he spotted a cyclopian, he kicked his horse into a short gallop and ran the brute down.

He was bearing down on one such enemy, the cyclopian's back to him, when the creature lurched over and groaned, apparently grabbing at its groin. Out from the side came a familiar, dashing halfling, the wide brim of his hat drooping low under the weight of snow.

Oliver ran about the brute, stabbing it repeatedly with his rapier.

Luthien was thrilled and surprised, so much so that he hardly noticed a second brute coming in at the halfling's back.

"Oliver!" he cried out, and he feared that he was too late.

But the ever-alert halfling was not caught unawares. He spun away from the brute he was fighting, down to one knee, and stabbed as the cyclopian whipped its sword high above his head. The rapier tip sank deep, into the one-eye's groin. Like its companion before it, the brute bent low and groaned, and Oliver's next thrust put a clean hole in its throat.

The halfling looked up then, as Luthien's horse pounded by, the young Bedwyr finishing off the first cyclopian Oliver had stung with one vicious swipe of *Blind-Striker*.

"I have lost my horse!" Oliver cried at his friend.

"Behind you!" came Luthien's reply as yet another Praetorian Guard, a huge cyclopian brandishing a spiked club, charged at Oliver's back.

Oliver whirled about and dropped; Luthien charged by, slicing his sword up at the brute. To its credit, the cyclopian got its club up to deflect *Blind-Striker*, though

Luthien's momentum as his mount passed ripped the weapon from the one-eye's hand. The brute couldn't block Oliver's thrust, again low, aimed at that most sensitive of areas.

Luthien turned and finished the defenseless cyclopian as it doubled over.

"Why do you keep hitting them there?" demanded Luthien, a bit disgusted by Oliver's tendency for low blows.

"Oh," huffed the halfling as though he was wounded by the accusation. "If you were my size, you would swing for the eyeball?" Luthien's shoulders drooped and he sighed, and Oliver snapped his fingers in the young Bedwyr's direction.

"Besides," Oliver said coyly, "I thought you were fond of cabarachee shots." Luthien's eyes narrowed as he caught the reference to Katerin that night in the Dwelf. "This one-eye," Oliver pressed on, "perhaps he will fall in love with me." The snickering halfling glanced down at the brute, dead on the field. He shrugged and looked back at Luthien. "Well, perhaps he would have."

A rush of cavalry stormed past the friends then, one rider skidding his horse to a stop near Luthien. "The one-eye leaders," the man said breathlessly, "on ponypigs, getting away!"

Luthien turned his mount about and reached down to take Oliver's hand.

"But my pony!" the halfling protested as Luthien yanked him up behind the saddle. Oliver gave a shrill whistle and peered all about, but the snow was thicker now, blowing fiercely, and the yellow pony could not be seen.

The battle had stretched out along the fields far to the north, with the cyclopians in full flight. Luthien and his cavalry group, some twenty riders, ignored the running cyclopian infantry, concentrating instead on catching up to the ponypigs.

Ponypigs could move well, especially on the muddy fields, but not as well as horses, and soon Belsen'Krieg and his dozen remaining escorts were in sight.

On came the cavalry, crying for Eriador and Caer MacDonald. The cyclopian leaders knew that they were caught, knew that they could not outrun the horses, and so they turned, ready to meet the charge.

Luthien saw the huge one-eyed general, and Belsen'Krieg saw him. It seemed somehow as if they were removed from the field then, or that all of the others were, for the young Bedwyr put his mount in line, and so did the cyclopian leader, and no fighter on either side moved to intercept or interfere.

Luthien pulled up; so did Belsen'Krieg. They sat staring at each other, hating each other.

"Get off," Luthien said to Oliver.

The halfling considered the huge cyclopian, barely a dozen yards away. Oliver could see the hatred between these two, the rivalry, leader against leader. "Time to go," he agreed, and rolled off the rump of Luthien's mount, turning a complete somersault to land gingerly on his feet—well, almost, for he hit a particularly slick patch of ground and his feet flew out from under him, landing him unceremoniously on his backside. The embarrassed halfling glanced around, near to panic, but none of the others took any notice.

"Caer MacDonald!" Luthien growled at the cyclopian leader.

Belsen'Krieg tilted his huge head as he considered the words, then brightened with understanding. "Montfort," he corrected.

Luthien yelled out and charged; Belsen'Krieg pacing his every move. Their great swords rang loudly as they passed, with no substantial damage, though Luthien's arm tingled from the weight of the cyclopian's blow.

Oliver realized a problem then. He was standing alone in the middle of the field, and suddenly the huge brute was closer to him than was Luthien! The halfling whimpered and considered his rapier, seeming so puny against that mounted monstrosity, but to his ultimate relief, the brute did not even notice him, just wheeled the ponypig about and began the second pass.

Again their swords slashed across up high, connecting in the air between them. But Luthien had changed his grip this time, and *Blind-Striker* rotated down with the momentum of Belsen'Krieg's mighty swing, Luthien ducking and nearly getting his head shaved as the cyclopian's blade barreled through.

The agile Bedwyr had allowed his sword to roll right out of his hand, and he caught it almost immediately, his grip reversed. He thrust it straight out, aiming at Belsen'Krieg's thigh, but he wasn't quite quick enough and *Blind-Striker* drove deep into the ponypig's flank instead.

The powerful mount rambled past and Luthien had to let go of his reins and grab his sword hilt in both hands to avoid losing the weapon. He did hold on to the blade, and it did tear free of the passing ponypig, but Luthien got yanked from his horse in the process. He splashed down in the muddy field, struggling up in time to see Belsen'Krieg extracting himself from his downed mount.

"Now you die!" the cyclopian promised, stalking over without the slightest hesitation. The brutish general's great sword slashed, then came in a rapid backhand, and Luthien barely got his weapon up to parry.

Belsen'Krieg pressed the attack with an overhand chop and a straight thrust; Luthien blocked and hopped aside at the last moment.

The cyclopian came on savagely, but Luthien was up to the task, letting Belsen'Krieg play out his rage, deflecting or dodging every attack. Every once in a while, the young Bedwyr found a slight opening and *Blind-Striker* penetrated Belsen'Krieg's defenses, but the young Bedwyr had to be quick and retract the blade immediately, ready to block the next vicious attack.

Though Luthien saw the thin lines of blood on his adversary, he understood that he was really doing very little damage. He felt like a buzzing wasp biting at a giant, an impossible match. Luthien pushed down any ensuing panic, telling himself that the wasp could win.

But only if it was perfect.

It went on for some time, Luthien dodging and stinging, but Belsen'Krieg seemed to feel nothing, and his attacks did not slow with exhaustion. This one was good, Luthien realized, far better than any cyclopian he had ever faced. And strong! Luthien knew that if he missed a single parry, if this brute connected even once, he would be cleaved in half.

And then it happened; Luthien, circling, stepped on a patch of uneven ice and skidded down to one knee. Belsen'Krieg was on him immediately, the great sword chopping down.

Up came *Blind-Striker*, horizontally above Luthien's head. Belsen'Krieg's sword hit it near the hilt and was stopped, but Luthien's arm buckled under the tremendous weight of the blow and he dropped his blade. He wasn't seriously wounded, he believed, but the pain was intense.

He grabbed up *Blind-Striker* in his left hand and thrust ahead, trying to force the one-eyed monster back. He got Belsen'Krieg in the belly, but not enough to stop the brute.

Luthien scrambled to get his blade up, but was knocked forward suddenly, as someone, something, ran up his back.

Springing from Luthien's shoulders, Oliver caught Belsen'Krieg by surprise. The cyclopian's eye widened, a wonderful target, but Oliver, off balance as Luthien slid to the side, missed it, his rapier stabbing Belsen'Krieg's cheek instead.

The cyclopian screamed and flailed his huge arms, falling back from the fight. He straightened out as Luthien and Oliver picked themselves up, standing side by side.

"You are a one-eyed, ugly thing," Oliver taunted. "You would not know the value of friends!"

As if to accentuate the halfling's point (and Oliver had timed things that way), a shining white stallion, long coat glistening with wetness, thundered right behind the cyclopian, slamming the huge brute across the shoulders and launching him headlong, face-first into the mud.

Belsen'Krieg came up sputtering to find himself surrounded by Luthien and Oliver, and now Katerin O'Hale, magnificent atop Riverdancer, her red hair darkened with wetness and snow gathering on her shoulders. Her smile was wide and bright, her green eyes sparkling more than the ice crystals forming at the ends of her thick hair, as she considered the situation, the victory that was won this day.

Belsen'Krieg looked about for support. He saw his last undercommander lurch over and slide slowly off a ponypig, its falling bulk revealing the victorious horseman behind it, sword red with blood. More than a dozen of Luthien's cavalry remained, along with the few Katerin had brought with her, including one slight woman riding a yellow pony that had little hair in its tail.

Oliver grinned at the sight of his beloved Threadbare, but turned serious at once when he faced the cyclopian leader.

"I think you should surrender," he remarked.

Belsen'Krieg looked around for a long while. Luthien could practically hear the creature's thoughts—the caged animal looking for an escape. There was none to be found. Luthien wasn't sure what Belsen'Krieg would do, which way the brute would turn, but then, unexpectedly, the one-eye threw his huge sword to the ground.

As one, the group relaxed, Luthien taking a stride toward the cyclopian leader. His sword arm still ached, but not so much that he could not take up *Blind-Striker*, flexing his muscles and grimacing through the pain.

Out came a knife, and daring, wild Belsen'Krieg charged ahead.

"Luthien!" Katerin and Oliver yelled together. Before the word had even left their mouths, Luthien's free left hand whipped across, catching the cyclopian by the wrist. Luthien could hardly move Belsen'Krieg's massive arm, but he used the support to shift himself instead, inside the angle of the rushing dagger. And as he moved, his own sword jabbed ahead, creasing Belsen'Krieg's breastplate, cutting through the armor, into the brute's lungs.

They held the macabre pose for a long moment, then Belsen'Krieg growled—and the mouths of those witnessing the event dropped open in disbelief—and began forcing his knife hand toward the young Bedwyr.

Luthien tucked his shoulder down against his sword hand and jerked at the blade, and Belsen'Krieg's movement came to an abrupt halt. Again they held the pose, unblinking, their faces barely a few inches apart.

"One up," Luthien growled, and the dying Belsen'Krieg had no response, for indeed the young Bedwyr had been one step ahead of him throughout the battle.

Luthien jerked his blade again, then felt it sinking down as Belsen'Krieg's legs slowly buckled, bringing the brute to his knees. Luthien felt the strength go out of Belsen'Krieg's massive arm; the knife dropped to the ground.

Luthien pulled *Blind-Striker* free, but even without the support, Belsen'Krieg fell no farther. The dead cyclopian leader knelt on the field.

Already the snow began to gather about him.

CHAPTER 17

IMPLICATIONS

THE BATTLE—THE rout—ended swiftly, with half of Belsen'Krieg's force killed and the other half running off blindly into the open fields. Losses to the Eriadorans were remarkably light; the folk of Port Charley could count their dead on the fingers of six hands, though Luthien's group, which had thrown itself into the cyclopian throng, was more battered.

Both Eriadoran armies gathered back together on the field near to where the Port Charley encampment had been. They tended their wounded, finished off any cyclopians who were sorely hurt, and put all the one-eye prisoners in line. Fortunately there weren't many prisoners, less than a hundred altogether, and these, having seen their proud Praetorian Guards routed so horribly, were little trouble.

The storm grew around them all, the day darkening, though it was near to noon. Brind'Amour organized the march with all of his archers in front. They fought a small skirmish as they crossed Felling Run, a couple of volleys of arrows mostly. The cyclopians responded by hurling heavy spears, but, with typical cyclopian accuracy, not a single Eriadoran was hit.

There wasn't much fight left in those entrenched Avon soldiers—they were beginning to break and flee before the Eriadorans ever got to the river. For the rest of that day, the biggest obstacle facing the army of Eriador was in getting back to the shelter of Caer MacDonald as the blizzard came on in full about them.

Back on Riverdancer, Luthien heard the cheers as he approached the walled city, for news of the rout had preceded the returning army. The young Bedwyr had lost a couple of friends this day, a woman and two men who frequented the Dwelf, but his sadness was tempered in the belief that his friends had not died in vain. They had won the day; Eriador had won the day! The victorious army along with their allies of Port Charley poured into the city, scattering among the streets, breaking up into small groups that they might recount the day's glorious events.

Luthien, Katerin, and Oliver went back to the apartment in Tiny Alcove to catch up on the events of the last few weeks. The young Bedwyr was thrilled to see his dearest friends again, particularly Katerin. He hadn't realized how much he had missed the woman. Of course he thought of Siobhan and their encounter the previous evening, but he hadn't really yet figured out what it all meant.

All that Luthien knew at the time was that he was glad, so glad, to see Katerin O'Hale once more.

Some time later, they were joined at the apartment by Brind'Amour, Siobhan, and Shuglin, who had also been quite busy that day.

"We killed every cyclopian running the streets of Caer MacDonald," the dwarf assured them. "No more fires."

Brind'Amour, reclining in the most comfortable of the three chairs in the small sitting room, hoisted a cup of wine in toast to that welcome news. Siobhan and Oliver, likewise seated and sipping wine, joined in, as did the other three, hoisting mugs of golden honey mead.

Seated on the stone hearth, Luthien looked across the open fireplace at Katerin, and they were warmed by more than the flames that burned between them.

"Well," Shuglin corrected himself, shifting closer to the hearth, "no more *unwanted* fires!"

That brought a slight chuckle from the group.

"We still have several thousand cyclopians running free across the countryside," Oliver remarked.

"Out in the blizzard," Katerin snorted.

"We will catch those who survive the storm," Siobhan said grimly.

Luthien nodded; on the way back into Caer MacDonald, pursuit groups had been arranged. The fleeing cyclopians would be hunted down.

"There are no towns nearby, except for Felling Downs," Siobhan went on. "And the brutes will find no shelter there, for the houses have all been razed. Likely, they will turn for Port Charley."

Luthien was hardly listening, more concerned with the half-elf's serious tone. The hard day's battle had been won, but Siobhan would not allow herself a break in the intensity. Yes, for Siobhan the rebellion was paramount, all-consuming. She would do whatever it took to free Eriador and free her people from Greensparrow.

Whatever it took, like bedding the Crimson Shadow? Luthien shook the notion away the moment he thought of it, scolding himself for thinking so little of Siobhan. There was something real between himself and the half-elf, something wonderful and warm, and though they both knew that it would never be more than it was now, Luthien vowed then and there that he would not look back on his lost relationship with Siobhan with doubt or remorse. He was a better man for knowing her; his life was happier because she remained a part of it. And in looking at her now, Luthien believed with all his heart that she felt the same way.

He turned his gaze from Siobhan, who continued talking of the duties still before them, across the hearth to Katerin. She had been staring at him, he realized, for she blushed (something rarely seen on Katerin's tanned cheeks) and turned her green eyes away.

Luthien gave a small smile to hide the pain and closed his eyes, holding fast his image of the woman from Hale as he rested his head back. He dozed then, as the conversation continued, even intensified, about him.

"Our fearless leader," Oliver remarked dryly, noticing Luthien's pose and rhythmic breathing.

All five had a laugh at Luthien's expense. Katerin reached across to shake him.

"Let him sleep," Siobhan bade her. Immediate tension filled the air between the two women as Katerin turned to regard the half-elf.

"He has labored day and night," Siobhan went on, ignoring the woman's visage, an expression that revealed the rivalry between the two.

Katerin straightened and dropped her arm to her side.

"Well, of course those cyclopians who fled this day will be of little consequence," Brind'Amour interjected, somewhat loudly and importantly, forcing all eyes to turn to him. "Many will die in the storm and those who do not will be in little condition to fight back when we catch up with them. They'll make to the west, of course, to their fleet, which is no longer their fleet!"

"Can Port Charley resist them?" Oliver asked in all seriousness, for most of that town's hardy souls were in Caer MacDonald.

"Few cyclopians will ever get there," Siobhan promised.

"And we'll get enough fighters there before the brutes arrive," Brind'Amour was quick to add. "They will be dogged every step, and we know the faster ways. No, they'll be little trouble. The army of Avon that came to our shores is defeated."

"But what does that mean?" Shuglin asked the question that was on everyone's mind.

Dead silence. In considering the long-term implications of this day's victory, each of them realized that it might, after all, be only a small thing, a flickering reprieve in the darkness that was Greensparrow.

"It means that we have won a battle," Brind'Amour said at length. "And now we have a fleet to hinder any further invasion through Port Charley.

"But Greensparrow will take us more seriously now," the wizard warned. "The snow is deep, and that favors us and awards us some time, but the days are warmer now and it will not last for long. We can expect an army marching out from Malpuissant's Wall soon after the melt, and likely another force coming through the passes of the Iron Cross, both of them greater than the force we just defeated on the field."

What had been a celebration quickly dissolved, stolen by the grim dwarf's necessary question and the obvious truth of the wizard's reminder.

Brind'Amour scrutinized each of his companions. These five, he knew, were representative of the Eriadorans. There was Katerin, proud Katerin, desperate for a return to the days of Eriador's freedom, Eriador's glory. Most of the islanders were like her—on Bedwydrin, Marvis, and Caryth—as were the folk of Port Charley and the tribes north of Eradoch, in the area of Bae Colthwyn.

There was Siobhan, angry Siobhan, stung by injustice and consumed by thoughts of revenge. So representative of the sophisticated people of Montfort—no, Caer MacDonald; it could be called that now—the wizard thought. She was the architect of it all, the cunning behind the rebellion, proud, but not too proud to allow the intrusions of a wizard when she understood that those intrusions would benefit her people.

There was Shuglin, whose people had suffered most of all. This one had moved past anger, Brind'Amour knew, and past resignation. Those dwarfs who had died in their suicidal ambush out by the fallen wall had been neither angry nor sad. They did as they believed they had to do, in the simple hope that Eriador, and their people, would have a better lot for their sacrifice. There he was, that blue-bearded dwarf, the purest of soldiers. Brind'Amour believed that if he had ten thousand like Shuglin, he could sweep Greensparrow and all of Avon from the face of the world.

There was Oliver, the epitome of Eriador's many foreign rogues. The rough land was a favored destination for those who could not fit in, either in Avon or Gascony, or even in lands farther removed. Oliver's value on the field could not be doubted, nor could his value as Luthien's trusted companion. But the true worth of Oliver, and of the many others who would no doubt surface as the rebellion spread, would be found in his knowledge of other places and other people. Should this rebellion, this war, reach a level where Gascony saw fit to become involved, Oliver's understanding of that place would prove invaluable. Oliver the diplomat? Brind'Amour considered that possibility for some time.

And there, last, was Luthien, still dozing with his back against the stone of the hearth. He was all of them, Brind'Amour realized. Proud as an islander, angry as one of Caer MacDonald, a pure, unselfish soldier, and the figurehead that Eriador desperately needed. After his exploits in the battle, Luthien had become undeniably the cornerstone on which Eriador would succeed or fail. Already the tale of "Luthien's Gamble" was spreading far from the city walls, mingling with the stories of the Crimson Shadow, the mysterious enemy to all that evil Greensparrow represented. Who would have guessed that the young man from Bedwydrin could rise so fast to such notoriety?

"I would have!" Brind'Amour answered his own question suddenly, and unintentionally, aloud. Embarrassed, the wizard cleared his throat many times and glanced about.

"What was that?" Luthien asked, stretching as he came awake.

"Nothing, nothing," the wizard apologized. "Just exercising my jaw at the mind's request, you know."

The others shrugged and let it go at that, except for shrewd Oliver, who kept his gaze on the wizard as though he was reading Brind'Amour's every thought.

"You know," the halfling began, drawing everyone's attention, "I was once in the wild land of Angarothe." Seeing that his proclamation apparently didn't impress anybody, the halfling quickly explained. "A hot and dusty land some distance to the south of Gascony."

"The War of Angar?" inquired Brind'Amour, more worldly than the others, despite the fact that he had spent most of the last few centuries asleep in a cave.

"War of anger?" Luthien snickered.

"Angar," Oliver corrected, appearing insulted. "Indeed," he answered the wizard. "I fought with deBoise himself, in the Fourth Regiment of Cabalaise."

The wizard cocked an eyebrow and nodded, seeming impressed, though the reference meant absolutely nothing to the others in the room. Oliver puffed with pride and looked about, but quickly deflated as he realized the ignorance of his audience.

"The Fourth of Cabalaise," he said with some importance. "We were in deepest Angarothe, behind the Red Lancers, the largest and most terrible of that country's armies."

Brind'Amour met the curious gaze of each of the others and nodded his understanding, lending gravity to Oliver's tale, though the wizard highly doubted that Oliver had ever been anywhere near to Angarothe. Few Gascons who had gone to that wild land had ever returned. But Brind'Amour did know the tale of deBoise and the Fourth, one of the classic victories in the history of warfare.

"We could not win," Oliver went on. "We were two hundred against several thousand, and not one of us thought that we would come out of there alive."

"And what did you do?" Luthien asked after a long and dramatic pause, giving the halfling the necessary prompt.

Oliver snapped his fingers in the air and blew a cocky whistle. "We attacked, of course."

"He speaks truly," Brind'Amour interjected before the expressions of profound doubt could grow on the faces of the other four. "DeBoise spread his line along the foliage marking the perimeter of the enemy encampment, each man with a drum. They used sticks to bang against trees, imitated the calls of huge elephants and other such warbeasts, all to make their enemy believe that they were many more, an entire army."

"The Red Lancers were weary of battle," Oliver added. "And they had no good ground to wage such a fight. And so they retreated to a mountain."

"DeBoise watched them and dogged them with empty threats, every step," Brind'Amour finished. "By the time the leaders of the Red Lancers came to understand the bluff, the Fourth had found the reinforcements it needed. The Red Lancers of Angarothe came off the mountain, thinking to overwhelm the small force, but were themselves overwhelmed. The only Gascon victory of the campaign."

Oliver turned a sour look on the old man at that last statement, but it melted away quickly, the halfling too eager to announce his own part in the strategic coup. "They wanted to call it Oliver's Bluff," he asserted.

Brind'Amour did well to hide his chuckle.

"A fine tale," Shuglin said, obviously not too impressed.

"But does it have a point?" Katerin wanted to know.

Oliver huffed and shook his head as though the question was ridiculous. "Are we not like the Fourth Regiment of Cabalaise?" he asked.

"Say it plainly," Shuglin demanded.

"We attack, of course," Oliver replied without hesitation. That widened more than a few eyes! Oliver paid no heed to their incredulity, but looked at the wizard, where he suspected he would find some support.

Brind'Amour nodded and smiled—he had been hoping all along that one of the others would make that very suggestion and save him the trouble. The wizard realized that he was more valuable agreeing with plans than in convincing the rebels to follow plans he had constructed.

Katerin rose from the hearth and slapped her hands against the back of her dusty breeches. "Attack where?" she demanded, obviously thinking the whole notion ridiculous.

"Attack the wall," Brind'Amour answered. "Malpuissant's Wall, before Greensparrow can run his army of Princetown north."

Suddenly the prospect didn't seem so absurd to Luthien. "Take Dun Caryth and cut the land in half," he put in. "With the mountains and the wall, and a fleet to guard our ports, we will force Greensparrow to attack us on ground of our choosing."

"And the daring conquest will make him think that we are stronger than we are," Oliver added slyly.

Siobhan's green eyes sparkled with hope. "And stronger we shall be," she asserted, "when the northern lands learn of our victory here, when all of Eriador realizes the truth of the rebellion." She looked around at the others, practically snarling with eagerness. "When all of Eriador comes to hope."

"Oliver's Bluff?" Brind'Amour offered.

No one disagreed and the halfling beamed—for just a moment. Suddenly it occurred to Oliver, who of course had not really been with deBoise in Angarothe, that he had set them all on a most daring and dangerous course. He cleared his throat, and his expression revealed his anxiety. "I do fear," he admitted, and felt the weight of Luthien's gaze, and Siobhan's, Shuglin's, and Katerin's as well, upon his little round shoulders. "They have wizard types," the halfling went on, trying to justify his sudden turn. He felt that he had to show some doubt to avoid blame in the face of potential disaster. But if this did go off, and especially if it proved successful, the halfling dearly wanted it to be known as Oliver's Bluff. "I am not so keen on the idea of daring a group of wizard-types."

Brind'Amour waved the argument away. "Magic is not what it used to be, my dear Oliver," he assured the halfling, assured them all. "Else Morkney would have left Luthien in ashes atop the Ministry and left you frozen as a gargoyle on the side of the tower! And I would have been of more use on the field, I promise." There was conviction in the wizard's words. Ever since he had left the cave that had served for so long as his home, Brind'Amour had realized that the essence of magic had changed. It was still there, tingling in the air, though not nearly as strong as it had once been. The wizard understood the reason. Greensparrow's dealing with demons had perverted the art, had made it something dark and evil, and that, in turn, had weakened the very fabric of the universal tapestry, the source of magical power. Brind'Amour felt a deep lament at the loss, a nostalgia for the old days when a skilled wizard was so very powerful, when the finest of wizards could take on an entire army in the field and send them running. But Brind'Amour understood well enough that in this war with Greensparrow and the king's wizard-dukes, where he was the only wizard north of the mountains, an apparent lack of magical strength might be Eriador's only hope.

"To the wall, then," he said.

Luthien looked at Katerin, then to Shuglin, and finally, to Siobhan, but he needed no confirmation from his friends this time. Caer MacDonald was free, but it could not remain so if they waited for Greensparrow to make the next move. The war was a chess game and they were playing white.

It was time to move.

CHAPTER 18

WARM WELCOME

THE SNOW LET up the next day, leaving a blanket twenty inches deep across the southern fields of Eriador, with drifts that could swallow a man and his horse whole, without a trace.

A huge force left Caer MacDonald anyway, mostly comprised of the folk from Port Charley, in pursuit of those seven thousand Praetorian Guards who had fled the battle. Wearing sheepskin mittens and thick woollen cloaks, with many layers of stockings under their treated doeskin boots and carrying sacks of dry kindling, the Eriadorans were well equipped for the wintry weather, but those cyclopians who had run off most certainly were not. Tired and hungry, many of them wounded and weak from loss of blood, that first frozen and snowy night took a horrible toll. Before they had gone two miles from Caer MacDonald's gates, the Eriadorans came upon lines of frozen bodies and shivering, blue-lipped cyclopians, their hands too numb and swollen for them even to hold a weapon.

And so it began, a trail of prisoners soon stretching several miles back to Caer MacDonald's gates. By midafternoon, more than a thousand had come in, and returning couriers estimated that two or three times that number were dead on the snowy fields. Still, a large force remained, making a direct line for Port Charley.

Brind'Amour used his magical sight to locate them, and with the wizard directing the pursuers, many cyclopians were caught and slaughtered.

Undercommander Longsleeves, still carrying wounds from the bridge collapse and with the head of an elvish arrow stuck deep in his shoulder, led the main host of some three thousand Praetorian Guards. They were dogged every step and had not the strength to respond to the attack in any way. Somehow they persevered and trudged on, cannibalizing their own dead and hunching their backs against the stinging, blowing snow.

Soon they were down to two thousand, their numbers barely larger than the force pursuing them, but the weather improved steadily and the snow diminished by the hour. Purely out of fear, Longsleeves kept them moving, kept them driving, until at last the tall masts of the Avon ships in the harbor of Port Charley came into view.

Among the cyclopian ranks there was much rejoicing, though every one of them understood that with the city in sight the force pursuing them would likely come on in full.

What the Avon soldiers didn't realize was that, while they were eyeing the masts for salvation, spotters among the folk within Port Charley were eyeing the cyclopians, locating shots for the crews, who had become quite proficient with the catapults on the captured ships.

One by one, the vessels loosed their flaming pitch and baskets of sharpened stones. Longsleeves would have called out a command to charge the city, but as fate would have it, the very first volley, a burning ball of sticky black tar, buried the undercommander where he stood, burned away his pretty hair, pretty sleeves, and his muttonchops.

Confused and frightened, the leaderless one-eyed brutes ran every which way, some charging Port Charley, others turning back east, only to meet old Dozier and his army. The slaughter was over within the hour, and it took only one of the captured ships to sail the remaining cyclopians to the north, where the Diamondgate would serve as their prison.

Back in Caer MacDonald, the preparations for the march to Malpuissant's Wall were well under way. A two-pronged movement was decided upon. Shuglin and his kin would go into the Iron Cross to guard the passes and hopefully to locate more of their own to bring into the rebellion. The main force, led by Brind'Amour himself, would strike out around the perimeter of the mountains.

The sheer daring of the move became apparent as those days of preparation slipped by. The force would not be so large, with the folk of Port Charley back in their city, and with so many dead and wounded. The Praetorian Guards, in such numbers, were simply too dangerous to be kept within the city, and so they, like their kin who had been caught on the field outside of Port Charley, would be carted west and then shipped north to the Diamondgate, from which there could be no escape.

That gave Luthien and Brind'Amour only a few thousand soldiers to work with, and it became quite apparent that Oliver's Bluff would depend upon how many reinforcements the Eriadorans might find as the days wore on. Word was spreading to the more northern towns, they knew, and cheers reverberated across the countryside for the freeing of Caer MacDonald. But they were asking much if they expected many farmers to come and join in the cause. The planting season was fast approaching, as was the prime fishing season for those Eriadorans who made their living at sea. And even with the stunning victories, both in taking the city, then in holding it against an army of Praetorian Guards, the Eriadorans had lived long enough under the evil Greensparrow's rule to understand that this fight was a long way from won.

"Oliver and I will go," Luthien announced to Brind'Amour one morning as the two walked the city wall, observing the preparations, overseeing the assembly of wagons and the mounds of supplies.

The wizard turned a curious eye on the young man. "Go?" he asked.

"Out before the army," Luthien explained. "On a more northerly arc."

"To roust up support," the wizard reasoned, then went very quiet, considering the notion.

"I will not be secretive about who I am," Luthien said. "I go openly as the Crimson Shadow, an enemy of the throne."

"There are many cyclopians scattered among those hamlets," Brind'Amour reminded. "And many merchants and knights sympathetic to Greensparrow."

"Only because they prosper under the evil king while the rest of Eriador suffers!" Luthien said, his jaw tight, his expression almost feral.

"Whatever the reason," Brind'Amour replied.

"I know the folk of Eriador," Luthien declared. "The true folk of Eriador. If they do not kill the cyclopians, or the merchants, it is only because they have no hope, because they believe that no matter how many they kill, many more will come to exact punishment upon them and their families."

"Not so unreasonable a fear," Brind'Amour said. The wizard was merely playing the role of nay-sayer now; he had already come to the conclusion that Luthien's little addition to the march was a fine move, a daring addendum to a daring plan. And they would likely need the help. Malpuissant's Wall had been built by the Gascons centuries before to guard against just such a rebellion, when the southern kingdom, after conquering Avon, had decided that it could not tame savage Eriador. The wall had been built for defense against the northern tribes, and would be no easy target!

"But now they will know hope," Luthien reasoned. "That is the measure of the Crimson Shadow, nothing more. What I do while wearing the cape long ago became unimportant. All that matters is that I wear the cape, that I let them think I am some hero of old returned to lead them to their freedom."

Brind'Amour stared long and hard at Luthien, and the young man became uncomfortable under that familiar scrutiny. Gradually the wizard's face brightened, and he seemed to Luthien then like a father, as Luthien hoped his father would be.

In all the excitement of the last few weeks, Luthien realized that he had hardly considered Gahris Bedwyr since Katerin's arrival with *Blind-Striker*, the Bedwyr family sword, bearing news that the rebellion was on in full on Isle Bedwydrin. How fared Gahris now? Luthien had to wonder. Homesickness tugged at him, but a mere thought of Ethan, his brother whom Gahris had sent away to die, and of Garth Rogar, Luthien's barbarian friend, ordered slain in the arena after Luthien had defeated him, stole that notion. Luthien had left Isle Bedwydrin, had left Gahris, for good reason, and now frantic events gave him little time to worry about the man he no longer considered to be his father.

He looked at Brind'Amour in a different light. Suddenly the young Bedwyr needed this wise old man's approval, needed to see him smile as Gahris had smiled whenever Luthien won in the arena.

And Brind'Amour did just that, and put his hand on Luthien's shoulder. "Ride out this day," he bade the young man.

"I will go to Bronegan, and all the way to the Fields of Eradoch," Luthien promised. "And when I return to you on the eastern edges of Glen Albyn, I will carry in my wake a force larger than the force which soon departs Caer MacDonald."

Brind'Amour nodded and clapped the younger Bedwyr on the back as Luthien sped off to find Oliver and their mounts that they might head out on the road.

The old wizard stood on the wall for some time watching Luthien, then watching nothing at all. He had set Luthien on this course long ago, the day in the dragon's cave when he had given the young man the crimson cape. He was responsible, in part at least, for the return of the Crimson Shadow, and when he considered Luthien now, so willing to take on the responsibility that had been thrust his way, Brind'Amour's old and wheezy chest swelled with pride.

The pride a father might have for his son.

CHAPTER 19

PASSAGE OF SPRING

"HE DOES THE right thing," Siobhan remarked, coming up on the wall beside Katerin. Katerin didn't turn to regard the half-elf, though she was surprised that Siobhan had chosen this particular section of the wall, so near to her.

Below the pair, Oliver and Luthien rode out from the gates, Oliver on his yellow pony and Luthien tall and proud on the shining white Riverdancer. They had already said their farewells, all that they had cared to make, and so they did not look back. Side by side, they trotted their mounts across the courtyard to the fallen outer wall, the area still dotted with several cyclopian corpses that the burial details hadn't been able to clear away, black-and-silver lumps in the diminishing snow.

"They have a long ride ahead of them," Siobhan remarked.

"Who?" Katerin asked.

Siobhan glanced at her skeptically and took note that her gaze was away to the east, to the horizon still pink with the new dawn. Pointedly, the proud woman did not look at Luthien.

"Our friends," Siobhan answered, playing the foolish, adolescent game.

Now Katerin did look to Luthien and Oliver, just a casual glance. "Luthien is always on the road," she answered. "This way and that, wherever his horse takes him."

Siobhan continued to study the woman, trying to fathom her purpose.

"That is his way," Katerin stated firmly, turning to look at the half-elf directly. "He goes where he chooses, when he chooses, and let no woman be fool enough to think that he will remain for her, or by her." Katerin looked away quickly, and that revealed more than she intended. "Let no woman be fool enough to think that she can change the ways of Luthien Bedwyr."

The words were said with perfect calm and control, but Siobhan easily read the underlying bitterness there. Katerin was hurting, and her cool demeanor was a complete façade, while her words had been uttered in just the right tones to make them a barbed arrow, shooting straight for the half-elf's heart. Rationally, Siobhan understood and knew that Katerin had spoken out of pain. In truth, the half-elf was not insulted or wounded in any way by Luthien's departure, for in her mind, she and the young Bedwyr had come to terms with the realities of their relationship.

Siobhan remained silent for a long moment, considered her sympathy for Katerin and the words the woman had just thrown her way. The verbal volley had been strictly out of self-defense, Siobhan knew, but still she was surprised that Katerin would attack her so, would go to the trouble of trying to make her feel worse about Luthien's departure.

"They have a long ride ahead of them," Siobhan said once again. "But fear not," she added, with enough dramatic emphasis to grab Katerin's gaze. "I do know that Luthien does well on long rides."

Katerin's jaw slackened at the half-elf's uncharacteristic use of double entendre and Siobhan's sly, even lewd, tone.

Siobhan turned and slipped easily down the ladder, leaving Katerin, and the specter of Luthien and Oliver riding away to the north and east.

Katerin looked back to the now-distant riders, to Luthien, her companion all those years back in Bedwydrin, where they had lost their innocence together, in the ways of the world and in the ways of love. She had wanted to hurt Siobhan, verbally if not physically. She cared for the half-elf, deeply respected her and in many ways called Siobhan a friend. But she could not ignore her feelings of jealousy.

She had lost the verbal joust. She knew that, standing up on Caer MacDonald's wall in the chill of an early spring day, watching Luthien ride away, her face scrunched in a feeble attempt to hold back the tears that welled in her shining green eyes.

"You are so very good at running from problems," Oliver remarked to Luthien when the two were far from Caer MacDonald's wall.

Luthien eyed his diminutive companion curiously, not understanding the comment. "Likely, we're running into trouble," he replied. "Not away from it."

"A fight with cyclopians is never trouble," Oliver explained. "Not the kind that you fear, at least."

Luthien eyed him suspiciously, guessing what was to come.

"But you have done so very well in avoiding the other kind, the more subtle and painful kind," Oliver explained. "First you send Katerin running off to Port Charley—"

"She volunteered," Luthien protested. "She demanded to go!"

"And now, you have arranged to be away for perhaps two weeks," the halfling continued without hesitation, ignoring Luthien's protests.

Those protests did not continue, for Luthien realized that he was guilty as charged.

"Ah, yes," Oliver chided. "Quite the hero with the sword, but in love, alas."

Luthien started to ask what the halfling might be gibbering about and deflect Oliver's intrusions, but he was wise enough to know that it was already too late for that. "How dare you?" the young Bedwyr asked sharply, and Oliver recognized that he had opened a wound. "What do you know of it?" Luthien demanded. "What do you know of anything?"

"I am so skilled and practiced in the ways of *amour*," the halfling replied coolly.

Luthien eyed his three-foot-tall companion, the young Bedwyr's expression clearly relating his doubts.

Oliver snorted indignantly. "Foolish boy," he said, snapping his fingers in the air. "In Gascony, it is said, a merchant is only as good as his purse, a warrior is only as good as his weapon, and a lover is only as good as—"

"Oliver!" Luthien interrupted, blushing fiercely.

"His heart," the halfling finished, looking curiously at his shocked companion. "Oh, you have become such a gutter-crawler!" Oliver scolded.

"I just thought . . ." Luthien stammered, but he stopped and waved his hand hopelessly. With a shake of his head, he kicked Riverdancer into a faster canter, and the horse leaped ahead of Threadbare.

Oliver persisted and moved his pony to match the Morgan high-lander's speed. "Your heart is not known to you, my friend," he said as he came up alongside Luthien. "So you run, but yet, you cannot!"

"Oliver the poet," Luthien said dryly.

"I have been called worse."

Luthien let it go at that, and so did Oliver, but though the conversation ended, Luthien's private thoughts on the matter most certainly did not. Truly the young man was torn, full of passion and full of guilt, loving Katerin and Siobhan, but in different ways. He did not regret his affair with the half-elf—how could he ever look upon those beautiful moments with sadness?—and yet, never had he wanted to hurt Katerin. Not in any way, not at any time. He had been swept up in the moment, the excitement of the road, of the city and the budding rebellion. Bedwydrin, and Katerin, too, had seemed a million miles and a million years removed.

But then she had come back to him, a wonderful friend of another time, his first love—and, he had come to realize, his only love.

How could he ever tell that to Katerin now, after what he had done? Would she even hear his words? Could he have heard hers, had the situation been reversed?

Luthien had no answers to the disturbing questions. He kept a swift pace toward the northernmost tip of the Iron Cross, trying to put Caer MacDonald far behind him.

The snow that had so hampered the cyclopians and left so many one-eyes dead on the field as they tried to flee became a distant memory, most traces of white swallowed by the softening ground of spring. Only two weeks had passed since the battle, and the snow, except in the mountains, where winter hung on stubbornly, was fast receding, and the trees were thickening with buds, their sharp gray lines growing red and brown and indistinct.

Luthien and Oliver had been out of Caer MacDonald for five days, and now, with several hundred soldiers filtering in from the west to join the campaign, Port Charley folk mostly, Brind'Amour began his march. Out they marched in long lines, many riding, but most walking, and all under the pennants of Eriador of old—the mountain cross on a green field.

At the same time, Shuglin and his remaining dwarfs, some two hundred of the bearded folk, left Caer MacDonald's southern gate, trudging into the mountains, their solid backs bent low by enormous packs.

"Luthien has passed through Bronegan," the wizard said to Katerin, who was riding at his side.

The young woman nodded, understanding that this was fact and not supposition, and not surprised that the wizard could know such things.

"How many soldiers has he added?" she asked.

"A promise of a hundred," the wizard replied. "But only to join with him if he returns through the town with many other volunteers in tow."

Katerin closed her eyes. She understood what was going on here, the most unpredictable and potentially dangerous part of the whole rebellion. They had won in Caer MacDonald and had raised the pennants of Eriador of old, which would give people some hope, but the farmers and the simple folk, living their quiet existence, hardly bothered by Greensparrow and matters politic, would only join in if they truly believed not only in the cause but in the very real prospect of victory.

"Of course they need to see the numbers," Brind'Amour said, as though that news should neither surprise nor dismay. "We expected that all along. I hate Greensparrow above all others," the old wizard said, chuckling. "And am more powerful than most, yet even I would not join an army of two, after all!"

Katerin managed a weak smile, but there remained a logical problem here that she could not easily dismiss. Not a single town north of Caer MacDonald, not another town in all of Eriador, except perhaps for Port Charley, could raise a significant force on its own. Yet the towns were independent of each other, under no single ruler. Each was its own little kingdom; they were not joined in any way, had not been even in the so-called "glorious" days of Bruce MacDonald. Eriador was a rugged land of individuals, and that is exactly what Greensparrow had exploited on his first conquest, and exactly what he would likely try to exploit again. The young woman tossed her shining red hair and looked around at the mass moving in fair harmony behind her. Here was a strong force—enough to take the wall, likely. But if Greensparrow struck back at them, even when they were secured behind the wall, even with the barrier of the mountains, even with the newly acquired fleet to hamper the king's efforts, they would need many more soldiers than this.

Many more.

"Where will Luthien turn?" Katerin asked, unintentionally voicing the question.

"To the Fields of Eradoch," Brind'Amour answered easily.

"And what will he find in that wild place?" Katerin dared to ask. "What have your eyes shown you of the highlanders?"

Brind'Amour shook his head, his shaggy white hair and beard flopping side to side. "I can send my eyes many places," he replied, "but only if I have some reference. I can send my eyes to Luthien at times, because I can locate his thoughts, and thus use his eyes as my guide. I can find Greensparrow, and several others of his court, because they are known to me. But as it was when I was trying to discern the fleet that sailed north from Avon, I am magically blind to matters wherein I have no reference."

"What have your eyes shown you of the highlanders?" Katerin pressed, knowing a half-truth when she heard it.

Brind'Amour snickered guiltily. "Luthien will not fail," was all that he would say.

CHAPTER 20

THE FIELDS OF ERADOCH

TO THE CASUAL observer, the northwestern corner of Eriador was not so different in appearance from the rest of the country. Rolling fields of thick green grass—"heavy turf," the Eriadorans called it—stretched to the horizon in every direction, a soft green blanket, though on a clear day, the northern mountains could be seen back to the west, and even the tips of the Iron Cross, little white and gray dots, poked their heads above the green horizon far in the distance to the southwest.

There was something very different about the northeast, though, the Fields of Eradoch, the highlands. Here the wind was a bit more chill, the almost constant rain a bit more biting, and the men a bit more tough. The cattle that dotted the plain wore coats of shaggy, thick fur, and even the horses, Morgan Highlanders like Luthien's own Riverdancer, had been bred with longer hair as a ward against the elements.

The highlands had not seen as much snow this winter as normal, though still more fell here than in the southern reaches of Eriador, and the snow cover was neither complete nor very deep by the time Luthien and Oliver crossed through MacDonald's Swath and made their way into the region. Everything was gray and brown, with even a few splotches of green, as far as their eyes could see. Melancholy and dreary, winter's corpse, with still some time before the rebirth of spring.

The companions camped about a dozen miles east of Bronegan that night, on the very edge of the Fields of Eradoch. When they awakened the next morning, they were greeted by unusually warm temperatures and a thick fog, as the last of the snow dissipated into the air.

"It will be slow this day," Oliver remarked.

"Not so," Luthien replied without the slightest hesitation. "There are few obstacles," he explained.

"How far do you mean to go?" the halfling asked him. "They have left Caer MacDonald by now, you know."

Oliver spoke the truth, Luthien realized. Likely, Brind'Amour and Katerin, Siobhan and all the army had already marched out of the city's gates, flowing north and west, along the same course Luthien and Oliver had taken. Until they got to MacDonald's Swath. There, they would cross and go to the south, into Glen Albyn, while Luthien and Oliver had turned straight north, across the breadth of the swath, to Bronegan, and now, beyond that and into Eradoch.

"How far?" Oliver asked again.

"All the way to Bae Colthwyn, if we must," Luthien replied evenly.

Oliver knew the impracticality of that answer. They were fully three days of hard riding from the cold and dark waters of Bae Colthwyn. By the time they got there and back, Brind'Amour would be at the wall, and the battle would be over. But the halfling understood and sympathized with the emotions that had prompted that response from Luthien. They had been greeted warmly in Bronegan, with many pats on the back and many toasts of free ale. Yet the promises of alliance, from the folk of Bronegan and from several other nearby communities who sent emissaries to meet with Luthien, had been tentative at best. The only way that these folk of the middle lands would line up behind the Crimson Shadow, in open defiance of King Greensparrow, was if Luthien proved to them that the whole of Eriador would fight in this war. Luthien had to go back through Bronegan on his journey south, or at least send an emissary there, and if he and Oliver had not mustered any more support, then they would ride alone all the way back to Glen Albyn.

And so they were in the highlands, to face perhaps their most critical test of the unity of Eriador. The highlanders of Eradoch were an independent group, tough and hardy. Many would call them uncivilized. They lived in tribes, clans based on heritage, and often warred amongst themselves. They were hunters, not farmers, better with the sword than the plow, for strength was the byword of the Fields of Eradoch.

That fact was not lost on the young Bedwyr, the general who had engineered the defeat of Belsen'Krieg outside of Caer MacDonald. All the highlanders, even the children, could ride, and ride well, on their powerful and shaggy steeds, and if Luthien could enlist a fraction of the thousands who roamed these fields, he would have a cavalry to outmatch the finest of Greensparrow's Praetorian Guards. But the highlanders were a superstitious and unpredictable lot. Likely they had heard of Luthien as the Crimson Shadow, and so he and Oliver would not be riding into Eradoch unannounced. Their reception, good or bad, had probably already been decided.

The pair rode on through most of that day, Luthien trying to keep them headed northeast, toward Mennichen Dee, the one village in all the region. It was a trading town, a gathering point, and many of the highland clans would soon be making their way to the place, with excess horses and piles of furs to swap for salt and spices and glittering gemstones brought in by merchants of the other regions.

The fog didn't lift all that day, and though the pair tried to keep their spirits high, the soggy air and the unremarkable ground (what little of it they could see) made it a long and arduous day.

"We should camp soon," Luthien remarked, the first words either of them had spoken in some hours.

"Pity us in trying to build a fire this night," Oliver lamented, and Luthien had no words to counter that. It would indeed be a cold and uncomfortable night, for they'd not begin a fire with the meager and soaked twigs that they might find in the highlands.

"We'll make Mennichen Dee tomorrow," Luthien promised. "There is always shelter available there to any traveler who comes in peace."

"Ah, but there's the rub," the halfling said dramatically. "For do we come in peace?"

The ride seemed longer to Luthien, who again had no real answers for his unusually gloomy friend.

They traveled on as the sun, showing as just a lighter patch of gray, settled into the sky behind them, and very soon, Luthien felt that subtle tingle of alarm, that warrior instinct. Something just beyond his conscious senses told him to be on guard, and the adrenaline began to course through his veins.

He looked to Oliver and saw that his halfling companion, too, was riding a bit more tensely in the saddle, ready to spring away or draw his blade.

Riverdancer's ears flattened and then came back up several times; Threadbare snorted.

They came like ghosts through the fog, gliding over the soft grass with hardly a sound, their bodies so wrapped in layers of fur and hide, and with huge horned or winged helms upon their heads, that they seemed hardly human, seemed extensions of the shaggy horses they rode, seemed the stuff of nightmares.

Both companions pulled up short, neither going for his weapon, transfixed by the spectacle of this ghostly ambush. The highlanders, huge men, every one of them dwarfing even Luthien, came in from every angle, slowly tightening the ring about the pair.

"Tell me I am dreaming," Oliver whispered.

Luthien shook his head.

"Sometimes, perhaps, you should do only as you are told." Oliver scolded. "Even if it is a lie!"

The highlanders stopped just far enough from the pair so that they remained indistinguishable, seeming more like monsters than men. Oliver silently applauded their tactic—they knew the ground, they knew the fog, and they certainly knew how to make an appearance.

"They want us to move first," Luthien whispered out of the side of his mouth.

"I could fall on the ground and tremble," the halfling offered sarcastically.

"They kill cowards," Luthien said.

Oliver considered the honest emotions flitting through his mind at the ominous presence sitting barely a dozen yards away. "Then I am doomed," he admitted.

Luthien snickered despite the predicament. "We knew what we were riding into," he said at length, to remind himself and bolster his resolve.

"Greetings from Caer MacDonald," he called in as strong a voice as he could muster. "The city that was unrightfully placed under the name of Montfort by a man who would claim kingship of all Avon and all Eriador."

For a long while, there came no response. Then one rider moved up through the passive line, walking his black horse past the others and close enough for Luthien and Oliver to see him clearly.

The young Bedwyr's face screwed up with curiosity, for this one appeared to be no highlander. He was large, yet he wore no furs or hide, but rather a complete suit of black-plated armor, the likes of which Luthien Bedwyr had never before seen. It was creased and jointed, with metal gauntlets fastened securely into place. Even the man's feet were armored! His helm was flat-topped and cylindrical—Luthien noted that there were two eye slits and not one; this was no cyclopian—and he carried a huge shield, black like his armor and emblazoned with a crest that Luthien did not know: a death figure, skeletal arms spread wide, an upturned sword in one hand, a downward-pointing sword in the other. A pennant with a similar crest flew from the top of the long lance he held easily at his side. Even the man's horse was covered in armor—head and neck and chest and flanks.

"Montfort," the man declared in a deep voice. "Rightfully named by the rightful king."

"Uh-oh," Oliver moaned.

"You are not of the highlands," Luthien reasoned.

The armored man shifted on his horse, the beast prancing nervously. Luthien understood that his words had somewhat unnerved the man, for his guess had been on the mark. The man was not of Eradoch, and that meant whatever hold he had over the highlanders would be tenuous indeed. He had come to some measure of power and influence by sheer strength, probably defeating several of the greatest warriors of Eradoch. Anyone who could best him would likely inherit his position, and so Luthien already had his sights set on the man.

But with the man's imposing size and all that armor, the young Bedwyr was not so fond of that possibility.

"Who are you, then, you who tinkles in a hard spring rain?" Oliver asked.

"A hard spring rain?" Luthien whispered incredulously to the halfling.

"Tinkle, tinkle," Oliver whispered back.

The armored man squared his shoulders and brought himself up to his full height. "I am the Dark Knight!" he declared.

The companions thought on that one for a moment.

"But you would have to be," Oliver reasoned.

"You have heard of me?"

"No."

The Dark Knight grunted in confusion.

"You would have to be," Oliver reiterated. "Is that not why it is called night?"

"What?" the exasperated man asked.

"Unless there is a moon," Luthien offered.

Oliver smirked, pleasantly surprised. "You are getting very good at this," he offered to his friend.

"What?" the knight demanded.

Oliver sighed and shook his head. "So silly tinkler," he said. "If you were not dark, you would be the day."

They couldn't see the man's face under the metal helm, but they both imagined his jaw drooping open. "Huh?" he grunted.

The two friends looked to each and exchanged helpless shrugs. "Peasant," they said in unison.

"I am the Dark Knight!" the armored man declared.

"Charge straight in?" Luthien offered.

"Of course," Oliver replied, and they both whooped, Luthien drawing *Blind-Striker* and kicking Riverdancer into a great leaping start. Threadbare didn't follow, though, Oliver sitting passively.

Luthien knew that he was in trouble as soon as the knight's lance dipped his way, as soon as he realized that the long weapon would slip past his guard, and probably through his chest, before he ever got close enough to nick his opponent's horse on the tip of its nose. He brought his sword arm down and grabbed up Riverdancer's bridle in both hands—only riding skills, not fighting skills, could save him now.

Luthien waited until the last possible second, then cut Riverdancer to the left, angling away from the knight, and the strong and agile steed responded, cutting hard, clumps of turf flying from its hooves. The knight apparently expected the move, though, for he, too, shifted, turning his lance enough to nick Luthien across the shoulder, a painful sting. The young Bedwyr grimaced and whipped his hands across the other way, yanking hard on Riverdancer's reins.

Again, the mighty horse responded, digging hooves deep into the sod. Luthien started to bring *Blind-Striker* up, but felt a twang in his right shoulder. Quick-thinking and quick-moving, the young Bedwyr caught up the sword in his left hand instead, and lashed out, striking hard along the center of the lance. Then he shifted his angle and swiped a vicious backhand that slammed the edge of the blade against the knight's breastplate.

The sword bounced harmlessly away.

The two riders pounded away from each other, the knight discarding his snapped lance and Luthien straightening in the saddle, taking up his sword in his right hand again and testing its grip. He noted the approving looks of the highlanders as he turned Riverdancer about, just short of their ranks. It was going well so far, the young Bedwyr realized, for they admired his courage, and probably they admired his horse. Riverdancer was much shorter than the Dark Knight's steed, but wider and stronger. And Riverdancer was a Highland Morgan, as fine a steed as had ever been bred on the Fields of Eradoch. Gahris Bedwyr had paid a small fortune for the shining white mount, and in studying the approving nods now coming his way, Luthien realized that the horse had been worth every gold coin.

The opponents squared off once more. The Dark Knight reached for his sword, and had it half out of its scabbard, but then a sour look crossed his face. He regarded the sword for a moment, then slid the weapon away, taking up a flail instead. He lifted it above his head, swinging it effortlessly, the spiked iron ball spinning lazily on its heavy black chain. Better than the lance, Luthien thought, for at least he would be close enough to strike before he got struck this time.

Luthien sighed and wondered what good that might do. He had hit his opponent hard the first time, a blow that should have felled the man. Yet the Dark Knight hadn't even grunted at the impact, and if he was feeling any pain now, he wasn't showing it.

On came the man, and Luthien shrugged and dug his heels into Riverdancer's powerful flanks. They passed close this time, close enough for Luthien to feel the puff of steam from the nostrils of the Dark Knight's towering steed.

Luthien snapped off a short backhand, catching the knight under the arm as he lifted his spinning flail for a swing. Up went *Blind-Striker* in a quick parry, just deflecting the iron ball before it crunched Luthien's skull.

This time, Luthien didn't allow the pass. He knew that he had the advantage in mounts here, and so he turned Riverdancer tightly, coming around behind the Dark Knight's steed. In a moment, he was pacing his opponent once more, and he got in three hard strikes with his sword before the armored man could turn about to retaliate. They ran the line together, side by side, hammering at each other. Luthien's hits were mostly clean, while *Blind-Striker* took the momentum from the flail each and every time. Still, the heavy ball battered the young Bedwyr, and Luthien's sword seemed to have little effect as it rebounded off the other's heavy plating.

Finally, each of them breathing heavily, the opponents broke apart, Luthien cutting Riverdancer fast to the side. He could not win this way, he knew, for the mounted battle was too frenzied for him to find a crease in the knight's armor. The Dark Knight apparently knew it, too, for he swung his mount about, aiming for Luthien.

"Pass!" he demanded, and on came the thundering charge once more.

Luthien bent low and whispered into Riverdancer's ear. "I need you now," he said to the horse. "Be strong and forgive me." Off they charged, kicking up the sod, angling for another close pass.

Luthien hunched his shoulders close to Riverdancer's strong neck and turned his mount right into the path of the charging opponent. The Dark Knight straightened in surprise, his horse breaking stride.

Exactly what Luthien had prayed for.

The young Bedwyr did not slow at all. Riverdancer plowed headlong into the Dark Knight's steed, bowling the horse over so that it practically sat on the ground before it was able to regain any semblance of balance. The armored knight held on dearly, accepting the hit as Luthien thrust *Blind-Striker* around the tumbling horse's neck.

Luthien, knocked dizzy from the impact of the powerful steeds, held on dearly as well. He focused squarely on his target, had known what he needed to do before he had ever begun the charge. His one attack, the sword thrust, was not for the knight's breastplate—what would be the point?—or even for the slits in the man's helmet, which were out of reach as the knight leaned defensively backward. Luthien swung at the man's fingers, so that he dropped the reins. As the staggering Riverdancer shuffled to the side, Luthien looped those reins about his sword and tugged with all his strength, and the knight's horse lurched violently.

Luthien nearly overbalanced and tumbled off the other side of his horse, but held on stubbornly, looking back just in time to see the Dark Knight unceremoniously slide off the rear flank of his mount, thudding hard to the ground.

Luthien slipped off Riverdancer and nearly fell facedown as the world continued to spin about him. He staggered and stumbled his way to his supine opponent, the man trying futilely to rise in his heavy armor. The flail whipped across, catching the young Bedwyr off balance.

Luthien's eyes widened in surprise and he hurled himself backward, slipping in the mud to fall unceremoniously to the ground.

The knight rolled and managed to get up as Luthien rose, the two facing off.

"Your attack was immoral," the Dark Knight declared. "You struck my horse!"

"My horse struck your horse," Luthien corrected indignantly.

"There are rules of combat!"

"There are rules of survival!" Luthien countered. "How am I to fight one armored such as yourself? What risks do you take?"

"That is the advantage of station," the Dark Knight roared. "Come on, then, *sans equine*."

Sitting not far away, Oliver cocked his head curiously at the armored man's demeanor. That last statement was a Gascon saying, reserved for nobles mostly, meaning competition, not always combat, without horses. Who was this knight? Oliver wondered.

Luthien approached cautiously. He could hit the man a dozen times to little effect, but one swipe of the flail would cave in his skull, or reduce his ribs to little bits. And his right arm was hanging loose, still feeling the sting from the lance cut. The two circled and launched measured strikes for a few passes, then the Dark Knight roared and came in hard, whipping his flail across and back.

The man couldn't move so well in that encumbering armor, though, and Luthien easily danced aside, swatting the knight on the back of the shoulder. The knight turned and tried to follow, but the agile Luthien was always a step ahead of him, *tap-tapping* with *Blind-Striker*, as much to prod the man on as to inflict any real damage. Already the young Bedwyr could hear the man panting inside that heavy suit.

"An honorable man would stand and fight!" the Dark Knight proclaimed.

"A stupid man would stand and die," Luthien countered. "You speak of honor, yet you hide behind a wall of metal! You see my face, yet I see no more than dark orbs through the slits of a helm!"

That gave the man pause, for he stopped abruptly and lowered his flail. "A point well taken," he said, and to Luthien's amazement, he began to unstrap his heavy helmet. He pulled it off and Luthien grew even more amazed, for the man was much older than Luthien had expected, probably three times the young Bedwyr's age! His face was rugged and wide, skin leathery and creased by deep lines. His gray hair was cropped short, but he wore a huge mustache, also gray, a line of bushy hair from mid-cheek to mid-cheek. His eyes, dark brown, were large and wide-spaced, with a thick nose between, and only his chin was narrow, jutting forward proudly.

The Dark Knight tossed his helmet to the ground. "Now," he said, "fight me fairly, young upstart."

He charged once more, and this time, Luthien met the rush, *Blind-Striker* whipping across, its angle and timing perfect to intercept the flail across the chain, halfway between the ball and the handle. The ball wrapped tightly around Luthien's sword. He tugged hard, thinking to take the weapon from the man, but the Dark Knight proved incredibly strong, and though Luthien had the advantage of angle, the older man held on.

Luthien felt the throb in his shoulder, but forgot about it as the Dark Knight's armored left hand came across in a vicious hook, slamming Luthien right in the face. Warm blood rolled down from Luthien's nose and over his lip, tasting salty-sweet.

The young Bedwyr staggered back a step, then wisely threw himself forward before the man could land a second weighted punch. The Dark Knight did snap his knee up, and while Luthien was wise enough to turn one leg in to protect his groin, he took the hit on the thigh.

Luthien responded by jamming his open palm up under the Dark Knight's chin, breaking the clench. The young Bedwyr leaped back, tugging and scrambling frantically, pulling hard on the knot the flail's chain had become.

He got punched again, in the chest, then again, right on his wounded shoulder. He reacted in kind and grimaced at the sudden throbbing in his hand after banging it hard off the Dark Knight's unyielding breastplate.

A left hook crashed in just under Luthien's ribs. He ran to the side, throwing his momentum into the tangle of weapons, trying to change the angle, or to push the flail handle back over the older man's hand, forcing him to let go.

Finally, *Blind-Striker* slid free of its tangle, so quickly that Luthien skidded right past his opponent and stumbled down to one knee. The Dark Knight turned to follow, whipped the flail in a circular motion over his head. His thought was to seize the moment and attack immediately, but *Blind-Striker*'s blade was much finer and stronger than the Dark Knight had anticipated, and the flail was an old weapon, as old as its wielder. The iron chain, weakened by age and by the finest blade in all of Eriador, split at one link and the studded ball flew through the air.

Across the way, Threadbare hopped to Oliver's command, and the halfling deftly lifted his hands, protected by his fine green gauntlets, to basket-catch the object.

The Dark Knight, apparently oblivious to the loss of his weapon, roared and rushed ahead, waving the handle and half a chain. He slowed only upon noticing Luthien's suddenly amused expression.

"Excuse me, good sir knight," came the halfling's call from behind. The Dark Knight turned slowly, to see Oliver dangling the lost flail ball by the end of its broken chain. The knight looked from Oliver to his weapon, his face screwed up with disbelief. Then he saw the horizon suddenly, and then the gray sky, as Luthien kicked his legs out from under him.

The young Bedwyr was atop him, straddling his breastplate, the tip of *Blind-Striker* at the man's throat.

"I beg of you," the Dark Knight began, and Luthien thought it out of character for this one to whine. "Please, good sir, allow me to offer a final prayer to God before you kill me," the Dark Knight explained. "You have won fairly—I offer no protests, but I ask that I might make my final peace."

Luthien didn't know how to react, so surprised to hear such talk from one of Greensparrow's professed followers. "Who are you?" he asked.

"Of course, of course, my name," the Dark Knight said. "And I, of course, must know yours before you kill . . ." The man sighed and let that thought go.

"I am Estabrooke of Newcastle," he declared. "Lord Protector, First of the Sixth Cavaliers."

Luthien looked over at Oliver, his lips silently mouthing, *"First of the Sixth?"* The young Bedwyr had heard of the group before, a band of knights dedicated as personal bodyguards of the king of Avon and of the governors of the six major cities in that southern kingdom. Luthien had thought the group disbanded with the arrival of Greensparrow, for the cyclopians now served as Praetorian Guard. Apparently, he thought wrong.

Luthien paused, understanding that he had to consider this matter very carefully. He lifted *Blind-Striker* away from the knight's throat and wiped the blood from his face, all the while staring at the curious old man lying supine below him.

"You are a long way from Newcastle," Luthien said.

The man straightened himself, seemed to regain a bit of his dignity despite his predicament. "I am on a mission," he declared. "The first for a cavalier since . . ." His face screwed up as he tried to remember. It had indeed been a long time.

"Well, no matter," Estabrooke said at length. "I have prayed. You may state your name and kill me now." He took a deep breath and locked his dark brown eyes on Luthien's cinnamon-colored orbs. "Have at it," he said matter-of-factly.

Luthien looked all around. Of course he would not kill this man, but he wanted to figure out how his action, or inaction, might be viewed by the rugged highlanders ringing him.

"I never heard the claim of a challenge to the death," Luthien said, stepping aside and extending his hand. The Dark Knight looked at him skeptically for a moment, then accepted the grasp, and Luthien helped him to his feet.

"I will see to our horses," Estabrooke offered, walking away as he noticed Oliver's approach.

Luthien saw the halfling, too, and with the blood still running from his bent nose, he wasn't very pleased. "You said that you would charge right in," the young Bedwyr scolded.

"I never said that," Oliver corrected.

"You *implied* it!" Luthien growled.

Oliver blew a deep breath and shrugged. "I changed my mind."

Their conversation came to an abrupt end a moment later when the ring of mounted highlanders suddenly converged, huge horsemen and wicked weapons, two-headed spears and axes with blades the size of a large man's chest, pinning the pair helplessly together.

Luthien cleared his throat. "Good sir Estabrooke," he began. "Might you talk to your . . . friends?"

CHAPTER 21

GLEN ALBYN

EXCITED WHISPERS CIRCULATED among the Eriadoran soldiers as they set their camp in the wide vale of Glen Albyn, northeast of the Iron Cross. They had nearly crossed the glen; Dun Caryth, the anchoring point of Malpuissant's Wall, was not yet in sight, but the mountain that harbored the fortress certainly was. The battle was no more than two days away, might even be fought on the next afternoon.

The Eriadorans believed that they could take Dun Caryth and all the wall with just the force from Caer MacDonald, the five thousand that had settled into Glen Albyn. Their hopes soared higher, for the whispers spoke of more allies. Luthien was on the way back to them, it was said, along with a thousand fierce riders of Eradoch and a like number of farmers-turned-warriors from the smaller hamlets of central Eriador. All the land had risen against Greensparrow, so it seemed to the soldiers as they set their camp that night.

Too many issues swarmed Katerin's thoughts and she could not sleep. Eriador had risen and would fight for freedom, or for death. It was something the proud woman of Hale had dreamed of since her youngest days, and yet, with the possibility of this fantasy looming right before her eyes, Katerin felt the joy tainted.

She had lost Luthien. She heard the whispers of friends talking behind her back, and though there was no malice, only sympathy in their quiet words, that stung Katerin all the more. She knew that Luthien and Siobhan were lovers, had known it for some time, but only now, with the rebellion nearing its end and the prospects of life after the war, did Katerin come to appreciate the weight of that truth.

She walked alone, quietly, past the guards and the groups huddled about campfires, many engaged in games of chance, or in soft songs from Eriador of old. Some took notice of her passing and waved, smiling broadly, but they understood from Katerin's expression that she meant to be alone this night, and so they granted her the desired solitude. Katerin walked right out of the northern perimeter of the encampment, out into the dark fields where the stars seemed closer suddenly, and there she stood alone with her thoughts.

The war was barely six months old, would likely not last another six months, and what, then, would be left for Katerin O'Hale? Win or lose against Avon, it seemed to Katerin that life without Luthien would not be complete. She had traveled nearly two hundred miles to be with him, and had gone nearly two hundred more on missions, including this march, for his army and his cause, and now it seemed to the young woman that all her efforts would be for naught.

Her sniffle was the only sound, and that was taken from her by the wind.

She was surprised, and yet, deep in her heart, she was not, when a slender form, much smaller than her own, walked quietly up beside her.

Katerin didn't know what to say. She had come out here to think of what could not be, to come to terms with the realities of her life, and here was Siobhan, apparently following her right out of the camp.

Siobhan!

Katerin didn't look at her, couldn't look at her. She sniffled again and cleared her throat, then turned abruptly back for the encampment.

"How very stubborn and very stupid you will be if you let the man who loves you, and the man whom you love, get away," Siobhan said suddenly, stopping Katerin dead in her tracks.

The red-haired woman wheeled about, eyeing her adversary skeptically. *How stupid will you be to let me have him?* she wondered, but she did not speak, too confused by what Siobhan might be hinting at.

Siobhan tossed her long and lustrous wheat-colored tresses over her shoulder, looked up at the stars, and then back at Katerin. "He is not the first man I have loved," she said.

Katerin could not hide the pain on her face at hearing the confirmation of their passion. She had known it was true, but in her heart had held out some last vestige of hope.

"And he will not be the last," Siobhan went on. Her gaze drifted back up to the stars, and Katerin didn't hate her quite so much in that moment, recognizing the sincere pain that had washed over her fair, angular features. "I will never forget Luthien Bedwyr," the half-elf said, her voice barely a whisper. "Nor you, Katerin O'Hale, and when you are both buried deep in the earth, I, young still by the measures of my race, will try to visit your graves, or at least to pause and remember."

She turned back to Katerin, who stood, mouth agape. Tears rimmed Siobhan's green eyes; Katerin could see the glistening lines that had crossed the half-elf's high cheekbones.

"Yes," Siobhan continued, and she closed her eyes and breathed deeply, feeling the warm breeze and tasting the first subtle scents of the coming spring. "I will mark this very night," she explained. "The smells and the sights, the warmth of the air, the world reawakening, and when in the centuries to come I feel a night such as this, it will remind me of Luthien and Katerin, the two lovers, the folk of legend."

Katerin stared at her, not knowing what to make of the unexpected speech and uncharacteristic openness.

Siobhan locked that stare with her own and firmed her jaw. "It should pain you that Luthien and I have loved," the half-elf said bluntly, catching Katerin off her guard, turning her emotions over once again. "And yet," Siobhan continued unabashedly, "I take some of the credit, much of the credit, for the person the young Luthien Bedwyr has become. This person can understand love now, and he can look at Katerin O'Hale through the eyes of a man, not the starry orbs of a lustful boy."

Katerin looked away, chewing on her bottom lip.

"Deny it if you will," Siobhan said, moving about so that the young woman had to look at her. "Let your foolish pride encase your heart in coldness if that is what you must do. But know that Luthien Bedwyr loves you, only you, and know that I am no threat."

Siobhan smiled warmly then, a necessary ending, and walked away, leaving Katerin alone with her thoughts, alone with the night.

Luthien and Oliver were camped on the fields south of Bronegan that night, part of a force nearly half the size of the army in Glen Albyn. After the victory over the Dark Knight, Estabrooke had indeed talked to his "friends" as Luthien had asked, giving Oliver and Luthien some breathing room and some time.

Noble to the core, Estabrooke promptly and openly ceded to Luthien his earned leadership position over the thousand assembled riders. Luthien eyed the man with concern as he did so, understanding that such a transition would not be easy.

Kayryn Kulthwain, a huge and fierce woman, the finest rider in all of Eradoch and the one Estabrooke had defeated in open challenge just a few days before, immediately reclaimed that position. By the ancient codes of the riders, the title could not be passed from outsider to outsider.

Luthien, son of an eorl and somewhat trained in the matters of etiquette, understood the basic traditions of Eradoch. Estabrooke had ascended to a position of leadership by defeating the leader of the gathered rulers, but that position would have never been more than temporary.

Very temporary. Estabrooke was an outsider, and as soon as the highlanders could have determined a proper order of challenge, the Dark Knight would have been forced to battle and win against every one of the riders, one after another. And if any of them had defeated Estabrooke on the field, there would have been no mercy.

"Is Kayryn Kulthwain the rightful leader?" Luthien had asked those around him.

"By deed and by blood," one man answered, and others bobbed their heads in agreement.

"I came not to Eradoch to lead you," Luthien assured them all, "but to ask for your alliance. To ask that you join with me and my folk of Caer MacDonald against Greensparrow, who is not our king."

The men and women of Eradoch were not a complicated folk. Their lives were straightforward and honest, following a narrow set of precepts, basic guidelines that ensured their survival and their honor. It was all Luthien had to say. When he turned back for Bronegan, the riders of Eradoch were not behind him, they were beside him—and it seemed to both Luthien and Oliver that the fiercely independent folk of Eradoch had wanted to join all along, but had been bound otherwise by the Dark Knight.

Now the two friends, the knight, and the riders were camped south of Bronegan, along with hundreds of farmers who had taken up arms for the cause, eager to join once they learned that Eradoch had come into the alliance.

Luthien sat with Oliver long into the night, the halfling wrapped in blankets and working furiously to clean his marvelous clothing, and to polish his belt buckle and his rapier. Oliver had put his purple breeches too close to the fire to dry, and Luthien watched in silent amusement as the foppish trousers began to smolder.

The halfling shrieked when he noticed, yanking the breeches away and putting a nasty stare on his content friend.

"I meant to tell you," Luthien offered innocently.

"But you did not!" Oliver stated.

Luthien shrugged, much as Oliver had shrugged earlier that same day, after Luthien's painful encounter with the Dark Knight. "I changed my mind," the young Bedwyr said, imitating his diminutive friend's Gascon accent.

Oliver picked up a stick and heaved it at him, but Luthien got his arm up in time to deflect it—though the movement pained his injured shoulder. He laughed and groaned at the same time.

As if on cue, Estabrooke, seeming only half the size of the imposing Dark Knight without his full suit of armor, walked into the light of their fire, carrying a small bowl. "A salve," he explained, moving near to Luthien. "Should take the sting out of your wounds and clean them. Allow them to heal properly, you see." Like a protective mother, the older man bent over Luthien, scooping up a handful of the smelly gray salve.

Luthien tilted his head so that his thick hair shifted away from the shoulder, giving the older man the opportunity to apply the stuff. All the while Luthien and Oliver watched the man closely, still not quite understanding why Estabrooke, First of the Sixth Cavaliers, was even in Eriador at that time. Luthien hadn't broached the subject up to now, for the day had been one of rushed travel and impromptu alliances. The young man could not wait any longer.

"Why are you here?" he asked bluntly.

Estabrooke's look was incredulous. His lips pursed, sending his huge mustache out so far as to tickle the tip of his nose. "I am a Lord Protector," he answered, as though that should explain everything.

"But King Greensparrow, he is in Gascony," Oliver reasoned. "Why would he think to send you so far to the north?"

"Greensparrow?" Estabrooke echoed. "Oh, no, not that one! Duke Paragor, it was, Duke of Princetown and all that."

"When?" Luthien interrupted.

"I was visiting—fine city, that Princetown. The best of zoos, and the gardens!"

Oliver wanted to hear about the zoos, but Luthien kept his priorities. "The duke?" the young Bedwyr reminded.

Estabrooke looked at him curiously, seeming for a moment as though he did not understand. "Yes, of course, Paragor, skinny fellow," the Dark Knight said finally, recollecting his original train of thought. "Should get his face out of those books and into some pie, I say!

"Two weeks," he added quickly to defeat Luthien's mounting scowl. "Called me in for a grand banquet, then asked me to come north, to Era . . . Eradoy. I say, what was the name you gave to this place?"

"Eradoch," Oliver answered.

"Yes, Eradoch," Estabrooke continued. " 'Go to Eradoch,' so said Paragor. Put the ruffians in line. Long live the king, and all that, of course. It was necessary to oblige, being a Lord Protector of the First of the Sixth, of course, and Paragor being an emissary of the rightful king of Avon."

It made perfect sense to Luthien and Oliver. Duke Paragor saw the trouble brewing in Eriador and was close enough to the northern land to understand the value of the riders. The duke would not have impressed the fierce highlanders, and neither would his most usual cohorts, wizards and cyclopians. But then Estabrooke, a knight of the old school, a man of the sword and of indisputable honor, arrives in Princetown and the emissary is found.

"But why did you turn sides?" Oliver had to ask.

"I have not!" Estabrooke insisted as soon as be figured out what the halfling was implying. "Your friend beat me in fair challenge, and thus I am indebted to him for one hundred days." He looked to Luthien. "Of course you understand that you cannot use me as a weapon against my king. My sword is silent."

Luthien nodded and smiled, quite pleased. "In that time, good sir knight," he promised, "you will come to know the truth of your King Greensparrow and the truth of what we in Eriador have begun."

Now it was the half-elf's turn to mourn the loss of Luthien, though Siobhan had known since that windy and rainy night in Caer MacDonald that their love would not be. It was official now, final, as it had to be.

Still, it hurt, and so Siobhan decided that she, too, would find no sleep this night. She meandered for a while around the encampment, pausing long enough to join in the singing at one campfire, the gaming at another. Making her way toward the southeastern end, she came in sight of Brind'Amour's rather large tent. A lantern was burning inside, and the shadows showed the old wizard to be awake.

He was clapping his hands, a smile stretching from ear to ear, when Siobhan entered. She noted that he had just draped a cloth over a circular item atop a small pedestal—his crystal ball, she realized.

"You have seen Luthien," Siobhan reasoned. "And know now that the rumors of his force are true."

Brind'Amour looked at her curiously. "Oh, no, no," he replied. "Too much fog up there. Too much fog. I think I saw the boy earlier, but it might have been a highlander, or even a reindeer. Too much fog."

"Then we cannot confirm—" Siobhan began.

"Rumors usually hold some measure of truth," the wizard interjected.

Siobhan paused and sighed. "We will need to form two sets of tactics," she decided. "Two plans of battle. One without help from Luthien, and another should he ride in with his thousands."

"No need," Brind'Amour said cryptically.

Siobhan looked at him unblinkingly, in no mood for the wizard's games.

Brind'Amour recognized this and wondered for an instant what might be so troubling the half-elf. "Word of our victory in Caer MacDonald precedes us," he explained at once, anxious to bring a smile back to the fair Siobhan's face. "The pennant flying above Dun Caryth is the mountain cross on the green field!"

It hit Siobhan too unexpectedly and she screwed her face up, trying to decipher what Brind'Amour might be talking about. Gradually, it came clear to her. Brind'Amour had just claimed that the fortress anchoring Malpuissant's Wall was under the flag of Eriador of old! "The wall is taken?" the half-elf blurted.

"The wall is ours!" the wizard confirmed, lifting his voice.

Siobhan couldn't even speak. How could such a victory have been handed to them?

"The majority of those living at Dun Caryth and in the various gate towers all along the wall were not cyclopian, nor even Avon citizens, but Eriadorans," the old wizard explained. "They were servants to the soldiers, mostly, craftsmen and animal handlers, but with easy access to the armories."

"They heard of the Crimson Shadow," Siobhan reasoned.

Brind'Amour put his arms behind his head and leaned back comfortably against the center pole of his tent. "So it would seem."

CHAPTER 22

EYES FROM AFAR

HE WAS SO thin as to appear sickly, skin hanging loosely over bones, eyes deep in dark circles. His once thick brown hair had thinned and grayed considerably, leaving a bald stripe over the top of his head. The rest he combed to the side and out, so that it appeared as if he had little wings behind his ears.

Frail appearances can be deceiving, though, as was the case with this man. Duke Paragor of Princetown was Greensparrow's second, the most powerful of the seven remaining dukes. Only Cresis, leader of the cyclopians, and the only duke who was not a wizard, was higher in line for the throne: a purely political decision, and one that Paragor was confident he could reverse should anything ill befall his king.

Paragor wasn't thinking much about ascension to the throne this day, however. Events in Eriador were growing increasingly disturbing. Princetown was the closest and the most closely allied of the Avon cities to that rugged northern land, and so Paragor had the highest stakes in the outcome of the budding rebellion in Eriador. Thus this wizard, proficient in the arts of divining, had watched with more than a passing interest. He knew of Belsen'Krieg's defeat on the fields outside of Montfort; he knew that the Avon fleet had been captured wholesale and sailed north. And he knew of his own failure, Estabrooke, who had been sent north with the intent of keeping the Riders of Eradoch out of the Crimson Shadow's fold.

That very morning, a surly Duke Paragor had watched a thousand riders follow the Crimson Shadow into the swelling rebel encampment in Glen Albyn.

"And all of this with Greensparrow away on holiday in Gascony!" the duke roared at Thowattle, a short and muscular cyclopian with bowed legs, bowed arms, and only one hand, having lost the other and half the forearm as well while feeding one of his own children to a lion in Princetown's famed zoo. The one-eyed brute had fashioned a metal cap and spike to fit over his limb, but the stump was too sensitive for such a device and so he could not wear it. Even with the loss, Thowattle was the toughest cyclopian in Princetown, unusually smart, and unusually cruel, even for one of his race.

"They are just Eriadorans," Thowattle replied, spitting the name derisively.

Paragor shook his head and ran the fingers of both hands through his wild hair, making it stick out all the farther. "Do not make the same mistake as our king," the duke cautioned. "He has underestimated our enemy to the north and the breadth of this uprising."

"We are the stronger," Thowattle insisted.

Paragor didn't disagree. Even if all of Eriador united against Greensparrow, the armies of Avon would be far superior, and even without the fleet that had been stolen, the Avon navy was larger, and manned with crews more acclimated to fighting from such large ships. But a war now, with many of Avon's soldiers away in southern Gascony, fighting with the Gascons in their war against the Kingdom of Duree, would be costly, and crossing the mountains or Malpuissant's Wall, fighting on the Eriadorans' home ground, would help to balance the scales.

"Fetch my basin," Paragor instructed.

"The one of red iron?" Thowattle asked.

"Of course," Paragor snapped, and he sneered openly when Thowattle's expression turned to doubt. The cyclopian left, though, and returned a moment later carrying the item.

"You've been using this too much," Thowattle dared to warn.

Paragor's eyes narrowed. Imagine a cyclopian scolding him concerning the use of magic!

"You told me yourself that divining is a dangerous and delicate act," the cyclopian protested.

Paragor's stare did not relent, and the cyclopian shrugged his broad shoulders and fell silent. Paragor would not discipline him for his insolence, and indeed the duke heard the truth in the cyclopian's words. Divining, sending his eyes and ears out across the miles, was a delicate process. Much could be seen and revealed, but often it was only half truths. Paragor could locate a specific familiar place, or a specific familiar person—in this case, as in the last few, it would be Estabrooke—but such magical spying had its limitations. A real spy or scout collected most of his information before he ever got to the target, and could then use whatever he learned from the target in true context. A wizard's eye, however, normally went right to the heart, blinded to all the subtle events, often the more important events, surrounding the targeted person or place.

Divining had its limitations, and its cost, and its trappings. Great magical energy was expended in such a process, and like a drug, the act could become addictive. Often during this process, more questions were formed than answers given, and so the wizard would go back to his crystal ball, or his enchanted basin, and send his eyes and ears out again, and again. Paragor had known of wizards found dead, drained of their very life force, slumped in their chairs before their divining devices.

But the duke had to go back again to Eriador. He had seen the defeat at Port Charley, the massacre on the fields of Montfort, and the ride of Eradoch, and all of it was inevitably leading his way, to Malpuissant's Wall, which was under his domain.

Thowattle placed the basin on a small round table in the duke's private study, a scarcely furnished and efficient room containing only the table, a large but rather plain desk and chair, a small cabinet, and a wall rack of several hundred compartments. The cyclopian then went to the cabinet and took out a jug of prepared water. He began to pour it into the basin, but it splashed a bit and an angry Paragor pulled the jug from his one hand, slapping him aside.

Thowattle just shook his ugly head skeptically; he had never seen the duke so flustered.

Paragor finished filling the basin, then produced a slender knife from under the voluminous folds of his brownish-yellow robes. He began to chant softly, waving one hand over the basin, then he stabbed his own palm and allowed his blood to drip into the water.

The chanting continued for many minutes, Paragor slowly lowering his face to within an inch of the bowl, peering deeply into the swirling red waters.

Peering deeply, watching the forming image . . .

"An easy victory," a young man—the Crimson Shadow! Paragor realized by the cape he wore—was saying. He was in a large tent, surrounded by an odd crew: a foppish halfling, an old man that Paragor did not know, and three women, all very different in appearance. One was tall and strong, with hair the color of a rich sunset, another was much smaller of frame—perhaps with the blood of Fairborn—with angular features and long wheat-colored tresses, and the third was a rugged woman, dressed in the furs of a highlander. Paragor knew this one, Kayryn Kulthwain, the woman Estabrooke had beaten to take control of the folk of Eradoch.

"But this army was up for a fight," the foppish halfling replied in a thick Gascon accent. "And now we have no fight for them!"

Paragor didn't quite understand, but he didn't let his mind wander at that time. He sent his gaze to the edges of the basin, seeking the object of his divining. There was Estabrooke, seated passively on a stool, resting against the side of the tent. What had happened to so quiet the commanding cavalier? the wizard-duke wondered. The resignation on Estabrooke's face might be the most unsettling thing of all!

Gradually Paragor realized that he was meandering from his course. Already he could feel the weight of the magic; his time was short. Near the center of the tent, of the basin, the Crimson Shadow was speaking once more.

"As the fingers of a hand have the folk of Eriador assembled," he said, waxing poetic and holding his own hand up in the air. "Come together into a fist."

"A fist that has punched King Greensparrow right in the nose," the old man said. "A solid blow, but have we really hurt him?"

"Eriador is ours," the red-haired woman declared.

"For how long?" the old man asked cynically.

That set them all back on their heels. "Greensparrow is in Gascony, that much we know," the old man continued. "And Greensparrow will return."

"The plan was yours, I remind you," the halfling protested.

"It did not go as planned."

"The objective was gained more easily," the halfling said.

"But not with the same effect as Oliver's Bluff" the old man snapped right back. "We are not done, I fear. Not yet."

"What is left?" the halfling asked.

"Forty-five miles is not so far a march in the spring," the old man said slyly.

The image in the divining basin faltered, Paragor's concentration destroyed by the sudden shock. Blanching white, the skinny wizard-duke fell back from the bowl. Princetown—the upstart fools were talking of marching to Princetown!

Paragor understood the peril. This was no small force, and Greensparrow had not acted quickly enough. The armies of Avon were not assembled for march and were nowhere near Princetown. And what other fight had the group declared already won?

Malpuissant's Wall?

The skinny duke ran his fingers through his hair again repeatedly. He had to think. He had to sit down in the dark and concentrate. He knew a little, but not enough, and he was tired.

Such were the limitations, and the cost, of divination.

"Princetown," Siobhan reasoned, following Brind'Amour's logic. "The Jewel of Avon."

"The stakes just rose for Oliver's Bluff," Brind'Amour confirmed.

"Greensparrow, he will never expect it, and never believe it," Oliver said. Then in quieter tones so that only Luthien could hear him clearly, he added, "Because I am standing right here and I do not believe it."

"Princetown is isolated," Brind'Amour explained. "Not another militia of any size within two hundred miles."

Siobhan wore a confused expression, half doubting the possibility, half intrigued by it. "They could send another fleet," she pointed out, "around the wall to cut us off from our home ground."

"They could," Brind'Amour conceded. "But do not underestimate the willingness of those Eriadorans who have not yet joined with us. The folk of Chalmbers, a fair-sized town, are not blind to the events along the mountains and along the wall. Besides," the old wizard added slyly, rubbing his wrinkled fingers together, "we will strike quickly, within the week."

Oliver understood that this might be his one chance to become a part of history, with his name attached to the daring assault. He also understood that the possibility existed that he, and all the rest of them, would be slaughtered on a field south of Eriador. Quite a risk, considering that the original objective of the rebellion (which, in fact, had only begun by accident!) had already been apparently attained. "Princetown?" he asked aloud, drawing attention. "To what point?"

"To force a truce," Brind'Amour replied without hesitation. The old wizard didn't miss the cloud that then crossed Luthien's face.

"Did you think to take it all the way?" Brind'Amour scoffed at the young Bedwyr. "Did you think to go all the way into Avon and conquer Carlisle? All of Eriador would have to march south, and we would still be outnumbered more than three to one!"

Luthien didn't know how to respond, didn't know what he was thinking or feeling. The completion had come easily—the wall was theirs and, for all practical purposes, Eriador was out from under Greensparrow's shadow. Just like a snap of Oliver's green-gauntleted fingers. But for how long? Brind'Amour had asked. It seemed to Luthien then that the fight was far from over, that Greensparrow would come back after them again and again. Could they ever truly win? Perhaps they should take it all the way to Carlisle, Luthien thought, and end the dark shadow that was Greensparrow once and for all time.

"The common folk of Avon would join with us," he reasoned, a hint of desperation in his resonant voice. "As have the common folk of Eriador."

Brind'Amour began to argue, but Oliver interrupted with a raised hand. "I am schooled in this," the halfling explained, begging the wizard's pardon.

"They would see us as invaders," Oliver said to Luthien. "And they would defend their homes against us."

"Then why is Princetown different?" Luthien asked sharply, not pleased at hearing the obvious truth.

"Because it is merely Oliver's Bluff," the halfling said, and then came the predictable snap of his fingers. "And I want to see the zoo."

"Only then do we offer a truce to Avon's king," Brind'Amour explained. "With Princetown in our grasp, we'll have something to barter." Luthien's expression was doubtful, and Brind'Amour understood. The young man had grown up on an isolated island, far from the intrigue of the world's leaders. Luthien was thinking that, if Greensparrow was so powerful, the king could merely march northeast from Carlisle and take Princetown back by force, but what Luthien didn't understand was the embarrassment factor. The only chance Eriador had of breaking free of Avon was to become such a thorn in Greensparrow's side, such an embarrassment to him in his dealings with the southern kingdoms, particularly Gascony, that he simply didn't want to have to bother himself with Eriador anymore. Princetown conquered might just accomplish that; then again, the wizard had to admit, it might not.

"So there we have it," Brind'Amour said suddenly, loudly. "We take Princetown and then we offer it back."

"After we let the animals go," Oliver added, drawing amused smiles from all in the tent.

Simple and logical, it outwardly sounded. But not one of the planners, not Luthien nor Oliver, Katerin nor Siobhan, Kayryn Kulthwain nor even Brind'Amour believed it would be that simple.

The army came upon Malpuissant's Wall, among the most impressive structures in all of Avon, the next day. It stood fifty feet high and twenty feet wide, stretching nearly thirty miles from the eastern edge of the Iron Cross all the way to the Dorsal Sea. Gatehouses had been built every five hundred yards, the most impressive of these being the fortress of Dun Caryth. She reached out from the last sheer wall of the rugged mountains, blending the natural stone into the worked masonry of the wall. Half of Dun Caryth was aboveground, soaring towers and flat-topped walls brimming with catapults and ballistae, and half was below, in tunnels full of supplies and weapons.

In viewing the place, Luthien came to appreciate just how important this easily won victory had been. If his army had gone against the Praetorian Guards of Dun Caryth, they would have suffered terrible losses, and no siege could have lasted long enough to roust the brutes from the fortress. The uprising had come from within the fortress walls, though, and Dun Caryth, and all of Malpuissant's Wall, was theirs.

Their welcome was warm and full of celebration, the Eriadorans all feeling invulnerable, as if Greensparrow's name was no more than a curse to be hurled at enemies.

Brind'Amour knew better, but even the wizard could not help but be caught up in the frenzy when the victorious armies came together. And it was good for them, realized the wizard-turned-general: celebration further sealed their alliance and ensured that the less predictable folk, like the Riders of Eradoch, were fully in the fold.

So they enjoyed that day at the wall, swapped their stories of hard-won victory, and of friends who had given their lives. The army from Caer MacDonald, and from the northern fields, camped on the plain north of Dun Caryth that night.

Feeling invincible.

Back in his palace in Princetown, Duke Paragor paced the carpeted floor of his bedchamber. He was tired, his magic expended, but he wanted to call to Greensparrow.

Paragor shook his head, realizing what that distant communication would offer. Greensparrow would dismiss the whole affair, would insist that the upstarts in Eriador were a mob and nothing more.

Paragor considered his options. The nearest dukes, fellow wizards, were in Evenshorn, far to the south, and in Warchester, all the way around the southern spur of the Iron Cross, on the banks of glassy Speythenfergus. It would take them weeks to even muster their forces, and weeks more for their armies to trudge through the mud and melting snows to get to Princetown. The wizard-dukes could get to Paragor's side, of course, by using their magic—perhaps they could even bring along a fair contingent of Praetorian Guards. But would they really make a difference against the force he believed would be coming down from Eriador? And what of his own embarrassment if he called to them and begged them, and then the unpredictable Eriadorans did not come?

"But I have other allies!" Paragor snarled suddenly, startling Thowattle, who was sitting on the rug in a corner of the lavish room.

Thowattle studied his master carefully, recognizing the diabolical expression. Paragor meant to summon a demon, the cyclopian realized, or perhaps even more than one.

"Let us see if their will for war can be slowed," the wicked duke continued. "Perhaps if the Crimson Shadow is slain . . ."

"That would only heighten the legend," the wary cyclopian warned. "You will make a martyr of him, and then he will be more powerful, indeed!"

Paragor wanted to argue the point, but found that he could not; the unusually perceptive one-eye was right again. Paragor improvised—there were ways to kill a man's spirit without killing the man. "Let us suppose that I can break the will of the Crimson Shadow," Paragor offered, his voice barely above a whisper.

Perhaps he could break the man's heart.

CHAPTER 23

COLLECTING ALLIES

IT WAS A bare room, empty of all furnishings save a single brazier set upon a sturdy tripod near the southeastern corner. Each of the walls bore a single sconce holding a burning torch, but were otherwise plain and gray, as was the ceiling. The floor, though, was not so unremarkable. Intricate tiles formed a circular mosaic in the center of the room, its middle area decorated as a pentagram. The circle's outer perimeter was a double line, and within these arching borders were runes of power and protection.

Paragor stood within the circle now, with Thowattle by the brazier, the cyclopian carrying a small crate holding many compartments strapped about his burly neck. The duke himself had placed the tiles, every tiny piece, years before—a most painstaking process. More often than not, Paragor would have finished one section and upon inspection discover that it was not perfect. Then he would have to rip up all the tiles and start again, for the Circle of Sorcery, the protection offered the wizard against whatever evil demon he summoned, had to be perfect. The design had stood the test for several years, against many demons.

Paragor stood absolutely still, reciting the long and arduous chant, a call to hell itself interspersed with thousands of protection spells. Every so often, he lifted his left hand toward Thowattle and spoke a number, and the cyclopian reached into the appropriate compartment of his crate, took out the desired herb or powder, and plunked it into the burning brazier.

Sometimes the component created a heavily scented smoke, other times, a sudden burst of flame, a miniature fireball. Gradually, through the hours of the sorcerous process, the fires in the brazier began to mount. At first, there had been no more than a lick of flame; now a fair-sized fire raged in the middle of the brazier, the heat of it drawing sweat on the already smelly cyclopian.

Paragor seemed oblivious to it all, though in truth, he and his magic were the true source of the brazier's life. There were two types of sorcery: lending and true summoning. The first, lending, was by far the easier route, wherein the wizard allowed a demon to enter his body. The true summoning, which Paragor now attempted, was much more difficult and dangerous. Paragor meant to bring a demon in all its unholy majesty into this room, and then to loose it upon the world, following a strict set of instructions given it by the wizard.

Demons hated servitude and hated more those who forced it on them, but Paragor was confident in his sorcery. He would bring in Kosnekalen, a minor fiend, and one he had dealt with successfully on several occasions.

The flames in the brazier went from orange to yellow to bright white, their intensity and fury growing as Paragor shifted dancing. The wizard spun about his circle, never crossing the line, calling out emphatically, throwing all of his heart into the chant, an unholy tenor, his voice breaching the gates of hell.

He stopped suddenly, thrusting his left hand out toward Thowattle, calling for six, three times, and the cyclopian, no novice to this awful experience, reached into the sixth compartment of the sixth row, extracting a brown, gooey substance.

Into the brazier it went and the flames burned hotter still, so hot that the cyclopian had to back away several steps. Inside the circle, Paragor fell to his knees, his left hand extended, tears mixing with sweat on his sallow features.

"Kosnekalen!" he begged as black crackles of lightning encircled the white fires, as the flames reached a new level of life.

Thowattle fled to the northwestern corner and huddled, terrified, on the floor, covering his eyes.

A forked tongue flicked from the flames and behind it, a dark shadow appeared, a huge head capped by great curving horns. A monstrous, muscled arm reached out the side of the fires, followed by a leathery wing—a huge leathery wing!

Paragor's face went from pain to ecstasy to curiosity. Kosnekalen was a lithe demon, man-sized, with tiny tipped horns, but this fiend was much larger and, the wizard could already sense, much more powerful.

Clawed fingers raked the air as a second arm came forth, and then, in a burst of sheer power, the flames spewed forth the fiend, a gigantic, twelve-foot-tall monstrosity with smoking black flesh and scales. Its face was serpentine, long and wicked fangs jutting over its lower jaw, drool dripping beside them and hissing like acid as it hit the stone floor. Three-clawed feet scraped impatiently on the floor, drawing deep lines in the stone.

"Kosnekalen?" Paragor asked, his voice barely above a whisper.

"I called for Kosne—" the wizard began.

"I came in Kosnekalen's place!" the demon roared, its horrid voice, both grating and squealing, echoing off the bare walls.

Paragor tried hard to collect his wits. He had to appear in command here, else the demon would crash out of the room and go on a rampage, destroying everything in its path. "I require only a single service," the duke began. "One that should be pleasurable . . ."

"I know what you require, Paragor," the demon growled. "I know."

Paragor straightened. "Who are you?" he demanded, for he had to know the demon's name before he could demand a service of it. This could be a tricky and dangerous moment, the practiced sorcerer understood, but to his surprise, and his relief, the demon willingly replied.

"I am Praehotec," the beast said proudly. "Who was with Morkney when Morkney died."

Paragor nodded—he had heard a similar tale from Kosnekalen. Kosnekalen had been more than happy to tell the tale in great detail, and Paragor had sensed that there was a great rivalry between the fiends.

"I was denied a pleasure then," the evil Praehotec went on, barely sublimating its boiling rage. "I will not be denied that pleasure again."

"You hate the Crimson Shadow," Paragor reasoned.

"I will eat the heart of the Crimson Shadow," Praehotec replied.

Paragor smiled wickedly. He knew just how to open that heart to the fiend.

Paragor's vision had been narrowly focused on the events to the north of Princetown, in Glen Albyn and farther north, in Bronegan and the Fields of Eradoch, but that focus, those self-imposed blinders necessary for such divining, hadn't allowed him a view to the northwest, into the mountains of the Iron Cross.

Shuglin stood tall in those mountains, watching to the east, toward the wall and the city of Princetown. He and his remaining kin, less than three hundred of the bearded folk, had gone out from Caer MacDonald when the army had marched, but had traveled south into the heart of the towering mountains, where the snow still lay thick, where winter had. not yet relinquished its icy grasp. Shuglin had gone to guard the mountain passes, though the dwarf and Brind'Amour, who had sent him, knew that those passes would be blocked for more than a month still, and maybe longer than that.

Brind'Amour was the only non-dwarf who knew the real mission behind Shuglin's dangerous march. That hope had been realized less than a week out from Caer MacDonald, in a deep, deep cavern high up from the city. For many years, the beleaguered dwarfs of Montfort, now Caer MacDonald, had heard rumors of their kin living free among the peaks of the Iron Cross. Most of the dwarfs were old enough to remember mountain dwarfs who had come into the city to trade in the days before Greensparrow, and one of the group, an old graybeard who had been enslaved in the mines since the earliest days of Greensparrow's reign, claimed to be from that tribe, the descendants of Burso Ironhammer. That old graybeard had survived twenty years of hard labor in the mines, then the fierce battles of Montfort. It was he, not Shuglin, who had led the troupe into the snow-packed passes, through secret tunnels, and ultimately into the deep cave, the realm of Burso's folk.

What Shuglin and the other city dwarfs found in that cavern made their hearts soar, made them know, for perhaps the first time, what it was to be a dwarf. Far below the snow-covered surface, in smoky tunnels filled more with shadow than light, the dwarfs had met their kin, their heritage. DunDarrow, the Ingot Shelf, the place was called, a complex of miles of tunnels and great underground caverns. Five thousand dwarfs lived and worked here, in perfect harmony with the stone that was the stuff of their very being. Shuglin looked upon treasures beyond anything he could imagine; piles of golden and silver artifacts, gleaming weapons, and suits of mail to rival those of the mightiest and wealthiest knights in all of the Avonsea Islands.

Though these were city dwarfs, they were welcomed with open arms by the king of the mines, Bellick dan Burso, and hundreds of the mountain folk gathered each night in several of the great halls to hear the tales of the battle, to hear of the Crimson Shadow and the victory in Montfort.

Now wrapped in thick furs, Shuglin stood on a high pass, waiting for King Bellick. The dwarf king, younger than Shuglin, with a fiery orange beard and eyebrows so bushy that they hung halfway over his blue eyes, was not tardy, and the eagerness of his step as he came onto the ledge gave Shuglin hope.

The city dwarf knew that he would be asking much of this king and his clan. Shuglin was glad that the king was a young dwarf, full of fire, and full of hatred for Greensparrow.

Bellick moved up to the ledge beside the blue-bearded dwarf and gave a nod of greeting. "We daren't trade with Montfort since the wizard-king took the throne," Bellick said, something Shuglin had heard a hundred times in the two days he had been at DunDarrow.

Bellick gave a snort. "Many haven't seen the outside-the-mountains land in score of years," the dwarf king continued. "But we're loving the inside-the-mountain land, so we're contented."

Shuglin looked at him, not quite believing that claim.

"Contented," Bellick reiterated, and his voice didn't match the meaning of the word. "But we're not happy. Most have no desire to go out to the flatlands, but even they who are content are not liking the fact that we cannot go safely outside the mountains."

"Prisoners in your own home," Shuglin remarked.

Bellick nodded. "And we're not liking the treatment of our kin." He put his hand on Shuglin's strong shoulder as he spoke.

"You will come with me, then," the blue-bearded dwarf reasoned. "To the east."

Bellick nodded again. "Another storm gathers over the mountains," he said. "Winter will not let go. But we have ways of travel, underground ways, that will get us to the eastern edges of DunDarrow."

Shuglin smiled, but tried hard to keep his emotions hidden. So perhaps he was not out of the fighting yet, he mused. He would return to Luthien and Siobhan's side, with five thousand armed and armored dwarven warriors in his wake.

Luthien sat alone on the stump of a tree and let the melancholy afternoon seep into his mood. Oliver had been right, he knew. Over the last few weeks, Luthien had been running away from his emotions, first by sending Katerin to Port Charley, then by traipsing off with Oliver on the roundabout circuit to Glen Albyn. He could continue to justify his cowardice in the face of love by focusing on his bravery in the face of war.

But he did not. Not now. There was great excitement in the Eriadoran camp, with whispers that they would soon cross through Malpuissant's Wall and march south, but for Luthien, the battle suddenly seemed secondary. He believed that they could win, could take Princetown and force Greensparrow to grant them their independence, but what then? Would he become king of Eriador?"

And if he did, would Katerin be his queen?

It all came inescapably back to that. Sitting on that tree stump, looking up at the indomitable Dun Caryth, dark against a gray sky that was fast fading to black as the sun dipped low, Luthien found himself at odds, caught somewhere between responsibilities to the kingdom and to himself. He wanted to be the Crimson Shadow, the leader of the rebellion, but he also wanted to be Luthien Bedwyr, son of an eorl on an island far to the north, fighting only bloodless battles in the arena and romping through the woods with Katerin O'Hale.

He had come so far, so fast, but the journey would not be worth the cost if that price included the loss of his love.

"Coward," he berated himself, standing up and stretching. He turned about, facing the encampment, and started his march. He knew where Katerin would be, in a small tent across the way, on the northern edges of the wide camp, and he knew, too, that he had to face her now and put an end to his fear.

By the time he got to Katerin's tent, the sun was gone. A single lantern burned inside the tent, and Luthien could see Katerin's silhouette as she pulled off her leather jerkin. He watched that curvy shadow for a long while, full of admiration and passion. Siobhan was right, Luthien knew. He cared for the half-elf deeply, but this woman, Katerin, was his true love. When the wild rush of the rebellion was ended, even if they proved victorious, it would be a hollow win indeed for Luthien Bedwyr if Katerin would not stand with him.

He should go right into that tent and tell her that, he knew, but he could not. He walked off into the darkness, cursing himself, using every logical argument to try to overcome his fear.

It took him two hours to muster the courage to return, now carrying a lantern of his own, his clothing soaked by the mist that had come up and his bones chilled by the breeze.

"Straight in," he whispered determinedly, his stride quick and direct. "Katerin," he called softly when he got to the tent flap. He pushed it aside and stuck his head in, then brought the lantern around.

Then he froze with horror.

Katerin sprawled diagonally across her cot, her shoulders hanging over the edge, her head and one arm against the ground. It took Luthien several seconds to digest that sight, to shift his gaze even a bit.

To see the gigantic demon crouched in the shadows at the bottom of Katerin's cot, the beast's sheer bulk filling the corner of the tent.

"Do you remember, foolish man?" Praehotec snarled, and came forward a squatting step.

In one swift motion, Luthien set the lantern down and drew *Blind-Striker*, giving a yell and rushing forward wildly. His charge surprised the demon, who was more accustomed to watching men cower and run away.

Luthien smashed *Blind-Striker* across one of Praehotec's upraised arms, drawing a line of hissing, sputtering gray-green blood that smoked as it hit the ground.

Screaming and slashing, Luthien's fury would not relent. He didn't think of the creature he battled, didn't fear for his own death. All he knew was that Katerin, dear Katerin, was down, possibly dead, killed by this evil beast.

The flurry continued for many moments, a dozen strikes or more, before Praehotec loosed a ball of sparking lightning that launched Luthien backward, slamming him into a tent pole. He was up immediately, hair dancing on ends, cinnamon eyes narrowed as he fought against twitching muscles to tighten his grip on the sword.

"I will burn the skin from your bones," Praehotec wheezed, a grating, discordant voice. "I will—"

Luthien screamed at the top of his lungs and hurled himself forward. The demon whipped a huge wing out to intercept, taking a blow on its massive chest but buffeting and deflecting Luthien enough that the young man's weapon could not dig in.

Luthien tumbled to the side, gained control of the roll and spun about, slashing frantically, for he knew that the demon would be following.

Praehotec, out of range, sneered at him, but then the demon started suddenly, coming up a bit out of its crouch, its huge shoulders lifting the entire tent.

Luthien saw a glimmer, a rapier blade, sticking through the back of the tent, right over Katerin's cot, aimed precisely at Praehotec's rear end.

"Ahah!" came a triumphant cry from outside the tent.

Praehotec waved a clawed hand and a gout of flame disintegrated the material of the tent in that direction, revealing a very surprised Oliver deBurrows.

"I could be wrong," the halfling admitted as the demon turned.

An arrow whipped over Oliver's shoulder, thudding into the demon's ugly, snakelike face.

Praehotec roared, an unearthly, ghastly sound, and the hair on the nape of Luthien's neck tingled. The young Bedwyr rushed right in, his terror overcome by the thought of Katerin.

He scored a single hit with *Blind-Striker*, and then he was slapped away, tumbling, the whole world spinning. Lying flat against a corner, Luthien shook his head and forced himself to his knees, to see the demon approaching steadily, acidic drool dripping from its fanged maw.

Another arrow, and then another, zipped in to strike the fiend, but Praehotec seemed to take no notice of them. Oliver darted in, and then back out, stabbing with his blade, but Praehotec didn't care.

Paragor had instructed the beast not to kill Luthien, but mighty Praehotec took no commands from puny humans.

Luthien, believing that he was doomed, scrambled about, trying to find his dropped sword. He came up to his knees and balled his fists, determined to go out with sheer fury. Then he was blinded by a sudden brightness. Luthien fell back, thinking the demon had struck again with its magic.

He was wrong.

Brind'Amour followed his lightning bolt into the tent, and Praehotec, stung badly by the blast, and by the continuing stream of arrows from the other direction, knew that the game was at its end. The fiend leaped up and scooped the unconscious Katerin in one powerful arm.

"Think well the consequences of marching on Princetown!" the beast roared.

Brind'Amour stopped his next casting, for Katerin was in the way. Siobhan hit the fiend's back again with an arrow, but Praehotec straightened, lifting its free arm up high and thrashing the frail tent aside. Huge leathery wings beat furiously and the demon lifted away, climbing into the night sky.

"Katerin!" Luthien cried, trying to find his sword, trying to chase the beast down. He ran out unarmed and leaped high, catching one of Praehotec's clawed feet.

The other foot kicked him, sent him spinning away into unconsciousness.

A glowing spear appeared in Brind'Amour's hand and he hurled it up at the demon, scoring a sparking, explosive hit; two more arrows hummed from Siobhan's great bow, sticking painfully into the demon's legs.

But Praehotec was too strong to be brought down by the missiles. Away the beast flew, bearing Katerin, to the helpless cries of protest from the companions and from many others in the encampment who came to learn of the commotion.

Cries of protest and agony. Music to the fiend's ears.

CHAPTER 24

BECAUSE HE MUST

"HE TOOK HER!" Luthien shouted, growing increasingly frustrated, even desperate, with the rambling conversation in Brind'Amour's tent some time later. They—the wizard, Oliver, Siobhan, and Kayryn—were discussing the implications of the demon's raid. Now the focus was on whether or not they should still march to Princetown, or if the abduction of Katerin signaled a desire for a truce.

Estabrooke was in the tent, too, the knight sitting on a stool off to the side, thoroughly despondent.

"It is important to remember that the demon did not kill her," Brind'Amour replied to Luthien, the wizard trying to remain calm and comforting. "She is a prisoner, and will be more valuable to . . ."

"To whom?" Oliver wanted to know.

Brind'Amour wasn't sure. Perhaps King Greensparrow had discovered their progress and had reached out to them from Gascony. More likely, though, the wizard believed that the fiendish emissary had come from much closer, from Paragor, duke of Princetown.

"We cannot remain paralyzed on the field," Siobhan put in, and Kayryn added her support, going over to stand beside the half-elf. "This is no paid army, but men and women who have farms to tend. If we sit here waiting, we will lose many allies."

"Duke Paragor of Princetown took her," Brind'Amour decided. "He knows that we are coming, and knows that he cannot hold against us."

"We will have to alter some of the planning," Siobhan replied. "Perhaps we could send in spies, or offer a truce to the duke when we are right before his walls."

The calculating conversation began to make Luthien's blood boil. Paragor had stolen Katerin, but these friends spoke of larger plans and larger things. To Luthien

Bedwyr, there was nothing more important in all the world, not even the freedom of Eriador, than Katerin's safe return. Brind'Amour and Siobhan would plan accordingly, doing whatever they could to help ensure the safety of the captured woman, but their primary concern was not for Katerin but for the rebellion.

As it should be, Luthien logically realized, but he could not follow such a course. Not now. He waved his arms in defeat, looked to the crestfallen Estabrooke, and stormed from the tent, leaving the others in a moment of blank and uncomfortable silence.

"Exactly what Duke Paragor was hoping for," Brind'Amour remarked. The wizard wasn't judging Luthien, merely making an observation.

"You know where he means to go?" Siobhan asked.

"He is already on his way," Oliver replied, understanding the young man too well. No one doubted the claim.

Brind'Amour wasn't sure how to respond. Should he try to dissuade Luthien? Or should he offer support, fall in with Luthien's obvious thinking that Katerin's safety should now be paramount? Brind'Amour was truly torn. He knew that he could not rush off in pursuit of the demon, for the sake of Katerin or anyone else. His responsibility was to no one person, but to Eriador as a whole.

"He should go," Siobhan said unexpectedly, drawing everyone's attention. She looked at the tent flap as she spoke, as though she was watching Luthien riding off even then. "That is his place."

When she looked back to the others, she noticed Oliver most of all, the halfling eyeing her suspiciously.

"More fuel for the legend of the Crimson Shadow," Siobhan insisted.

"Or does the woman scorned wish her lover dead?" Oliver asked bluntly.

Brind'Amour winced—the last thing they needed now was to be fighting amongst themselves!

"A fair question," Siobhan replied calmly, diffusing the tension. "But I am no woman, no human," she reminded the halfling. "Katerin is in peril, and so Luthien must go after her. If he does not, he will spend the rest of his days thinking himself a coward."

"True enough," Brind'Amour offered.

"We will not be led by a coward," Kayryn of Eradoch said coldly.

Oliver, as frustrated as Luthien had been, looked at them, one after the other. They spoke the truth, he knew; their reasoning was sound, but that did little to comfort the halfling. He had been beside Luthien from the beginning, before Brind'Amour had given the young Bedwyr the crimson cape, before whispers of the Crimson Shadow had ever passed down the back streets of Montfort. Now Luthien was doing as he must, was going after the woman he loved, and so Oliver, too, had to follow his heart and follow his friend.

He gave a curt bow to the others and walked from the tent.

Estabrooke, a noble man, a knight whose entire existence was founded on stringent principles, silently saluted the halfling and the brave man who had gone before Oliver.

Luthien paced Riverdancer easily along the edge of shadow cast by Malpuissant's Wall. The sun was low, breaking the horizon to the east, casting a slanted but narrow shadow into Eriador. Not as black as the shadow which had crossed the young Bedwyr's heart. It seemed to Luthien as if all the world had stopped the night before—as if everything, the rebellion, the coming invasion, had simply ceased, caught in a paralysis, a numbing of the spirit that would remain until Luthien reclaimed Katerin from the clutches of the demon and its evil master.

He wanted to hurry, to break Riverdancer into a powerful run, but he did not wish to attract too much attention, either from friends who might try to stop him, or from spying enemies who would warn the duke of Princetown.

He and his horse were by then a common sight to the guards at the gatetower closest to Dun Caryth, and so they let him cross through the wall into Avon without incident.

To Luthien's surprise a foppish halfling on a yellow pony was on the other side of the wall, sitting quietly, waiting for him.

"At least you waited until the morning," Oliver huffed and sniffled, looking thoroughly miserable, his little nose bright red. He sneezed, a tremendous sneeze for one so small, then brought a bright yellow-and-red checkerboard handkerchief up to wipe his nose and goatee.

"You have been out here all night?" Luthien asked.

"Since you left the meeting," Oliver replied. "I thought you would go straightaway."

Luthien didn't manage a smile, though he was touched by the halfling's loyalty. He didn't want Oliver along this time, however. He didn't want anyone along. "This is for me to do," he said firmly, and when Oliver didn't reply, Luthien made a ticking noise in Riverdancer's ear and gave a slight prod and the great shining stallion trotted off to the south.

Oliver and Threadbare paced him, the little pony scampering along to match Riverdancer's longer strides.

Luthien's scowl had no effect, and when he kicked Riverdancer to a faster trot, Threadbare, too, picked up speed. Finally, Luthien pulled his mount up short and sat staring at the halfling. Oliver looked at him curiously and sneezed again, showering the young man.

"This is for me to do" Luthien said again, more firmly.

"I do not argue," Oliver lisped.

"Me, alone," Luthien clarified.

"You could be wrong."

Luthien sighed and looked all about, as if trying to find some way out of this. He knew how stubborn Oliver could be, and he knew how fast that deceptive little beast Threadbare could run.

"Do you know anyone else so small enough to fit under the hem of your hiding cape?" Oliver asked logically.

Luthien stared at his friend for a long moment, then threw his hands up in defeat. In truth, the. concession came as a huge relief to the young Bedwyr. He was determined to go after Katerin, and it frightened him to take another on the perilous, probably suicidal, journey, yet he realized that Oliver's place was indeed beside him, as his place would have been beside Oliver if the halfling's love had been whisked away in the night. So now he would have company for the long ride and the adventures to follow, a trusted friend who had gotten him out of many predicaments.

Before the pair began to move once more, they heard the sound of hooves behind them. They looked back toward the wall to see two riders, one large and wearing a horned highlander helm and the other small of frame.

"Siobhan," Oliver reasoned, and as the pair approached, Luthien saw that the halfling had guessed right. Now the young Bedwyr grew frustrated. He could rationalize having Oliver along, but this was getting out of hand!

Siobhan and the rider pulled up beside the companions.

"You are not going," Luthien offered, a preemptive strike against any argument to the contrary.

Siobhan looked at him curiously, as though she didn't understand. "Of course I am not," she said matter-of-factly. "My duty is to Eriador, and not to Luthien, or to Katerin."

For some reason that Luthien couldn't quite figure out, that statement hurt more than a little.

"But I condone your course," the half-elf went on. "And I wish you all speed and all victory. I expect to see you, and you," she said, looking at Oliver, "and Katerin, waiting for us when we breach Princetown's gate."

Luthien felt better.

"I have brought this," Siobhan went on, extending her hand to reveal an amber-colored stone the size of a chicken egg. "From Brind'Amour," she explained as Luthien took the stone. "When your task is complete, or when you are most in need, the wizard bids you to hurl it against a wall and speak his name three times."

Luthien felt the stone for some time, marveling at how light it was. He wasn't sure what the stone was all about, but he had seen enough of Brind'Amour's magic to understand that this was no small gift. "What of him?" the young Bedwyr asked, looking at the highlander.

"Do you mean to ride into Princetown?" the half-elf asked.

Luthien was beginning to catch on.

"Malamus will ride with you as far as the eastern end of Glen Durritch, almost in sight of Princetown," Siobhan continued. "And there he will wait with your mounts." Unexpectedly, the half-elf then slid down from her saddle, handing the reins to Malamus. "For Katerin," she said to Luthien. "My walk to the wall is not so far."

She nodded to Luthien, then to Oliver, and patted the rump of her horse as she started back for Malpuissant's Wall, back to the duties that would not allow her to accompany them.

Luthien watched her with sincere admiration. Siobhan wanted to go, he realized. Though she and Katerin were rivals in some respects, they also shared a deep regard for each other.

The young Bedwyr looked from Siobhan's back, to her gifts, to Brind'Amour's gift, and then to Oliver, sitting patiently, waiting for Luthien to lead on.

The night had been dark, but the day was dawning brighter.

Back atop the gatehouse at Malpuissant's Wall, Estabrooke, the First of the Sixth Cavalier, watched the small forms on the southern field, the Eriadorans in Avon, invading the proud knight's homeland. The image of the demon, of evil Praehotec, was still sharp in the old knight's mind. For twenty years Estabrooke had lived in the shadow of Greensparrow, hearing the tales of atrocities, of allegiances with demonkind. Some said that the horrible plague which had broken Eriador's will for war twenty years before had been brought on by the Avon king, but Estabrooke had dismissed such rumors as peasants' folly.

Some said that Greensparrow was a sorcerer of the darkest arts, a demon friend, a fiend himself.

But Estabrooke had dismissed such rumors, all the rumors.

Now the knight of the throne, the noble cavalier, had seen with his own eyes. The rumors had come true for poor, torn Estabrooke. They had materialized into a demonic, evil shape that the noble warrior could not shake.

He watched Luthien and Oliver ride off. Secretly, and though it were against everything the man had devoted his life to defending, Estabrooke hoped that they would succeed, would bring Katerin back safely and leave Duke Paragor, the same duke who had sent the cavalier to Eriador, dead in a pool of blood.

CHAPTER 25

GHOSTS

THE HIGHLANDER, MALAMUS, spoke not a word on the two days of riding it took the companions to get into Glen Durritch, the wide and shallow vale just southeast of Princetown. Here, there were no more trees for cover and only a single road, a brown snake winding through the thick green turf.

Luthien, playing the role of general again, studied the land, imagined a battle that could be fought and won here. The ground sloped up to the left and to the right, into rolling, tree-covered hills. Perfect cover and high ground. Elven archers could hit this road from those trees, he realized, and down here, there was no cover, no place to hide from the stinging, deadly bolts.

So intent was the young Bedwyr that he was caught fully by surprise when Oliver's rapier tapped him on the shoulder. Luthien pulled up on Riverdancer's reins and looked back to see the halfling dismounting.

"The western end of Glen Durritch," Malamus explained. Oliver motioned with his chin to the west and Luthien squinted against the low-riding sun. Mountains loomed dark and cold, not so far away, and before them . . .

What? Luthien wondered. A sparkle of white and pink.

Oliver walked by him. "Five miles," the halfling said. "And I do not like to walk in the dark!"

Luthien slipped down from Riverdancer and gave the reins over to Malamus. The highlander matched Luthien's gaze for a long moment. "The blessing of Sol-Yunda go with you, Crimson Shadow," he said suddenly and turned about, pulling hard with his massive, muscled arm to swing all three riderless mounts with him. "I await your return."

Luthien just grunted, having no reply in light of his surprise. Sol-Yunda was the god of the highlanders, a private god whom they said watched over their kin and held no regard for anyone else, friend or foe. The highlanders hoarded

Sol-Yunda as a dragon hoarded gold, and for Malamus to make that statement, to utter those seven simple words, was perhaps the most heartening thing Luthien Bedwyr had ever heard.

He stood and watched Malamus for a few moments, then turned and sprinted to catch up with Oliver as the halfling plodded along, toward the spec of white and pink below the line of dark mountains.

Less than an hour later, the sun low in the sky but still visible above the Iron Cross, the friends came close enough to witness the true splendor of Princetown and to understand why the place had earned the nickname as the Jewel of Avon.

It was about the same size as Caer MacDonald, but where Caer MacDonald had been built for defense, nestled in between towering walls of dark stone, Princetown had been built as a showcase. It sat on a gently rolling plain, just beyond the foothills, and was widespread and airy, not huddled like Caer MacDonald. A low wall, no more than eight feet high, of light-colored granite encompassed the whole of the place, with no discernable gatehouses or towers of any kind. Most of the houses within were quite large; those of wood had been white-washed, and the greater houses, those of the noblemen and the merchants, were of white marble tinged with soft lines of pink.

The largest and dominant structure was not the cathedral, as in most of the great cities of Avonsea. That building was impressive, probably as much as Caer MacDonald's Ministry, but even it paled beside the fabulous palace. It sat in the west of Princetown, on the highest ground closest to the mountains, four stories of shining marble and gold leaf, with decorated columns presented all along its front and with great wings northeast and southeast, like huge arms reaching out to embrace the city. A golden dome, shining so brightly that it stung Luthien's eyes to look upon it, stood in the center of the structure.

"This duke, he will be in there?" Oliver asked and Luthien didn't have to follow the halfling's gaze to know which building Oliver was talking about. "We should have kept our horses," the halfling remarked, "just to get from one end to the other."

Luthien snickered, but wasn't sure if Oliver was kidding or not. The young Bedwyr couldn't begin to guess how many rooms might be in that palace. A hundred? Three hundred? If he kicked Riverdancer into a full gallop, it should take him half an hour to circle the place but once!

Neither companion spoke, but they were both thinking the same thing: how so oppressive a kingdom could harbor such a place of beauty. This was grandeur and perfection; this was a place of soaring spirits and lifting hearts. Was there more to the Kingdom of Avon than Luthien, who had never been to the south before, understood? Somehow, the young Bedwyr simply could not associate this spectacle of Princetown with what he knew of the evil Greensparrow; this fabulous city spread wide before him seemed to mock his rebellion and, even more so, his anger. He knew that Princetown was older than Greensparrow's reign, of course, but still the city just didn't seem to fit the mental image Luthien had conjured of Avon.

"My people, they built this place," Oliver announced, drawing Luthien from his trance. He looked to the halfling, who was nodding as though he, too, was trying to figure out the origins of Princetown.

"There is a Gascon influence here," Oliver explained. "From the south and west of Gascony, where the wine is sweetest. There, too, are buildings such as this."

But not so grand, Luthien silently added. Perhaps the Gascons had built, or expanded, Princetown during their occupation of Avon, but even if Oliver spoke truthfully, and the architecture was similar to those structures in southwestern Gascony, Luthien could tell from Oliver's blank stare that Princetown was far grander.

Shaken by the unexpected splendor, but remembering Katerin in the clutch of the demon and focusing on that awful image, Luthien motioned to the north and started off at a swift pace; Oliver followed, the halfling's gaze lingering on the spectacle of Princetown. From somewhere within the city, near to the palace, it seemed, came a low and long roar, a bellow of pure and savage power. A lion's roar.

"You like cats?" Oliver asked, thinking of the zoo and wishing that he could have visited Princetown on another, more inviting, occasion.

The sky was dark and dotted with swift black clouds by the time the companions had circled Princetown, moving along the granite wall back to the south, toward the palace. They came around one sharp bend in the wall, and Luthien stopped, perplexed. Looking to the west, he discovered Princetown's dirty secret.

From the east, the place had looked so clean and inviting, truly a jewel, but here, in the west, the companions learned the truth. The ground sloped down behind the palace and the eight-foot wall that lined the city proper encircled into a bowl-shaped valley filled with ramshackle huts. Luthien and Oliver couldn't see much in the darkness, for there were not many fires burning down below, but they could hear the moans of the poor, the cries of the wretches who called a muddy lane their home.

Luthien found the sights and sounds heartening in a strange way, a confirmation that his conclusions of Greensparrow and the unlawful and ultimately evil kingdom were indeed correct. He sympathized with the folk who lived in that hidden bowl west of the city's splendor, but their existence gave him heart for the fight.

Oliver tugged on his cloak, stopping him.

"Close enough," the halfling whispered, pointing up to the side of the palace, looming dark and tall not so far away.

"Here now!" came a bellow from the wall, a guttural, cyclopian voice, and both friends dropped into a crouch, Luthien pulling the hood of his cape over his head and Oliver scampering under the folds of the magical crimson garment.

On the wall, several lanterns came up, hooded on three sides to focus the beam of light through the fourth. Luthien held his breath, reminding himself repeatedly that the cape would hide him as the beams crossed the field before him and over him.

"Get back to your holes!" the cyclopian roared and from the wall, several crossbows fired.

"I would like it better if the one-eyes could see us," Oliver remarked.

The barrage continued for several volleys and was then ended by a shared burst of grunting laughter from the wall. "Beggars!" one cyclopian snorted derisively, followed by more laughter.

Oliver came out from under the crimson garment and straightened his great, wide-brimmed hat and his own purple cape. He pointed to the south, toward the towering palace wall, and the pair moved on a few dozen yards.

Oliver went right up to the wall, listening intently, then nodding and smiling at the sound of snoring from above. He pushed his cape back from his shoulder and reached into the shoulder pouch of his "housebreaker," a harness of leather strapping that Brind'Amour had given him. Oliver wore the contraption all the time, though it was hardily noticeable against his puffy sleeves and layered, brightly colored clothing. It seemed to be no more than a simple, unremarkable harness, but like Brind'Amour himself, the looks were truly deceiving. This harness was enchanted, like many of the items it contained: tools of the burglary trade. From that seemingly tiny shoulder pouch, Oliver produced his enchanted grapnel, the puckered ball and fine cord. But before he could unwind and ready the thing, Luthien came over and scooped him up.

Oliver understood; the wall was only eight feet high, and Luthien could hoist him right to its lip. Quickly, the halfling looped the grapnel openly on his belt, within easy reach, and then he grabbed the lip of the wall, peering over.

A parapet ran the length of the wall on the other side, four feet down from the lip. Oliver looked back to Luthien, a wicked grin on his face. He put a finger over pursed lips, then held it up, indicating that Luthien should wait a moment. Then the halfling slipped over the wall, silent as a cat—a little cat, not the kind they had heard roaring earlier.

A moment later, while Luthien grew agitated and wanted to leap up and scramble over, Oliver came back to the wall and held out his hand to his friend. Luthien jumped and caught the lip of the wall with one hand, Oliver's hand with the other. He came over low, slithering like a snake, rolling silently to the parapet.

Luthien's eyes nearly fell from their sockets, for he and Oliver were right between two seated cyclopians! The startlement lasted only a moment, stolen by the simple logic that Oliver had been up here and knew the scene. On closer examination, Luthien realized that neither of these brutes was snoring any longer. Luthien looked to Oliver as the halfling wiped the blood from his slender rapier blade on the furred tunic of one dead brute.

Barely thirty feet away, the other group, the ones who had fired at the companions, continued a game of dice, oblivious to the invasion.

Oliver slipped under Luthien's cape and the two started off slowly, away from the dicing band, toward the looming wall of Princetown's palace.

They had to slip down from the wall and cross a small courtyard to get to the building, but it was lined with manicured hedgerows, and with Luthien's cape helping them, they had little trouble reaching the palace. Oliver looked up at the line of windows, four high. Light came from the first and second, but the third was much dimmer and the fourth was completely dark.

The halfling held up three fingers, and with a final glance around to make sure that no cyclopians were nearby, he twirled his grapnel and let fly, attaching it to the marble wall beside the third-story window.

The marble was as smooth as glass, but the puckered ball held fast, and after testing it. Oliver scampered up. Luthien watched from below as the halfling again went to his harness, producing a suction cup with a wide arm attached. Oliver listened at the window for a moment, then popped the cup onto it and slowly but firmly moved the compass arm in a circle, against the glass.

Oliver came back down a moment later, bearing the cut glass. "The room is emp—" he began, but he stopped and froze, hearing the approach of armored guards.

Luthien stepped up and swooped his cape over Oliver, then fell back against the wall, the halfling in tow.

Half a dozen cyclopians, wearing the black-and-silver uniforms of Praetorian Guards, came around the corner in tight formation, the one farthest from the wall carrying a blazing torch. Luthien ducked low under his hood, bending his head forward so that the cowl would completely block his face. He held his confidence in the enchanted cape, but could only hope now that the brutes wouldn't notice the fine cord hanging down the side of the palace wall, and hope, too, that the cyclopians didn't accidentally walk right into him!

They passed less than four feet away, right by Oliver and Luthien as though the two weren't even there. Indeed, to the cyclopians, they were not, purely invisible under the folds of the crimson cape.

As soon as the brutes were out of sight, Luthien moved out of hiding and Oliver jumped to the cord, climbing quickly, hand over hand. Luthien braced the rope for a moment, allowing Oliver to get up to the second story, then the young Bedwyr also took a tight hold and began to climb, wanting to be off the ground as quickly as possible.

It seemed like many minutes drifted by, but in truth, the two friends were inside the palace in the space of a few heartbeats. Oliver reached out through the hole in the window and gave three sharp tugs on the cord, freeing the puckered ball and pulling it in behind him. Gone without a trace—except for the circle of cut glass lying on the grass and the image of a shadow, a crimson shadow, indelibly stained upon the white wall of the palace.

Luthien settled himself and waited for his eyes to adjust to the shift in the level of darkness. They were in the palace, but where to go? How many scores of rooms could they possibly search?

"He will be near the middle," reasoned Oliver, who knew his way around nobility fairly well. "In the rooms to one or the other side of the dome. That dome signals the chapel; the duke will not be far from it."

"I thought the cathedral was the chapel," Luthien said.

"Duke-types and prince-types are lazy," Oliver replied. "They keep a chapel in their palace home."

Luthien nodded, accepting the reasoning.

"But the dungeons will be below," Oliver went on. He saw the horrified look crossing his friend's face and quickly added, "I do not think this Duke Paragor would put so valuable a prisoner as Katerin in the dungeons. She is with him, I think, or near to him."

Luthien did not reply, just tried hard to keep his breathing steady. Oliver took that as acceptance of his reasoning.

"To the duke, then," Oliver said, and started off, but Luthien put a hand on his shoulder to stop him.

"Greensparrow's dukes follow no law of God," the young Bedwyr reminded him, suddenly wondering if the halfling's reasoning was sound. "They care not for any chapel."

"Ah, but the palace was built before Greensparrow," the halfling replied without the slightest hesitation. "And the old princes, they did care. And so the finest rooms are near to the dome. Now, do you wish to sit here in the dark and discuss the design of the palace, or do you wish to be off, that we might see the truth of the place?"

Luthien was out of answers and out of questions, so he shrugged and followed Oliver to the room's closed door, distinguishable only because they saw the light from the corridor coming through the keyhole.

That hole was about eye-level with the halfling, and he paused and peeked through, then boldly opened the door.

In the light, Luthien came to see that Princetown's palace was as fabulous on the inside as on the outside. Huge tapestries, intricately woven and some with golden thread interlaced with their designs, covered the walls, and carved wooden pedestals lined the length of the corridor, each bearing artwork: busts of previous kings or heroes, or simple sculptures, or even gems and jewels encased in glass.

More than once, Luthien had to pull Oliver along forcibly, the halfling mesmerized by the sight of such treasures within easy grasp.

There was only one treasure that Luthien Bedwyr wanted to take from this palace.

Gradually, the companions neared the center of the palace. The hallways became more ornate, more decorated, the treasures greater and more closely packed together, giving credence to Oliver's reasoning concerning the likely location of the duke. But so, too, did the light grow, with crystal chandeliers, a hundred candles burning in each, hanging from the ceiling every twenty paces along the corridor. Many doors were thrown wide, and all the side rooms lit; though it was very late by then, near to midnight, the palace was far from asleep. A commotion caught the pair, particularly Luthien, off guard; the young Bedwyr even considered turning around and hiding until later. But Oliver would hear none of that. They were inside now, and any delay could be dangerous for them and for Katerin.

"Besides," Oliver added quietly, "we do not even know if the party will end. In Gascony, the lords and ladies are known to stay up all the night, every night."

Luthien didn't argue, just followed his diminutive companion into the party. Merchants and their prettily dressed ladies danced in the side rooms, often sweeping out into the hall to twirl through the next open door, joining yet another of the many parties. Even worse for Luthien and Oliver, Praetorian Guards seemed to be around every corner.

The halfling thought that they should walk openly, then, and pretend to be a part of it all; Luthien, realizing that even the magical crimson cape could not fully shield them from this growing mob, reluctantly agreed. He was well dressed, after all, especially with the fabulous cape shimmering over his shoulders, and Oliver always seemed to fit in. And so they half walked, half danced their way along the corridors. Oliver scooped two goblets of wine from the first cyclopian servant they passed who was bearing a full tray.

The atmosphere was more intoxicating than the wine, with music and excited chatter, promises of love from lecherous merchants to the many fawning ladies. Oliver seemed right at home, and that bothered Luthien, who preferred the open road. Still, as he became confident that their disguise, or lack of one, was acceptable in this company, particularly with Oliver's foppish clothing and his own magnificent cape, Luthien grew more at ease, even managed a smile as he caught in his arms one young lady who stumbled drunkenly out of a room.

Luthien's smile quickly disintegrated; the painted and perfumed woman reminded him much of Lady Elenia, one of Viscount Aubrey's entourage who had come to Dun Varna, his home on faraway Isle Bedwydrin. Those two ladies who had accompanied Aubrey, Elenia and Avonese, had started it all; their bickering had precipitated the death of Garth Rogar, Luthien's boyhood friend.

Luthien stood the woman up and firmly straightened her, though she immediately slumped once more.

"Ooh, so strong," she slurred. She ran her fingers down one of Luthien's muscled arms, her eyes filled with lust.

"Strong and available," Oliver promised, figuring out the potential trouble here. He stepped in between the two. "But first, my strong friend and I must speak with the duke." The halfling looked around helplessly. "But we cannot find the man!"

The woman seemed not to notice Oliver as he rambled along. She reached right over his head to again stroke Luthien's arm, not fathoming the dangerous glare the young Bedwyr was now giving her.

"Yes, yes," Oliver said, pulling her arm away, pulling it hard to bend her over so that she had to look at him. "You might rub all of his strong body, but only after we have met with the duke. Do you know where he is?"

"Oh, Parry went away a long time ago," she said, drawing frowns from the companions. A million questions raced through Luthien's mind. Where might Paragor have gone? And where, then, was Katerin?

"To his bedchamber," the lady added, and Luthien nearly sighed aloud with relief. Paragor was indeed in the palace!

The lady bent low to whisper, "They say he has a lady there."

Oliver considered her jealous tones and, understanding the protective, even incestuous, ways of a noble's court, the halfling was not surprised by what was forthcoming.

"A foreigner," the lady added with utter contempt.

"We must find him then, before . . . before . . ." The halfling searched for a delicate way to phrase things. "Before," he said simply, with finality, adding a wink to show what he meant.

"Somewhere that way," the lady replied, waggling a finger along the corridor, in the same direction the companions had already been traveling.

Oliver smiled and tipped his hat, then turned the woman about and shoved her back into the room from whence she came.

“These people disgust me,” Luthien remarked as the pair started off once more.

“Of course,” Oliver outwardly agreed, but the halfling remembered a time not so long ago when he, too, had played these noble party games, usually lending a sympathetic shoulder for those ladies who had not snared the richest or the most powerful or the most dashing (though Oliver always considered himself the most dashing). Of course they were disgusting, as Luthien had said, their passions misplaced and shallow. Few of the nobles of Gascony, and of Avon, too, from what the halfling was now seeing, did anything more substantial than organize their drunken parties, with the richest foods and dozens of young painted ladies. These frequent occasions were orgies of lust and greed and gluttony.

But, in Oliver’s thinking, that could be fun.

The pair grew more cautious as they continued toward the center of the palace, for they found fewer partygoers and more cyclopians, particularly Praetorian Guards. The music dimmed, as did the lighting, and finally, Luthien decided that they should drop the façade and hide under the protection of the magic cape.

“But how are we to find information to lead us to the man?” Oliver protested.

It was a good point, for they still had no idea of which room might be Duke Paragor’s, and no idea if this “foreigner” the lady had spoken of was even Katerin. But Luthien did not change his mind. “Too many cyclopians,” he said. “And we are increasingly out of place, even if we were invited guests to the palace.”

Oliver shrugged and hid under the cape; Luthien moved to the side of the corridor, inching from shadow to shadow. A short while later, they came to a stairwell, winding both up and down. Now they had a true dilemma, for they had no idea of which way to go. The fourth floor, or the second? Or should they remain on this level, for the corridor continued across the way?

The companions needed a measure of luck then, and they found it, for a pair of servants, human women and not cyclopian, came bustling up the stairs, grumbling about the duke. They wore plain white garb—Oliver recognized them as cooks, or as maids.

“E’s got ’imself a pretty one this night,” said an old woman, a single tooth remaining in her mouth, and that bent and yellow, sticking out over her bottom lip at a weird angle. “All that red hair! What a firebrand, she be!”

“The old wretch!” the other, not much younger and not much more attractive, declared. “She’s just a girl, she is, and not ’alf ’is age!”

“Shhh!” the one-tooth hissed. “Yer shouldn’t be spaking so o’ the duke!”

“Bah!” snorted the other. “Yer knows what he’s doin’. He sends us away fer a reason, don’t yer doubt!”

“Glad I am then, that we is done fer the night!” said one-tooth. “Up to bed wit me!”

"And down to bed with the duke an' the girl!" the other shrieked, and the two burst out in a fit of cackling laughter. They walked right beside the companions, never noticing them.

It took all the control Luthien could muster for him to wait until the pair had passed before running down the stairs. Even then, Oliver tried to hold him back, but Luthien was gone, taking three steps at a time.

Oliver sighed and moved to follow, but paused long enough to see that the cape had left another of its "crimson shadows" on the wall beside the stairwell.

Their options were fewer when they came down to the next level. Three doors faced the stairwell, each about a dozen feet away. The two to the sides were unremarkable—Luthien could guess that they opened into corridors. He went to the third, curbed his urge to charge right through, and tried to gently turn the handle instead.

It was locked.

Luthien backed up and snarled, meaning to burst right through, but Oliver was beside him, calming him. From yet another pouch of his remarkable housebreaker, the halfling produced a slender, silver pick. A moment later, he looked back from the door at Luthien and smiled mischievously, the lock defeated. Luthien pushed right past him and went through the door, coming into yet another corridor, this one shorter, incredibly decorated in tiled mosaics, and with three doors lining each side.

One of those, the middle door to Luthien's left, had a pair of burly Praetorian Guards in front of it.

"Hey, you cannot come in here!" one of the brutes growled, approaching as it spoke and moving its hand to the heavy cudgel strapped to its belt.

"My friend here, he needs a place to throw up," Oliver improvised, jabbing Luthien as he spoke.

Luthien lurched forward, as though staggering and about to vomit, and the horrified cyclopian dodged aside, letting him stumble past. The brute turned back to complain to Oliver, but found a rapier blade suddenly piercing its throat.

The other Praetorian, not seeing the events behind Luthien, moved to slap the apparently drunken man aside. Luthien caught the hand and moved in close, then the guard went up on its toes, its expression incredulous as *Blind-Striker* sunk into its belly, angled upward, reaching for its lungs and heart.

Oliver shut the door to the stairwell. "We must hope that we are in the right place," he whispered, but Luthien wasn't even listening and wasn't waiting for any lockpicking this time. The young Bedwyr roared down the corridor, cutting to the right, then back sharply to the left, slamming through the door into Duke Paragor's private bedchamber.

Paragor was inside, sitting with his back to his desk in the right corner of the room, facing the bed, where Katerin sat, ankles and wrists tightly bound, a Praetorian flanking her on either side.

Something else, something bigger and darker, with leathery wings and red fires blazing in its dark eyes, was in the room as well.

CHAPTER 26

THE DEMON AND THE PALADIN

LUTHIEN'S FIRST INSTINCTS were to go to Katerin, but he kept his wits about him enough to realize that the only chance he and Katerin had was to be rid of the wizard quickly, and hopefully the wizard's demon along with the man. The young Bedwyr took one running step toward the bed, then cut sharply to the right, cocking back *Blind-Striker* with both hands.

The wizard jumped up and shrieked, throwing his skinny arms in front of him in a feeble attempt at defense. Luthien cried out for victory and brought the sword in a vicious arc, just under the flailing arms, and the young man snarled grimly as the sword struck against the wizard's side, boring right across. He saw the wizard's robes, brownish-yellow in hue, fitting for the sickly looking man, fold under the weight of the blow, saw them follow the blade's path.

Blind-Striker had moved all the way around, left to right, and the robes with it, before Luthien realized that Paragor was not there, that the wizard somehow was no longer in these robes. The young Bedwyr stumbled forward a step, overbalancing as his sword found nothing substantial to hit. He caught himself and wheeled about, the brownish-yellow robes folded over his blade.

He saw a shimmer across the room against the wall beyond the foot of the bed, as Paragor came back to corporeal form, wearing robes identical to the ones wrapped over Luthien's sword. He saw Praehotec, eyes blazing, rage focused squarely on Luthien, coming over the bed, rushing right past Katerin and barreling over one of the cyclopians as he went, the fiend's great wings buffeting both Katerin and the other one-eyed guard.

Luthien knew that he was dead.

Like his companion, Oliver thought the key to this fight would be in slaying the wizard. And like his companion, Oliver came to understand that getting to

Paragor would not be easy. At first, the halfling started right, following Luthien. Then, seeing that Luthien would get the attack in, Oliver had cut back toward the middle of the room, toward Katerin. The halfling's eyes bulged when he realized Paragor's magical escape, and how they bulged more when Oliver saw Praehotec, gigantic and horrid Praehotec, coming over the bed!

With a squeak, Oliver dove down, crossing under the tumbling cyclopian and slipping under the bed as the demon charged out. The agile halfling recovered quickly, in a roll that turned his prone body about, and he scrambled right back out the way he had come in so that he could stab at the downed one-eye with his rapier. He scored a hit, then a second and a third, but the stubborn brute was up to its knees, bellowing like an animal, turning around to face the halfling.

Oliver stuck it once again as it turned, and then the halfling let out a second squeak and faded back under the bed, the enraged cyclopian in close pursuit.

From the very beginning, Katerin had not been a model prisoner, and she kept up her reputation now. She accepted the hit as Praehotec passed, the demon's wing knocking her flat to the bed and blasting her breath away. Her instincts yelled for her to go to Luthien, to die beside him, for she knew that he could not defeat this monstrous beast. But her wits told her to inflict as much pain on wretched Paragor as she could, and so as she went flying downward, she tensed her muscles and threw herself into the fall, hitting the cushioned bed with enough force to bounce right back to a sitting position. The second cyclopian, half on the bed and half off, dazed by the weight of Praehotec's wing, was more concerned with its companion, who was scrambling under the bed, than with Katerin.

The brute felt her arms come across its broad shoulders, the chain binding her wrists scraping its face as her wrists came down in front of its burly neck. In a split second, the cyclopian felt Katerin's feet against its upper back, and she was pushing and tugging with all of her strength, her chained wrists tight across the one-eye's throat.

The dominant thought in Paragor's mind as he easily vanished from in front of Luthien's mighty swing was that he had erred in keeping Praehotec so long. Before he ever came back to his corporeal form, the wizard knew that the demon would be going after Luthien, meaning to kill the young man and tear him apart, to punish the young Bedwyr, this legendary Crimson Shadow, for its defeat on the high tower of the Ministry.

Thowattle's warnings of turning the young man into a martyr echoed in Paragor's mind, and so his first attack, a beam of searing, crackling, white energy, was aimed not at Luthien, nor any of his companions, but at Praehotec.

The demon was close enough to Luthien by then that the wizard's attack appeared to be an errant casting. The white bolt slammed Praehotec's leathery wing, doing no real damage to the beast, but stopping its charge, slamming the monster against the far wall.

Luthien, fighting hard to curb his terror, lunged forward, thrusting *Blind-Striker* with all his strength. The mighty sword had been forged by the dwarves of the Iron Cross in ages past, its blade of beaten metal folded a thousand times. Now, after centuries of use, it was better than when it was forged, for as the blade wore down, each layer was harder than the previous. It sank deep into demon flesh. Luthien ignored the hot, greenish gore that erupted from Praehotec's torn torso and pushed on, throwing all his weight behind the attack. *Blind-Striker* went in right up to its jeweled and golden hilt—the sculpted dragon rampant. The sharpened points of the sculpture's upraised wings, the formidable crosspiece of the weapon, gouged small holes in the demon's flesh.

Luthien, snarling and screaming, looked up into the demon's fiery eyes, thinking he had won, thinking that no beast, not even a monster of the Abyss, could withstand such a strike.

Praehotec seemed in agony, green gore oozing from the wound, but gradually a wicked grin widened across the monster's serpentine face. A trembling, clawed hand reached out to Luthien, who backed off to arm's length only, not daring to withdraw the blade. A long, low growl came from the pained demon's maw; Praehotec's trembling, weakened hand caught Luthien by the front of his tunic and pushed him, the twelve-foot giant extending its long arm, driving Luthien back step by step, and since the young Bedwyr didn't dare let go of *Blind-Striker*, the sword followed, sliding from the wound.

When Praehotec's arm was fully extended, *Blind-Striker* was only a few inches deep in the monster's chest. Luthien yanked it all the way out and snapped it straight up, nicking the bottom of Praehotec's jaw. Before he could do any more harm, though, the demon clenched its hand tighter and yanked its arm out to the side, hurling Luthien back by the door.

The young Bedwyr came up in a roll to see Paragor casting straight at him. Through the open door Luthien dove, pulling it closed behind him.

The door slammed all the faster when Paragor's blast of lightning hit it, splitting the wood right down the middle so that splinters followed Luthien out into the hall. Luthien was up again in an instant, meaning to charge right back in, but he had to dive aside as the door exploded and Praehotec burst through.

Luthien skittered behind the beast, back in front of the door. He saw Katerin on the bed, tugging for all her life, the cyclopian gasping and clawing at her hands and wrists. He saw the second brute, dodging futilely side to side as it tried to squirm under the bed, as Oliver's darting rapier poked it again and again.

"Get out!" Luthien cried to Oliver and he pulled the amber gemstone from his pouch and sent it skidding under the bed, hoping the halfling would see it and find the chance to take Katerin along with him if that stone was indeed an escape.

Paragor was approaching, dark eyes focused right on Luthien, as though nothing or no one else mattered in all the world. The duke's hair flared in wild wings behind his ears, and he seemed inhuman, as monstrous as the beast Praehotec.

Luthien accepted that he was overmatched, but he didn't care. All that mattered was that Katerin and Oliver might escape, and so the young Bedwyr spun about, snarling with fury and slashed *Blind-Striker* across Praehotec's back, right between the wings.

The demon howled and whipped around, clawed hand raking. But Luthien was already gone, rolling to the side, and Praehotec's great hand caught nothing but the door jamb and remaining pieces of the door, launching a volley of splinters right into Paragor's face.

"Fool!" the duke yelled, hands going to his bloody face. "Do not kill him!"

Even as Paragor yelled his instructions, *Blind-Striker* came in again, a crushing blow to the side of the crouching demon's head. Praehotec let out a wail, and no commands the wizard-duke could utter then, no reasoning, would have contained the fiend's fury. Praehotec wheeled wildly, filling the corridor with its huge form, preventing Luthien from skipping behind this time.

They faced off, the demon still in a crouch, its wings tight to its back so they would not scrape against the walls. The corridor was small and rather narrow, had been built for defense, and its ceiling was not high enough to accommodate the tall fiend. Praehotec was at no disadvantage, though; it could fight this way easily enough.

Luthien, too, went into a crouch, backing down the hall as the demon stalked him. Clawed hands came at him, and all the young Bedwyr could do was whip his sword back and forth, parrying. Luthien nearly tripped over one of the dead cyclopians, and knew that if he had, his life would have come to a sudden and violent end.

Regaining his footing and looking up at his foe, Luthien watched in blank amazement as two dagger-length beams of red light emanated from Praehotec's blazing eyes. The serpentine maw turned up into another of those awful grins as the demon crossed its eyes to angle the beams. As soon as the light beams touched, a third beam burst forth, a red line that hit Luthien square in the chest, hurling him backward.

He fought for his breath, felt the burn, the spot of sheer agony, and saw the grinning beast still approaching. He tried to backpedal, all his sensibilities told him to flee, but the door held firm behind him, and it could only open one way, into the corridor.

Had Luthien been thinking clearly, he might have stepped aside and thrown it wide, then run out into the palace proper. But he could not stop and reason, not with the pain and with Praehotec so close, great arms reaching for him. And then his chance was lost altogether as Praehotec worked more magic, swelling and twisting the door in its jamb so that it would not open at all.

"Will you fall down and die, you ugly offspring of a flounder and a pig?" Oliver shouted, poking the cyclopian yet again. He had pierced the creature twenty times, at least. Its face, its chest, and both its reaching hands spotted bright lines of blood. But the brute didn't cry out, didn't complain at all, and didn't retreat.

Something skittered beside Oliver and he heard Luthien call out for him to escape. Without even knowing what it might be, the halfling instinctively scooped up the bauble. Then he changed tactics. He poked at the cyclopian again, but fell back as he did so, allowing the brute to get further under the bed. When it had squeezed in all the way, Oliver, much smaller and more maneuverable in the tight quarters, poked it hard in the forehead, then scampered out the other side, coming to his feet to find Katerin still tugging with all her strength, though the strangled brute was no longer fighting back.

"I think you can stop now," the halfling remarked dryly, bringing Katerin from her apparent trance. "But if you really want to fight," Oliver continued, dancing away from the bed as the crawling cyclopian swiped at him, "just wait a moment."

Oliver danced away; Katerin stood up. She looked at the door, and so did the halfling, watching Paragor's back, the wizard apparently picking at his face, as he exited the room.

Then Katerin's attention was back to the immediate problem: the cyclopian reemerging from under the bed. She crouched and waited, and as the brute stood up, she called to it. As soon as it turned, Katerin leaped and tumbled, hooking her chained wrists under the one-eye's chin and rolling right over the brute's shoulder.

She came around and down hard to her knees on the floor, tugging the cyclopian viciously behind her, bending back its back and neck. She hadn't planned the move, but thought it incredibly clever and deadly indeed, but the cyclopian was stronger than she realized, and she was not heavy. The brute's bloody hands reached back over its shoulders and clasped Katerin by the elbows, then tugged so hard that the sturdy woman gave out a scream.

Oliver, busy examining the amber gem, casually strolled right in front of the engaged one-eye. The brute, straining to look back at Katerin, didn't even notice him.

"Ahem," the halfling offered, tapping his rapier on top of the brute's head.

The cyclopian visibly relaxed its hold on Katerin and slowly turned to face front, to stare into the tip of Oliver's rapier.

"This is going to hurt," Oliver promised, and his blade darted forward.

The brute let go and grabbed wildly, trying to intercept, but the halfling was too quick and the rapier tip drove into the cyclopian's eye.

Oliver walked away, examining the stone once more, trying to recall all that Siobhan had said when she had given it to Luthien. Katerin, her arms free once more, for the blinded brute was wailing and thrashing aimlessly, turned herself over to face the creature's back, twisting the chains tight about its neck.

Had the powerful cyclopian grabbed her again, it might have been strong enough to break the strangling hold, but the one-eye was beyond reason, insane with pain. It thrashed and jerked, rolled to one side and then the other. Katerin paced it, her bindings doing their deadly work.

Oliver wasn't watching. He moved to the bottom of the bed and hurled the amber gemstone at the wall, calling three times for Brind'Amour. It shattered when it hit, but before a single piece of it could fall to the floor, it became something insubstantial, began to swirl as a fog, becoming part of the wall, transforming the wall.

Oliver recognized the magical tunnel and understood that he and Katerin could get away. "Ah, my Brind'Amour," the halfling lamented, and then he looked from the potential escape route to the shattered door. None of the three, not Luthien, the demon, or the wizard, was in sight.

"I hate being a friend," the halfling whispered, and started toward the door.

Before he had gone three steps, though, two forms came rushing through the amber fog into the room. Oliver's jaw drooped open; Katerin, finishing her latest foe, dared to hope.

Brind'Amour and Estabrooke.

The parries came furiously and in rapid succession, *Blind-Striker* whipping back and forth, left and right, always intercepting a hand just before it raked at Luthien—or just after, before the demon could gain a firm hold or sink its terrible claws in too deep. Luthien couldn't keep it up; he knew that, and knew, too, there was no way for him to launch any effective counter measures.

Beams of red light began to extend from Praehotec's blazing eyes.

Luthien screamed, put one leg against the door and hurled himself at the beast, rushing in between the extended, grasping arms. He came in high, but dropped low as Praehotec crossed its eyes, the beams joining and sending forth another jarring bolt that flashed over Luthien's head and slammed into the door, blasting a fair-sized crack.

Luthien stabbed straight out, scoring a hit on Praehotec's belly. Then he slashed to his right, gouging the demon's great wing, and followed the blade, rolling around the beast, trying to go between Praehotec and the wall and get into the larger area of the corridor.

Praehotec turned, and though the giant couldn't keep up with Luthien's scrambling, the beast did swing a leg fast enough, lifting a knee into Luthien's side and slamming him painfully against the corridor wall.

Luthien bounced out the other side, still scrambling on all fours, scraping his knuckles and gasping for breath, trying to make it back to the door of the wizard's room, though he didn't even have his head up, so bad was the pain.

He saw the hem of the wizard's brownish-yellow robes, a sickly color for a sickly man.

Luthien forced himself to his knees, threw his back against the wall, and squirmed his way up to a standing position. Before he ever fully straightened, before he ever truly looked Paragor in the eye, he heard the crackle of energy.

Blue lines of power arced between Paragor's fingers, and when he thrust his hands toward Luthien, those lines extended, engulfing the man in a jolting, crackling shroud.

Luthien jerked spasmodically. He felt his hair standing on end, and his jaw chattered and convulsed so violently that he bit his tongue repeatedly, filling his mouth with blood. He tried to look at his adversary, tried to will himself toward the wizard, but his muscles would not react to his call. The spasms continued; Luthien slammed the back of his head against the wall so violently that he had to struggle to remain conscious.

He hardly registered the movement as Praehotec finally turned and advanced, a clawed hand reaching for his head.

With a roar of victory, the beast grabbed for its prey, meaning to squash Luthien's skull. But the energy encircling the young Bedwyr sparked on contact and blew the demon's hand aside. Praehotec looked at Paragor, serpentine face twisted with rage.

"You cannot kill this one!" the duke insisted. "He is mine. Go to his lover instead and take her as you will!"

Luthien heard. Above all the crackling and the pain, the sound of his own bones and ligaments popping as he jerked about, he heard. Paragor had sent Praehotec to Katerin. He had given the demon permission to kill Katerin . . . or worse.

"No," Luthien growled, forcing the word from his mouth. He straightened, using the wall for support, and somehow, through sheer willpower, he managed to steady himself enough to look the evil duke in the eye.

Both Paragor and Praehotec stared at the young Bedwyr with a fair amount of respect, and so it was Luthien, gazing over the duke's shoulder, who noticed the blue-robed wizard at the open doorway to the duke's bedchamber.

Brind'Amour's hands moved in circles as he uttered a chant. He took a deep, deep breath and brought his hands back behind his ears, then threw them forward, at the same time blowing with all his might.

Luthien got the strange image of the wizard as a boy, blowing out the candles upon his birthday cake.

There came an explosion of light, and a great and sudden burst of wind that flattened Luthien against the wall at the same time as it blew out the arcing energy emanating from Paragor's hands, freeing the trapped young Bedwyr.

Paragor stumbled, then turned about, glaring at this new adversary, recognizing him as the old man he had seen in the divining basin. Now, with the display of power from the man, Paragor pieced things together.

"You," he snarled accusingly, and Brind'Amour knew that the wizard-duke, who knew the stories of the ancient brotherhood and had no doubt been warned of Brind'Amour by Greensparrow, at last saw him for who he really was. With a primal scream, Paragor lifted his hands, and they glowed that sickly brownish-yellow color. The wizard-duke charged, his hands going for the old man's throat.

By the time Luthien gained enough of his senses to look up, he was lying on the floor, a sheet of golden light suspended in the air above him. He saw the giant, shadowy form of Praehotec through that veil, saw the demon's huge foot rise up above him.

Luthien closed his eyes, tried to grab his sword, but could not reach it in time, and screamed out, thinking he was about to be crushed.

But then it was Praehotec who was screaming, terrible, awful wails of agony, for as the demon's foot entered the sheet of golden light, it was consumed, torn and ripped away.

Brind'Amour's hands, glowing a fierce blue to match his own robes, came up to meet the duke's charge. He caught Paragor's hands in his own and could feel the disease emanating from them, a withering, rotting touch. Brind'Amour countered the only way he knew how, by reciting chants of healing, chants of ice that would paralyze Paragor's invisible flies of sickness.

Paragor twisted and growled, pressing on with all his might. And Brind'Amour matched him, twisted and turned in accord with each of the duke's movements. Then Paragor yanked one hand away suddenly, breaking the hold, and slapped at Brind'Amour's face.

The old wizard intercepted with a blocking arm, accepting the slap, and his forearm, where his unprotected skin was touched by the evil duke, wrinkled and withered, pulling apart into an open sore. Brind'Amour responded by slamming his own palm into Paragor's nose, and where the blue touched

Paragor's skin, it left an icy, crystalline whiteness, the duke's nose and one cheek freezing solid.

Gulping for breath, the evil duke grabbed Brind'Amour's hand with his own and the struggle continued. Paragor tried to pull Brind'Amour to the side, but to the duke's surprise, the old wizard accepted the tug, even threw his own weight behind it, sending both of them tumbling down the hall, away from Luthien and Praehotec.

Luthien gawked at the spectacle, as Praehotec, unable to stop the momentum, sank more and more of its foot, then its ankle, into the light.

No, Luthien realized then, not light. Not a sheet of singular light, as he had first thought, but a swirling mass of tiny lights, like little sharp-edged diamonds, spinning about so fast as to appear to be a single field of light.

How they ate at the demon flesh, cutting and gobbling it into nothingness!

Everything turned red then, suddenly, as Praehotec loosed another of its powerful eye bolts, and an instant later, Luthien felt the demon's blood and gore washing over him. He twisted and squirmed and looked up to find Brind'Amour's protective barrier gone, along with half of Praehotec's leg. The demon's acidic lifeblood gushed forth, splattering the wall and floor and Luthien.

He took up his sword and rolled out from under the wounded demon, came up to his knees just as Oliver, rapier held before him, came gliding past with Estabrooke, the Dark Knight's great sword glowing a fierce and flaming white.

Luthien tried to rise and join them, but found that he hadn't the strength, and then Katerin was beside him, bracing his shoulders, hugging him close. She kissed him on the cheek—and he saw that she had taken a cudgel from one of the dead guards.

"I must go," she whispered, and she scrambled up and ran off, not toward Oliver, Estabrooke, and the demon, but the other way.

Luthien looked back to see Brind'Amour and Paragor rolling and thrashing, alternately crying out. The sight brought the young Bedwyr further out of his stupor; he could control his muscles once more, but how they ached! Still, Luthien knew that he could not sit there, knew that the fight was not yet won.

"Ick!" Oliver said, skidding to a stop before he hit the puddle of demon gore.

Praehotec, leaning against the wall, didn't seem to notice the halfling. It looked right over Oliver's head to the shining sword and the armored man, this cavalier, this noble warrior, a relic of a past and more holy age. The demon recognized what this man was, the most hated of all humankind.

"Paladin," Praehotec snarled, drool falling freely to the floor. Out came the great leathery wings as the beast huffed itself up to its most impressive stance, straight and as tall as the corridor would allow, despite its half-devoured leg.

Oliver was impressed by the fiend's display, but Estabrooke, crying to God and singing joyfully, charged right in and brought his sword down in a great sweeping strike. The halfling watched his courage, knew the demon's word, and understood what this man they had met on the fields of Eradoch truly was. "Douzeper," the halfling muttered.

Estabrooke sheared off Praehotec's raised arm.

The demon's other arm came around, battering the man; twin beams became one before Praehotec's eyes, flashing out, searing through the knight's armor, aimed at his heart. The stump of the demon's other arm became a weapon as Praehotec whipped it back and forth, sending a spray of acidic blood into the slits of Estabrooke's helm.

Still Estabrooke sang, through the blindness and the pain, and he slashed again, gouging a wing, digging into the side of the demon's chest with tremendous force.

Praehotec, balanced on just one foot, rocked to the side and nearly tumbled. But the beast came back furiously, with a tremendous, hooking blow that rang like a gong when it connected with the side of Estabrooke's helm and sent the cavalier flying away, to crumple in the corner near to the battered door.

Finally, the wizards broke their entanglement, each scrambling to his feet, dazed and sorely stung. Several lesions showed on Brind'Amour's skin and the sleeves of his beautiful robes were in tatters. Paragor looked no better, one leg stiff and frozen, icy blotches on his face and arms. The duke shivered and shuddered, but whether it was from the cold or simple rage, Brind'Amour could not tell.

Both were chanting, gathering their energies. Brind'Amour let Paragor lead, and when the duke loosed his power in the form of a bright yellow bolt, Brind'Amour countered with a stroke of the richest blue.

Neither bolt stopped, or even slowed, the other, and both wizards accepted the brutal hits, energy that struck about their heads and shoulders and cascaded down, grounding out at their feet, jolting them both.

"Damn you!" Paragor snarled. He seemed as if he would fall; so did Brind'Amour, the older wizard amazed at how strong this duke truly was.

But Paragor was nearing the end of his powers by then, and so was Brind'Amour, and it was not magic, not even a magical weapon, that ended the battle.

Katerin O'Hale crept up behind the wizard-duke and slammed the cyclopian cudgel down onto the center of his head, right between the hair "wings." Paragor's neck contracted and his skull caved in. He gave a short hop, but this time he held his footing only for a split second before falling dead to the floor.

■ ■ ■

There was no rest, no reprieve, for Praehotec. Before the demon could turn around, Oliver's rapier dug a neat hole between the ribs of its uninjured side, and more devastating still was the fury of Luthien Bedwyr.

Luthien did not know that word Praehotec had uttered—"paladin"—but he knew the truth of Estabrooke, knew that the man was not just any warrior, but a holy warrior, grounded in principles and in his belief in God. To see him fall wounded Luthien profoundly, reminded him of the evil that had spread over all the land, of the sacrilege in the great cathedrals, where tax rolls were called, of the enslavement of the dwarfs and the elves. Now that fury was loosed in full, defeating any thoughts of fear. Luthien slashed away relentlessly with *Blind-Striker*, battering the demon about the shoulders and neck, pounding Praehotec down onto the sheared leg, which would not support the beast's great weight.

Praehotec tumbled to the ground, but Luthien did not relent, striking with all his strength and all his heart. And then, amazingly, Estabrooke was beside him, that shining sword tearing horrible wounds in the demon.

Again Praehotec's rage was aimed at the cavalier. The demon kicked out with its good foot and at the same time opened wide its maw and vomited, engulfing Estabrooke with a torrent of fire.

The knight fell away, and this time did not rise.

Luthien's next strike, as soon as the fires dissipated, went into the demon's open maw, drove through the back of Praehotec's serpent mouth, and into the beast's brain. Praehotec convulsed violently, sending Luthien scrambling away, and then the battered beast melted away and dissolved into the floor, leaving a mass of gooey green ichor.

Luthien rushed to Estabrooke and gently turned up the faceplate of the fallen knight's helm.

Estabrooke's eyes stared straight up, unseeing, surrounded by cracked skin, burned by demon acid. Luthien heard banging on the door, cyclopian calls for Duke Paragor, but he could not tear himself away from the grievously wounded man.

Somehow Estabrooke smiled. "I pray you," the knight gasped, blood pouring from his mouth. "Bury me in Caer MacDonald."

Luthien realized how great a request that was. Estabrooke, this noble warrior, had just validated the revolution in full, had asked to be buried away from his homeland, in the land that he knew to be just and closer to God.

Luthien nodded, could not speak past the lump in his throat. He wanted to say something comforting, to insist that Estabrooke would not die, but he saw the grievous wounds and knew that anything he might say would be a lie.

"Eriador free!" Estabrooke said loudly, smiling still, and then he died.

"Douzeper," Oliver whispered as he crouched beside Luthien. "Paladin. A goodly man."

The banging on the door to the outer corridor increased.

"Come, my friend," Oliver said quietly. "We can do no more here. Let us be gone."

"Lie down and pretend that you are dead," Brind'Amour said suddenly, drawing both friends from the dead cavalier. They looked at each other, and then at the wizard, curiously.

"Do it!" Brind'Amour whispered harshly. "And you, too," he said, turning to Katerin, who seemed as confused as Luthien and Oliver.

The three did as the wizard bade them, and none of them were comfortable when their skin paled, when more blood suddenly covered Katerin and Oliver, who had not been splattered and beaten, as had Luthien.

Their startlement turned to blank amazement when they regarded the wizard, his familiar form melting away, his white hair turning gray and thinning to wild wings over his ears and his head disappearing altogether. As soon as his blue robes turned brownish-yellow, the three understood, and as one, they looked down the hallway to see the dead duke now wearing the form of Brind'Amour.

The wizard clapped his hands together and the door, swollen by Praehotec's magic, shrunk and fell open before the blows of the cyclopians, led by Paragor's lacky, Thowattle. The brutes skidded to a stop, overwhelmed by the grisly scene, two dead cyclopians, three mutilated humans and one halfling, and a mess of bubbling green and gray slime.

"Master?" Thowattle asked, regarding Brind'Amour.

"It is over," Brind'Amour replied, his voice sounding like Paragor's.

"I will clean it at once, my master!" Thowattle promised, turning to leave.

"No time!" Brind'Amour snapped, stopping the one-armed brute in its tracks. "Assemble the militia! At once! These spies wagged their tongues before I finished with them and told me that a force has indeed gathered at Malpuissant's Wall."

The three friends, lying still on the floor, had no idea of what the old wizard was doing.

"At once!" Thowattle agreed. "I will have servants come in to clean . . ."

"They stay with me!" Brind'Amour roared, and he waggled his fingers at the three prone friends and began a soft chant. Luthien, Oliver, and Katerin soon felt a compulsion in their muscles, and heard a telepathic plea from their wizard friend asking them to follow along and trust. Up they stood, one by one, appearing as zombies.

"What better torment for the doomed fools of Eriador than to see their heroes as undead slaves of their enemy?" the fake duke asked, and Thowattle, always a lover of the macabre, smiled wickedly. The brute gave a curt bow and its cyclopian companions followed suit. Then they were gone, and Brind'Amour, with a wave of his hand, closed the door behind them and swelled it shut once more.

"What was that about?" Oliver asked incredulously, for a moment, even wondering if this was really Brind'Amour, and not Paragor, standing in the hall.

"Glen Durritch," Brind'Amour explained. "Even as we sit here and banter, our army, under Siobhan's direction, has taken the high ground all about Glen Durritch. My excited cyclopian fool will give orders to double-time to Malpuissant's Wall, to meet with the Eriadorans there."

"And the Princetown garrison will be slaughtered in the glen," Luthien reasoned.

"Better than fighting them when they're behind city walls," the devious wizard added. Brind'Amour looked back at Oliver. "You and I once spoke of your value to Eriador beyond the battles," he said, and Oliver nodded, though Luthien and Katerin had no idea of what the two were talking about.

"The time has come," Brind'Amour insisted, "though I will need the rest of the night to recuperate and regain any measure of my magical powers."

Brind'Amour looked closely at Estabrooke then, and sighed deeply, truly pained by the sight. He had spoken with the cavalier at length over the last couple of days, and was not surprised when Estabrooke had insisted on sitting beside him, waiting in case the magical tunnel should open. Brind'Amour hadn't hesitated in the least about letting the knight accompany him, fully trusting the man, realizing the goodness that guided the knight's every action. Estabrooke's death was a huge loss to Eriador and to all the world, but Brind'Amour took heart that the man had redeemed his actions on behalf of the evil Paragor, had seen the truth and acted accordingly.

"Come," Brind'Amour said at length, "let us see what niceties Paragor's palace has to offer to four weary travelers."

CHAPTER 27

DIPLOMACY

LUTHIEN DIDN'T KNOW how to approach her. She sat quiet and very still on the bed in the room she had commandeered, across the hall and down one door from Duke Paragor's bedchamber. She had let him in without argument, but also without enthusiasm.

So now the young Bedwyr stood by the closed door, studying Katerin O'Hale, this woman he had known since he was a boy, and yet whom he had never really seen before. She had cleaned up from the fight and wore only a light satin shift now, black and lacy, that she had found in a wardrobe. It was low cut, and really too small for her, riding high on her smooth legs.

An altogether alluring outfit on one as beautiful as Katerin, but there was nothing inviting about the way the woman sat now, back straight, hands resting in her lap, impassive, indifferent.

She had not been wounded badly in the fight and had not suffered at the hands of Duke Paragor. No doubt the abduction had been traumatic, but certainly Katerin had been through worse. Since the fight, though, after those first few moments of elation, the woman had become quiet and distant. She had reacted to Luthien as her savior for just a moment, then moved away from him and kept away from him.

She was afraid, Luthien knew, and probably just as afraid that he would come to her this night as that he would not. Until this moment, Luthien had not truly considered the implications of his relationship with Siobhan. Katerin's jealousy, her sudden outburst that night at the Dwelf, had been an exciting thing for Luthien, a flattering thing. But those outbursts were gone now, replaced by a resignation in the woman, a stealing of her spirit, that Luthien could not stand to see.

"I care for Siobhan," he began, searching for some starting point. Katerin looked away.

"But not as I love you," the young man quickly added, taking a hopeful stride forward.

Katerin did not turn back to him.

"Do you understand?" Luthien asked.

No response.

"I have to make you understand," he said emphatically. "When I was in Montfort . . . I needed . . ."

He paused as Katerin did turn back, her green eyes rimmed with tears; her jaw tightened.

"Siobhan is my friend and nothing more," Luthien said.

Katerin's expression turned sour.

"She was more than my friend," Luthien admitted. "And I do not regret . . ." Again he paused, seeing that he was going in the wrong direction. "I do regret hurting you," he said softly. "And if I have done irreparable harm to our love, then I shall forever grieve, and then all of this, the victories and the glory, shall be a hollow thing."

"You are the Crimson Shadow," Katerin said evenly.

"I am Luthien Bedwyr," the young man corrected. "Who loves Katerin O'Hale, only Katerin O'Hale."

Katerin did not blink, did not offer any response, verbal or otherwise. A long, uncomfortable moment passed, and then Luthien, defeated, turned toward the door.

"I am sorry," he whispered, and went out into the hall.

He was down at the other end, nearing his door, when Katerin called out his name behind him. He turned and saw her standing there, just outside of her door, tall and beautiful and with a hint of a smile on her fairest of faces.

He moved back to her slowly, guardedly, not wanting to push her too far, not wanting to scare her away from whatever course she had chosen.

"Don't go," she said to him, and she took his hand and pulled him close. "Don't ever go."

From a door across the hall, barely cracked open, a teary-eyed Oliver watched the scene. "Ah, to be young and in Princetown in the spring," the sentimental halfling said as he closed his door after Luthien and Katerin had disappeared.

The halfling waited a moment, then opened the door again and exited his room, dressed in his finest traveling clothes and with a full pack over his shoulder, for though it was night, Oliver had a. meeting with Brind'Amour, and then a long, but impossibly quick, road ahead.

The next morning, the proud Princetown garrison marched out of the city to much fanfare. The long line moved swiftly, out to the east and south, meaning to swing through the easy trails of Glen Durritch and then turn north to Malpuissant's Wall, where they would put down the rebels.

But the rebels were not at the wall. They were waiting, entrenched in the higher ground of the glen, and the Princetown garrison never made it out the other side.

The length of the cyclopian line was barraged with missile fire, elvish bowstrings humming, each archer putting three arrows in the air before the first had ever hit its mark. After the first few terrible moments, the cyclopians tried to form up into defensive position, and the Riders of Eradoch came rushing down upon them, cutting great swaths through their lines, heightening the confusion.

Then there was no defense, no organized counterattack, and the slaughter became wholesale. Some cyclopians tried to run out the eastern end of the glen, but the jaws of the fierce Eriadoran army closed over them. Others, near the back of the long line, had an easier time getting out of the glen's western end, but they found yet another unpleasant surprise awaiting them, for in the mere hour they had been out of the city, an army of dwarfs had encircled Princetown.

Not a single cyclopian got back to the city's gates that fateful morning.

Greensparrow shifted in his seat, a smile painted on his face, trying to appear at ease and comfortable, though the high-backed and stiff, stylish Gascon chair was anything but comfortable. The Avon king had to keep up appearances, though. He was in Caspriole, in southwestern Gascony, meeting with Albert deBec Fidel, an important dignitary, one of the major feudal lords in all of Gascony.

For some reason that Greensparrow could not understand, deBec Fidel had turned the conversation to events in Eriador, which Greensparrow truly knew little about. As far as the vacationing king of Avon was aware, Belsen'Krieg was in Montfort, though the last message from one of his underling wizards, Duchess Deanna Wellworth of Mannington, had hinted at some further trouble.

"What do you mean to do?" deBec Fidel asked in his thick accent, his blunt question catching Greensparrow off his guard. Normally deBec Fidel was a subtle man, a true Gascon dignitary.

"About the rebels?" the Avon king replied incredulously, as though the question hardly seemed worth the bother of answering.

"About Eriador," deBec Fidel clarified.

"Eriador is a duchy of Avon," Greensparrow insisted.

"A duchy without a duke."

Greensparrow controlled himself enough not to flinch. How had deBec Fidel learned of that? he wondered. "Duke Morkney failed me," he admitted. "And so he will be replaced soon enough."

"After you replace the duke of Princetown?" deBec Fidel asked slyly.

Greensparrow gave no open response, except that his features revealed clearly that he had no idea what the lord might be speaking about.

"Duke Paragor is dead," deBec Fidel explained. "And Princetown—ah, a favorite city of mine, so beautiful in the spring—is in the hands of the northern army."

Greensparrow wanted to ask what the man was talking about, but he realized that deBec Fidel would not have offered that information if he had not gotten it from reliable sources. Greensparrow's own position would seem weaker indeed if he pretended that he did not also know of these startling events.

"The entire Princetown garrison was slaughtered on the field, so it is said," deBec Fidel went on. "A complete victory, as one-sided as any I have ever heard tell of."

Greensparrow didn't miss the thrill, and thus, the threat, in deBec Fidel's voice, as though the man was enjoying this supremely. An emissary from Eriador had gotten to the man, the wizard-king realized, probably promising him trade agreements and free port rights for Caspriole's considerable fishing fleet. The alliance between Avon and Gascony was a tentative thing, a temporary truce after centuries of countless squabbles and even wars. Even now, much of Greensparrow's army was away in lands south of Gascony, fighting beside the Gascons, but the king did not doubt that if Eriador offered a better deal concerning the rich fishing waters of the Dorsal Sea, the double-dealing Gascons would side with them.

What had started as a riot in Montfort was quickly becoming a major political problem.

Behind one of the doors of that very room, his ear pressed against the keyhole, Oliver deBurrows listened happily as deBec Fidel went on, speaking to Greensparrow of the benefits of making a truce with the rebels, of giving Eriador back to Eriador.

"They are too much trouble," the feudal lord insisted. "So it was when Gascony ruled Avon. That is why we built the wall, to keep the savages in the savage north! It is better for all that way," deBec Fidel finished.

Oliver's smile nearly took in his ears. As an ambassador, a Gascon who knew the ways of the southern kingdom's nobles, the halfling had done his job perfectly. The taking of Princetown might nudge Greensparrow in the direction of a truce, but the not-so-subtle hint that mighty Gascony might favor the rebels in this matter, indeed that the Gascons might even send aid, would surely give the wizard-king much to consider.

"Shall I have your room prepared?" Oliver heard deBec Fidel ask after a long moment of uncomfortable silence.

"No," Greensparrow replied sharply. "I must be on my way this very day."

"All the way back to Carlisle," Oliver snickered under his breath. The halfling flipped an amber gemstone in his hand, agreeing with Greensparrow's sentiments, thinking that it might be time for him, too, to be on his way.

CHAPTER 28

THE WORD

LUTHIEN AND KATERIN sat astride their mounts on a hill overlooking the shining white-and-pink marble of Princetown. The sun was low in the eastern sky, beaming past them, igniting the reflected fires along the polished walls of the marvelous city. In the famed Princetown zoo, the exotic animals were awakening to the new day, issuing their roars and growls, heralding the sunrise.

Other than those bellowing sounds, the city was quiet and calm, and the panic that had begun after the news that Duke Paragor was slain and the garrison slaughtered had settled.

"Brind'Amour told the Princetowners that neither the Eriadoran nor the dwarfish army would enter the city," Luthien remarked. "They trust in the old mage."

"They have no choice but to trust in him," Katerin answered. "We could march into the city and kill them all in a single day."

"But they know we will not," Luthien said firmly. "They know why we have come."

"They are not allies," Katerin reminded him. "And if they had the strength to chase us away, they would do so, do not doubt."

Luthien had no reply; he knew that she was right. Even though he knew of Brind'Amour's intention of retreating back to Eriador, Luthien had hoped that, after the massacre in Glen Durritch and if the folk of Princetown embraced the Eriadoran cause, they might continue this war, indeed might take it all the way to Carlisle. It had been as Oliver had predicted on that day of planning the attack. The Princetowners were calm now, trusting, praying that the threat to their personal safety was ended, but they made no pledges of allegiance to the Eriadoran flag.

"And know, too," Katerin said grimly, pounding home her point, "that our army will indeed enter the city and lay waste to any who oppose us if we find another of Greensparrow's armies marching north to do battle."

Luthien hardly heard the words, because he had not wanted to hear them, and also because he noticed Oliver upon Threadbare, riding up the hill to join them. Also, to the left, the south, and still very far away, Luthien noticed the expected entourage approaching the captured city. Several coaches moved in a line, all streaming pennants, fronted and flanked by cyclopians upon ponypigs, the one-eyes smartly dressed in the finest regalia of the Praetorian Guard. Luthien did not recognize all of the pennants, but he picked out the banner of Avon and figured that the rest were the crests of the southern kingdom's most important families, and probably the banners of the six major cities, as well. Most prominent among the line, along with the banner of Avon, was a blue pennant showing huge hands reaching out to each other across a gulf of water.

"Mannington, I think," Katerin remarked, watching the same show and picking out the same, prominent banner.

"Another duke?" Luthien asked. "Come to parley or work foul magic?"

"Duchess," came a correction from below as Oliver hustled his pony toward the pair. "Duchess Wellworth of Mannington. She will speak for Greensparrow, who is still in Gascony."

"Where have you been?" Luthien and Katerin asked together, for neither had seen the halfling in the five days since Duke Paragor was dispatched.

Oliver chuckled quietly, wondering if they would even believe him. He had used Brind'Amour's magical tunnel to cross a thousand miles, and then a thousand miles back again. He had met with dignitaries, some of the most important men in Gascony, and had even, on the occasion of passing the man in the hall, tipped his great hat to King Greensparrow himself! "It was time for me to go home!" the foppish halfling roared cryptically, and he would say no more, and Luthien and Katerin, too involved in speculating about the meeting that would soon take place, did not press the point.

Luthien had wanted to attend that parley, but Brind'Amour had frowned upon the notion, reminding the young Bedwyr that the coming negotiator was probably a wizard and would be able to recognize the young man, perhaps, or at least to relay information about Luthien to the king in the south. As far as Greensparrow and his cronies were concerned, Brind'Amour realized that Eriador would be better served if the Crimson Shadow remained a figure of mystery and intrigue.

So Luthien had agreed to stay out of the city and out of the meeting. But now, watching the line of coaches disappearing behind the gray granite wall, the young Bedwyr wished he had argued against Brind'Amour more strongly.

By all measure, Duchess Deanna Wellworth was a beautiful woman, golden hair cut to shoulder length and coiffed neatly, flipped to one side and held in place by a diamond-studded pin. Though she was young—certainly she had not seen thirty winters—her dress and manner were most elegant, sophisticated, but Brind'Amour sensed the power and the untamed, wild streak within this woman. She was an enchantress, he knew, and a powerful one, and she probably used more than her magic to get men into difficult situations.

"The fleet?" she asked abruptly, for from the moment she had sat down at the long, oak table, she had made it clear that she wanted this parley concluded as quickly as possible.

"Scuttled," Brind'Amour answered without blinking.

Deanna Wellworth's fair features, highlighted by the most expensive makeup, but not heavily painted in typical Avon fashion, turned into a skeptical frown. "You said we would deal honestly," she remarked evenly.

"The fleet is anchored near to the Diamondgate," Brind'Amour admitted. The old wizard drew himself up to his full height, shoulders back and jaw firm. "Under the flag of Eriador free."

His tone told Wellworth beyond any doubt that Greensparrow would not get his ships back. She hadn't really expected Eriador to turn them over, anyway. "The Praetorian Guards held captive on that rock of an island?" she asked.

"No," Brind'Amour answered simply.

"You hold near to three thousand prisoners," Wellworth protested.

"They are our problem," Brind'Amour replied.

Deanna Wellworth slapped her hands on the polished wood of the table and rose to leave, signaling to the Praetorian Guards flanking her. But then the other negotiator across the table from her, a blue-bearded dwarf, cleared his throat loudly, a not-so-subtle reminder of the additional force camped in the mountains, not far away. Princetown was lost, and the enemy was entrenched in force, and if an agreement could not be reached here, as Greensparrow had instructed, Avon would find itself in a costly war.

Deanna Wellworth sat back down.

"What of the cyclopian prisoners taken in Glen Durritch?" she asked, her voice edged in desperation. "I must bring some concession back to my king!"

"You are getting back the city," Brind'Amour said.

"That was known before I was sent north," Deanna protested. "The prisoners?"

Brind'Amour looked at Shuglin and gave a slight chuckle, an indication of agreement, and he explained with a wide and sincere smile, "We have no desire to march a thousand one-eyes back into Eriador!"

Deanna Wellworth nearly laughed aloud at that, and her expression caught Brind'Amour somewhat off his guard. It was not relief that fostered her mirth, the wizard suddenly realized, but agreement. Only then did the old wizard begin to make the connection. Mannington had always been Avon's second city, behind Carlisle, and a seat of royalty-in-waiting.

"Wellworth?" Brind'Amour asked. "Was it not a Wellworth who sat upon Avon's throne, before Greensparrow, of course?"

All hint of a smile vanished from Deanna's fair face. "An uncle," she offered. "A distant uncle."

Her tone told the keen-minded wizard that there was much more to this one's tale. Deanna had been in line for the throne, no doubt, before Greensparrow had taken it. How might she feel about this rogue wizard who was now her king? Brind'Amour dismissed the thoughts; he had other business now, more pressing and more important for his Eriador.

"You have your gift for your king," he said, thus bringing the meeting to conclusion.

"Indeed," Deanna replied, still tight-lipped after the inquiry about her royal lineage.

Luthien and Katerin watched, Oliver and Siobhan watched, and all the army of Eriador and all the dwarfs of the Iron Cross watched, as Brind'Amour, Shuglin beside him, and Duchess Deanna Wellworth close behind, ascended the tallest tower in Princetown, the great spire of the cathedral. When he was in place, his voluminous blue robes whipping about him in the stiff breeze, the wizard spoke out, spoke to all the folk of the land, Eriadoran and Avonite alike, in a voice enhanced by magic so that it echoed to every corner of Princetown.

"The time has come for the folk of Eriador to turn north," the old wizard declared. "And for the dwarfs of the Iron Cross to go home."

And then he said it, the words that Luthien Bedwyr and Katerin O'Hale had waited so very long to hear.

"Eriador is free!"

EPILOGUE

"A KINGDOM? A democracy?" Oliver spat derisively. "Government, ptooey!" They had been on the road for a full week, and though spring was on in full, the weather had been somewhat foul—not the expected weather considering the glorious return to Caer MacDonald. Now, with the walls of the mountain city finally in sight, the Ministry sitting huge and imposing up on the hill, their conversation had turned to the coronation of free Eriador's king.

There had never been a doubt in Luthien's mind about who that should be. Several of the folk had called for the Crimson Shadow to take up the reins as their leader, but Luthien knew his talents and his limitations. Brind'Amour would be king, and Eriador would be better off for it!

"Ptooey?" Katerin echoed.

"Government," Oliver said again. "Do you know the difference between a kingdom and a democracy?"

Katerin shrugged—she wasn't even certain what this concept of democracy, which Brind'Amour had raised soon after they had all crossed back in to Eriador, exactly was.

"In a kingdom," the halfling explained, "a man uses power to exploit man. In a democracy, is the other way around."

It took Luthien and Katerin a long moment to catch on to that remark.

"So, by your reasoning, Eriador would be better off without a king?" Luthien asked. "We can just let the towns run themselves . . ."

"They will anyway," Oliver put in, and Katerin had to agree. Few of Eriador's proud folk would bend to the will of anyone who was not of their particular village.

"Still, we need a king," Luthien went on determinedly. "We need someone to speak for the country in our dealings with other lands. It has always been that way, long before anyone ever heard of Greensparrow."

"And Brind'Amour will keep the people of Eriador together," Oliver agreed. "And he will deal fairly with the dwarfs and the elfish-types, of that I do not doubt. But still, government . . ."

"Ptooey!" Luthien and Katerin spat together, and the three enjoyed a hearty laugh.

The coronation of King Brind'Amour went off perfectly, on a bright and sunny day less than a week after the army had rolled back into Caer MacDonald. If there were any who disagreed with the choice, they were silent, and even the rugged highlanders seemed pleased by the pomp and the celebration.

Brind'Amour had ascended to the role of leader now, with the battles of swords apparently ended and the diplomatic duels about to begin, and Luthien was glad for the reprieve, glad that the weight and responsibility had been lifted from his shoulders.

Temporarily, Luthien held no illusions that his duties had ended, or that the war had ended. He had discussed the matter at length with Brind'Amour, and both of them were of the mind that Greensparrow had so readily agreed merely to buy himself some needed time. Both of them knew that there might remain yet a larger battle still to be fought.

Luthien thought of Estabrooke then, who had given so many years in service to the Kingdom of Avon. He thought of Estabrooke, who would be buried in Caer MacDonald. A lifelong service to Avon, and the noble knight had asked to be buried in Eriador. Luthien would have to think long and hard on that irony.

But all such dark thoughts were for another day, Luthien told himself as the decorated coach approached the platform that had been constructed in the wide plaza near to the Ministry. Brind'Amour, looking regal indeed in huge purple robes, with his shaggy hair and beard neatly trimmed and brushed, stepped out of that coach and ascended the stairs to the joyful cries of the thousands gathered.

Gathered to mark this day, Luthien reminded himself, forcing all thoughts of Greensparrow far from his consciousness.

This day. Eriador free.

ABOUT THE AUTHOR

R. A. Salvatore's first book, *The Crystal Shard*, was published in 1988; in 1990 his third novel, *The Halfling's Gem*, hit the *New York Times* bestseller list. Since then he has written more than sixty novels, which have sold more than thirty million copies worldwide. In addition, Salvatore has numerous game credits, making him one of the most important figures in modern epic fantasy. Among his books are numerous titles in the saga of dark elf Drizzt Do'Urden, the Coven series, the Crimson Shadow trilogy, and many more.

Salvatore spends a good deal of time speaking to schools and library groups, encouraging people, particularly young people, to read. He enjoys a broad range of literary writers, from James Joyce to Dante and Chaucer, and counts among his favorite genre literary influences Ian Fleming, Arthur Conan Doyle, Fritz Leiber, and J. R. R. Tolkien. Salvatore makes his home in Massachusetts, with his wife, Diane, and their dogs. His gaming group still meets on Sunday nights.

He is currently working on more novels set in the Demon wars and Dark Elf series.

THE CRIMSON SHADOW

FROM OPEN ROAD MEDIA

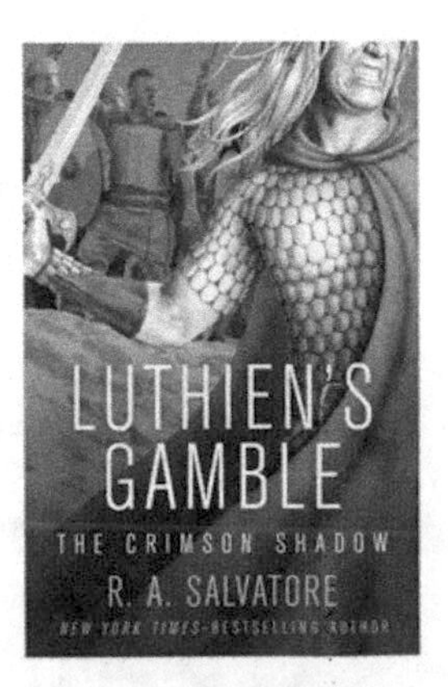

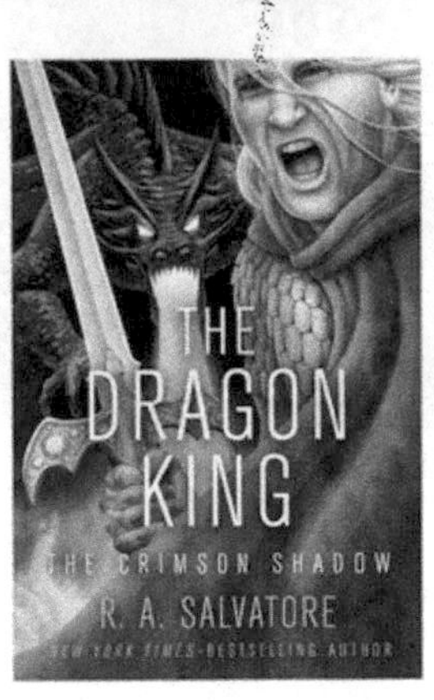

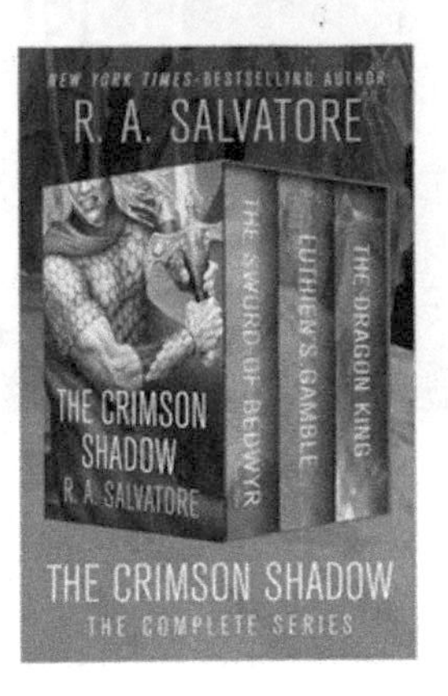

OPEN ROAD
INTEGRATED MEDIA

CPSIA information can be obtained
at www.ICGtesting.com
Printed in the USA
BVHW071920160519
548331BV00001B/1/P